Beyond the Forest

Kay L. Ling

ISBN: 978-1539729235

To my sister, Marie Clapsaddle, my biggest fan, who provided invaluable feedback for this book and shaped the plot in subtle ways.

Join us online to find out about the exciting sequel to _Beyond the Forest_!

Shadowglade

by Kay L. Ling

Visit us at

http://www.kaylling.com/newsletter.html

for more about gemstones and a sneak peek at Lana's upcoming adventures.

Contents

Chapter 1

Et wouldn't be fair to take the credit. Although Lana hated to admit it, this little, black gemstone had gotten her through a very tough day.

Holding the gem tightly for the second time this afternoon, Lana Grayson felt the warmth radiating from it and drew the gem's powers. New energy chased away her weariness. Stress drained from her body. Her mind felt clearer. The effects would only last a few hours, but she'd be home by then. She took a deep breath, let it out slowly, and opened her hand to look at the stone. Most people didn't believe in gem lore and she couldn't blame them. She had been a skeptic herself.

As she put the gem back in the tray she looked at it thoughtfully. No, it didn't look like much, but it was deceptively more than it appeared. Sometimes people were the same way. If you looked beneath the surface, you discovered they were capable of a lot more than you thought.

Lana glanced at the round clock marked "Grayson Jewelers" over the front door. Five forty-five. Only fifteen minutes to go. Even with three salespeople, Fridays were hectic, and she had worked most of the day alone. Never again, she promised herself. Customers had come in two and three at a time even though it was a dismal rainy day, and the phone hadn't stopped ringing. She had been tempted to call in one of the part-timers—or worse, Dad. Instead, she had turned to gems for help. In a few minutes she would clean up and call it a day. Hematite or no, she was ready—more than ready—to go home. She slid the gem tray into the showcase, yanked the glass door shut, and glanced over her shoulder at the closed office door. Arlene Dietz had come in, finally, at four o'clock, and had seen the customers waiting, but had gone straight to her office—and *stayed* there. What kind of manager acted that way?

Lana sprayed glass cleaner on the jewelry counter and rubbed savagely. The damp paper towel's shrill squeak, squeak, squeak matched her mood. In a few months, when *she* was manager, she wouldn't hide in the office and let the staff do all the work. Taking over the store at twenty-two, fresh out of gemology school, would be a big responsibility, but if she didn't assume ownership, Dad would sell the store, ending five generations of Grayson ownership. She couldn't let that happen. Ed or Alex could have owned the business years ago if they'd wanted to. Gems and jewelry didn't interest them. They'd rather work for someone else and get a salary, and that was just as well. She loved her older brothers dearly, but seriously, letting them run a jewelry store would be like letting the Amish run a car dealership.

Wincing at the lingering smell of ammonia, she stashed the glass cleaner and picked up the receipt book. Not a bad day, she decided as she flipped through the receipts—no diamond sales, but a little of everything else. Dad's specialty had been diamonds, but actually, other gems were far more interesting. Colored gems could do things—fascinating things—that no one taught in gemology school.

The front door swung open, accompanied by jangling bells, and a petite young woman in jeans and a red jacket darted inside as if blown in by a gust of autumn wind. Fallen leaves skipped along the sidewalk outside the store's rain-spattered windows. The woman paused, a white rectangular gift box in her hand.

Lana sighed inwardly. Why did someone always come in at closing time? She hoped that thought didn't show on her face because she didn't want to seem rude, but it had been a long day. She pasted a smile on her face and willed it to look sincere. "Hi, can I help you?"

The woman walked to the counter and set down the box. "I hope so. I'd like to have a ring made to match a bracelet I bought a while ago. I heard you do that here."

"Yes, we do. We have a large inventory of loose gemstones, from common to exotic." Despite being young, the woman had dark hollows under her eyes, deep lines around her mouth, and a weary sag to her shoulders that suggested life had dealt her some unpleasant blows. Lana tried not to stare and turned her attention to the box on the counter. "Let's start by taking a look at your bracelet," she suggested.

The woman opened the box, revealing a silver bracelet with eight, pale green aventurine stones. Lana glanced up and met her eyes. "It's beautiful!" What a wonderful piece. Silver links shaped like interwoven vines connected the stones. Few people had even *heard* of aventurine. Most people owned the common, familiar gems like garnets, topaz, and amethyst.

"Do you have gemstones like these?" the customer asked.

"Sure. We don't sell a lot aventurine, but we do carry them."

"Are they expensive? I didn't spend a lot on the bracelet."

"No, they're not," Lana said, and the woman looked relieved.

Lana checked the pricelist under the counter. A couple hours ago she'd used rhodonite gems to enhance her eyesight so she could grade diamonds without magnification. Now she could easily read the tiny print. She quoted the price per carat and said, "I'll show you some ring settings. When you find one you like, I'll show you gems that fit." She placed a group of settings on the counter, and the woman reached for one that had a vine and leaf motif.

"I can't believe you have one with vines! It's perfect! Look how well it matches my bracelet."

"It really does! If that one suits you, would you like to look at gems now?"

"Yes, please."

Lana found one that was a perfect match. "How about this one?" Holding the gem in her tweezers, she tilted it under the overhead lights.

The customer bent to study the stone, and Lana scrutinized her again. She appeared to be in her late twenties, and she was thin, but not fashionably thin—gaunt was the word that came to mind. Her mousy brown hair, salon-streaked with blonde highlights, looked brittle and unhealthy. She wore too much make-up, particularly eye make-up, as if trying to compensate for her otherwise lackluster appearance. A troubling sadness surrounded the woman. A pale circle around the ring finger on her left hand suggested that she had recently removed an engagement or wedding ring. That might explain why she seemed so sad—and why she'd bought the bracelet. Folklore ascribed special abilities and powers to each kind of gem. Aventurine might hold something she needed.

Lana moved the gem closer to the bracelet. "It's a good match. The green is the same intensity."

"You're right. It's perfect. I bought the bracelet in St. Thomas on a cruise a few months ago but I've never worn it." The woman took it out of the box and laid it on the counter. "I never buy jewelry spur-of-the-moment. I don't know what got into me. I simply couldn't pass it by." She ran her fingers over the gems in a way that reminded Lana of someone stroking a cat. "They're such a beautiful color." The woman glanced at her watch. "I know it's almost closing time. Can you finish the ring today, or should I come back on Monday?"

"It won't take long. I can set the stone while you wait."

Tucking a long strand of wavy chestnut brown hair behind her ear, Lana carried the gemstone and setting to her workbench at the back of the store. Why make the customer come back again when this was such a simple job? Dinner would have to wait a little longer. She dropped into her chair and adjusted her desk lamp. Seating the stone and tightening the prongs only took a couple minutes. When she finished, she examined the ring carefully, gave the setting a quick buff with her polishing cloth, and carried the finished ring to the customer. "Here, try it on."

The woman put on the ring and studied it from various angles. "Perfect! I love it! I like things to match. I didn't have any green rings to go with the bracelet, much less anything with the same stone."

"Let's see how they look together." Lana leaned across the counter, drew the bracelet around the woman's wrist and fastened the clasp. As she held the woman's wrist to admire the ensemble, her fingers touched the gemstones and her eyes widened. The stones! Their energy was amazing! Her fingers tingled. The sensation was like touching a low-level electrical charge, and she hadn't even tried to draw the gems' power. No wonder the customer had felt drawn to the bracelet! Lana let go, trying to hide her surprise. What exceptional gems, she thought with a touch of envy. Too bad their owner couldn't fully use or appreciate them. "Very nice. They look great together," she said as calmly as possible.

A voice from behind her said, "Let's have a look at the finished ring."

Lana frowned. It was just like Arlene to show up when no one actually needed her.

The plump, white-haired woman charged across the showroom floor, stepped behind the counter, and crowded Lana out of the way to get a better look at the ring. "You couldn't have made a better choice," Arlene announced with the air of someone who is the ultimate authority on such things. "The ring compliments your bracelet perfectly without being an exact match."

Lana held her tongue. Two years ago, Dad had retired and promoted Arlene to manager while Lana finished gemology school. The position had gone to the woman's head like a glass of wine on an empty stomach, even though Dad had made it clear that the promotion was only temporary. Clearly, Arlene intended to enjoy her authority while she could. Lana often told the part-time clerks, "Just smile. Don't argue. Stay out of her way. Never swat a hornet unless you plan to kill it."

"Lana probably didn't show you our pendent selection," Arlene said, gesturing toward the next showcase. "We have several pendants with this vine motif."

"No, thank you. This will be all for today." The customer stepped back from the counter and brushed imaginary lint from her jacket, but Arlene was harder to brush off.

"If you're *sure*. A pendant would be a nice finishing touch for your ensemble. Lana would be happy to show them to you."

Lana was tempted to give Arlene a silencing jab in the ribs. More often than not Arlene's aggressive sales tactics drove customers away, but you'd never convince her of that and Lana didn't try.

The customer edged further down the counter and said to Lana, "Tell me again, what's the name of this stone?"

Before Lana could open her mouth Arlene cut in, "It's called aventurine."

"Aventurine is a stone from the quartz family," Lana said. "In folklore, it served as a lucky talisman. It brings prosperity, and gives the wearer confidence, imagination, and creativity."

Arlene heaved a sigh. She might as well have said, "There you go again with your folklore drivel." She had complained so many times about Lana discussing folklore with customers that Lana had pretty much given up, but a lot of customers found it fascinating.

"Confidence? I could use a big dose of that right now. And a lucky talisman sure couldn't hurt," the customer added with a wan smile as she slipped the empty gift box into her purse.

Lana shot Arlene a look that said, "*You see? People like gem lore*," but Arlene just scowled and stalked away.

Lana walked the customer to the cash register, rang up the sale and handed her the receipt. "Enjoy your new ring. Buying a piece of jewelry is always a nice pick-me-up."

"Thank you. It's been a bad month. More like a bad year." The woman stuffed the receipt in her jacket pocket and glanced at her new ring. When she looked up, tears welled in her eyes and she blinked them away. "I need a little cheering up."

Lana groped for a soothing reply, but before she could think of anything that didn't sound trite, the woman was walking out the door. The bells jangled cheerfully behind her, as if promising that her life would improve.

Arlene, muttering under her breath, started rounding up the jewelry that went into the safe overnight. Lana returned to the sales counter and put away the rest of the ring settings. A mug of cold coffee sat on a stool, its murky surface reflecting the store lights. Maybe she'd had three sips all day, and that had been as close as she'd come to having lunch. She went to the restroom, dumped it down the sink, and then started carrying jewelry displays to the safe.

"I'm leaving now," Arlene said, brushing by her at the office door. "Lock up when you're done."

"Sure. Have a good weekend."

Arlene kept walking. No reply, unless you counted a grunt. Typical. Lana felt sorry for Arlene's husband. Arlene would be retiring in a few months and she was sure to load her husband down with home improvement projects, then hover over him, berating him when he didn't finish fast enough.

For a moment Lana stood inside the doorway of the walnut paneled office—the office that would soon be hers—trying to control her annoyance. Better days were coming, she promised herself. Sure, she'd be working longer hours but it would be worth it. She walked to the safe, slid the diamond ring displays inside, shut the heavy door and spun the combination lock. She could finally go home, ditch these heels, and treat her feet to a pair of well-worn slippers.

As she lifted her brown, fleece-lined jacket off the coat tree and shrugged into it, she looked around the office. The scent of leather-bound books and lemon polishing oil made her think of rainy summer days here as a kid helping Dad. Dad had given her odd jobs, but more often than not "helping" meant sitting at his desk looking at loose gemstones and matching them up with pictures in his books. Happy memories surrounded her here, and unlike her brothers, she valued the store's legacy. It was quite an accomplishment—a family business lasting five generations. She wouldn't be the youngest owner, but she *would* be the first woman, and she was proud of that.

She wouldn't change a thing in this office. It had gorgeous walnut paneling and built-in bookcases. The desk and a few of the furnishings had belonged to first owner, Elias Grayson. Her favorite piece was the old regulator clock, with *Grayson Jewelers Time for Cherished Memories* in gold letters on its door.

Lana walked behind the walnut desk, reached to the top shelf of the bookcase and took down a thick volume, its brown calfskin binding worn and soiled from use. The flyleaf was marked *Elias Grayson, 1872, Grayson Jewelers*. Newspaper clippings from the store's early years lay between the first pages and she was glad Elias had thought to save them.

Grayson Jewelers had gotten off to a rocky start. In the early 1880s, Elias's wife, Helen, had died of pneumonia. Rather than remarrying to provide a mother for his young son, Elias had tried to raise the boy alone while running the store. A few years later, he had gone on one of his frequent business trips and never returned. What could have happened to him? Had he fallen sick and died alone in an unfamiliar city? Had someone robbed and killed him when he was carrying jewels? Maybe he'd had an accident and lost his memory. She hoped he hadn't simply run away from his responsibilities.

Lana returned the book to the shelf and frowned. No one would ever know the truth. Henry had been twelve at the time. She couldn't imagine how frightened and lonely he must have felt. Well-meaning relatives could never take a father's place, but an aunt and uncle had taken Henry in and run the store until he was eighteen. Putting his unhappy childhood behind him, Henry had become a successful businessman. Lana admired him for that. He hadn't wallowed in self-pity and used his disastrous childhood as an excuse for failure.

Nothing else had threatened the store's survival until Dad had developed heart problems in his early sixties. Her brothers hadn't wanted the store, and Dad had pushed himself a few more years, hoping she'd grow up to have the ambition her brothers lacked.

Lana zipped up her jacket. In a few months she'd have loads of responsibilities and few, very few, carefree moments. Was that really what she wanted? For years she had dreamed of running the store and she still wanted to, but now that the dream was about to come true, she had a more realistic view of what it would be like. With a last look back, she shut the office door behind her.

* * *

Recently, Lana had found a second floor apartment in a 1930s home a couple miles from the store. Quite frankly, it wasn't much to look at, but it was roomy and cheap. Right now, with student loans to pay off, cheap was important.

She unlocked the door, took off her shoes and coat in the narrow hallway, and headed to her rather disappointing kitchen. It was functional, but just barely. It had flimsy cabinets, limited counter space, and the refrigerator door opened the wrong way so there was no place to set anything. But she was willing to forgive all that because the dining area had a huge window that overlooked a park-like back yard. Few homes in the village had this much land. It was almost like living in the country.

Her landlady, Lillian, who lived downstairs, was an unexpected bonus. Lana's grandparents had passed away years ago, so Lana had claimed Lillian as her surrogate grandmother. The woman was like a brownie-baking Wikipedia. She knew, well, practically everything—timesaving household tips, home remedies, gardening, and the current *New York Times* bestseller list. Try to stump her. Good luck. Lillian was always baking "too much for one," and Lana was the happy beneficiary. Although she was a decent cook herself, she happily accepted Lillian's free treats.

Once a week they chatted over a cup of coffee in Lillian's kitchen. Lana hated to admit it, but sometimes she'd rather be with Lillian than her own friends. Erika and Karin could be so annoying. They complained about their boyfriends and asked her opinions, but how often did they take her advice? Her best friend Emily griped about office politics but thrived on tension and conflict. Face it—spending time with Lillian was much more relaxing. As a menopause baby, everyone important in Lana's life had been a lot older, so being around older folks felt natural. Her parents had been in their sixties when she'd graduated from high school.

Lana rummaged through the refrigerator, juggling several plastic containers until she found the foil-covered plate with last night's pork chops. Leftovers were great. She didn't mind eating her favorite foods three or four days in a row. At home, her mother had cooked most of their meals. Every day was an adventure since Mom liked to try new recipes. Lana called them "experiments." Some were pretty good, but others were spectacular failures, and sadly, Mom couldn't always tell the difference.

After reheating her dinner, she flopped into a chair at the kitchen table. Nothing could make her move until she had eaten. These pork chops would be history in five minutes. She sighed with annoyance when the phone rang. Probably those wretched telemarketers. They always called at dinnertime. She had gotten rid of most of them, explaining in her "little old lady voice" that she was ninety-two and in a nursing home. Usually the recitation of her illnesses, along with the pills she took every day, made them hang up on *her*. If not, her shrill cries of, "*Nurse! Bring the bedpan! Hurry!*" sent them over the edge. She stabbed a forkful of salad and let the phone go to voice mail.

"I'm so sorry, Lana." Her head snapped up when she recognized Emily's voice. "I know I promised we'd get together tomorrow. I was looking forward to dinner and shopping, but I can't make it. I have to go to Nicole's for the weekend. Her due date is Friday and they haven't finished the baby's room. Rain check for next weekend?"

Not again. Every time they made plans something came up at the last minute. It was so frustrating. Lana's last boyfriend, Jake Harris, had been nearly as unreliable. Handsome or not, she'd said goodbye to him and his lame excuses after the third offense. Emily's excuses were always legit, though, so it was hard to be mad at her. Besides, they'd been friends since grade school. Oh, well. Lana speared a piece of pork chop, trying to convince herself that she didn't care. She wouldn't let it ruin her weekend. Time alone might be just what she needed. Forty hours at the jewelry store, plus helping her aging parents with chores every Saturday—and all too often on weeknights—took a lot out of her. Ed and Alex were no help. They could barely keep up with their *own* house and yard work. "We'd be lost without you," they told her. "Good thing you have free time to help Mom and Dad." Yeah, she had free time because she had sacrificed most of her social life, but it was hard to be resentful when they were so appreciative.

She loaded the dishwasher and stretched out on the couch with a stack of decorating magazines. Every wall in the entire place was a boring, uninspired, beige or white. For a person who loved color, it was intolerable. Thankfully, Lillian had given her permission to paint—just not black or anything crazy that was hard to cover. She flipped through the first magazine but nothing inspired her. Paint colors that matched her favorite gems would be fun, she thought as she picked up the next magazine. Too bad paint couldn't duplicate gems' *abilities* as well.

For thousands of years people had believed that gems could influence moods and attitudes, and provide luck, protection and healing, but somewhere along the way people had stopped believing. To be perfectly honest, she had been dubious at first, but folklore books described gem powers from intuition to invisibility, and the way she saw it, even if only a tenth of the claims were true, gem powers were worth pursuing. Reading had led to experimentation—holding gems, trying to feel their power. In the beginning she hadn't felt much, but perseverance—okay, sheer stubbornness—had paid off. The sensations and emotions had grown stronger. Now she had mastered several powers—nothing on the order of invisibility, but useful skills.

The clerks at the store said gem lore was bunk. When they touched gemstones they didn't feel a thing. Lana knew they got minimal benefits anyway, but nothing on the order of what she got from tapping into and controlling the deeper levels of energy.

How far could she take her powers? How much of the folklore was true? Could people really master skills like invisibility?

She skimmed through several magazines before finding her ideal bedroom: pale green walls the color of aventurine with darker green woodwork like malachite. Simple white draperies, capped by white valances with tiny green flowers and a matching bedspread, contrasted well with the green.

Perfect. Aventurine walls and malachite trim. She wore malachite a lot. The alternating dark and light green bands appealed to her, and its folklore was fascinating. For one, malachite brought success in business. That seemed to be true. How many times had she picked a piece of jewelry out of an entire showcase, a piece the customers hadn't even noticed, and it was just what they wanted? Malachite was also the guardian stone of travelers, providing protection and power, and able to detect impending danger. One legend claimed that malachite broke into pieces when danger was near. Okay, that sounded pretty crazy, but it might be true.

She glanced at her watch. Time for bed. She rolled off the couch and yawned as she headed for the bedroom. She'd promised her parents she'd help them with chores first thing in the morning, but that should only take a couple hours. Hopefully, she'd sleep better tonight. She set the alarm for seven. Lately, something unpleasant nagged just beneath her consciousness, and she often lay awake trying to figure out what it was. Was it Arlene's increasing coldness and faultfinding? Something to do with her parents? Apprehension about taking over the store? Nothing she could think of felt right.

A clammy film of perspiration coated her skin when she finally drifted off to sleep. She woke and found the sheets wound around her like clinging fingers trying to hold her back from her dreams. She tried to fall back to sleep, but sleep wouldn't come. She couldn't get comfortable in any position and it was impossible to banish idle thoughts from her mind. With a frustrated sigh she rolled over and flipped on her bedside lamp. She had used gems to cure headaches and minor injuries. Gems could probably cure insomnia.

She walked across the room and went through the gem trays on her desk. Folklore claimed opalite jasper could induce sleep, and she had a nice sized specimen, around three carats. She picked up the translucent, white gem with rainbow hues, and then she spotted another candidate. Lapis lazuli was supposed to improve sleep and cure insomnia but it also stimulated extrasensory perception. Actually, that was an ideal mix of abilities for what she needed. Once she fell asleep the lapis might work on her subconscious. When she woke, maybe she'd know what had been troubling her. It was worth a try. She picked up the dark blue stone flecked with gold, and carried both gems back to bed.

Holding the gems loosely, she lay still, feeling them grow warm as she drew their power. After a few minutes she tried to relax and empty her mind. Before long, she fell back to sleep.

* * *

A dog's insistent barking woke Lana at six o'clock. Her heart raced as she sat up, fighting off a haze of sleep. Swinging her legs over the edge of the bed, dizziness washed over her. She sat motionless, waiting for it to pass. What was the matter with her? The barking dog disturbed her in a way she couldn't quite explain.

A few deep breaths cleared her head enough for her to stand. Still a bit unsteady, she stumbled across the room and braced her palms against the window frame. Cars swished by on rain-soaked pavement. The sky was a colorless shade best described as dismal. There was no activity at the houses across the street. No sign of a dog, either. An aggravated yelp, fainter this time, came from farther down the street. Dogs—she didn't like them. Especially big dogs, though she couldn't say why.

So much for sleeping in, she thought, thoroughly annoyed. The alarm wasn't due to ring for another hour, and she'd been sleeping soundly. In fact, she'd been in the midst of a vivid dream, but now it had evaporated. She pushed the alarm to the off position, snatched a fleecy, navy blue top from her dresser and jammed her legs into a pair of jeans.

In the kitchen she turned on the radio, managing to dance and cook at the same time. Another benefit of living alone—no one laughed when she looked like an idiot. And on a day like today, when she was in a black mood until she'd had her morning coffee, she wasn't snapping at anyone. Her hearty breakfast of ham and eggs, washed down by strong coffee with lots of cream, did wonders for her mood.

Thanks to a genetic twist of fate she, instead of her brothers, had inherited Dad's appetite. At 5'7" and 130 pounds, no one would call her overweight, but she was hardly petite. She could do serious damage to a buffet line, and her friends hated the fact that she never gained weight. Ten years from now, she might gain weight just by walking past the refrigerator, but for now, she planned to enjoy her good fortune. Mopping floors and vacuuming for her parents would burn through some of these calories.

Sipping her second mug of coffee, she stared out the window at the back yard. Autumn had finally arrived—her favorite time of year. Bright yellow and orange leaves showed among those that were still green, and some had already fallen.

Lana caught her breath.

Her dream! She remembered it now.

She was hiking in County Forest Park. Dappled light shone through the treetops, casting shadows across the winding paths that led through maples, aspens and birch. The park was nearly deserted, and it was easy to avoid other hikers. In a mood to explore, she wandered off the familiar, marked trails. Deep in the woods she found something curious—troubling was a better word—and she debated whether to keep it. Lana frowned. What had it been? She couldn't remember. She took a gulp of coffee and sighed in frustration. Well, it didn't matter, she supposed. It was only a dream, and not a particularly *useful* dream at that. It didn't explain her sleepless nights. At least she'd slept soundly for a change, so holding the gems had accomplished *something*. She thought for a moment. Could the troubling object in her dream represent the problem, whatever it was, that was keeping her awake? She had never been one to assign meanings to dreams, but it was an interesting theory. Maybe a hike at County Forest Park was just what she needed. It would give her time to relax and think. She might discover what had been troubling her, but if not, she'd get some fresh air and exercise.

She stood and looked out the window. Yes, why not?

The worst that could happen was nothing.

Chapter 2

Lana came home from her parents' house and changed to go hiking. After pulling on comfortable faded jeans, she found her green T-shirt with the silk-screened photo of the Grand Canyon. Her parents had bought it during their trip to see Aunt Lucy and Uncle George, whose new house, an hour from the Grand Canyon, had an awesome stone fireplace and a huge deck that overlooked rocky hills and a rushing stream. It must be heaven to live in a place like that. Imagine waking to that view every day! Someday she'd visit them. Her friend Emily's aboveground pool just didn't cut it for a cool vacation.

Lana always carried a pouch of gems, but she didn't usually wear jewelry hiking. For some reason she felt like wearing malachite today, so she pawed through two jewelry boxes, pulled out a malachite ring and pendant, and a cuff bracelet with a massive oval malachite that spanned the width of her wrist. No outfit was complete without jewelry, she told herself with a grin as she threaded the pendant onto a sterling chain. The malachite looked even greener with the Grand Canyon T-Shirt. She leaned closer to her dresser mirror. The green shirt made her eyes look intensely green. She frowned at the freckles scattered across her nose and debated covering them with make-up, but decided not to. Her friends said she had an appealing "outdoorsy" look. Why fight it? Besides, make-up was a time-wasting pain in the butt. She ran a brush through her thick waves. If she had any vanity, it was her hair. She hadn't cut it in years. It was the one touch of femininity, other than her beloved jewelry, that offset her tomboyish style. Grabbing her purse and brown coat, she galloped down the stairs.

* * *

County Forest Park was no Grand Canyon but it was a beautiful place to hike, and even though it was a public park, the nice thing was, you could still feel alone with nature here. Sure, she liked people, but there were times, especially after a busy week at the store, when she craved solitude. She got out of the car, anxious to walk the narrow, winding trails. She loved the hushed embrace of the trees.

The park boasted some of the biggest trees in the state. From what she had read, in the 1700s, a Revolutionary War officer had received a land grant of 10,000 acres for services rendered, and in the 1870s, one of his descendants had deeded part of it to the county—the part that was too hilly and full of rocks to be farmed or logged. So this land had retained its unspoiled, natural beauty. Trails wound through hills covered in aspens, pines, locust, beech and maples. She loved it all: the hills and ravines, the swampy low spots, the narrow, trickling brooks. And especially the acres of old pine forest with its carpet of rust-colored needles.

Lately, she'd been too busy to hike. That was just wrong, she told herself firmly, because she needed to come here. Something about the wind sighing through the trees and the sun filtering through the leaves rejuvenated her. She breathed in air scented with damp soil and pine needles, and exhaled her anger, frustration and disappointments. It was cheap therapy. And at this time of year, she could usually hike without seeing anyone, so it was almost like having the park to herself.

Walking toward the trails, she passed weatherworn picnic tables, a small open pavilion with more tables, and several slightly rusty grills that had seen more than their share of charcoaled hot dogs and hamburgers.

Behind the picnic area, three trails led into the woods. She knew where each one led and chose the one on the right. Even in the early days, when she had first started coming here, she had never gotten lost. Her internal compass always led her back to her car. She glanced at her watch. Two o'clock. The park closed a half hour before dark. Plenty of time for a long hike.

Since the whole object of coming here was to be alone, she always hiked the least-traveled trails. In several areas a trail split, with the upper section following a ridge, and the lower following a stream or a swampy bird habitat. It was easy to switch trails and avoid other hikers.

Bursts of laughter and snatches of conversation rose on the wind. She spotted three girls and two boys jogging along a lower trail, but none of them looked up. They probably didn't know she was here.

She wasn't sure how long she had walked—maybe ten or fifteen minutes—when she noticed a path on her left that she'd never seen before. The groundcover, some kind of ivy, was matted, and here and there dirt showed through. She knew every marked trail and this wasn't one. What could be more intriguing than an undiscovered path? Especially after the strange dream she'd had. The trees looked far enough apart for her to easily walk through, so she might as well see where the path went.

A few yards in, the path narrowed and became harder to distinguish but she kept going. After several minutes of dodging branches and ducking under tree limbs, she stopped to catch her breath. The silent forest was so dense, the leafy canopy nearly blocked out the afternoon sun. The dusky gloom felt restful and soothing, as if the gently swaying boughs overhead were absorbing light and noise. She thought with a sigh of contentment that this was one of the most peaceful places she had ever found.

Unmarked trails often led to piles of branches waiting to be mulched, but there weren't any piles so far. The path hadn't intersected any of the marked trails and, as far as she could tell, this path really didn't go anywhere or serve any purpose. She swept back her hair and started out again. She'd walk a little further before turning back.

Just after the next bend she came to a small clearing and stopped short. A campfire. Well, the remains of one, anyway. Ash and charred wood showed through the dirt. What moron would start a fire here? Each trailhead had a sign marked: NO CARS, SMOKING, HORSES. If smoking wasn't permitted, campfires certainly weren't. She shook her head, annoyed. Probably teenagers. So many of them ditched their parents at the picnic shelters, and then ran off with their friends. Years ago, she'd done the same thing, but she'd known better than to start a fire in the woods.

Circling the campfire, she examined the exposed, charred wood. Something half-buried glistened in the sunlight and she dropped to one knee to get a better look. No, it wasn't wood or a piece of charcoal—something shiny and black. Like a rock. Brushing away the dirt, she picked up the stone and turned it over in her hands. Strange, it was unnaturally heavy for its size. And touching it produced an odd sensation. Her hands were starting to feel numb. She looked at the stone with narrowed eyes. She had never seen anything quite like it. It was a translucent black stone. As she rotated it, iridescent flecks of silver twinkled like light from distant stars.

Her dream came back to her. Was this the troubling object she'd found?

She dropped the stone and rubbed her hands briskly. Sensation returned, but slowly, and it was creepy to think that her hands had gone numb. An inner voice whispered, *bury the stone and leave it here.* But how could she—gems and minerals were her life. If she took it home she could look it up in her reference books. It had to be something really rare. She picked up the stone and slipped it into her pocket.

Retracing her steps, she came out on the original marked trail and resumed her hike. The unplanned detour had taken at least a half hour, and as she started to climb a series of steep hills, she was already looking forward to plopping down on the familiar bench at the top of the fourth hill. She reached the crest, breathing hard, and her heart sank. "Rats," she mumbled. A family had already beaten her to the bench, but maybe they wouldn't stay long. She could really use a break. Her legs ached and she was dying to sit down and catch her breath.

Two dark-haired boys, maybe eight and ten, sat with their mother, looking so bored and dejected that Lana couldn't help but feel sorry for them. Mom looked equally unhappy. Dad, his cell phone to his ear, asked irritably, "Can't it wait till Monday? I left that file at the office. Tell him I'm out of town for the weekend."

Maybe it wouldn't be so bad to live in a world without computers or cell phones. She never brought her phone here. The last thing she wanted was someone calling her when she was trying to relax.

She pretended to study the path ahead, the rock-strewn hills that fell away on either side of the trail, the slow progress of clouds across the sky—anything, so she didn't look like she was waiting impatiently to sit on the bench.

The man ended his phone call but the family didn't show any signs of leaving. She felt awkward waiting any longer, so she gave up and started walking.

For the rest of the day her only companions were birds, squirrels, and an unsuspecting snake that lay by a rotting log she had chosen as a seat. It darted away and hid in a clump of rocks, but she didn't scream or run away. Although she didn't particularly *like* snakes, she wasn't afraid of them. Years ago, the boys next door had been famous for trying to frighten her with frogs, mice, and snakes, expecting her to run away screaming. She had stood her ground. Once, she had even touched a big garden snake to prove she wasn't afraid. It had felt smooth and cold, like Mom's purse. The boys had looked at her with new respect after that. She smiled at the memory. Actually, she hated bugs and spiders more than snakes.

The sun's rays, slanting through the leaves, felt soothing and warm even though the breeze was a bit chilly. For a moment she closed her eyes and simply listened to the rustling leaves. Here in this quiet place she could empty her mind of everything but the forest and shed all her stress. No overbearing Arlene, no duties to aging parents, and no too-busy friends to disappoint her. A deep sense of relaxation settled over her and a few times she caught herself nodding off. Something finally roused her, maybe squirrels chasing each other, or a birdcall. Whatever it was, she stretched and glanced at her watch. It had stopped, she noticed with surprise. Fully awake now, she looked at the darkening sky. How long had she sat here? Considering how dark it was, her watch must have stopped a couple hours ago. She jumped to her feet. The park would close in a few minutes and she was probably a mile or more from her car. If the rangers spotted her, she was sure to get a scolding. Digging into the gem pouch she wore on her belt, she pulled out gems for strength and stamina, and held them tightly as she started to run.

By the time she reached the last of the four hills, she felt amazingly alive and refreshed. The air smelled like damp soil. Every limb and branch stood out boldly against the darkening sky. Her footfalls came unusually clear and distinct to her ears.

She reached the parking lot, still jogging, but even with the benefit of her gems she was getting a pain in her side and she finally slowed to a walk. Her car was the only one left. No surprise, there. Just then a black SUV marked "Parks and Recreation" pulled in, checking for stragglers. She waved to say she was leaving. The ranger gave her a stern look as if to say, "Why are you still here?" and then rolled up his window and circled to the exit. Clouds of dust rose as he pulled onto the paved road. No doubt he was anxious to go home, especially on the weekend.

She unlocked the door of her old blue Toyota and slid behind the wheel. Maybe it wasn't her dream car, but it was reliable and she didn't have car payments. She turned the key in the ignition.

Nothing happened.

What? Why wouldn't the car start? It *had* to start! She twisted the key again.

Nothing.

Of all the times to pull a stunt like this! The Toyota had *never* been temperamental and this was *no* time to start. Flinging the door open, she walked around and lifted the hood. The battery cables were attached, so that wasn't the problem. Maybe a wire had come loose in the electrical system? She scanned the engine compartment. No, nothing looked detached. What else was she supposed to look for? She let out an angry hiss. Who was she kidding? This was a waste of time. She had no *idea* what she was looking for. Slamming the hood shut, she climbed into the car and glared at the windshield. Now what? The park ranger was long gone. In a few minutes he'd be home having dinner. Lucky him. No dinner for *her* tonight.

She slumped in resignation. Face it. She wasn't going anywhere tonight.

Chapter 3

How ironic. She'd been so excited to come here, and now she wanted nothing more than to be home, safe, watching TV or curled up on the couch with a book. She stared out the car window. The forest felt so forsaken after dark. The hushed solitude had seemed wonderful this afternoon. Now, it just felt ominous. She opened her gem pouch and found rhodonite and rhodochrosite, both known for enhancing eyesight, and drew their power. In addition to allowing her to see distant objects more clearly, the gems would improve her peripheral vision and greatly enhance her night vision.

The night sky was clear, lit by the stars and a three-quarter moon. As her vision sharpened she scanned the trees along the edge of the parking lot and tried not to imagine nameless horrors lurking there.

Time to decide what to do. She rubbed her chin thoughtfully. Which was worse, spending the night locked in the car, or sleeping in the dark, creepy woods where at least she could stretch out? Neither alternative sounded very appealing. If she stayed in the car, she wouldn't have to worry about bugs, snakes, or animals—just people. No one was likely to come here after dark, but she couldn't rule it out. Sleeping in the car, even with the doors locked, would leave her trapped and vulnerable. She imagined waking to see a face peering through the windshield. The hair on the back of her neck stood up. Okay, that decided it. Sleeping in the woods had to be better. At least she could run and hide. And quite honestly, she probably wouldn't see anything scarier than a fox or a coyote.

It was so unfair. What were the chances of being stranded the one place she never took a cell phone? From now on, she'd bring the phone and leave it in the car. She popped open the glove compartment and grabbed her flashlight. With any luck, the blue blanket that doubled as a ground cloth for picnics and a beach blanket was still in the trunk. She got out, gave the traitorous Toyota a black look, and opened the trunk. Good. The blanket was there—a bit tattered and grass stained, but who cared?

No point carrying anything she wouldn't use. Pocket change, snack foods, the weird stone and her purse, could all stay here in the trunk. She tossed in anything that would weigh her down, then put on her jacket and grabbed the blanket.

Starting across the parking lot, she switched on the flashlight and gave a sigh of relief when it actually worked. Perfect. Bright enough to keep her from tripping over roots or stones on the trails. She strode toward the trailhead. Maybe this wouldn't be so bad after all. Someday she'd laugh about her County Forest adventure.

On the trail, she indulged in an old childhood game, placing one foot in front of the other as quietly as possible, pretending to be an Indian. Despite her caution, twigs crunched underfoot and she winced at the sound. Apparently she wouldn't make a very good Indian. She'd be awfully hungry after scaring off all the game. As if to prove her point, something farther up the trail scampered away. Twigs snapped in the underbrush.

The rutted path led up a hill and then descended sharply, forking at the bottom. She chose the path on the left, remembering a grassy clearing that would make a nice overnight camp.

The heavy, damp air smelled of wet moss and leaves. Except for her labored breathing, everything was strangely quiet. Unnaturally quiet.

Shouldn't there be crickets or other insect noise? Something seemed wrong, but she couldn't say what. For a moment she stood perfectly still like a deer that senses a hunter. Everything looked and sounded different at night. That was all it was. Flicking the flashlight over the trail, she strained to see beyond its beam.

She started walking again, a little faster now. Not that she was scared. It just made sense not to dawdle. She'd find her camping spot, and then she'd settle down and try to get some sleep.

The trail skirted a shallow streambed. A narrow channel of water flowed sluggishly through the mud. In the spring, the stream ran swiftly, filling and often over-flowing its banks, but now twigs and leaves lay exposed in sodden, rotting clumps.

An owl hooted mournfully. Leaves rustled overhead. Lana scanned the trees on the far bank, unaccountably nervous. For the last few minutes she'd felt that someone or something was watching her. Who would be here after hours? Shining her flashlight over the brush and trees on both sides of the trail, she continued cautiously.

But the uncomfortable feeling persisted, no matter how she tried to ignore it, and she fought a childish urge to whistle or hum a tune— anything to break the silence. Her breath came in shaky, shallow gasps, the tension growing stronger with each step. Poised to run at the slightest hint of danger, she forced herself to glance over her shoulder to prove nothing was following her.

Just ahead, a different trail went up a steep hill. She hesitated a moment and then switched trails, annoyed with herself. What was the matter with her? This trail led away from the camping spot she'd had in mind. Now she'd have to find a different place to camp. She walked a few yards, and then giving in to a sudden urge to run, she sprinted up the hill.

At the top of the hill she stopped, sweating and winded, and shone her flashlight down toward the streamside trail. The darkness seemed thicker there. Shadows clawed at her light and slithered away. A chill breeze rustled through the treetops. Dead leaves skittered around her feet. She licked dry lips, unwilling to train the light on that trail any longer. Why did she feel she had narrowly escaped something dark and terrible?

And that it was still watching her?

Squaring her shoulders, she turned, training her light on the trail ahead. If she didn't rein in her over-active imagination she'd be in for a long, sleepless night. Moving her flashlight in a high, sweeping arc she was relieved to see rows of huge pines standing like military ranks. She knew where she was now, and even in the dark this part of the woods had a wholesome, inviting look. The lack of underbrush and the wide spacing between trees made a path almost unnecessary, but there was a path. A trail marker—a green metal arrow—had been tacked to a nearby tree.

She had come here so many times she could picture the lay of the low, rolling hills. She started forward, and even in the dark with just a flashlight to light the way, the broad trail was easy to follow. Breathing in the sweet tang of pine, she slowed her pace and began to relax. The dense carpet of fallen needles cushioned her footsteps, so she could stop worrying about making noise. As long as she skirted fallen branches rather than stepping on them, she would barely make a sound.

It was quiet here, but not unnaturally silent like the streamside trail. A hushed symphony of insect noise surrounded her. Pine boughs stirred gently in the breeze, whispering a soothing lullaby. After walking at least a mile, she stopped to drink in the atmosphere. This had always been her favorite part of County Forest Park, and it was positively magical at night. Her flashlight could only illuminate a small area, but wherever she shone her light, powerful boles rose far overhead, their limbs spreading in a dense canopy that shut out the rest of the world. She stretched out her arms and turned in a slow circle, smiling. If an enchanted forest existed, it would feel just like this—an unearthly place where time stood still.

The ground was soft, thanks to the dense mat of needles. This would be a good place to camp. She swept her flashlight over the trail. Ahead, a log bridge spanned a wide, shallow ditch. She played her light over the ditch. It was probably wet and swampy down there, but the land on the other side looked flat and dry. She crossed the log bridge in four long strides. A small clearing a few yards away looked like an ideal place to camp.

After finding a spot free of roots, twigs and broken branches, she spread out the blanket, toed off her sneakers and sat. In a way, this was kind of exciting—being on her own after hours, camping in the wild. Not that she'd do it again on purpose. In fact, if someone rescued her right now, she'd happily go home and crawl into her warm bed.

In the distance, a lone owl hooted. The breeze died away and the boughs stopped rustling, leaving a hush so complete that all she could hear was her own breathing.

Up until now she hadn't felt cold—at least not much—but now that she wasn't walking, the air felt damp and her jacket wasn't very warm. It would be a lot colder by morning. Without matches or a lighter, she couldn't start a fire, but if she did have a way, she'd be tempted—park rules or no. The campfire she had stumbled across, who had made it? The same people who had left behind the unusual stone?

And when had they been here? In the daytime?

Or after hours?

She switched off her flashlight and set it on the ground. Anyone who ignored a rule that forbid campfires might ignore other rules as well—like park hours. Pulling part of the thin blanket over herself, she curled up on her side and shut her eyes. If only she had a pillow and a sleeping bag. Even then it would be hard to sleep after the uneasy feeling she'd had on the streamside trail—that feeling of eyes watching in the dark. For all she knew, she wasn't safe even here. She pulled the flashlight under the blanket.

An hour or more passed before she felt herself drifting off to sleep. In that hazy plane of consciousness she thought she heard distant voices, branches snapping, a whistle like a signal, but it was just a dream, she told herself groggily.

When she rolled over a while later, the flashlight jabbed into her ribs and her dream of camping in the Grand Canyon dissolved. She felt headachy and confused. Opening her eyes a sliver, she blinked in the moonlight. A cold gust swept through the pines, and branches shivered overheard, needles rustling. Distant voices pierced the night air. Voices! She sucked in a breath, shivering.

She couldn't make out the words, but something about the voices sounded wrong. The tone was odd. Guttural. Rasping. Inhuman, she thought with a mounting sense of panic.

Inhuman? That's crazy.

Throwing back the blanket, she turned on the flashlight. She'd risk using a light for a couple minutes. Where were her sneakers?

Her eyes dropped to her arm and the malachite bracelet.

Malachite: guardian stone of travelers. A stone that can detect impending danger.

She leapt to her feet, heart racing.

Malachite will break into pieces when danger is near.

That had sounded like a farfetched claim. Until now.

Her malachite stone had cracked in two.

Chapter 4

The strange, guttural voices drew closer, punctuated by angry shouts. Lana frantically looked around. She found her sneakers, shoved her feet into them, and tied them hastily. Snatching up the flashlight and blanket, she drew a deep breath. *Don't panic. Stay calm. Think.* Where could she hide? The trees were spaced too far apart to provide much cover. Climb a tree? No, that would never work. The branches were all too high.

You can't stand here dithering. Get moving!

She ran—hopefully in the opposite direction of the voices. More shouts. Then silence. She tried to run noiselessly, but it was impossible, even on a carpet of pine needles. Dry twigs crunched underfoot, and her breath rasped in her throat.

An eerie horn-blast pierced the brief silence, and she gasped in alarm. Who used hunting horns these days? All she could think of was an English foxhunt. And she hoped she wasn't the fox. After a few seconds, a horn with a different pitch answered, then a third. She had to ditch the blanket. It was slowing her down. Worse, it was sure to snag on branches or underbrush.

Pausing long enough to roll the blanket tightly, she wedged it under some fallen branches. What should she do about the flashlight? Running by moonlight was suicidal, even with her enhanced night vision, but using a light would give her away. She switched it off, stuffed it into her jacket pocket, and plunged deeper into the woods.

I have to stay ahead of them—whoever they are.

The voices and horns sounded closer no matter which direction she went or how fast she ran. Coincidence? Was someone looking for her? Tracking her? Suddenly her sense that someone had been watching her in the lowlands didn't seem so silly.

She could keep running until she dropped, but trying to outrun them didn't seem to be working. It was time to hide. If she was very quiet, they might pass by. The strange voices were disturbing. Just who or what was she was running from? She crouched behind a tree.

Not far away, a dog snarled and then gave several sharp, angry barks. Her heart nearly stopped. A dog! That was a game changer, especially if it found her blanket. She couldn't hide long with a dog tracking her scent, and she'd never outrun it. A wave of nausea swept through her. She didn't stand a chance now.

A soft whistle sounded behind her. She turned, breathless and shaking.

What she saw was impossible—a little man about three-and-a-half feet tall with a dark, shaggy beard. She strained to see in the darkness. His features, while not unpleasant, were clearly not human. He wore loose-fitting pants and a long tunic. All she could think of was *Gnome*. With an unmistakable look of panic, he motioned for her to follow. Was he trying to help her? Why? Did she really care? This was all so unreal. She supposed it couldn't hurt to follow him. Still, she hesitated.

The echoing blast of hunting horns came again, closer now. The little man bolted into the trees. Whoever he was, wherever he planned to take her, it had to be better than staying here. She ran after him. How would she ever keep up? He dodged between trees and jumped over fallen branches, never slowing, despite having only the moon and stars for light.

After a few minutes they broke through the edge of the pine forest. Now they ran between huge oaks, maples and beech. How much farther? Where was he going? Would he just keep running until they dropped of exhaustion?

They passed through a grove of beech trees, and just beyond he stumbled to a halt in front of a massive oak. Panting, Lana stopped beside him. Movement caught her eye and she jumped, stifling a shriek. A hand reached out from *inside* the tree.

Impossible!

Her guide laid a hand on her back and pushed gently. "We must go inside," he said in a surprisingly deep voice. "Hurry!"

Inside? How do we get inside a tree? The hand sticking through the tree waggled as if saying, "Come *on!*" It stretched farther still, and even though none of this made any sense, she reached out and took it. After a push from behind, and a tug from inside, she was *inside the tree!*

The white-haired gnome facing her had apparently pulled her in. He surveyed her critically. Her escort came in and stood beside the older gnome. Neither spoke.

Which was good, because she was utterly speechless.

Several mind-bending, impossibilities vied for her attention. First, the tree itself—a towering, round room, at least fifty feet across, lit from the base of the tree to the top by veins of dim light shining from the walls. How could the tree be hollow? And how could the interior be several times the size of the outside? The room, comfortably warm for a chilly evening, smelled like fresh air after a hard rain. Near one wall, roots twisted up from the floor and spread out to form small tables and stools.

On the opposite side of the tree room, a group of gnomes sat around a heap of glowing stones. Unlike a wood or coal fire, the stones didn't give off smoke or ash. The gnomes' conversation was so boisterous it was a wonder she hadn't heard them from outside. They didn't look up. They probably hadn't even noticed her.

What odd little beings. They weren't ugly or frightening but they clearly weren't human. Bushy brows like untrimmed hedges sat over their deep-set eyes. Their bulbous noses were too long by human standards of beauty, and their chins, which jutted out prominently, nearly touched their chests since they had very short necks. Many of the males had shoulder-length hair, without much regard for style, and their beards surely hadn't seen a pair of scissors for years. The women wore waist-length hair held back by a simple leather thong. Males and females dressed alike in loose-fitting trousers and tunics in colors that blended with nature: tan, rust, brown, green and black.

Lana's rescuers didn't say a word, as if waiting for her to catch her breath and take in her surroundings. Finally, her escort said sternly, "I don't know why you're here after dark, but you were in danger. You're lucky I found you."

The white-haired gnome scowled at him. "It wasn't wise to bring her here, but it's done now."

"If I had left her behind, what would have become of her?"

This was awkward. The white-haired gnome must be one of the leaders, and he wasn't happy about her being here. Who or what had they rescued her *from?*

The old gnome answered her question before she found the courage to ask. "At night, beings from a world called Shadow come to this forest. We gnomes would never hurt you, but the breghlin would. Never come here after dark."

Another world? She certainly hadn't expected *that!* A hundred questions raced through her mind.

"My name is Raenihel," the old gnome continued. "I'm the leader of our clan. We watch over this land, just as our ancestors have done for many generations. This is Gliaphon, one of our scouts."

She had a tendency to babble when she was nervous, and she didn't want to say the wrong thing and offend her rescuers. Should she apologize or just explain why she was here? "My name is Lana. I would have left the park—I *wanted* to—but my car wouldn't start so I camped in the woods."

"That was dangerous, but of course you didn't know that," Gliaphon said. "Just beyond our Tree Home is a membrane that separates your world from ours. At night the membrane weakens enough for us to cross. We'll go back through that portal at dawn, as will the breghlin, since we don't wish to be seen."

A portal between worlds. Here. In County Forest Park. Her voice came out a little shaky. "I heard voices and horns. I'm pretty sure someone was tracking me."

Raenihel nodded. "The breghlin, no doubt. Long ago they were gnomes like us, but now their features are so hideous they barely resemble us, and they are brutal, evil creatures."

Gliaphon added, "They delight in every sort of mischief and cruelty. If they saw you, they'd blow their horns and summon others to hunt you."

Lana shivered. Her quiet day in the park had taken an unpleasant twist.

"Don't worry," Gliaphon said, "You're safe here. They can't come in."

"This is all so strange," she murmured, "I had no idea." By day County Forest Park was completely safe. After dark, its character changed completely. She started to shake. The idea of monstrous beings from another world hunting her was too much.

"Wait here a moment," Raenihel told her, his expression softening. He walked to the circle of gnomes and interrupted their conversation. She couldn't make out what he said, but they all turned to look at her, and then Raenihel motioned for her to join them.

"Come," Gliaphon said. "Raenihel is stern but kind. If he seemed ill tempered, blame it on the burden of his responsibilities. He will introduce you to the others. Don't be afraid. We gnomes are more familiar with humans than you are with us."

She felt awkward as she approached their circle. Did she look as odd to them as they did to her?

"This is Lana," Raenihel announced, "a guest under our protection." He didn't attempt to introduce her to each of the gnomes. She glanced around the circle and smiled, unnerved by their scrutiny.

Gliaphon said in her ear, "We have unusual names. I can introduce you to everyone later if you like."

"Now you must have a cup of fialazza with us," Raenihel said. It sounded more like a command than a suggestion. "You'll find it calming."

The gnomes moved aside and opened a space for her, Gliaphon, and Raenihel to sit. She and her escorts sat down cross-legged like the others. Her eyes flicked from face to face, and when she didn't see anything menacing in their expressions, she started to relax. A young female picked up a wooden goblet and poured red liquid into it from a flask. The gnomes passed the goblet from hand to hand until it reached her. She stared into the cup warily. There was no telling what this stuff was. Raenihel nodded encouragement and the others watched with amused smiles.

I've got to drink it. The gnomes saved my life. How can I act as if I don't trust them?

Cautiously, she took a sip. The fluid was slightly sweet and tasted like fruit, but it wasn't any flavor she could identify. After several more sips, it was clear that the drink wasn't intoxicating, but Raenihel was right, it made her feel calm and relaxed. At the same time, it sharpened her senses and heightened her awareness, rather like a gem power. Amazing! She could make a fortune if she could reproduce this stuff!

She leaned closer to Gliaphon and said, "You said the breghlin couldn't come in here. Are they a threat to your people?"

"Yes, if they find us in the open where there are no trees for refuge. Breghlin live in the barren wastelands. We live in forested hills." He frowned, as if searching for the right words. "The breghlin can't *Walk Like the Wind*, which is the way we travel if we need to avoid danger. You see, we woodland gnomes can pass from tree to tree by using our minds to access their multi-dimensional space."

She tried to digest that. Gnomes could pass through the insides of trees and stay out of the breghlins' reach. She was sitting in a multi-dimensional room right now, so he had to be telling the truth, but what an odd concept. "Raenihel said you're a scout. Do you watch for breghlin, or are you watching for humans?"

"We watch for changes in this forest of any kind. The area surrounding your side of the portal is a special place. We call it the Amulet. It protects your world from those who don't belong."

"Protects us? How?"

"The Amulet confines intruders within its boundaries so they can't go any further. Lately, breghlin have been coming through the portal every night, which is unusual. Something has changed and that's troubling. We must keep watch."

Lana sipped her fialazza. She was glad he was willing to confide in her, but his answers left her worried and confused. "When I walked through the lowlands, I felt someone watching me. The feeling went away after I climbed the hill to the pine forest. I felt safer there, so I tried to sleep. Noises woke me—voices and hunting horns. I didn't hang around to see who it was. I grabbed my stuff and ran." She looked around the circle. The gnomes had all stopped talking and were listening to her. "I heard a dog bark. I think it must have found my blanket. Now it has my scent and—"

Raenihel stiffened. "A dog, you say? Here at night?"

Gliaphon nodded. "Yes, I heard it, too. But don't jump to conclusions, Raenihel. It might be a normal dog."

Lana's heart thudded dully in her chest. What did he mean—it might be a *normal* dog?

The gnomes whispered among themselves.

Raenihel looked increasingly alarmed. "The park closes at night and visitors don't leave their dogs behind. A dog here at night? Yes, I fear the worst."

"What do you mean, it might be a *normal* dog?" Lana asked sharply. "What *else* would it be?"

Gliaphon and Raenihel exchanged furtive glances, and then Raenihel stroked his beard and stared at the glowing stones. "Very well, I will tell you the legend. The dog we speak of is a black wolfhound, but once it was human. During the full moon the beast's human mind returns, and it bays at the moon in torment, or so the legend says."

Another gnome broke in. "If the wolfhound is here—"

A pointed look from Raenihel silenced him.

"We should investigate," said a gray-haired gnome across the circle, ignoring any signals from Raenihel. "The wolfhound is a sign."

Gliaphon leaned closer to Raenihel and whispered something that Lana could barely hear, but it sounded like, "The woman could be a help."

Investigate? Go look for a wolfhound that used to be human? Count me out. I'm afraid of normal dogs!

"We *must* know whether the wolfhound is here," the gray-haired gnome insisted. "We should search tonight. If we find it, we'll send someone to warn the other clans."

Several gnomes agreed. The entire company rose, talking at once.

"You're *all* going?" Lana asked, alarmed. Which was worse, being left behind or being asked to go?

"We could use your help, Lana," Gliaphon said. "Will you go with us?"

"What help could I be? What if it attacks us?"

"It won't attack. Actually, it's not the *dog* we fear, it's someone else." Raenihel looked reluctant to say more.

His cryptic answer was less than satisfying. "*You* may not be afraid of the wolfhound, but *I* am. I'm afraid of dogs."

"We won't force you to come, but if you do, Gliaphon and I will take your hands and we will *Walk Like the Wind* through the trees. That way, the wolfhound can't catch us."

Her mind raced. What should she do? She didn't want to go, but she didn't want to stay here alone. If the gnomes didn't come back for hours, she'd just have to wait, trapped in this tree. On the other hand, staying here was probably safer than looking for an enchanted wolfhound.

For the second time tonight she had to make a choice between two alternatives that she didn't like. Her decision to camp in the woods had seemed safer than staying in the car and look where *that* had gotten her.

She drank more fialazza and felt herself relax, and after a moment she decided this was all rather exciting and sort of fun, despite being dangerous. She swallowed her remaining fialazza in three big gulps and set down her cup with a thud. *Decide. Now.* She stood and took a deep breath. "Okay, I'll go," she said, hoping she wouldn't regret it.

Gliaphon and Raenihel stood on either side of her. She placed her hands in theirs and took a deep breath. In the next moment, she understood why the dog could never catch them.

Chapter 5

Lana and the gnomes passed from one tree into the next like a leaf blown by the wind. Glimpses of tree rooms flickered by as she clung to the gnomes' hands. What would happen if they let go of her? Slightly woozy, she closed her eyes. When the sensation of movement stopped, she found the courage to look. She and her escorts stood at the far edge of the pine forest looking down a hill. Raenihel and Gliaphon let go of her.

"Are you all right?" Gliaphon whispered.

Good question. She swayed on wobbly legs. "I'm fine. Just a little dizzy. That was amazing!" She wanted to discuss her experience, but Raenihel's clan stood a few feet away looking down at the lowlands, understandably anxious to begin the search.

What would the gnomes find down there? The breghlin and the dog had probably returned to a campsite near the streamside trail. The gnomes were sure to search there, and they couldn't do that from inside a tree, so they would be vulnerable in the open. After the premonition of danger she'd felt along that trail, well, that was the last place she wanted to go.

Raenihel motioned the group forward. It was too late to back out now. She stayed close to Raenihel and Gliaphon as they walked down the hill, and at the bottom, she breathed a sigh of relief when they forged into the trees instead of heading for the streamside trail. She glanced back. The rest of the gnomes followed, moving as silently as the Indians she had imitated earlier. Not a twig snapped underfoot and their earth-toned clothing blended into the forest like camouflage, especially at night. She tried to imitate their stealth, but leaves crunched underfoot and twigs snapped as she pushed through the underbrush. She frowned in annoyance. Every creature in the forest probably heard her coming.

Tall trees, a couple hundred years old, grew beside long-dead trees that thrust up bare, leafless branches to the night sky. Rotting limbs covered in moss littered the ground. She shrank from a fungus the size of a dinner plate growing from a blackened stump. Huge vines like clinging snakes encircled some of the larger trees. She knew poison oak and poison ivy when she saw it and steered clear of trees with vines.

The ground itself was treacherous after dark. Innocent patches of ivy concealed rocky outcroppings. Stray roots poked through the soil, sure to trip careless travelers. Dry ground gave way unexpectedly to swampy patches that almost sucked off her sneakers. No wonder the park rangers had created marked trails for hikers. The streamside trail might be safer after all, she decided as she nearly tripped over a fallen branch. Good thing the gnomes had superior night vision. As long as she stuck close to Raenihel and Gliaphon, she might get through this in one piece. The gnomes walked slowly, not because they were groping in the dark. They were looking for signs of the hound. She sighed in frustration. So far, there had been no sign of the mysterious wolfhound. If only they would find someone's lost mutt wandering in the woods so they could end this futile search and go home.

Dry leaves muttered overhead. The air grew colder the farther they walked, and gusts of wind like icy hands slipped beneath her clothing and probed her shivering body. She jumped every time a limb creaked ominously or a leaning tree moaned in the wind. The forest was unsettling after dark, even under the best of circumstances. Several times the gnomes stopped to examine footprints or animal tracks, but they found nothing alarming. The footprints were human, not breghlin, and the animal tracks were just deer.

If breghlin were here, they must be on the other side of the stream. She scanned the far bank. For all she knew, they could be hiding in those trees right now. From the gnomes' description, breghlin were hideous, misshapen ogres, and she didn't want to see one in person. Against her will she imagined them sitting around a campfire gnawing the bones of some hapless gnome. Worse, dragging *her* unconscious body through the woods and roasting her on a spit. *Stop it! You're letting your imagination run wild!*

She stared at the trees on the other side of the stream, wishing her fears were groundless, but if Gliaphon hadn't come along and the breghlin *had* caught her, well, it was best not to think about that. A few days ago she'd loved every inch of this forest, but not anymore. It was the habitat of monsters.

She stumbled, glimpsing movement from the corner of her eye. *What was that? Something moved between those trees!* Heart racing, she stopped, straining to see in the darkness, but of course now that she was watching, nothing moved. Whatever it was, if there had been anything at all, it was probably gone now. *Just watch the woods ahead. Never mind the streambank.* With her luck, she'd run smack into a breghlin while staring at the woods across the stream.

Eventually, younger gnomes moved into the lead and Raenihel and Gliaphon didn't object. Maybe it was better this way. Someone else could be the advance scouts for a while. If it were up to her, she'd turn back now. How long before the gnomes gave up and went home? There was no sign of the dog, and hunting for it was a waste of time. She hugged herself for warmth and kept walking. The effects of the fialazza were wearing off—along with her taste for adventure.

The young gnomes walked a lot faster, and much to her alarm, the gnomes fanned out to cover a wider area. Lana stayed with Raenihel and

Gliaphon. They walked slower than the young gnomes did, but even so, she could barely keep up. Raenihel glanced back now and then to make sure she was still there. His expression was always inscrutable, but when Gliaphon looked back, he looked frightened. Could he see or sense something she couldn't? It was hard to stay focused when she was tired, cold and hungry, but she had to try.

Blocking out physical distractions—the cold, her sore feet, and hunger—she wrapped her fingers around the malachite bracelet and concentrated on the stone. The familiar jittery feeling began to churn in the pit of her stomach. *It's not my imagination. We're being watched.*

The gnomes emerged from the trees and crossed the streamside trail, then paused by the sluggish water as if deciding whether to cross. Dead leaves, tangled twigs, and clumps of rotting grass littered the banks. What had been a cheerful bubbling stream in the spring was now a tired channel of slow-moving, murky water. At its narrowest point, the water was still seven or eight feet across, but she was pretty sure it wasn't deep. She hoped the gnomes wouldn't cross the stream. The land on the other side disturbed her. Something dark and brooding waited in the woods. She could feel it. Whatever it was, the gnomes were heading straight toward it.

Choosing the shallowest part of the muddy stream, several gnomes started across. She couldn't stay here by herself. She had to follow. Were they crossing the stream to confront the evil she sensed, or were they unaware of the danger? She glanced at her malachite bracelet. The crack down the middle of the stone was noticeable despite the green stripes, a reminder that their lives might be in danger.

Malachite. Guardian stone of travelers.

She stepped into the stream. Frigid water closed over her ankles, soaking her sneakers. Her sense of dread grew stronger with each step as she waded through water up to her knees.

Malachite provides protection, power, and security.

On the other side, she climbed the bank to higher ground and waited for the others to cross. The wind, which had blown with irregular gusts, now intensified, as if trying to push them back across the stream. Her soaked pant legs clung uncomfortably, magnifying the cold. She leaned into the wind and clutched herself for warmth. It wasn't safe to be out in the open. They needed to be near trees so they could retreat inside in case of danger, and along the stream bank there was nothing but weeds and scrub brush.

The last of the gnomes slogged through the stagnant water and climbed to the top of the bank. They stamped their feet to dislodge the clinging mud, and then drew their clothing tighter about themselves in a futile effort to ward off the biting wind. No one spoke. She looked around. Who was in the lead, and where did they plan to go?

A wailing howl shattered the silence. She sucked in a startled breath and froze, staring into the darkness. All around her the gnomes stood motionless. The howl died away, and then it came again—a mournful, unearthly baying that echoed through the woods. As if on cue, the gnomes broke into a run. Gliaphon motioned frantically for her to follow—hardly necessary; she was already running.

Gusts of wind whipped loose strands of hair into her eyes. There wasn't much cover. Where could they hide? The gnomes converged on a decaying, fallen tree buried in tall weeds and scrub brush—the only possible hiding place—and dove into the brush. She followed, burrowing deep, ignoring the brambles and twigs that scratched her face and hands. Gasping for breath, she peeked over the rotting tree.

A female gnome near Lana whispered, "That was no normal dog. I'm sure it was the cursed hound."

Oh, great. If the legend was true, they faced something worse than a vicious dog—as if that weren't bad enough.

Ahead, a faint light appeared deep in the woods. Lana watched transfixed as the light moved toward them, growing brighter as it came and illuminating the trees with an unnatural, bluish-white glow. An unreasoning dread gripped her, choking off her breath. *Hiding isn't good enough. We need to run!* She wanted to, but her body felt like lead and refused to move.

The light expanded, wider and wider. It shone through an opening in the trees directly across from their hiding place. Its eerie florescence lit a wide swath of forest.

A tall, pale woman walked out of the woods. A glowing crystal rested on her palm—the source of the eerie light. Thick, wavy black hair reached down to her waist. Her perfectly sculpted features should have been beautiful, but her obsidian eyes looked like dark, bottomless pools. Her skin was unnaturally white, the bloodless hue of death. She was beautiful, but she didn't look human. Pendants that held gems lay against her black gown, and on each arm she wore several bracelets set with gems.

"I have returned. This forest is mine." The air vibrated with energy, and even though the voice was low and restrained, Lana could feel the power behind it. This was a voice of death and destruction—a voice that could make rocks crumble to dust. The evil, the hatred, which radiated from the woman, was nearly tangible, and when she spread her arms every plant and blade of grass within several feet shriveled and turned brown. Lana's mouth dropped open in stunned amazement.

The woman's eyes passed slowly over the brush where the gnomes were hiding.

Lana shivered and held her breath, but something drew her attention from the woman. What was happening? With mounting panic she realized that sensation was draining from her arms and legs. She was growing increasingly numb. When she tried to wriggle her fingers, she could barely move them. Her whole body felt as heavy and immovable as the dead tree in front of her. In fact, she could barely turn her head to see the gnomes. Raenihel and Gliaphon gaped open-mouthed in a trance-like stupor, and the others within her line of vision looked equally overcome.

It took all her strength to turn her head toward the terrifying woman, and it was becoming difficult to breathe.

The barefoot woman walked straight toward Lana, stepping on twigs and stones without flinching. Her eyes, darker than a starless night, did not *reflect* light; they *extinguished* it.

She regarded Lana coldly. "You don't belong here, human. Why are you here after dark?"

Lana couldn't answer even if she wanted to. Her lips wouldn't move.

Branches snapped. Something black sprang from the trees and bounded forward. In a few powerful strides, the wolfhound reached the woman's side. The huge, shaggy black dog looked at Lana with shining eyes, and all Lana could do was stare in horror. *This dog! I've seen it before! How is that possible?*

A jumble of images came flooding back. Some were just vivid nightmares, but many of the things she remembered she felt certain had really happened. At night, this dog had looked through her window. A few times it had gotten into the house and had stood over her bed, thinking thoughts into her mind. Her mind raced with questions. How old had she been when this dog first appeared? When had the nightmares started? Her early teens? Why had it singled her out and what did it want? She had never seen this woman before, only the wolfhound. Where did the woman fit in?

Maybe it was the shock of seeing the dog, or the flood of distracting memories, but something was happening. She realized that her fingers tingled and she could move them a little. Her arms and legs burned with a pins and needles sensation. The paralysis was starting to fade.

Malachite. Guardian stone of travelers. Protection, power, and security.

Could the bracelet be helping her? After all, even though she couldn't actually hold the malachite, it was touching her body. Before, the stone had cracked to warn her of danger. Then, when she was about to be captured, Gliaphon had found her. Had the malachite drawn him? Just how did the stone work? She wasn't sure, but if there was any chance that the stone was helping her, she needed to focus her mind and draw its energy.

Her whole body began to feel hot, and then the pins and needles sensation eased. She tensed her muscles and felt them respond. Maybe, just maybe, she could escape.

Half expecting her body to betray her, she lurched to her feet. A rush of adrenalin surged through her. She whirled and stumbled over two gnomes huddled together in the brush. Bending down she frantically shook the closest one. "Try to move! Run!" She didn't want to abandon them, but she couldn't stay. If they couldn't snap out of their paralysis, there was nothing she could do for them.

The wolfhound howled; the woman screamed in fury; the ground beneath Lana's feet shook like an earthquake.

She ran blindly.

Branches fell, stones flew up from the ground, and the wind pelted her with dirt and leaves. At any moment the wolfhound or the woman would probably catch her. She had no idea where she was going. Cold, wet and hungry, her odds of escape weren't very promising.

When she finally slowed from exhaustion, deep in the woods, a small hand grabbed hers.

And then the forest disappeared.

Chapter 6

Lana opened her eyes inside the Tree Home, dizzy and out of breath. "Thank you," she gasped. "I couldn't have run much further." She let go of Raenihel's hand.

A few gnomes stood nearby, and two more burst in, wild-eyed and panting. After a moment, more gnomes arrived.

Raenihel began to pace, visibly shaken. "It's just as I feared," he said darkly. "The wolfhound was a sign."

The gnomes gathered around him, faces tense, but they didn't say a word. Raenihel finally stopped pacing and turned to Lana with tears in his eyes. With a sweep of his hand that included the other gnomes, he said, "You broke the trance. Bless you, Lana! I hope everyone escaped."

Then everyone began to talk at once.

"When you shook me, Lana, my mind returned from the dark place."

"I heard you shout, 'Run!' and it broke my trance."

"We should never have crossed the stream."

"Well, we didn't expect to be caught in the open!"

"When Raenihel shoved me, I could feel my arms and legs again."

"I ran for the nearest trees, expecting to be struck down at any moment."

Overwhelmed, Lana interrupted. "Who *was* that woman?"

"Sheamathan. She's a woodspirit. The last of her kind," Raenihel answered, "or so we've been told. She's the embodiment of death and corruption. Long ago she turned many of the gnomes to evil."

Lana frowned. "You mean the ones that became the breghlin?"

"Yes," Raenihel replied, looking pleased that she understood.

"Where did she come from?" Lana asked. She had so many questions she didn't know where to begin. She wanted to know about the woman, but actually, she was even more interested in the dog.

One of the gnomes said, "She comes from our world—from Shadow."

Again, the gnomes began to talk at once—bits and pieces of information. It was hard to make heads or tails of it.

"She'd enslave us all if she could."

"She's ruined most of our land with her blight."

A gnome with a white, waist-length beard said, "Our world wasn't always called Shadow. *She* calls it that. She says it's a shadow of its former self and laughs about it."

"Long ago, it was a beautiful place."

"But she corrupted and destroyed it."

"And it will happen here, in the Fair Lands! Wait and see!"

"That's right. The woodspirit will rule The Fair Lands unless someone powerful can stop her," a young male agreed bitterly.

Lana thought back. What had the woodspirit said? *"I have returned. This forest is mine."* So, the woodspirit had been here before. It was all so confusing. She threw her hands up in dismay. "Please! One at a time!"

"I suppose it was selfish to take you with us," Raenihel said, looking rather distracted. "If the wolfhound was here, there was a good chance Sheamathan was as well. Our lore says that a strong human mind can break the woodspirit's control." He frowned. "We, on the other hand, are powerless in her presence."

Lana glared at him. "You took me along in case you needed me to *save* you? You put me in danger based on *folklore*?" Unbelievable. How could he do such a thing? "What if you were wrong and I was just as susceptible to her power?"

Raenihel hung his head. "Gnomes can't withstand her power, but we thought you could. It was foolish of me, and unfair to you."

"I'll say!" She felt like shaking him. Sure, one of the gnomes had done her a good turn—maybe even saved her life—but returning the favor should be up to her, after knowing all the risks. Had she broken the paralysis just because she was human? Did she have an extraordinarily strong mind? Or had the malachite protected her? There was no way to know.

Raenihel said, "Years ago, Sheamathan entered this forest but was driven out—otherwise she would have turned your world into a poisoned wasteland back then, just like ours."

Lana shook her head. "Driven out? How?"

"By a great gem master called the Challenger."

"And what became of this, um, Challenger?"

Raenihel shrugged, looking uncomfortable. "No one knows. The legend is silent about that. After the woodspirit left your world no one ever saw the Challenger again. The fact that the woodspirit has returned to the Fair Lands means something is wrong. Clearly, the Challenger's power to prevent her from returning has been broken."

A grim silence fell over the group. The formerly talkative gnomes suddenly had nothing to say. They looked so miserable that Lana couldn't help but feel depressed. She looked around. Gliaphon and some of the other gnomes hadn't come back.

"The others should be back by now. I'm afraid they've been captured," one of the females said quietly.

"Yes," Raenihel agreed with a frown. "Sheamathan will take anyone she captures to her castle in Shadowglade. Or worse, to her work camps."

"We have to look for them," a young, auburn-haired gnome said. "Maybe they're injured or unconscious and she didn't find them."

Raenihel nodded. "All right, Artham. Take two others and search near the fallen tree where we hid."

Lana hoped Artham wouldn't ask her, but she wouldn't be surprised if he did. The gnomes mistakenly thought she was powerful. She didn't want to face Sheamathan again, and she was afraid of the wolfhound. The gnomes didn't know her history with the dog. If they did, they'd understand, but she wasn't sure she should tell them.

Artham pointed to a young, powerfully built fellow who stood at least two inches taller than the rest. "I'll take Terrilem."

Terrilem wore tall black boots and a rust colored tunic over black trousers. A thick, black beard softened his broad, rather blocky face. His eyes flickered with a mixture of pride and determination. "Thank you, Artham. If our friends are still in this world, we'll bring them back."

Lana thought gloomily, *And if they're not?*

"The human can come with us," Artham said to Raenihel without looking at her. "She proved a great help so far."

"I think we've already imposed enough on our guest," Raenihel said, looking embarrassed.

An uncomfortable silence hung in the air. If they thought she'd volunteer, they were wrong. "I've had my fill of adventures for one night," she said firmly. She shouldn't need an excuse. A simple no ought to be enough, but the tense silence was unbearable, and she felt the need to defend herself. "Look, breaking free from the woodspirit wasn't as easy as you think."

Disapproval showed in Artham's eyes. Terrilem frowned and looked away. How dare they expect her to risk her life? Not only were they not human, they didn't even belong here. Why were they here, anyway? Watchers, they said. What good were watchers? They reported back to their own clans. What help was that?

Artham shrugged. "I'll take Mattiger, then. Wish us luck."

Mattiger, an older gnome with gray hair, stepped forward. Then they were gone.

"Come sit by the fire, Lana," Raenihel urged kindly, taking her arm. "I'm sure you're cold and tired. Relax and have something to eat."

She let out a long breath. "Thank you. It doesn't seem right to rest while your people are in danger, but you're right, I'm tired and hungry and rattled by this whole experience. First, breghlin were hunting me, and now you're telling me that a being—a woodspirit—plans to come here and rule my world. Sorry, but it's too much to handle right now. I need a while to absorb it." It would all seem just as incredible tomorrow, or next week. Fortunately, gemstone folklore had introduced her to strange, inexplicable forces and conditioned her to question rather than dismiss things she didn't understand, so that would help.

Raenihel led her to the circle of glowing stones and sat. She joined him, sitting close enough to the stones to feel their warmth. Her wet, muddy pant legs might finally dry, and that would go a long way toward making her more comfortable. She looked around at the Tree Home, still amazed that such a place existed. Dim light shining from the walls illuminated the gnomes as they opened crocks and filled large earthenware bowls.

In a show of deference and respect, the gnomes served her first. They gave her an empty bowl and offered her an array of foods. She took helpings of mushrooms, turnips, assorted greens, potatoes, and salted venison. Then they poured her a cup of fialazza and she took it with a polite nod. Sipping the red liquid, she felt calmer and more focused. Maybe she *should* tell the gnomes her bizarre tale. She had seen Sheamathan's wolfhound throughout her lifetime. Would they believe her?

Listening to snatches of the gnomes' conversations, she ate everything in her bowl. As she ate the last of the salty meat, Raenihel said, "Tell my people why you are here at night and what happened to you earlier."

Another gnome said, "Yes. How did Gliaphon find you?"

She had given Raenihel a brief synopsis. Now, if they were in the mood for a story, she'd tell them everything.

"I took a long hike. After a couple hours, I found a quiet spot to rest, and I totally lost track of time. When I stopped daydreaming I ran all the way to the parking lot. By then, everyone was gone. The park ranger came through, but he didn't hang around. He figured I was leaving." She gave a short laugh and shook her head. "So did I, but my car wouldn't start. I never bring my cell phone here, so I couldn't call for help." She shrugged. "I was stuck here."

"Then you went back into the forest," Raenihel prompted. "You didn't want to stay in your car?"

"It sounds silly, but I thought I'd be safer in the woods." She laughed at the irony. "The parking lot made me nervous, so I camped in a forest full of breghlin."

"You didn't know the dangers," Raenihel said calmly. He refilled her fialazza.

She took a sip, then set it aside and rubbed her hands idly on her knees. "I had a camping place in mind, so I headed there with a blanket. I took the streamside trail through the lowlands, and I got the strangest feeling that someone was watching me. It bothered me so much I changed trails."

Several of the gnomes exchanged meaningful glances.

"When I climbed the hill to the pine forest, the atmosphere was completely different. I felt safe there. It seemed so peaceful."

"You have keen perception for a human," said a female near Lana. "It's quite unusual, isn't it, Raenihel?"

"Yes," Raenihel agreed. "Very unusual. And it may have saved her life."

Lana reached for her fialazza and drank. Good thing it calmed her or she might not make it through this story. "I felt safe enough to camp for the night, so I spread my blanket and tried to sleep. Well, that didn't last long. I woke after a little while. I heard voices in the distance, and whistling, like signals. No one is supposed to be here at night. I was in danger and I had *proof*—the stone in my bracelet had split in two." Setting down her cup, she pushed up her sleeve and held out her arm. Malachite had warned her of danger, as crazy as that sounded. But why should they believe the folklore? Maybe they'd laugh at her.

The gnomes leaned forward, staring wide-eyed at the large, striped, green stone. Conversation exploded around her. Raenihel grabbed her wrist and cried over the din, "Malachite! It's malachite!"

Lana gave him a startled look. "Yes, what do you know about it?"

"Forgive me. Where are my manners?" He let go of her wrist and the gnomes fell silent but he continued to stare at the stone. "Malachite is prized in Shadow. It's a rare, powerful stone." He looked up and said reverently, "Malachite is the guardian stone of travelers, a powerful, protective stone."

Her mouth fell open. Almost verbatim what she had read.

Raenihel said, "Our world has a few of the same gemstones as yours, such as malachite. But most are unique to our world and many are amazingly powerful."

Lana was stunned. "Really? More powerful than ours?"

He nodded. "Oh, yes. Partly due to their inherent properties, and partly because our world is simply more conducive to gem powers."

"More conducive? What do you mean?"

"Stones from your world become more powerful in ours," He paused, frowning slightly, and then laid his hand on her arm. "For instance, your bracelet would be far more effective if you wore it in Shadow. Even so, it warned you of danger and protected you. Perhaps it broke Sheamathan's control."

Lana took a deep breath and let it out slowly. Her ability to use gem powers had improved her life in many ways. If gems from her world became far more powerful in Shadow, that would be amazing. If gems native to Shadow were magnitudes more powerful than any of the gems in her world, that would be mind blowing!

"Please, go on with your story," the gnomes urged.

Where had she left off? She took a deep breath and continued. "Anyway, then I heard hunting horns and a dog barked. I ran but I couldn't find a good place to hide. I heard a soft whistle behind me, and there stood Gliaphon, motioning for me to come with him."

A stocky gray-bearded gnome smiled and asked, "And what did you think when you saw him?"

She laughed. "I was stunned! I didn't know what to think! I'd never seen anyone like him."

The gnomes chuckled good-naturedly.

"I really don't know how Gliaphon found me. You'll have to ask him." She immediately winced at her words. Poor Gliaphon. Where was he now? She continued hastily, "He must have heard the horns and wondered what the breghlin were tracking. And he probably heard the dog bark. Now I understand your worries about a dog being here at night. You know the wolfhound's history. Actually, I have some history with that dog, too."

"Really, how is that?" Raenihel asked, clearly surprised.

She laced her fingers together to keep her hands still. "When I saw the wolfhound tonight, it unlocked suppressed memories. Since my early teens I've had nightmares of a huge, shaggy black dog with frightening, intelligent eyes. And I've seen the dog when I was awake, too. On my street. Outside my bedroom window. A few times I woke and found it leaning over my bed." She stopped and took a shuddering breath. "This must all sound crazy. The dog speaks in my mind—or tries to, anyway. I block the words and refuse to listen." She looked up at the gnomes. "I swear it was the same dog I saw tonight."

She expected the gnomes to burst into excited conversation but they didn't. They probably thought she was making this up. It did sound crazy, even to her. Feeling embarrassed, she blinked back tears.

Raenihel took her hand and stroked it soothingly. "It's a mysterious tale, indeed, and very troubling."

The gnomes murmured their assent but were otherwise silent.

"Beings from Shadow can't enter the Fair Lands," Raenihel said tentatively, as if thinking the matter through while trying to explain it.

"They can't go any farther than the Amulet—the protective realm around the portal that keeps outsiders from entering your world. If the wolfhound is an enchanted human, then I suppose the Amulet wouldn't prevent it from entering your world." He paused and frowned thoughtfully. "If the legend is true, and the wolfhound's human mind returns during the full moon, perhaps during that time it can communicate with you."

"But why would the wolfhound single out Lana?" one of the gnomes asked with a troubled look.

Raenihel shook his head. "I have no idea. This is all quite puzzling."

At least they believed her.

"Do you still have the nightmares? And visitations?" an elderly gnome asked.

"Yes. I've just gotten better at blocking them from my memory." She was nearly certain her gemstones had created a protective mechanism that blocked the incidents from her conscious mind. She finally understood the uneasiness that had been keeping her awake. How many times had she felt haunted by a troubling dream that she couldn't quite remember? She frowned thoughtfully. The other morning she'd woken to a dog barking. The wolfhound? The enchanted dog's attempts to contact her in person or through dreams were becoming more frequent, but why?

Just then the search party returned without the missing gnomes, and their grim expressions said more than words. The seated gnomes leapt to their feet. Lana followed, sharing their despair even though she barely knew the lost gnomes.

Artham said bitterly, "There's no sign of them. They're gone."

Terrilem added, "The breghlin are gone, too. They must have followed Sheamathan back to Shadowglade."

"They're her scouts. They'll be back," Raenihel said unhappily. He rubbed his lined forehead. "Sheamathan's next step in accessing the Fair Lands will be the destruction of this forest."

"What should we do?" Artham asked.

"Right now, our first priority is our captured friends," Raenihel told him.

"How can we rescue them?" Terrilem demanded. "No rescue attempt has ever succeeded. Anyone who tries is captured or killed."

Raenihel said in a determined tone, "Nevertheless we must try."

Another elderly male spoke. "This is a dangerous new era. The Challenger's power over the woodspirit has been broken. We must find a new Challenger."

Artham said, "Fate has intervened." He turned, pointing at Lana. "Is it mere happenstance that this woman arrived on the very night Sheamathan returned to the forest?"

Lana bristled at Artham's presumption. The gnomes looked at her hopefully.

"But I—" was all she got out before Artham interrupted her half-formed protest.

"She saved us once."

She glared at him. "I barely—"

He spoke over her. "She has the ability to withstand Sheamathan's power."

It was infuriating to be the subject of the conversation but not allowed to speak.

The female who had sat near Lana during dinner cried, "Yes! And she bears one of the rare power stones! Look at her bracelet!"

Artham's brows shot up and he and Terrilem walked toward her. She didn't want to show them the bracelet, but really, what good would it do to refuse? The other gnomes had already seen it. She reluctantly pushed up her sleeve and held out her arm. Terrilem reached out to touch her but pulled back. Maybe he could feel her eyes boring into him. Artham merely bent over the stone. He let out a low whistle and said, "What a magnificent malachite! Where did you find it?"

She knew better than to say that malachite was common here. She was in enough trouble now. The gnomes already believed she had special powers and could rescue their missing friends. She snatched her arm away and said, "If you think I'm going to risk my life on a doomed rescue mission in another world, you're mistaken."

Artham took a step toward her and they locked angry gazes. "Why do you call it a doomed mission?" he demanded. "Don't you believe in your own abilities?"

"What do you know about my abilities?" she snapped. "Sheamathan almost captured me. Yes, I broke free. I was lucky. I might not be so lucky next time."

Artham gave an exasperated sigh. "Merely being human gives you some protection, and you have the malachite as well."

"So, because I'm human I have nothing to fear from Sheamathan?"

"Far less than we do."

"Tell that to Sheamathan's wolfhound!"

The other gnomes watched the verbal sparring with helpless fascination.

Artham sputtered, "But it's only a legend. We can't be certain the dog was ever human."

She smiled in victory. Artham's annoyance was proof she'd made a valid point. "*I* have reason to believe he *was*," she said coldly. Would she ever convince the gnomes that she wasn't their savior? "Here's what I know about your Challenger—you're looking in the wrong place for a *new* one!"

Finally Raenihel intervened. "My ancestors spoke with the Challenger. They claimed he was human, but I see now they were mistaken. We were wrong to assume that you could help us."

What a tactful insult. She tried not to show her resentment. Maybe she had that coming.

Artham stalked off and Terrilem followed. The rest of the gnomes stared at her with long faces.

"There's nothing more we can do tonight," Raenihel said. "But soon, someone must go to Shadowglade to find our missing brethren. At daybreak we'll return to Shadow and send messengers to warn the other clans that Sheamathan grows stronger and has passed through the portal again."

Maybe it was nervy to ask questions, especially after refusing to help them, but she was curious about the gnomes. "How many gnomes live in Shadow?"

"Hundreds of thousands, I suppose. We live in hiding, whether in Tree Homes or caves. Some parts of Shadow have suffered less from Sheamathan's blight. We call those places Safe Havens, since the land supports life, but it's somewhat of a misnomer since we aren't safe there, or anywhere. You see, Sheamathan uses the breghlin to capture gnomes to mine minerals and gems. Fortunately, only a few from my clan have been captured over the years." Raenihel smiled a bit self-consciously and added, "Some gnomes consider humans as dangerous as Sheamathan, but my clan does not share that view."

One by one the gnomes drifted away. Unrolling colorful, padded bedrolls, probably stuffed with leaves or moss, they lay down, preparing to sleep until dawn.

Lana said to Raenihel, "I'm sorry to let you down. Gliaphon probably saved my life and I'll always be grateful. Maybe it seems like I don't care about your friends but I—"

Mercifully he cut her off or she would have kept babbling. "Say no more, dear one. You've already done us a great service."

Raenihel spread two bedrolls along the wall. Lana lay down on the fleecy green mat he offered her, which was surprisingly soft and comfortable. It smelled like grass and wild flowers. The dim glow of the tree walls shed a soft, reassuring light, like a child's nightlight. Whispers, mixed with light snoring, soft gasps, and snuffling sounds, surrounded her in a strange but comforting symphony. Before long, despite the strangeness of her surroundings, she felt herself drifting off to sleep.

Chapter 7

Morning sunlight shone on Lana's face. She opened her eyes and looked up at a canopy of autumn leaves and a cloudless blue sky. *Blue sky!* She sat bolt upright. *I'm outside the Tree Home!* It would be easy to believe the events of the evening had been a dream, but no dream had ever been that detailed, and besides, she was sitting on the green bedroll Raenihel had lent her. This was the same tree she had fallen asleep inside; she was certain of that. The gnomes had probably returned to Shadow at dawn. Apparently they had deposited her outside, but she didn't remember a thing. Were they back in their Safe Havens now?

She wrapped her arms around her knees. Birds chirped, insects whirred, the leaves rustled gently. So peaceful. So soothing. The forest seemed its normal self this morning. If only she could forget last night, but forgetting wouldn't make it any less real. No, even if she could push everything else from her mind—the gnomes, the breghlin, the woodspirit—there was still the wolfhound. Her nightmare beast was real and capable of tracking her. It was better to know that, she supposed.

She knelt and rolled up her bedding. Stuffing the bedroll under her arm, she started for her car via the long route that went through the lowlands. She needed to replay the events of the evening, think it through, and come to grips with it.

At the place where she and the gnomes had forded the stream, she stopped and looked for the fallen tree. There! She and the gnomes had hidden behind *that* tree. The woodspirit had nearly captured her. Her heart beat faster at the thought. Sheamathan had stood with outstretched arms and everything growing around the woodspirit had shriveled and died. Who could do things like that? And what *worse* things could she do? Lana stood absently rubbing her malachite bracelet. Humans might escape Sheamathan's paralyzing control, but they wouldn't escape the destruction she'd bring here.

Lana turned and walked away. She had broken the gnomes' trance last night. Some of them had reached the nearest trees and escaped. But Gliaphon and a few others hadn't gotten away in time. Sheamathan had taken them captive. How could the gnomes fight a being who could paralyze them and put them in a mindless trace? In the past, they'd had an ally, the Challenger. She rubbed her forehead and frowned. Had he really been human? It probably didn't matter. He was gone and his power over the woodspirit had been broken. The gnomes must stay clear of the woodspirit and her breghlin servants; otherwise, they'd wind up in work camps. *Maybe I should worry less about the gnomes and more about what could happen here.* She shook her head sadly. The gnomes were deluded if they thought she could save them. She didn't know how to save her *own* world.

Breaking into a run, she ran all the way to the end of the trail, crossed the picnic area, and slowed to a walk as she reached the deserted parking lot. She glanced at her watch before she remembered that it didn't work, but oddly enough it was working again.

Time for a snack while she waited for the rangers. Unlocking the car, she tossed the bedroll into the back seat and then went to open the trunk. The first thing she saw as she lifted the lid was the strange stone. With all the excitement last night, she had forgotten all about it. She picked it up and tilted it at various angles. Fascinating. The shimmering silver flecks were so unusual. She'd never seen a stone like this. Why was it so unnaturally dense? And why, after holding it, even for a few seconds, did her hands feel numb? How did it *do* that?

She grabbed her purse and a few snacks and got back into the car, setting the stone on the dash.

She felt better after eating, but it was uncomfortably cold in the car. *How much longer till the rangers come?* She looked at the car clock, but of course it wasn't working—dead battery—so she checked her watch. The stupid thing had stopped again. When she got home the watch was going straight in the trash. Maybe she'd take a hammer to it first just to make herself feel better.

It was so aggravating to be stuck here. She hadn't tried to start the car this morning because it seemed pointless, but maybe she should try. There was no reason for her battery to be dead, and she couldn't imagine what else could be wrong. She dragged her keys from her purse and held her breath as she twisted the key in the ignition. "Come on! Start!" she ordered as if she could intimidate it into cooperating. Nothing happened. "Rats! Why won't you start?"

Frustrated, she reached for the stone to kill some time. Within seconds her hands felt cold and numb. *Heat. Heat is energy. What did they teach us in school? Heat energy, measured in calories, flows across the boundary between two objects.* But heat and energy didn't seem to be flowing between the stone and her hand. Why? Face it; the stone was unnatural. It was way too heavy, and the numb sensation was totally bizarre. Checking her books would be a waste of time. Raenihel had said there were different stones in his world. This had to be one of them. What other explanation could there be?

She gave it an appraising glance as something occurred to her. *Energy, or lack thereof? Time for another experiment.*

She carried the stone to the grass at the edge of the parking lot, left it there and went back to her car. This time when she turned the key the engine started without hesitation. "Yes!"

She looked at her watch. It was running again. No need for the hammer after all. This was starting to make sense. The stone interfered with energy—blocked it somehow. Maybe it siphoned off energy, too, but judging by the fact that her watch battery still worked, it was more likely that the stone just blocked the transference of energy. So, she couldn't drive off with the stone, but maybe she could carry it away. That would be her next experiment. Raenihel had said that the protective area, the Amulet, kept outsiders from entering her world. Did it only stop people? For all she knew, maybe *nothing* from outside could go through. If that were the case, what would happen to a foreign object when it reached the boundary? Would it just stop there? Disappear? Disintegrate? She would love to find out, but she couldn't take a chance with the stone.

But I have something else!

Grabbing the green bedroll from the back seat, she set it beside her. *Perfect! You're my guinea pig!* Wait. She was getting ahead of herself. First, she had to take care of the stone—hide it.

Taking no chances, she left the car running. She picked up the stone and looked around for a hiding place where no one would find it. Maybe in the woods. She walked to the nearest trailhead and saw a rotted stump that would be easy to identify. Perfect.

Using a broken branch with a sharp end, she dug a hole at the base of the stump, put her prize inside, backfilled, and smoothed the dirt. Standing by the hole, she stared at the ground. Yesterday had started out as a normal Saturday, and then she'd come here.

If I hadn't taken this stone I wouldn't have been stranded here. This crazy adventure would never have happened.

Why did *she* have to be the one to discover all of this? Why couldn't it be someone older and wiser—someone who would know what to do?

Leaves swayed gently in the breeze as she drove to the exit. By day, the forest looked so peaceful and safe.

She pulled onto the main road. Music was what she needed. Loud music. She didn't want to think about the portal, or the frightening world on the other side. She glanced toward the radio and noticed something.

The green bedroll was gone.

Chapter 8

Lana piled research books on the kitchen table, and then went to make a pot of coffee. Strong coffee. Of course she should sleep, at least a few hours, before hitting the books, but how could she? She was too anxious to prove beyond any reasonable doubt that the strange stone wasn't from this world. Any gemologist would feel the same way. She grabbed a banana and some yogurt while she waited for the coffee to finish brewing.

One hour turned into two, and then three before she closed the last book and leaned back in her chair, rubbing her forehead wearily. She had checked every book and magazine on this table, and she hadn't found anything that looked like the specimen from the park. The odd stone was clearly *not* from this world. She gave a rueful smile. Too bad she couldn't name her discovery after herself, but she couldn't even *show* the stone to anyone.

Her head hurt and her eyes felt dry. Little wonder after looking at several hundred pages and thousands of photos. A nap would help—an hour or two on the couch. She stretched out, closed her eyes, and was out immediately. When she woke it was nearly suppertime. She sighed in annoyance. How had she slept so long? At least her headache was gone, but now she'd wasted most of the day, and she had so many things she wanted to do. For one, she wanted to talk to Dad. Not about the weird stone, even though that would be fun, but about gemstones in general.

Despite their mutual interest in gemstones and jewelry, they had never discussed gem lore.

Dad was a down-to-earth, practical sort, so she avoided subjects like that. Not that he would outwardly poke fun at her. He was far too kind for that, but she didn't want him to think less of her. Still, she needed to know where he stood on the subject, and the only way to find out was to ask.

When she arrived at her parents' she saw Mom first and chatted for a few minutes. As expected, Dad was in his woodworking shop. He loved to restore old furniture. Few pieces were too damaged to be saved, he always said, and he enjoyed the challenge. Sometimes he rescued pieces left by the curb on trash day. He couldn't resist. They were like stray puppies that needed his love. Mom wasn't always so thrilled with his projects, but she humored him. Lana owned a few pieces that Dad had generously provided now that she had her own place.

Moving a can of varnish off a three-legged stool, she sat and watched her father refinish a small, two-drawer end table. He had stripped the old finish from the table and made a new leg to match the missing one. Now he was applying new stain and varnish. Even with a window open for ventilation, the workshop smelled like fresh-cut wood, turpentine, and varnish.

They exchanged pleasantries about the weather, and then chatted about her brothers, nieces and nephews. She wasn't sure how to segue into the subject of gem lore. When their conversation finally hit a lull, she took a deep breath and said, "You know how much I love gems, but we've never talked about my pet interest."

Dad paused, varnish brush in hand, and looked up with a smile. "What pet interest is that?"

"Gemstone legends and folklore." There was no going back now even though she felt awkward. "Since ancient times, people have believed that some gems have healing properties, and others affect moods and personality traits. They can bring love or luck. You know. That sort of thing."

"Well now," Dad said as he went back to work, "I've read about such things, but since it's just mythology, I never bothered to study it. Are many people interested in folklore these days?"

Dad wasn't an imaginative person like her, and she wasn't surprised that "mythology" didn't interest him. "It's more popular than it used to be. Some customers aren't into it, but quite a few are. Most of them go to gem and mineral shows. People who collect individual specimens tend to be interested in anything gemstone-related."

Dad gave her an appraising look. "I've never set up at gem and mineral shows. I was always too busy running the store. Arlene would complain if I added anything to her workload, but you could do a show."

Lana was momentarily at a loss for words. She hadn't been hinting. Quite honestly, she hadn't even *thought* of doing a show. The idea appealed to her, though. She'd be independent. No Arlene hanging over her shoulder. "I'll look into it if you think it's a good idea."

"Yes, absolutely." He laid down his brush, pushed a stack of newspapers off an old bentwood rocker and plopped into it, looking genuinely excited. "It's a great idea! I'm sorry I didn't think of it. Your talents are going to waste at the moment, but you need a little longer to get the feel of things before you take over the business. Gem shows would be a great way to get more experience." He gave her a conspiratorial wink. "If you want to sell common garnets and topaz you can, and if you want to peddle magic gems, you can do that, too!"

Lana laughed, more amused than offended by the magic gem remark. "So, you think gem lore is humbug, but you don't think I'm silly for studying it?"

"Silly? No. Come to think of it, your grandfather used to talk about such things. I never paid much attention. My mind was on the more practical aspects of the jewelry store. As you know, I learned most of my gem identification and stone-setting skills from Dad. Picked up the rest on my own. I never went to school like you did. I'm very proud of you. I hope you know that."

She smiled and sat a little straighter. Compliments always embarrassed her.

Dad leaned back in the chair and rocked absently with a distant look in his eyes. "I wish you had known your Grandpa Carl better, but you were barely seven when he passed. Your brothers, being so much older than you, got to listen to his stories about running the store back in the old days."

"So, was he interested in folklore?"

"I don't think he put much stock in it himself, but he told me a few tales. Stories passed down in the family."

"Do you remember any?"

"Most of the tales originated with Elias, I think, in the late 1800s. Carl said people used to believe that gems protected them from danger. There were other gems that gave people better eyesight, or took away ailments like arthritis or gallstones. One gemstone supposedly gave the user telepathic powers." He shook his head at the thought and gave a little laugh. "Another one was supposed to make a person invisible. Oh, and he told me several stories about poison."

"Poison?"

"If you were invited to someone's home for dinner, and you suspected foul play, you carried a gem that sweat moisture or turned dark in the presence of poison."

"Sweating gems. That's a new one. I'll have to add that to my files." She couldn't help feeling disappointed that most of her family viewed gem lore as fanciful tales. If any of them had taken it seriously, it had probably been Elias. "I love hearing family history," she said. "Especially anything to do with the store. Most people can't say they're part of a family business that's been around for five generations."

Dad absently brushed sawdust off his pant legs. "I'll admit, I found the business more duty than pleasure at first, but I was grateful for the start in life. I liked to be my own boss. Eventually I came to enjoy my work."

"I guess the family passion for jewelry skipped a generation, and I got it."

"Yes, I think so." He stopped rocking and sat forward in his chair. "Speaking of passed down, I should give you a few things now while I'm thinking about it. Things related to the store. You're the one who should have them, since you'll be taking over. Would you like that?"

"Like it! Are you kidding? Absolutely!"

Together they walked into the house. He took her to his den, pulled out the bottom right-hand desk drawer, and lifted out a slightly squashed cardboard box tied with a faded red ribbon.

"This box has some old pictures, a few letters, and a very early notebook with comments about gemstones. You'll probably find some of it interesting, especially the notebook."

How could she not find it interesting? This was her family's history. She would look at every picture and read every letter. Reverently, she took the box from his hands. She could hardly wait to get home and look inside.

Chapter 9

The kitchen table was a mess, so Lana went straight to her bedroom, settled onto her bed, and pulled the box onto her lap. This was more exciting than getting presents at Christmas. She lifted the lid and started with the top layer: old black-and-white photographs. Several pictures showed her grandfather or great-grandfather working in the store—tall, dignified men in suits. She'd seen other photos of them, years ago, so their faces looked vaguely familiar.

Most of the photos just showed the store, with no people in the photos. From the late 1800s through the early 1920s, Peterson's Pharmacy and Harold's Five and Dime had flanked Grayson Jewelers. Apparently both of those Main Street businesses had succumbed to The Great Depression because other names appeared on their brick facades in later photos.

She studied an interior photo. Even though the store had changed with the times, she recognized it. Wouldn't it be fun if she could see inside those old showcases? Everything would be antiques now. And look at those fancy brass chandeliers—impressive but a bit too ornate, especially for a small town jewelry store.

She picked up a photo of the office. Not much had changed. The paneling and bookcases were the same, and even those Hudson River style oil paintings she had admired for years. And there, over the file cabinet, hung the framed news story about the store. Look, the old regulator clock in exactly the same spot as today. She shook her head in amazement. This photo was a great find. Why was it laying in a musty old box? It deserved a place of honor. When she was manager, she'd have it framed and put it on her desk.

Under the photos lay a stack of letters, some in envelopes and some loose. One small envelope felt empty. She pulled out a note-size paper that only had numbers: 14 35 72. How odd.

She skimmed through all the letters to see which held general family news and which were about the store. The personal letters, discussing important events like engagements, weddings and funerals, were from relatives whose name she recognized. She'd read them all thoroughly, but not now. The notebook was waiting at the bottom of the box and she was dying to read it.

The last item before the notebook was a business correspondence. The curious note, written in neat, elegant handwriting read:

Elias,

I will proceed according to your recommendations:

Chalcedony, Malachite, Hematite, Aquamarine, Topaz, Sapphire, Jasper, and Sugalite.

A mixture of these should produce the desired benefits. I shall let you assess whether this proves true upon its completion, as you have more experience than I do in this regard.

Very Truly Yours,

Jules

She read the note again. Desired benefits? Not desired *appearance*, desired *benefits*. Could he be talking about gem lore properties? What an odd combination of gems. She tried to picture a piece of jewelry that incorporated all of those gemstones. Who was Jules? As far as she knew he wasn't a relative, so he must have been a customer or a friend.

Now for the item she was most eager to see: great-great-grandfather Elias's notebook. She lifted it out and flipped through the pages with growing excitement. This was even better than she'd hoped. It had lists of gemstones with detailed notes about their folklore. Finally! Someone in the family shared her passion for gem lore!

Bending over the ledger, grinning like an idiot, her hands trembled with excitement. Elias had made notations about healing properties as well as the stones' influences on mood and behavior. And look! He'd put a star beside some gems and a big X beside others. Hopefully, somewhere in the ledger he explained the marks or she'd drive herself crazy trying to figure it out.

Now *this* was interesting. Toward the back of the ledger he'd listed pairs of gems. There were also groups of four to six, like the group in Jules's letter. She might be wrong, but it looked as if he had grouped gems together because they had similar abilities. Other groups of stones didn't fit that pattern, but he must have had a reason for listing them together. She had a wild idea. What if combining unrelated stones *altered* their powers? She reread the note from Jules:

A mixture of these should produce the desired benefits. I shall let you assess whether this proves true upon its completion, as you have more experience than I do in this regard.

Were Elias and Jules experimenting with various stone combinations, trying to produce specific powers? What a fascinating project, if so. She read the message again. Interesting. She hadn't noticed before. *Elias* wasn't making the piece, *Jules* was, based on Elias's stone recommendations. So, maybe Jules was a fellow jeweler with an interest in gem lore.

She closed the ledger and rubbed the cover absently. For years she'd collected gems and her collection was quite impressive. If gems became more powerful in Shadow as Raenihel claimed, maybe hers could help the gnomes, especially if combining gemstones enhanced their abilities.

It was worth looking into. She didn't want to be the gnomes' new hero, but if her gems could form part of a defense strategy, she was willing to start with that and see what developed.

* * *

Two weeks passed in a blur of activity. When she wasn't working at the store, Lana delved into gem lore and researched the gem-and-jewelry-show circuit. The gnomes were never far from her mind, though, and that was starting to bother her. In a few months she'd be taking over the store. How could she run a store while keeping tabs on County Forest Park and the gnomes? She couldn't drop off her gem collection at the Tree Home and walk away. She didn't know if gnomes could draw out the gems' powers. Maybe Raenihel and his clan were like most of the humans she knew who touched gems and got no reaction.

Had anyone found Gliaphon or the others? She could still see the gnomes' expectant faces, looking at her so hopefully and believing that armed with only her malachite bracelet she could stand up to Sheamathan. There had to be a solution. She wasn't a believer in "fate" or "destiny" in the way some people thought of it—a fixed outcome that couldn't be changed. But she *did* believe she had stumbled into this strange adventure for a reason. Saturday, she would go back to the forest and look for the gnomes.

* * *

Shortly after noon on Saturday, Lana locked her apartment and ran down the stairs with food and water, a compact reference book on gems, a flashlight, her cell phone, rain poncho and an assortment of useful items in her backpack. This time she was ready for almost anything. Under her T-shirt she wore her pouch with assorted gemstones.

She opened the car door, feeling a touch of annoyance. Yesterday had been a beautiful, sunny day. Today, the sky was dreary and overcast, but she couldn't wait for better weather.

As she approached the entrance to County Forest Park, it was painfully obvious that something was wrong. Everywhere else the trees were turning color, showing vibrant shades of crimson, orange and yellow. Here, at least half the trees were bare, and the rest looked diseased. Their foliage had shriveled and turned a sickly yellowish-green with black spots. This was horrible. The park's forestry team must be baffled, especially since the disease had taken hold so suddenly. This blight couldn't be coincidence. The disease had started just after Sheamathan's arrival, and the gnomes had mentioned that the woodspirit's plan of attack would center on destroying the forest.

Lana drove into the park and headed for the farthest parking lot, blinking back tears. She loved this park and the blight sickened her. Crying about it wouldn't do any good, though. Anger would be more useful. Somehow, she had to stop the destruction.

Did Shadow look like this? According to the gnomes, Sheamathan had corrupted and destroyed most of the land and they were concerned about that, but right now, they were more concerned about their captured friends.

The park looked deserted, which wasn't surprising. The diseased forest was the last place anyone would go for an autumn walk. She parked, pulled her backpack out of the trunk, slipped it on, and started walking. Would the gnomes believe she had already decided to help them before she'd seen the blight?

The shortest route to the gnomes' Tree Home would take her through the pine forest that she loved so much. She was afraid to think what it looked like now. Everywhere, leaves spotted with black covered the ground. Moss on rocks and fallen logs, green two weeks ago, had turned brown. Only a few squirrels or chipmunks scampered through the leaves, and the wrens, sparrows, robins and other birds she usually saw were strangely absent. A mournful hush had fallen over her beloved forest.

When she finally reached the familiar evergreen-clad hills, she sighed with relief. So far, the towering pines had withstood the blight. They stood proud and steadfast as they always had. The fragrant carpeted path of fallen needles hadn't changed, either. But how long would this area remain free of disease?

The sky grew more overcast as she walked. The air felt humid, oppressive. She wiped a film of perspiration from her face and scanned the woods. It might be harder than she thought to find the Tree Home. The giant oak wasn't near any of the marked trails. Distinctive groups of rocks and trees, and the occasional fallen log, were her only reference points. Hadn't the tree been near a beech grove?

Just as she despaired of finding the right tree, she spotted its massive trunk. Running toward the tree, she swept aside branches that got in her way.

As she approached she called, "Is anyone there?" The gnomes probably weren't here this time of day, but she had to check. She called a little louder, "It's me. Lana. Is anyone there?" No response. How could they hear anyone outside, anyway? Maybe they sensed rather than heard visitors. Now what? It was pointless to stay here. She might as well check the campfire and see if anyone had been around. After that, she could photograph the stone she'd buried by the stump. The gnomes probably wouldn't arrive until after dark, so she'd come back then.

Thunder rumbled ominously in the distance. The first spatters of rain fell. *Great. Just great.* The forecast had mentioned scattered thundershowers, but usually she got lucky and it rained somewhere else. The wind was picking up, whistling through the trees. She glanced at the sky. Huge thunderclouds, driven by a swift wind, were moving in. What were her chances of making it back to the car before she got drenched? She took off her backpack. Might as well put on her rain poncho right now.

Leaves fell from branches overhead, and others rose from the ground, swirling together. An eerie gloom blanketed the forest. The rising full moon appeared briefly, quickly smothered by clouds. She struggled into the poncho and yanked the hood over her hair. No doubt about it, a cold front was moving in. The temperature had already dropped several degrees. She hastily entered the Tree Home's coordinates in her phone and started to walk.

Lightning flashed. Thunder boomed, and the gentle patter of rain came faster. This wasn't the safest place during a lightning storm. She walked quickly, head down, shoulders hunched, in a futile attempt to avoid the rain. Droplets splattered against her hood and dribbled down the poncho.

Branches snapped somewhere on her right. The sound was unmistakable, even over the relentless patter of rain. She stopped and stood perfectly still, listening. The sound came again—someone or something forging through the underbrush. At first she couldn't see anything. Then she glimpsed a dark form thirty or forty feet away. A deer? No, too small. Maybe a fox or coyote.

Her heart beat faster as another possibility suggested itself.

She broke into a run, trying not to slip on wet leaves as she dodged fallen limbs and jumped over exposed tree roots and rocks.

Was it following? She didn't want to look, but it was better to know. She glanced aside. The animal kept pace with her, running in a parallel course about thirty feet away.

The ground was slippery and treacherous. She dodged rocks and jumped muddy ditches, afraid she'd lose her footing if she didn't slow down. Lightning flashed again, illuminating the woods. Her breath caught in her throat. There was no mistaking it now—the animal was Sheamathan's wolfhound.

Why was it here? Her sides ached but she couldn't stop running. She had to stay ahead of it. The pine forest lay just ahead. It offered no real refuge, but the trees were widely spaced, the land more even. It would be easier to run there.

Snatches of nightmares flashed through her mind—the wolfhound outside her bedroom window. It wanted her to come to the window and let it in, but she wasn't that stupid. And yet, she remembered the wolfhound bending over her bed, speaking inside her head. Somehow it *had* gotten into the house. It knew her name. Her defense had been, *don't listen when it speaks. Think of something else. Crowd out the voice.*

Before she reached the first row of pines, lightning sliced the sky in a blinding flash. Thunder boomed, faded into an angry rumble, and then boomed again. The skies opened. Sheets of rain pelted her. A gust of wind whipped back her hood and rain stung her face, nearly blinding her. Strands of wet hair dripped in her eyes and clung to her face. She let out a moan of despair, wishing she were home, or anywhere but here. If only the rain would let up. Her flimsy poncho stuck to her like a coating of wet leaves.

Swiping rain from her eyes, she plunged into the pine forest. It ought to be drier here. Overhead, the dense network of pine boughs trapped most of the rain, but it was dark, so dark, she could barely see where she was going. Silently cursing the weight of her backpack, she raced forward.

Her foot snagged on an exposed root and she felt her leg twist. She tried to catch herself but went down hard on both knees, pitching forward, her palms bearing most of her weight. Pine needles stabbed into her. Wincing at the pain, she pushed herself off the ground and struggled to her feet. Her knees hurt like crazy but she had to keep going.

The wolfhound emerged from the trees and stood, watching her.

Her heart skipped a beat. She needed something to defend herself—a branch—anything. She looked around frantically, but there was nothing within reach.

Lana. Its voice spoke in her head. *I mean you no harm.*

The dog's intelligent eyes held her captive. She stared at the beast, her nightmare beast, her face frozen with dread. The wolfhound belonged to Sheamathan the woodspirit and answered to her. Why should she trust it? She'd resist its voice as she always had. It wouldn't trick her into opening her mind. *I won't listen! My gem powers are strong enough to block you!*

Maybe she wasn't defenseless. She had powerful gemstones: gems for courage, wisdom, and protection. Now when she most needed their help, she must trust her abilities to use them. Opening the pouch she grabbed a handful of gems and held them tightly. She kept a wary eye on the wolfhound as she concentrated, and before long its voice became so faint she could hardly hear it. *No time. Full moon. Listen to me,* she thought the dog said.

She shook her head defiantly, refusing to listen. The wolfhound turned and began to walk away, then it stopped and turned back and their eyes met. She knew she should look away, but somehow she couldn't. Its intelligent black eyes held a terrible sadness and longing. The wolfhound threw back its head and let out a tormented howl. That howl was as disturbing as the voice in her head. She bolted, despite her bruised legs and throbbing knees.

When she slowed and looked back, the wolfhound was gone.

Chapter 10

Lana kept running until her knees throbbed so badly the pain made her queasy, and then she stumbled to a halt. It was a wonder she'd made it this far. The pain was worse than when she had fallen. She picked up a sturdy branch, and leaning on it heavily, used it as a walking stick. Feeling like a resident in a nursing home, she plodded along the muddy trail. From time to time she looked back, but there was no sign of the wolfhound. Maybe she could finally relax.

Why had the dog come in the daytime? The gnomes weren't usually around then. Was it looking for her? If she hadn't been here, would it have gone to her home?

The rain was finally letting up, but her knees hurt too much for side trips. Her plan to walk to the campfire site, and the tree where she'd buried the stone, would have to wait. Right now, the only place she wanted to go was her car. She had to tend her knees.

As usual, her car was the only one in the lot. She slid behind the steering wheel, careful not to bump her knees, and turned on the radio.

Rolling up her pant leg, she inspected her injuries. Both knees looked puffy, but aside from that, the worst damage consisted of ugly brush burns that stung like mad. Walking would be painful for a few days. Between her sore knees, and her rattled nerves, she didn't want to go to the Tree Home tonight. But if she put it off, would she ever come back?

Sticking with her plan, she drove out of the park, pulled onto the shoulder of a side road, ate the dinner she'd packed, and waited for nightfall. Time passed all too slowly, and listening to the radio didn't help much.

She drove back to the park a few minutes earlier than planned, sick of waiting and a little stir-crazy. Another few minutes of staring idly out the windows and she'd have lost her mind.

Locking the car, she leaned against the fender and looked up at the sky. It had finally stopped raining. A cool breeze blew from the west, but it felt refreshing rather than chilly. The full moon shone between bands of clouds. Time to go. She held her rhodonite and rhodochrosite gems for a moment, and then put them back in the pouch.

Despite being committed to seeking out the gnomes, she felt a mixture of anticipation and dread as she shrugged into her backpack. She walked a few feet to decide whether she needed a walking stick. Her knees felt a lot better now. She headed off toward the trail, grateful for the GPS coordinates stored in her phone. This time it should be easier to find the Tree Home.

The silent forest didn't seem as ominous tonight. She shone her flashlight onto the path, hoping to spot stones, holes and roots before she tripped over anything and made her injuries worse.

Walking at a brisk but comfortable pace, she felt relaxed enough to enjoy the wind in the trees, the soothing drone of insects, and the sense of being one with nature. Even so, she was wary. It would be foolish to let down her guard. Would she ever relax here again after everything she'd learned? Not likely, she thought with a frown. Occasionally she swept the beam of her flashlight into the woods, lighting up the boles of the trees and dense patches of underbrush, just in case anything was lurking there.

Tonight, she was happy to say, she didn't feel watchful eyes tracking her, and even when she passed through the lowlands, premonitions of danger were thankfully absent.

After about fifteen minutes she consulted her map app again and whispered, "Yes!" It showed the Tree Home just ahead.

When she reached the tree, she pressed her hands against the rough bark, leaned close, and called softly, "Hello! It's Lana. Is anyone in there?" She waited a moment before calling again a little louder. "Hello! Raenihel? Are you there?" Good thing no one could see her talking to a tree. They'd think she was a lunatic. How long should she wait? Seconds seemed like minutes. She was about to give up when a small brown arm shot through the bark. A hand closed over her wrist and gave a sharp tug.

Suddenly she stood face-to-face with Raenihel.

"So," he said softly. "You came back." His lined face looked weary, his brown eyes unbearably sad. "The forest is dying."

"You said this would happen. I—well, I thought you were exaggerating. It's hard to believe this could happen, even after seeing it. Part of me wants to think there's some other *natural* explanation." He didn't say anything, just nodded. Feeling a little awkward she went on, "I've been worried about you. Have you found any of the missing gnomes?"

"No, Lana. We believe Sheamathan took them to Shadowglade, her stronghold. Lately more gnomes have been disappearing—captured no doubt, for her work camps." He gestured toward the gnomes sitting around the glowing stones. "My people drink fialazza to soothe their heartache, but that's no way to deal with our problems."

"It must be terrible to have no way to fight back, no way to defend yourselves."

"Weapons aren't much use against a being that can paralyze you," he said grimly. "As for the breghlin, we fight them when necessary, but we're often out-numbered. Staying out of reach in the Safe Havens is our best defense, but that isn't always possible. We have to grow food and hunt and live our lives as normally as possible."

A few gnomes looked up from their meals and saw her talking with Raenihel, but they avoided eye contact, so she was pretty sure what they thought of her. Artham and Terrilem were among the group, but thankfully, they seemed too preoccupied to notice her.

"Look," she said, coming straight to the point. "I want to help you, Raenihel, but I'm not your new Challenger."

"Then we must find one, or try to overthrow Sheamathan ourselves."

Unzipping the pouch at her waist, she took out her gemstones—some transparent, some opaque, some smooth, some faceted, in every color of the rainbow. She held them out to Raenihel. "I've been studying gem lore more intensively than ever. These stones, I think, have the powers we'll need." Raenihel's eyes grew wide. "You said my gems would be more powerful in Shadow. If that's true, I'd like to see it for myself."

At first, he looked too dumfounded to say anything. He stared at her outstretched palm and then hesitantly ran his trembling fingers over the colorful stones. Finally, he looked up at her. Tears glistened in his eyes. "You have wondrous treasures. Bless you for bringing these. You're willing to go to Shadow?"

She nodded. "Yes, if you think I should. I figured we could experiment. How much do you know about Fair Lands gems?"

"Only what I've learned from my ancestors, and perhaps their tales aren't very reliable."

"Your description of malachite's powers matched our folklore," she pointed out as she put the gems back into her pouch.

"That's encouraging, I suppose. Naturally, I know more about our gems than yours. As the leader of our clan, I've made it my business to learn as much as possible, but I don't consider myself an expert." He sighed heavily. "You see, gnomes are fascinated by gems, but we aren't born with the ability to draw out their powers."

Lana's heart sank. That meant the burden of whatever plan they came up with would fall on her. "Most people in *my* world don't have that skill, either," she told him. "They can't feel, let alone control, gemstones' powers."

Movement caught Lana's eye and she braced herself for a fight as Artham strode toward them. The confrontational look on his face set her teeth on edge.

"Lana has offered to help us," Raenihel said before Artham could speak.

"Apparently she's had a change of heart." Artham's eyes bored into hers, challenging her to look away.

She was *so* up for this fight. Glaring at him, and yes, stretching herself to her full height so she towered over him, which did seem a bit unfair, she said coldly, "Yes, I've had a change of heart. Partly because I'm worried about *my* world, and partly because I'm worried about *yours*. I may have a way to help." She took out the gemstones and showed him.

His expression turned from hostile to contrite. He didn't look at her when he said quietly, "You were able to use the malachite, so I assume you can use these?"

Not exactly an apology, but she'd overlook that. "Yes. I've been experimenting with gems for a while, but I'm still a novice. If I had someone to teach me I'd be more proficient by now. It takes time. Gem studies are a lifetime pursuit."

Artham's eyes took on a strangely guarded look. He didn't ask any more questions and he didn't try to touch the stones. At least Raenihel was excited about the gemstones. Who cared what Artham thought? She said to Raenihel, "It's amazing to think that your world has gemstones I've never seen, ones that are more powerful than these. I'd love to study them."

"Yes, amazing. No doubt," Artham muttered, frowning. He ran a hand through his curly auburn hair and shot Raenihel a troubled look.

Lana ignored Artham and plunged ahead. "Raenihel, can you show me some of your native gemstones and teach me what they do?"

Raenihel glanced at Artham before answering hesitantly, "Yes, I'll teach you what I know."

"Are you sure that's wise?" Artham asked under his breath.

What was the matter with them? Why were they acting this way? She was only trying to help. "I'm here to help you, but we won't get far if we don't trust each other. Out with it! Why don't you want to teach me?"

Raenihel looked uncomfortable. "Some people might have ulterior motives. It would be tempting to learn about our gems and then stay, hoping to become powerful."

Her face fell. "Oh. I never thought of that. That's terrible. I'm not like that. I don't use people."

"I believe you," Raenihel answered gently. "But I understand Artham's concern."

Artham said, "Seeking knowledge for a noble purpose has been known to devolve into an ugly quest for power."

"I'm not like that," she repeated stubbornly. But how could she be sure? Who really knew what darker impulses hid in one's heart?

"If we hope to overcome Sheamathan, we have to trust *someone*," Raenihel said to Artham, "We can't do it on our own."

"You said yourself, fate brought me here the night Sheamathan came to this forest," Lana reminded Artham pointedly.

"So I did," he conceded with a frown.

"We didn't expect Lana to come back, Artham, and here she is with Fair Lands gems, and more importantly, the ability to use them. This gives us a great advantage." When Artham didn't reply, Raenihel said firmly, "You can't deny she would be helpful in freeing our friends, and she may be able to prevent Sheamathan's incursion into the Fair Lands. If teaching Lana about our gems helps her—and us—we should teach her all we know."

"Yes, no doubt you're right." Artham sighed, resigned but clearly not happy about it. "I have no problem with her using Fair Lands gems in Shadow, but allowing her to learn about ours as well can be dangerous, as you well know. I suppose I must leave the past in the past and focus on the future. Do as you think best."

"If Lana is ready, I will take her to Shadow." Raenihel took Artham's arm and said in a reverent tone, "I will take the jeweled knife that was entrusted to our ancestors."

Artham nodded solemnly. "Gnomes will never master the Challenger's blade. Perhaps Lana can."

Lana felt a shiver run through her. The jeweled blade owned by the Challenger? It sounded intriguing, and she could hardly wait to see it, but how much good had it done its last owner? The legend said he had driven Sheamathan from the Fair Lands, but then he had disappeared. What had become of him? She kept her thoughts to herself. She didn't want to insult the gnomes. Apparently they thought the legendary blade was a great prize. As far as she was concerned, it was wise to be wary of powerful abandoned artifacts.

Chapter 11

Raenihel gave Lana a cup of fialazza to put her at ease, and then left her by the circle of glowing stones so he could pack for their journey. She had agreed to leave tonight. It would be wise to leave before she lost her nerve. Raenihel frowned. To be fair, it was *he* who might lose his nerve. *He* knew their destination in Shadow. Gnomes never willingly traveled to Shadowglade, Sheamathan's stronghold, but that was where he and Lana must go. He took a deep breath and willed his hands to stop trembling. All his life, he had heard that standing in the woodspirit's presence was worse than death itself. He had wondered how that could be possible until he had actually encountered Sheamathan in the forest. The intensity of her evil was overwhelming, and being held in thrall was an experience he hoped never to repeat. Going to Shadowglade was foolhardy indeed, but it had to be done.

Raenihel filled a wineskin with fialazza and wrapped several thick portions of dried venison, making sure he had enough for a few days. Although he was ashamed of his deception, he hid the extra rations at the bottom of his pack, and then packed the pouch of nuts, seeds and dried berries for a short trip on top. The deception was necessary, he told himself firmly. Lana believed that this would be the first of several short trips to study native gemstones. She wanted to learn all she could before confronting Sheamathan. While he understood her viewpoint, he couldn't allow that. Long studies and experimentation took time—time humans and gnomes didn't have. Besides, Artham was right—too much knowledge was as dangerous as too little. Humans who understood gem lore and had gem powers were too easily swayed by ambition and corrupted by power. It had happened before, and it might happen again. Lana must not linger in Shadow.

The woodspirit's power had grown. She had crossed through the portal and unleashed her destruction. Now, if history were any guide, the blight would expand outward through the Amulet in an ever-widening circle, altering and corrupting more and more land, so Sheamathan and her minions could occupy it.

Raenihel laid the Challenger's sheathed knife at the top of the pack and closed the flap. He didn't know much about the knife or how it worked, but that didn't matter. Sheamathan feared it. Despite all the years that had passed, he was certain she would recognize the knife, and merely seeing it might be enough to unsettle her plans. He knew all too well that Sheamathan hated to feel vulnerable. She thrived on control and domination.

He picked up the backpack and slipped the straps over his shoulders. Yes, they must implement his strategy immediately. If it wasn't successful there might be time to think of another plan.

* * *

Lana walked with Raenihel to the portal and stood in front of it, pretending this was just another day. Lana Grayson, gemologist, was going on a field trip. No big deal. She wet her lips and took a deep breath to steady her nerves. She couldn't see the portal, but the air vibrated with energy.

"Are you ready?" Raenihel asked.

Her voice was a little unsteady when she said, "Yes. Absolutely." Sure, she was nervous. Who wouldn't be? But visiting another world was too tantalizing to resist. She placed her hand in his and resisted the urge to close her eyes. She didn't want to miss anything. She wanted to etch this moment indelibly on her memory.

Raenihel stepped forward, pulling her with him.

There was a brief sensation of pressing against a resistant membrane and then they were through. She had expected it to be more dramatic. Raenihel had promised the transition would be simple and painless and he was right.

But there was no doubt that she had entered a different world. A distinctly different forest with impossibly tall trees surrounded her— trees of such great girth it would take half a dozen men to encircle one. These trees must be hundreds of years old, she decided with a sense of wonder, and they weren't varieties she recognized. Most had greenish-gray bark and many had patches of oily-looking black moss that clung like leeches to their trunks. A light breeze carried the tang of rotting wood and vegetation.

She looked up. Above the towering trees, the night sky shimmered with a peculiar, silvery haze that left the sky eerily darker than twilight, but not totally dark. Maybe it never got completely dark here, she thought as she studied the sky. A full moon that looked like the full moon at home shone through the haze. She had a million questions but Raenihel was already walking down a narrow dirt path. She frowned in annoyance. Although she hadn't expected a 'Welcome to Shadow' speech, or a running commentary on what she was looking at, a few words to put her at ease would be nice. She hurried after him. The forest had a forbidding look, as if it didn't care for strangers. The narrow, barely-discernible path suggested that few people traveled here. Probably for good reason, she thought darkly.

A repetitious snapping-clicking sound that she couldn't quite describe, much less identify, seemed to be coming from the underbrush along the trail. She tilted her head to listen. Some kind of insect? She grimaced, hoping she was wrong. She hated creepy-crawly things. She hadn't given a passing thought to what species besides gnomes and breghlin lived here. Of course there must be insect and animal life and whatever lived here was probably very different from home. *Get a grip, girl. You've been here all of five minutes and you're already wishing you'd stayed home. You can't learn anything useful about Shadow without seeing it firsthand.*

Quickening her pace, she hurried after the elderly gnome. He certainly walked fast for his age, she thought with a mixture of annoyance and respect. "Hey," she said to get his attention.

"Hmm," he said without slowing down or looking back.

"Does all of Shadow look like this?"

"Some looks better, some a great deal worse," he said, which wasn't particularly helpful. After a moment he added, "There are areas where the blight is less severe and we have tillable ground."

"I suppose even Sheamathan and her breghlin need to eat."

"Indeed, but diseased, rotting produce meets their needs and suits their tastes."

She hoped Raenihel planned to take her to parts of Shadow that looked nicer than this creepy place. "I don't know how you measure distance, so I don't know how to ask you this, but how big is Shadow? Like, is it as big as my whole world? The size of the United States? Or maybe more like New York State?" Her voice trailed off. He probably knew too little about her world to make a comparison.

"I really can't say. Most of us have ventured only a short distance from home, so we have seen little of our world. Breghlin troops are everywhere, but mostly in the open lands, so we remain in the forests in our Tree Homes or caves. Gnome Safe Havens are in the healthier parts of Shadow."

"Is that where we're going?" she asked hopefully. "A Safe Haven?"

"No. We're going to Shadowglade."

A chill settled over her. "Why there? Isn't that where Sheamathan lives? Aren't we supposed to be looking for gemstones?"

"There are gemstones everywhere, including Shadowglade." Raenihel stopped and turned to her with an uneasy expression. "You need to see more than gemstones. You need to see what Sheamathan is capable of doing to the Fair Lands, and nothing is more self-explanatory than Shadowglade."

"That's where the missing gnomes are, right?" Maybe he wanted her to see where Sheamathan had taken the gnomes so it would be easier to figure out how to rescue them.

"Most likely they're in work camps by now."

An overview of Shadow that included Sheamathan's stronghold made sense, but she had an uncomfortable feeling that her geology trip had just taken a dangerous detour.

The forest ended a few hundred yards ahead on the ridge of a rocky hilltop. As she and Raenihel trudged up the hill, the clicking sound she had noticed earlier grew louder, and she heard a sound like buzzing wings. With a growing sense of apprehension, she looked back. A few yards behind, black insects as large as her fist alternately crawled on jointed legs, and then spread their wings to fly, but they could only stay airborne for a foot or so, and then they fell back. Their crippled but determined effort to fly made her shudder. Their legs were too spindly for their thick bodies, and their wings were too small to bear their weight in flight. Two pairs of red eyes stared from their elongated heads topped by a pair of long, whip-like feelers. The clicking sound made sense now that she saw their powerful mandibles. She sucked in a horrified breath as hundreds of the grotesque insects surged from the underbrush. It was as if the creatures had followed her and Raenihel to the edge of the forest and wanted to make sure they left.

"Some of Sheamathan's handiwork," Raenihel said bitterly over his shoulder. "Come along."

Only a twisted mind could create such repulsive creatures, she thought in disgust. These insects could barely crawl, much less fly.

She and Raenihel broke through the trees and walked out into the open. The air was fresher, with less odor of decay, and the silvery sky looked brighter outside the forest. They looked down over a grim wasteland.

"We're going this way," he said, indicating a steep, treacherous path that snaked down to the lowlands. "Go slowly and watch your step."

That was good advice, she decided, because if she slipped, there was little to grab for support except stalks of prickly weeds, a few saplings, and scrub brush. She shrugged in resignation. If an elderly gnome could manage, she could. At least they were leaving behind the army of malformed insects.

Midway down she started to slide and caught frantically at whatever saplings and brush she could reach. Brush snapped, stones tumbled, and she slid several feet before skidding to a stop. Raenihel, as sure-footed as a mountain goat despite his age, looked over his shoulder, apparently deciding she was all right, and kept going. She should have given her knees time to heal before making this trip, she told herself as she started down the path again, but she hadn't expected to be climbing down a ravine. Actually, except for the brush-burns, her knees felt pretty good. The path wasn't as steep as they neared the bottom, and she made it the rest of the way without further mishaps.

Relieved to be on level ground, she looked around. Under the silvery night sky, the flatlands looked utterly bleak and depressing. An occasional dead tree stood with mournful limbs outstretched; otherwise the soil was bare except for scattered clumps of low, thorny bushes. Lagging a few steps behind, she stopped to examine one of the shrubs. Its yellowish-green, oval leaves had the same black blotches as the leaves in County Forest Park. Raenihel was right; this was a frightening demonstration of what could happen in her own world.

After about a mile they crossed a dry streambed and came to a series of hills covered in knee-high brown weeds. The air stank like spoiled meat. Lana broke off a few stalks and sniffed them, but they didn't smell like much, so the weeds weren't to blame. What could be making the unpleasant odor?

She discovered the hard way that the weeds hid a minefield of small, half-buried rocks. After tripping over a couple, she slowed, but it was impossible to avoid all of them. Many poked through the ground just high enough to throw her off balance. Following in Raenihel's footsteps was no help, either. She stumbled over most of the same rocks he did. Muttering under her breath, she made her own path and forged through the weeds, staring at the ground.

They had walked five minutes, maybe ten—it was hard to tell since they were walking so slowly—when she looked up and noticed several gray boulders among the weeds. The smell in this area was even worse. She tried to breathe through her mouth, which helped a little.

Something crunched underfoot. Definitely not a rock. She stopped and looked down through the weeds, shivering as her eyes fell on the skeleton of an animal she didn't recognize. What *was* this thing? It reminded her of a fox, but its head was large and flat with a snout like a pig. With any luck, she'd never run into a live one. She grimaced and reached for her flashlight to get a better look.

Nothing happened when she tried to turn on her flashlight, so she shook it, gave it a rap against her leg, and tried again. It still didn't work. Rats! The batteries were almost new, so it shouldn't go dead this soon. She'd have to make do with the flashlight app on her phone, and she'd better hurry before Raenihel got too far ahead. She pressed the power button. What? It didn't work either? *Great, just great.* With a sigh, she jammed the phone and flashlight into her pocket and hurried to catch up.

For no reason she could explain, a knot of fear formed in her stomach as she watched Raenihel picking his way through the weeds, giving wide berth to the rocks.

How much farther to Shadowglade? What would Raenihel say if she insisted on turning back now? And how would she ever get home without him? The idea of being abandoned here, whether by accident or design, was too terrible to consider. Raenihel would never intentionally hurt her, she told herself, wishing she completely believed it. He wanted to keep the Fair Lands safe so her world wouldn't suffer the destruction his had, and he wanted to rescue the captive gnomes. Both goals were compatible, weren't they? She frowned. When he'd taken her along to search for Sheamathan's wolfhound, as his ace in the hole in case the gnomes needed to be rescued, he'd put the gnomes' welfare ahead of hers. Sure, he'd apologized later. But was he really sorry? Had he learned his lesson?

I'm much too trusting. Before, I could run away and go home, but now I can't. What have I gotten myself into?

The strange forest with the mutant bugs didn't seem so frightening now. She was better off there. At least it was near the portal and there were places to hide.

As if reading her mind and wanting to put her more at ease, Raenihel stopped and opened his pack. Taking out a wineskin and a pouch of food, he handed her the wineskin. "Have some fialazza."

"Thanks," she said, buoyed by the sight of refreshments. She took a long drink. A wave of new energy coursed through her, and the drink heightened all of her senses. She took another gulp, enjoying the rush of sensations, and then she wrinkled her nose, realizing that a keener sense of smell was the last thing she wanted right now.

Raenihel seemed more interested in food than drink. He poured nuts and seeds into his palm and then offered her some. She wolfed down a handful and nearly choked as something high overhead let out a shrieking cry. She scanned the sky and caught a glimpse of something huge and dark that soared like a bat, but then it disappeared in the silvery haze. Too stunned to speak, she glanced at Raenihel, expecting an explanation. He wolfed down more nuts, then stuffed the pouch and wineskin into his backpack and said, "It would be best to keep moving."

He has a gift for understatement. She hurried after him. *If that thing saw us, it may be back.* Maybe he thought if he acted nonchalant she wouldn't worry. Instinctively she reached for her pouch, feeling the gemstones inside. She wanted to test their powers in Shadow, but not under pressure.

It was all she could do to keep up with Raenihel now, despite her longer stride. His sudden lack of concern about tripping over rocks told her all she needed to know. He was afraid, and if *he* was afraid, she should be, too.

Just as she was about to ask him to wait, he paused and turned to make sure she hadn't fallen too far behind. He didn't see the creature rise up behind the boulder, but he *did* see her eyes go wide. He looked behind him and gave a terrified gasp.

A few yards away, the serpentine creature wove slowly, studying them from behind the rock. Lana stood frozen. Any sound or movement might make it attack. Yellow eyes, in a broad, flat head as large as a human's, watched them with an intelligent gleam. Its body was covered in a geometric pattern of dark green and gray scales.

Raenihel stumbled backward, snatching her close to him, and his grip on her arm was painful. Leaning close to her ear he whispered, "A pythanium."

Her hearted thudded dully. "Wings? Do I see wings?" she whispered. Most of the creature's body was behind the rock and she wasn't anxious to see more of it.

Raenihel looked transfixed. "Yes, it has wings like a bat. Three sets."

The instinct to run was overwhelming. She tried to wrench away, but Raenihel held her too tightly. "I wouldn't make any sudden moves if I were you." Reaching slowly over his shoulder, he slipped a hand into his leather pack, came out with a dagger and unsheathed it. Inlaid gemstones covered the hilt. Beautiful, yes, but the blade looked none too big to attack a creature this size.

"Stay here," Raenihel ordered.

She nodded. Absolutely. She had no plans to go *near* that thing.

He approached the creature warily, edging forward, and when the creature didn't react he slowly lifted the knife over his head with both hands. This time the knife's artistry wasn't what caught her attention. The blade had begun to glow, growing brighter by the minute, and then it began to pulse. The serpent swayed, watching the knife, and then sank down behind the boulder until only its head showed above the rock. A long red tongue flicked from its mouth, testing the air, and then it hissed in warning, or perhaps in fear.

Lana couldn't take her eyes off the blade. If she felt strangely mesmerized by the rhythmic pulsing light, she wasn't alone. The serpent watched in a trancelike stupor.

Raenihel inched closer. Finally within striking distance, he stood still as if gathering his courage, and then he plunged the knife into the serpent, just below its head where it had no protective scales. The knife glowed through the pythanium's flesh, and dark red blood spewed out, spraying Raenihel. The incision hissed, and then the creature's flesh blackened around the knife, turning to cinders and ash.

Lana shuddered, sickened and yet fascinated as the pythanium's head dropped forward onto the rock and its eyes went dull. Raenihel yanked the knife free and, taking no chances, drove the blade through the pythanium's eye into its brain. When he pulled it out, the blade had stopped glowing. He wiped it on the hem of his tunic and sheathed it. Then, as if nothing had happened, he walked away. His voice came back on the breeze as Lana stood staring at the dead, winged-serpent, "I suggest you stay close. There may be more."

She hurried after him with newfound respect. He might be old and smaller than she was, but he was brave when he had to be.

The rocky ground gave way to a flat plain of barren, reddish soil that looked too poor to support any kind of life. Here and there, deep fissures split the ground. This land hadn't seen rain in a long time, she thought as she scanned the bleak terrain. The wind picked up, raising a choking haze of dust. She bent her head, pulled the neck of her T-shirt up to cover her mouth, and breathed through the fabric until the gusts subsided.

What a wretched place. Fine red particles of dirt caked her skin and clothes. She swept a hand over her head to brush away the dust. Her hair felt disgustingly stiff, and she was sure she must be a redhead by now. Raenihel certainly was, she noted with a trace of amusement. Red dust caked his white beard and shoulder-length hair and his clothing, too. His efforts to brush away the clinging dust hadn't done much good.

Not far ahead, the land dropped off into a ravine like the one at the edge of the forest. They walked to the edge to get a closer look. Crossing her arms tightly over her chest, she rubbed her arms to ward off a sudden chill.

Dead, leafless trees, blackened and shattered as if lightning had struck them, rose up inside a wall built of square, gray stone blocks. The wall seemed to stretch for miles. The ground, bare except for scrub brush and blackened trees, formed the courtyard of a massive two-story stone structure that was crude and ugly in its simplicity. Round towers pierced by narrow window slits stood at each corner. Apparently no one cared to look out on the blighted courtyard, she thought grimly, because the main structure had very few windows. Window slits for observation and defense were located at intervals across the second story.

A drawbridge extended over a moat. The stagnant water might not be deep, since it obviously didn't rain often here, but who knew what lived in it? On the opposite side of the moat, stone slabs led to a stairway, and at the top stood a set of massive iron doors.

No one needed to tell her she was looking at Shadowglade.

Suddenly feeling small and vulnerable, she crouched beside Raenihel who had already dropped to his knees. He was trembling, clearly as rattled as she was. It couldn't be easy for him to come here. She wasn't sure what to say, so she just waited for him to pull himself together.

As she shifted position, it occurred to her that crouching like this should be hard on her knees, but she wasn't in pain. She sat down and pulled up her pant leg. To her amazement, the final traces of puffiness were gone and the brush-burns, which had been a scabby red mess, had started to heal.

Raenihel finally noticed her examining her leg and asked, "Is something wrong?"

"No. Something is right—that shouldn't be." He gave her a puzzled look and she explained, "I fell and scraped my knees. I had some pretty nasty brush burns. Now, all of the sudden, they look a lot better."

Raenihel bent over her knee. "Remarkable. Do you think it's due to your gemstones?"

He was right. That had to be it. She nodded. "Yes, I think so." Unzipping her pouch, she took out the black hematite, white topaz, and purple sugalite—gemstones with the most healing lore. If her knees had already started healing without gemstones in direct contact, what would happen if she placed them directly on the injury?

She held the gems tightly until they grew warm, and then placed them on her knee. After a moment she looked up at Raenihel who was watching with rapt attention, and said, "My knee feels tingly."

When she removed the stones and moved her leg at various angles, her knee felt pain-free and stronger. All that remained of her brush-burns were faint pink marks. Amazing. Now for the other knee. Pulling up her other pant leg, she said, "This one's worse. When I fell, I came down hard on this knee."

She placed the healing stones on the bruised area and waited for the tingling sensation to pass. When she removed the stones, she smiled triumphantly. The red marks had faded to pink and the scabs were gone. "I can't believe it," she said, shaking her head and bending her knee a couple times. "Absolutely no pain or stiffness. Call this an unscientific test, but I'd say my gems' healing properties are greatly amplified here."

Raenihel nodded. "I'm not surprised. All your stones should exhibit stronger powers here."

"I hope you're right." She dropped the topaz and sugalite into her pouch, took out the pale blue aquamarine, and held it with the hematite.

"And these? What are their powers?" Raenihel asked.

"Besides healing, the black stone—hematite—gives strength, optimism and courage." She opened her palm to show him the stones. "Aquamarine gives courage, foresight and happiness, and it's supposed to reduce the effects of poison."

"Strength, courage and foresight," he repeated thoughtfully. "Valuable powers. Especially here near the woodspirit's castle." He studied her face and asked, "What sensations or emotions do you feel when you touch the stones?"

What was she feeling right now? Looking away, she closed her fingers over the stones and focused. A change in attitude. Less fear. An inexplicable assurance that somehow, although it seemed impossible, she would play a role in overcoming the woodspirit. Should she tell him that or keep it to herself? It hadn't occurred to her at first, but experimenting with Fair Lands gems here on Sheamathan's doorstep might not be a good idea. Fear could be useful. It was nature's way of keeping you from doing stupid, risky things. *Put away the gems before you get yourself into trouble.*

"The gems definitely have stronger powers here," she said. "I feel much calmer now." It wasn't much of an answer, but that was all she was willing to say. He probably knew she was holding something back, but to her relief he simply nodded and let the matter drop. His eyes took on a distant look, and then he turned away and stared moodily at the castle.

Uncurling her fingers, she looked down at the gems and felt a sudden chill.

Foresight.

Suddenly she knew Raenihel was about to tell her the *real* reason he had brought her here.

Chapter 12

"Sheamathan's power is overwhelming. It crushes my spirit, even at this distance," Raenihel said in a defeated tone as he looked at the castle.

Lana couldn't feel the woodspirit's influence the way he could, but her heart was heavy and she struggled with a sense of hopelessness.

He combed his fingers absently through his white beard. "Recently, the woodspirit's power has grown much stronger. We need to know why."

Her sense of foreboding grew as Raenihel unfastened his backpack and took out the sheathed knife. "Lana, this knife once belonged to the Challenger who drove Sheamathan from your world. The Challenger gave it to my ancestors for safekeeping nearly a hundred years ago. No one thought it would be needed again."

Human history was the same, she thought sadly. Whenever a war ended, people believed peace would last for generations, but it seldom did.

"I can't tell you much about the knife. It's a powerful weapon, but we don't know how it works or what it can do. Sheamathan would surely paralyze any gnome who attempted to use the knife against her, so we hid it and kept it safe. He turned it over thoughtfully in his hands and then looked up at her, his eyes dark with emotion. "The blight is spreading through the Amulet and it won't stop there. It will alter more and more of your world unless someone stops Sheamathan. We need to confront her. *Now.*"

Lana felt the blood drain from her face. Now? Was he kidding? Her mind spun with a list of excuses, but she could tell by his expression that he wouldn't listen to reason. "I'm still developing my gem powers," she said in her most reasonable tone. "Someday I'll be able to do a lot more, especially after I learn about Shadow gemstones. And then I—"

"There's no time!" Raenihel interrupted passionately. "And even if there were, would you risk becoming like the old fool, Folio? All his studying got him nowhere!" Raenihel's eyes blazed. "A curse upon him! He lives in isolation in Strathweed, compiling folios full of knowledge that might have saved my people from torment and bondage."

For a moment she was speechless. If studying gem lore wasn't the answer, what *was*? According to the gnomes, the Challenger had used some kind of power or enchantment to keep Sheamathan out of the Fair Lands. But after nearly a hundred years, Sheamathan had gotten around it somehow and had come through the portal again.

"So, what's your plan?" she asked, knowing she wouldn't like the answer.

"We must tell Sheamathan this," he said gravely. "A power exists that can drive her out of your world and destroy her. Not only must she abandon her conquest of the Fair Lands, she must release the enslaved gnomes in Shadow."

Lana threw up her hands. "That's your plan? You're going to bluff her?" Didn't he hear how ridiculous that sounded? She sighed in frustration. "Look, that's never going to work. She'll expect proof. You can't make a wild claim like that and expect her to believe you."

"We *have* proof—the Challenger's blade," Raenihel insisted stubbornly. "We know she fears it." He leaned forward, his voice lowering to a conspiratorial tone. "She began a quest to find it a few months ago. She sent emissaries throughout Shadow, asking questions, trying to learn who had it."

Yes, that certainly did seem strange. "Why now after a hundred years?" she asked, frowning.

He shook his head. "I'm not sure. Her sudden interest puzzles us, too. The knife is still a threat to her in the hands of someone with the power to use it. Great gem masters live very long lives. When she sees the knife, she'll think one of two things—the Challenger has returned, or a new Challenger has risen and claimed the knife. Either way, she's in danger." Raenihel reverently held out the sheathed knife. "That's what you must make her believe."

"*Me!*" Lana waved the knife away. "What about *you*? This is *your* plan!"

"My race isn't strong enough to resist the woodspirit's control. You saw what happened in the forest. If I confronted her with the knife, she would simply paralyze me."

Sheamathan had paralyzed Lana too, and it hadn't been easy to break free. Sure, studying and working with gems since then had strengthened Lana's abilities, but that didn't make her a match for the woodspirit. "Well, I'm not going in there alone! If I were crazy enough to go, I'd expect you to go with me!"

With a pained look he said, "I'm sorry to place this burden on your shoulders, but if you can't stop Sheamathan, we have no hope." His voice trailed off and he shook his head sadly. "Look around. This is what your world will look like. As for my world, the destruction will continue to spread. More gnomes will be captured for work camps and held in bondage for the rest of their lives."

She couldn't believe he thought his plan could work. Was he really that naïve? "Sheamathan will just laugh at your warning and kill me. What good will that do any of us?"

Raenihel gripped her arm, his expression earnest. "Even if she doesn't accept your message, she won't hurt you. She'll be curious about who you are and what you know. You overrate the danger and underestimate yourself." Lana gave him a doubtful look but he continued with unshakable conviction, "With only the malachite for protection, you broke free of her power and escaped. Now, you have many powerful gemstones that are all the more effective because they're in Shadow. And you have the Challenger's blade. Our legends say that evil creatures from Shadow can't touch a Fair Lands gem. It burns them like touching a hot coal. Remember the pythanium? When I drove the blade into its flesh, the wound sizzled and blackened. I believe the hilt of the Challenger's knife was inlaid with stones for two reasons. The gems hold great power, and evil creatures can't touch the knife."

Lana frowned thoughtfully. What Raenihel said made sense, but it was easier to be brave and optimistic when you weren't the one risking your life. "You put a lot of faith in legends," she said. The start of a headache throbbed dully in her temples. Her own bluster about fate and destiny sounded silly now. She looked down at the castle. If she was foolhardy enough to go, there was no telling what she'd encounter: Sheamathan's wolfhound, malformed insects, pythanium, breghlin and other horrors. A voice that sounded surprisingly like her own said, "All right, I'll deliver your message," but someone braver and more confident must have spoken. Yes, she wanted to help the gnomes, but this wasn't what she'd had in mind. She looked around at the bleak landscape. Anything that wasn't currently diseased had already died. Was this what her own community would look like someday?

With a sigh, she reached for the Challenger's blade. "I don't think your plan will work, but if I get out of this in one piece, we may learn something about Sheamathan that we can use against her." She stood and tucked the sheathed knife into her waist. "And if I can, I'll find out what happened to your missing friends."

Raenihel stood and took her hand. His fingers closed around hers in a firm grip. "No words can express my gratitude. Be careful, and trust your gem powers. I'll wait for you here."

She managed a half-hearted smile. "If this doesn't go well, you may have a very long wait."

* * *

Lana climbed down the steep hill, grateful for the cover of darkness. How had she gotten herself into this? And yet, what other choice *was* there? Raenihel couldn't confront the woodspirit himself. She understood his desperation; he was responsible for his clan but he couldn't protect them, and it must be awful to feel so helpless. His world had been green and alive. Now it looked like this.

She reached the bottom of the hill and sighed at the sight of the dismal terrain. More dry red soil and clumps of thorny brush. No grass, no flowers. This was starting to happen in *her* world. Someone had to do something about it, but it shouldn't be her. She was in way over her head.

Nearing the outer wall that surrounded the castle, she studied it critically. No toeholds between each block of stone. Much too smooth and tall to climb. Edging along, she came to a tall iron gate, but yanking on it proved useless. Just as she expected, it was locked.

Further along, thick vines grew up the wall, but their sharp barbs would cut her to shreds if she tried to climb them. Oily black moss grew between the stones' joints, eroding the mortar, and some of the stones looked loose. Could she exploit that defect? She spotted a half-buried object in the ground and it turned out to be a rusty trowel. Rusty or not, it was sharp. She spent a few minutes chiseling mortar and then gave up in disgust. What a waste of time. The stones were just too thick. Even if she loosened a stone completely, she wouldn't be strong enough to push it out of the wall.

Well, it couldn't hurt to keep the trowel. It seemed like a providential find. She continued down the wall. There had to be a way in, short of waving her arms and shouting so the guards would capture her. That wouldn't be a show of strength. No, she needed to find a way into the castle on her own and have a look around, and then demand to see Sheamathan.

Ah, what have we here? This looks more promising.

Good. A bricked-up doorway. The mortar was bad here too, and it would be a lot easier to knock out weathered bricks than a four-foot-thick stone. She attacked the mortar with her trowel and nearly whooped with joy when the mortar crumbled to dust. Grunting with exertion, she hacked at more of the mortar. Soon, a few bricks came loose and fell to the ground, raising a cloud of dust. She sneezed and wiped her nose, and then went back to work. After ten or fifteen minutes, sore and covered with dust, she had dislodged enough bricks to climb through the doorway.

On the other side she found the groves of dead trees she had seen from the hilltop. She ran to the closest trees. Their scarred boles and blackened branches looked even worse at close range. Huge knobbed roots thrust up from the ground. If she didn't watch where she was going, she'd trip over them. Darting from one grove to the next, she kept her head down and hoped no one was watching.

The drawbridge was down. That seemed odd at first but after all, why raise it? Who besides Sheamathan or her allies would come here? Sheamathan's enemies would be trying to *escape*, not get *in*, and they probably wouldn't get far.

The courtyard with its scrub brush and twisted, half-dead trees gave an unwelcoming first impression to anyone who crossed the drawbridge. Broad stone steps led to the imposing iron doors, which looked so forbidding who would want to enter?

Now or never. Before her instinct for self-preservation could stop her, she marched resolutely toward the drawbridge. Was Raenihel watching from the cliff? If so, was he half as scared as she was?

Her feet echoed dully on the thick wooden boards and she pulled her jacket tighter about herself, staring at her feet as she walked. In a few more strides she reached the end. Remarkably, she was still alive. Even now, she expected guards to appear or arrows to rain down from the watchtowers.

Feeling increasingly wary, she walked through the courtyard and skirted the front of the castle. How long could her luck last? When would guards show up and haul her away? But none appeared and she continued unchallenged. Not one to argue with good fortune she kept going, and turning the corner, started down the side of the castle, looking for an entryway. There had to be a way in, other than that terrifying front door.

At last, along the rear wall, she finally found a door—a small, partially open wooden door, half off its hinges. It couldn't be more than two-and-a-half feet wide and four feet high. Where could such a tiny door lead? She pushed it gently inward, then stooped and squeezed through. Although it was too dark to make out much, she didn't need her eyesight to discover the limited headroom. She rubbed her bruised scalp and moved cautiously forward.

What I wouldn't give for my flashlight now.

On a whim, she decided to see what would happen if she unsheathed the Challenger's knife. Maybe it would glow like before. She pulled the blade from its sheath. At first nothing happened, and then it began to glow. The blade's light revealed another small door, thirty feet away at the end of the narrow room. She must be in part of the cellar. The walls were made of stone blocks and the room smelled musty.

Whole timbers supported the low ceiling. Dust-covered shelves, holding wooden kegs, tools, and covered clay pots lined the walls.

Just as she started forward, the blade's light began to dim. She'd find herself in total darkness if she didn't hurry. It was hard to run in her stooped position. Darkness enveloped her before she reached the door. "Rats," she muttered as she stumbled forward.

Then she heard something. Whispered voices? She cocked her head and listened. Yes. She was certain of it. Holding her breath, she inched forward. She could barely make out the words, but it sounded like someone said, "Huh? Someone there?" Another voice replied, "Might be looking for us. Shhhh! Let's go."

It might not be safe to leave, but she couldn't stay here forever. Groping for the door, she fumbled with the latch. The door creaked open on stiff hinges.

Let's try this again. Feeling for the sheath at her waist, she inserted the knife and then drew it out again. The blade began to glow. Standing in the doorway, she looked around. This room was bigger than the last, and thank goodness the ceiling was normal height. The floor was filthy and she saw patches of dark stains that looked suspiciously like dried blood. Cautiously she stepped inside. Doors barred with heavy timbers lined the perimeter, but one stood open. Ahead on the right, a stone stairway curved upward, disappearing in the shadows.

Two choices. And not long to think before I run out of light.

Not fond of cellars, especially this one, she chose the stairway and climbed several steps before being plunged into darkness again. She kept climbing, feeling her way along the wall with her right hand, the useless knife in her left. The angled steps and curving wall were a challenge in the dark, and her heart beat faster as she climbed blindly with no way to know what lay ahead.

Maybe she should turn back now while she still could. Sheamathan was a powerful being who would never give up her ambitions without a fight. She'd insist on a face-to-face meeting with the Challenger—or whoever this new person was who could supposedly destroy her. Showing Sheamathan the knife and making veiled threats would never work.

A sudden premonition of danger, like a cold, restraining hand, broke in on her thoughts. She froze in place, and suddenly her blade began to glow. Her eyes widened. She had nearly reached the top of the stairs. Looking up, she saw a stone passageway. And something else—a pythanium, curled around a stone support column at the head of the stairs.

The winged serpent looked down at her with a near-human expression of hatred, and let out a long, angry hiss.

She almost dropped the knife. Her heart raced. *Show of strength,* she reminded herself. *Don't look afraid.* Maybe if she spoke in a calm, soothing tone, the creature wouldn't attack. "Hello. I'm looking for Sheamathan."

"Ssseee her you ssshall," it answered. Lana gasped and stepped backward, nearly falling down the stairs. An unsettling, *awareness* had shone in the serpent's yellow eyes, but she hadn't expected it to *speak*.

The creature unfolded its upper set of wings and spread them tentatively, but the other two sets remained tucked against its sides. Lana stood motionless. Any movement might prompt an attack. The pythanium studied her shrewdly, as if assessing her. A pair of short, muscular legs that had been folded against its body appeared beneath its upper wings, and she stared apprehensively at its clawed feet, which could easily pick up small prey or gouge out her eyes. She stood a little taller and met its gaze. Did she see a flicker of apprehension in its eyes?

The creature moved further up the pillar and from that safer distance looked down at her and her glowing blade. Summoning her courage, she climbed the last few steps.

Approaching footsteps clomped on the stone floors and echoed from the walls. She stiffened. It was probably too late to run, and besides, she had a message to deliver. From a connecting corridor, a light shone into her passageway. She blinked into the torchlight, momentarily blinded.

Above her, the pythanium hissed, "Breghlinssss will take you." Her attention snapped back to the hideous serpent. Weaving its head slowly, as if in time to some ghastly tune that only it could hear, it added, "You will *like* breghlinssssss." Its yellow eyes mocked her.

Yeah, I bet I will.

Four breghlin, two carrying torches, two holding iron pikes, marched toward her, swords at their sides. Taller and more muscular than gnomes, they were even more frightening than she had imagined. Her fingers tightened around the knife hilt.

All four breghlin had deep-set brown eyes, pocked, bulbous noses, sagging jowls, and wide mouths with thick, protruding lips. She caught a glimpse of broken stumps of yellowed teeth when one of the breghlin leered at her. Their skin looked lumpy, like something festered underneath, and their dark hair and beards were tangled and matted. Their gray uniforms were little better than filthy rags. They smelled like urine and rotting meat and the stench was nearly overpowering. She knew she should say something but she was too busy trying not to gag.

"It isss human," the pythanium announced helpfully, "and it wishesss to sssseee Ssssheamathan."

At last she found her voice, but she was so nervous she couldn't keep from babbling. "You must be breghlin. I've heard a lot about you. I'm Lana. Pleased to make your acquaintance."

"Come with us." If they were curious about her or her strangely glowing knife, they didn't let on. They formed ranks around her, one on either side and two behind. Off they marched. She sheathed her knife. It would be best to hide it until her meeting with Sheamathan.

This place must be ancient. The gray stone floor had been rubbed smooth, probably through centuries of wear. She looked up. In the flickering torchlight, the stone ceiling looked dark with soot, and cobwebs hung like dismal garlands from the ceiling and upper walls.

Her guards stopped at a majestic pillared doorway that opened to a torch-lit room. Inside, weird shadows danced along the walls. When the breghlin prodded her forward she swallowed her fear and walked inside, head high, trying to look unconcerned even though her heart was hammering.

Her eyes flicked around the throne room, avoiding its occupant. Huge stone columns with capitols shaped like coiled serpents supported massive ceiling beams. The serpents looked disturbingly realistic. Had they been *made* of stone, or *turned* to stone? The walls, built of square stone blocks dark with age and soot, looked ancient enough to have witnessed the dawn of time. Torches in iron brackets lined all four walls, and their wavering flames cast a shifting orange glow over the breghlin guards who stood six abreast on each wall.

I'm surprised she needs guards if she's so powerful.

At last, Lana forced herself to look at the woodspirit. Sheamathan sat on a throne on top of a stone dais, dressed in a gown so black it absorbed the torchlight. Her eyes bore such evident malice that Lana broke into a cold sweat. Braziers filled with burning coals surrounded the dais. Curling streams of smoke wove around Sheamathan like dark, cavorting spirits.

Fingers bit into Lana's arms. The guards marched her toward Sheamathan's throne.

What demented artist would design such a throne? Elaborate carvings covered every inch—pythanium, giant insects and hideous malformed birds and animals. Jewels imbedded in the creatures' eye sockets seemed to watch her—jewels with malevolent powers, no doubt. They flickered ominously in the torchlight.

Her small store of courage seeped away. She should never have come here. As if in agreement, stone gargoyles behind the dais leered down at her.

"You again," Sheamathan said with obvious distaste.

Grasping at anything to bolster her confidence, she reminded herself that the woodspirit hadn't paralyzed her this time. Her mind was clear even though she was frightened. She met the woodspirit's eyes and said as calmly as she could, "I came to deliver a message."

Sheamathan smiled condescendingly. "What could you possibly say that I would want to hear?"

"I'm sure it's nothing you *want* to hear." Her tongue felt too thick to speak and her mouth had suddenly gone dry, but she forced out the words. "There is a Challenger, a defender of the Fair Lands, who will not allow you to destroy my world. I warn you, release the gnomes you've enslaved. Stop destroying their world and stay away from the Fair Lands."

Sheamathan sat forward in her throne, her face pinched with anger. "Who sent you with this message? The Challenger is gone—powerless."

Lana lifted her chin defiantly. "Your power will be challenged again. The gnomes sent me here with a warning, and with proof."

Sheamathan's hands moved restlessly over the arms of her throne. "Show me your proof."

Drawing the Challenger's blade from its sheath with a flourish, Lana held it up and prayed that Sheamathan would react as Raenihel hoped.

The woodspirit's eyes widened briefly, her mouth twitched, and then she mastered herself and her face became a frozen mask.

The Challenger's blade began to glow.

The glow brightened to a near-blinding white light. For a terrifying instant, Lana almost let go. Clutching the hilt tightly, she held on for all she was worth, shielding her eyes as she continued to watch the woodspirit. The gemstones under her fingers grew hot. Energy burst through her in an unexpected explosion that set every nerve on fire. A tumult of emotions nearly overwhelmed her but after a moment they subsided, replaced by an unnatural calm. She looked into Sheamathan's startled eyes. *You're powerful, Sheamathan, but you're not invincible. Right now you're feeling uncertain and a little afraid, and you're not used to that.*

With new courage she looked at the throne's hideous carvings. The jeweled eyes flickered with power, but she wasn't afraid. Shifting her fingers on the hilt she turned her mind inward, surprised and confused. Before, she hadn't experienced anything of this magnitude. Did the blade's response depend on the danger?

Sheamathan broke in on her thoughts as the blinding light slowly faded to a more bearable intensity. "Why should *you* be the gnomes' messenger?"

"They protected me from your breghlin once. And we have similar objectives."

"You owe the gnomes a favor. How touching." The woodspirit's lip curled in disgust.

"So, what's your answer?" Lana demanded, not backing down. "What do you want me to tell the gnomes?"

Sheamathan's eyes flickered with hatred. "Tell them *this!*" She swept her arm in an arc.

A wall of energy slammed into Lana, lifting her off her feet and hurling her backward. Grunts and curses rang in her ears as the guards went down in a tangled heap, breaking her fall. She clung to the knife despite the chaos, determined not to let go of it. Scrambling to her feet, shaken but resolved to get the upper hand, she glared defiantly at Sheamathan. *Apparently I'm not the only one who believes in a show of strength.* "Very impressive," Lana said coldly. "I see you enjoy using your power to intimidate others." Hot anger surged through her. This evil being had terrorized the gnomes and destroyed their world because they were defenseless and couldn't fight back. It was Sheamathan's turn to feel defenseless.

"Power comes in many forms," she told the woodspirit. "For instance, this is a remarkable weapon." She waved the knife menacingly and its light began to intensify. "Maybe you would like to hold it yourself." Before the guards could stop her she walked to the dais.

When she reached the first step, Sheamathan turned her head from the brilliant light and lifted a warning hand, her face contorted with pain. "The gnomes have entrusted the knife to you. I would not think of touching it."

Because you can't. Now I have proof. At least one of Raenihel's legends is true.

"Take our guest to the Waiting Rooms," Sheamathan ordered.

The guards may have been frightened, but they did as they were told, regrouping around Lana.

"Make sure she arrives safely."

As Lana and her guards neared the entrance, more breghlin fell in step behind them.

Waiting rooms? Why do I have a bad feeling about this?

She glanced over her shoulder and smiled in spite of herself. *I must be really dangerous to need this many guards.*

They led her to the same stairway she had climbed before. The pythanium had left the safety of the column and lay along the wall at the head of the stairs. As she approached, it rose up, thrust its head forward and hissed angrily. Lana nearly laughed. The serpent was a lot braver when there was a troop of breghlin surrounding her. The light from her blade had faded to a soft yellow, but it hadn't gone out. One long stride brought her within striking distance. She thrust her blade within an inch of the serpent's face and said, "You'd make a very nice pair of shoes."

The pythanium jerked back with an unmistakable look of fear. It hissed again, but with less conviction.

Fingers closed around Lana's arm and yanked her away. "There now," the breghlin growled. "Enough of that." When she dropped her knife-hand, he let go of her arm.

Another breghlin let out a low whistle. "A darin' move, threat'nin' Sheamathan's pet."

No one spoke as the group passed through endless rooms and passageways on their way to the Waiting Rooms. A number of escape plans ran through her mind, but none seemed promising. She had the Challenger's blade, but she didn't like her odds. How could she take on all of the guards at once? She might kill one or two but then what? Before she could get away, the others would run her through with a sword or split her skull with a pike. In Raenihel's hands, the Challenger's blade had created a hypnotic pulsing light, but how had he done that? Quite possibly, *he* didn't know, either. Lana frowned. The knife didn't come with an owner's manual, and its behavior changed every time she used it. In time, she would learn its secrets, but that didn't help now.

Even if you could escape, you haven't learned anything about the missing gnomes. Are they in prison? Or in work camps?

The breghlin descended a flight of stairs and continued further into the bowels of the castle. Their boots thumped heavily on the stone floors, and the clank of their weaponry echoed off the low ceilings, reminding her that she had no hope of escape.

Cold seeped through the floors. The breghlins' torches illuminated patches of black moss on the walls. The familiar oily moss managed to thrive here despite little moisture or light.

Her throat felt raw from the torch smoke. The breghlins' stench in this confined space was unbearable. By now she was sure that "Waiting Room" was a euphemism for dungeon. Until today, she had never expected to see a real dungeon, much less find herself a prisoner in one.

Her guards turned a corner and herded her into a low-ceilinged room where two breghlin prison guards, dressed in grimy blue pants and shirts, sat on a ledge across from a row of empty cells.

"What have we here?" one of them asked, standing. His deep, raspy voice echoed mockingly off the walls and his dark eyes slithered over her, raising the hair on the back of her neck.

"Dunno," one of her escorts said. "Calls herself Lana. When we found her, she says to us nice as can be, 'You must be breghlin. Pleased to make your acquaintance.'"

She flushed as both prison guards roared with laughter. Around her, her escorts joined in the merriment. The breghlin who was still sitting on the ledge gleefully pounded his metal cup on the stone, spilling its contents. "Pleased, is she? Ya shoulda cut out her tongue!"

"Like to see you try," a gruff voice behind her replied. "She tried to stab Sheamathan's favorite pythanium. Threatened to turn its hide into a pair of shoes."

The prison guards looked at her with new interest. Their eyes dropped to her knife, which was still glowing softly.

The gruff voice added, "Spoke to the woodspirit, bold as ya like, and didn't cower a bit."

"Well, 'magin' that." The seated breghlin rose, walked to one of the empty cells, and with a key attached to his belt, opened a cell door. "Bring 'er here."

"Come an' get her," two of her escorts taunted in unison.

No one moved. Both sets of guards stood glaring at one another. This was ridiculous. She stepped forward and walked toward her cell. As soon as she passed through the open door, the prison guard slammed it shut behind her, looking relieved that she was safely inside.

With great dignity, she walked to the rear of the cell and sat on a stone slab covered with straw. This, apparently, was her couch, chair and bed. She rested her back against the wall, drew up her knees and wrapped her arms around them. Here she was in a castle in another world, locked in a dungeon. Today she had faced down a pythanium, a host of breghlin, and even the woodspirit. Already, she was getting used to being in danger and having her life threatened. A few weeks ago, in a situation like this, she would have given up hope of escape and waited for someone to rescue her. But rescue wasn't coming. Raenihel, the only one who knew she was here, was too terrified to come. It was up to her to think of a plan and rescue herself. And maybe she could actually do that.

In a few minutes her prison guards returned, along with others. The entire group gathered in front of her cell and stared as if she were an exhibit in a zoo. After a couple minutes they walked away, jostling one other and whispering.

What a crazy nightmare.

As if cued by the word nightmare, she heard the click, click, click of nails on stone, and her eyes widened. The black wolfhound entered her cellblock. It scanned the room, padded toward her cell, and sat, staring at her through the bars.

Chapter 13

Lana took a steadying breath. There was no reason to panic. She was behind bars. How could the wolfhound hurt her? Besides, in the forest she had used a handful of gemstones to drive it away, and now she had the Challenger's blade.

The dog didn't try to communicate. It merely sat and stared. She stared back. Was it trying to frighten her? Or was it waiting for *her* to say something? She had never initiated contact and she had always shut out its voice. Maybe she should try a different approach.

She stood and drew the Challenger's blade, and as soon as it began to glow, she felt bold enough to walk toward the cell door.

The light immediately faded, and the blade went dark.

She froze and looked at the traitorous knife. Wretched thing! How could it fail her when she needed it most? She clenched her teeth. Was she going to cower at the back of her cell, or was she going to face her nightmares? She started forward again. The gems in the hilt grew warm under her hand even though the blade was dark. So, the knife was doing *something*. Stopping within inches of the cell door, she demanded angrily, "Why do you torment me? What do you *want?*"

I need your help, the wolfhound said distinctly in her head.

The stern voice didn't frighten her this time. The gems continued to feel warm to her touch and she tightened her grip on the knife hilt.

Lana, please help me protect the gnomes' world, and your own. I never meant to frighten you. I'm not evil. Your fear convicted me before I could convince you otherwise.

"If you aren't evil, why do you serve Sheamathan?"

Sheamathan turned me into what I am today. This is not my true form. I don't want to serve her. I'm as human as you are.

She gave the dog a sidelong look. "The gnomes told me a legend. They said you used to be human. That doesn't mean you're not evil or that I should trust you. Maybe you were Sheamathan's rival and she turned you into a dog to get rid of you. You could be just as evil as she is. How would I know?"

The voice in her head responded sadly, *There's some truth to that. She did see me as a rival and wanted to get rid of me.* The dog's eyes dropped from Lana's face to the knife in her hand. *The knife is telling you I'm not evil. Look at the blade. It stopped glowing. It recognized immediately that I'm not evil and you're not in danger.*

Her eyes widened in surprise. There *was* a connection between the blade's light and the presence of danger or evil. In the basement, when she wasn't in danger, its light had faded quickly. During her encounter with the pythanium, which hadn't tried to harm her, the blade had glowed briefly. In Sheamathan's presence, the blade had burned white hot. When surrounded by breghlin, it had glowed with a pale but constant light.

"Assuming you're right—the Challenger's blade only glows in the presence of evil or danger—how did you know that?"

His answer blindsided her.

I made the knife.

A shiver ran through her as she leapt to an unthinkable conclusion. But it couldn't be—it just *couldn't.* He had created the knife, but that didn't mean he *was* the Challenger. This *dog* could *not* be the Challenger.

The wolfhound said, *Yes, Lana, I was the Challenger, but she was far more powerful. I might have been her equal someday—if I'd had more time.*

Lana shook her head in dismay. "The gnomes are in trouble if *you're* the Challenger." It sounded harsh, but it was true. The gnomes would be devastated. How could she tell them that their champion was none other than Sheamathan's wolfhound? "How can you help the gnomes or the Fair Lands when you're like *this*? And how could I possibly help you?"

You're right. Like this, there's nothing I can do. I have to regain my human form and confront Sheamathan again.

She gave the dog a skeptical look. "Forgive me, but it looks like last time things didn't go very well. The legend claims you're a great hero who drove Sheamathan out of the Fair Lands. It doesn't make much sense."

It comes down to knowledge and power, bluffs and bargains. Each side thinking they have the advantage and hoping to double cross the other. The events of the last century have been a tragic tale of ignorance, greed and—I'll admit it—blunders. He angled his head, and his eyes held such a sad look that she felt herself relax a little, but that didn't mean she trusted him. It would take more than this brief explanation to win her trust. *I've traveled between your world and Shadow for five generations and the story is still unfolding. Lana, you've met the gnomes and you have the Challenger's blade. A few months ago, I didn't think you'd ever get involved. Now, you're finally speaking to me.* His eyes shone with such fervent intensity she couldn't look away. *Help me. Help me end this tragic tale.*

"First the gnomes need my help. Now *you* need my help. I don't know whether to feel flattered or annoyed." When the wolfhound didn't say anything, she said, "I'm not sure I'm up to it."

I've watched you for years. I know you. I know you're capable.

Her eyes narrowed. "Well, I know next to nothing about you. You say you want to protect my world and help the gnomes and I'm supposed to take your word for it. You say you're not evil. Your proof? This knife didn't glow."

The wolfhound shifted anxiously, glancing toward the passageway. *Your guards will be back soon. I must go. There are hidden papers that describe my background and the history of the knife. I'll tell you where to find them—if you're willing to look.*

"I'll look. I'll read the papers. But that doesn't mean I'm promising to help you."

Fair enough. Letters and documents were hidden generations ago in your family's jewelry store, behind a panel in the office, in a hidden wall safe. The combination is 14-35-72. Remember those numbers. Your great-great-grandfather Elias helped me create the Challenger's blade. Once you read about our experiences, I think you'll pity both of us. My name is Jules DeLauretin.

Lana stared witlessly. A hidden safe? At the store? Elias Grayson had helped the wolfhound make the knife? Just when she thought things couldn't get any stranger. "Jules," she repeated slowly, thinking back to the odd letter with the list of gemstones. "I recognize your name." Slightly less wary of him now, she added, "I've already read one of your letters."

Voices and footsteps echoed down the corridor. Guards were coming. The wolfhound dipped his head respectfully, and then turned and padded from the room.

Lana looked down at the knife in her hand as if seeing it for the first time. The mysterious gemstone list suddenly made sense.

I will proceed according to your recommendations:

Chalcedony, Malachite, Hematite, Aquamarine, Topaz, Sapphire, Jasper, and Sugalite.

She had read the list many times, reflecting on the interesting choice of stones, but no matter how many times she had read it, the combination had always seemed strange. Turning the knife over in her hands, examining the hilt, she confirmed the presence of each stone on the list. So, it hadn't been a piece of jewelry. Jules had been making this knife—a knife with special abilities.

A mixture of these should produce the desired benefits. I shall let you assess whether this proves true upon its completion, as you have more experience than I do in this regard.

Elias probably had more expertise in gem powers than Jules, so naturally Jules would value Elias's opinion and turn to him for advice. How and why had Jules gotten mixed up with Sheamathan? The woodspirit was obviously far more powerful. No wonder things hadn't gone well.

And what about Elias? Had he come here and gotten into trouble? Why else would Jules expect her to pity both of them after reading the letters? Yes, it made sense. She dropped heavily onto her stone bed. Elias had gone away and never returned. She was willing to bet he had come to Shadow, and his fascinating adventure had turned into a nightmare. The letters and documents, written before his disappearance, might not *prove* her theory, but they might give hints. She could hardly wait to find the safe.

She laid her head in her hands and sighed. Unfortunately, she had to escape from Sheamathan's dungeon first.

Chapter 14

Lana woke slowly in a haze of pain and rolled onto her side, groaning at the painful kink in her neck. Her shoulders and back ached, and she realized with disgust that there was something prickly in her mouth. She opened her eyes a sliver, coughed, and spat out a piece of straw. *Straw?*

The room came into focus—a dingy, low-ceilinged stone cubicle with iron bars. The events of the previous day rushed back as she examined her surroundings by the light of flickering torches outside her cell. No, this wasn't a bad dream. This was real. Way too real.

How had she managed to sleep on a stone slab in this dreadful place? And how had she blocked out this stench? She grimaced at the pungent odor of sewage and smoke. By now her hair and clothes probably reeked of it. In a day or two she'd smell as bad as the breghlin.

Last night she'd been excited to find an iron grate covering an air vent in her ceiling, but the vent was useless. It might let out smoke, but it let in very little air. And it was too small to crawl into, so even if she could get the bolted grate off, she couldn't escape through it.

Deep, guttural voices, talking and laughing loudly, echoed in the passageway outside the cellblock. Hopefully the guards would stay there. She needed a few minutes alone. With a groan, she sat and swung her legs over the side of the stone slab. Never again would she complain about her cheap mattress, she promised herself as she rubbed the back of her neck. Or her boring, beige apartment. She'd give her right arm to be there now. But it was a world away. Literally.

Brushing dust and straw from her face, she walked to the cell door and looked out. Good. No guards. She grabbed a handful of straw from her "bed," and made use of the sewer grate in the floor. Just as she was walking away, a group of guards entered the cellblock. She faced them calmly.

"Look, she's awake," one said. His thick lips spread in a malicious smile as he studied her. She studied him in return, and he wouldn't have liked her assessment. Repulsive was the best word to describe him. Barrel-chested and bow-legged, he looked awkward and out of proportion. Pockmarks riddled his low, sloping brow and crooked, bulbous nose. It wouldn't surprise her if lice infested his matted black hair and beard. And then, of course, there was his stench.

As he clomped to her cell door, the others gathered behind him, staring at her with obvious curiosity. To prove she wasn't afraid, she walked up to meet them, but she wasn't crazy—she stayed a few feet from the door.

The bow-legged breghlin, apparently in charge, bowed with a sarcastic smile that revealed blunt, yellowed teeth. "Good day. Pleased t'have ya with us."

The breghlin all dissolved into harsh laughter, jostling one another and winking. Clearly she would never live down yesterday's, 'Pleased to make your acquaintance' comment. She felt her face flush.

"My name is R," the leader said when it had quieted down. "Since you'll be here a long time, I'll introduce ya to the group."

More jostling and snickering. The brute turned to his companions and indicated each in turn. "This here is L, and this is D. And this is W, G, and F."

As if on cue, the whole group chorused, "Pleased to make your acquaintance," and burst into laughter again.

Lana ignored their mockery. Let them have their fun. When the laughter died down she asked calmly, "Don't you have names?"

The leader squinted his eyes and frowned in confusion. "Whassa matter? Dontcha got ears?"

One of the others cut in, "Maybe somebody cracked 'er over the head yesterday."

The leader shoved his hideous face closer to the bars. She held her ground, resisting the urge to back away. "Crack on the head. Yeah, that might be it," he agreed.

She smiled. "No. You don't understand. Those aren't names. Those are just letters."

"What're letters?" one breghlin asked. The others shrugged.

"*She* calls us that. That's all that matters." He stepped back and the others crowded closer for a better look.

Lana tried not to wrinkle her nose at their odor or show her disgust. While planning her escape, it would be best to get on their good side. Pasting on a polite smile she explained, "Letters are a *part* of names. Like, my name is Lana. The first letter is L. L is not a name."

"Is too," growled L, looking offended.

It was hard to keep a straight face. She tried a different approach. "Well, I don't think it's fair you only have letters for names. You deserve proper names, don't you think?"

Two breghlin glanced at each other and nodded. The leader looked dubious and said darkly, "Seems if *She* calls us by these whatcha call— letter things—it oughta be OK."

"I could give you very nice *real* names. Using your letters," she told them. "Wouldn't you like that?"

The leader scowled. "Errr, I dunno."

"Oh, come on, R," chimed in the most hideous of the lot. "What's the harm? Let's have some fun."

"Yeah," two of the others groused, "We never have no fun."

"Oh, all right," R grumbled. "So, get on with it."

Lana motioned L forward and he approached the bars. His eyes widened and his protruding lips parted in anticipation. Summoning her most ceremonious tone, she pronounced, "You, oh L, shall I name Larry!" Then she bowed, trying not to smirk at the thought of naming this repellent creature Larry. Larry tried the name once aloud and stepped back, smiling to himself.

D came next without her summoning him. He grinned self-consciously and stared at the floor while she thought.

"Yes," she said after a moment. "I think the name would suit you nicely." D looked up expectantly and smiled broadly, showing one blackened tooth and several empty spaces between yellowed stumps.

"Your name," she said, pausing for effect, "shall be Danny." He practiced his new name silently, mouthing it over and over. She shooed him away. Somehow, these ridiculous names made the breghlin seem less frightening.

W, the breghlin who had urged R to let her give them new names, stepped up to her cell. She pretended to be deep in thought. It wouldn't do to come by their names too easily. "Hmm, a name for W," she mused aloud. "Let me see." W happened to be the most grotesque of the bunch. His entire face was pitted and scarred. He had no beard. A cut along his jawline had healed badly, leaving a pink bulge of scar tissue, like a worm attached to his face. His nose was nearly twice as large as the others.' Skin hung from his chin in a cascade of folds. By comparison, the other breghlin were almost attractive. W stared at her eagerly, brushing absently at his dirty uniform as if trying to look more presentable.

"You, W, shall henceforth be called Wally!" she proclaimed with a satisfied smile.

Finally warming to the naming process, the others nodded their approval and chanted, "Wally, Wally, Wally!" D gave him a friendly crack in the ribs. "Hey, Wally, pleased to make your acquaintance!" The group dissolved into hoots of laughter until R finally threw up his hands and barked, "Quiet! Enough of this nonsense!"

"No way, R," said F irritably. "They got a name an' I'm gettin' one too."

"You *got* a name," R said with an angry scowl.

"Naw," F protested. "That's just a letter. I want a *real* name, like *they* got."

R started to say something, but F shouldered his way past him. "Me next."

Lana studied him. "After looking at you and giving the matter careful thought, there is no doubt what your name should be," she said solemnly. If she ever got out of here alive, this would be a story to tell the gnomes. "Your name," she said, with a dramatic flourish of her hand, "Shall be Ferdinand!"

A chorus of "Ahhhhs" rose from the group.

The next breghlin was G. A smile tugged at Lana's lips as a name flashed through her mind. *Oh why not! They'll never know the difference.* "To you, G, I give the name, Grace." Lana nodded solemnly at Grace who nodded back. "Grace," said Grace.

"Grace," chorused the others.

What could she come up with as an encore after that? She had named them all, except R. He still looked none too enthused. She motioned him forward but he didn't budge. Fidgeting nervously, he wet his lips.

"Surely you, the leader of this group, don't want to be the only one without a name," she said reproachfully.

"I dunno. Maybe *She* wouldn't like it."

"Who's gonna tell her?" Grace asked.

R shrugged.

"Step forward. Receive your name," Lana commanded, giving him an encouraging smile.

Reluctantly, R edged toward the cell door. His shoulders sagged and his lower lip stuck out in a moody pout. What did you name a barrel-chested, bow-legged breghlin with a pockmarked forehead and crooked, bulbous nose? Her mind raced. She had to come up with a name before he became any more self-conscious. A word, rather than a name, popped into her head. Before she could stop herself, she blurted, "You, oh R, do I name Regurgitate!" She was sure they'd never heard that word; it had more than three syllables. Their eyes widened and their mouths dropped open at the splendor of the magnificent name.

The sound of approaching footsteps brought an end to her naming ceremony. A moment later, a battered and bruised gnome, accompanied by two, armed breghlin, walked into the cellblock.

"Got another one," one of the guards said, shoving the gnome forward.

R gave his group a meaningful look and said, "Back to work, an' not a word of this to anyone."

After the gnome's escorts left, Regurgitate and Wally stayed to process the new prisoner. The rest of the guards split up and went to other cellblocks. Lana stood near her cell door and watched as Wally prodded the gnome toward the row of cells. The gnome's green tunic and pants were dirty, ripped, and bloody. He'd put up quite a fight, by the looks of him. She wasn't sure how old he was—probably middle aged—and he was thinner than most. Straight brown hair fell over his broad forehead and his beard reached mid-way down his chest.

A deep gash on one cheek still oozed blood, and that could be a problem. Without proper treatment, which he wasn't likely to get here, the wound would get infected in this filthy place. The cuts and bruises on his right hand and arm didn't look as serious. Judging by the way he staggered as he walked, he was tired and weak.

The guard stopped at the cell beside hers. A key clattered in the latch, and then the iron hinges grated as the door opened.

"In the cage ya go," Wally ordered.

She cringed as the door clanged shut with such force that bits of dust pattered down in her own cell.

"You'll miss this cage when you get to the work camp," Wally said, chuckling unpleasantly as he left.

Should she try to talk to the gnome, or leave him alone to his misery? Now and then he let out a soft groan, and she could hear his labored breathing. Moving to the front corner of her cell, she said, "You're injured. Can I help?"

"Help? How?" The gnome's voice sounded firm and steady, even though he must be in pain.

To be honest, she wasn't sure what she could do for him. Mostly, she was just being sympathetic. "What happened to you?"

"I was captured by breghlin while hunting. I killed two of the five breghlin before they got me."

"Five against one? You're lucky to be alive."

"Lucky!" The gnome gave a humorless laugh. "Locked in a cell? About to be sent to a work camp?"

"My people have a saying—where there's life, there's hope."

"Not in Sheamathan's realm," the gnome replied bitterly. "I can feel her power. It's strong this close to her. But you're human. Are you immune?"

"Not entirely." How could she explain? Did she even understand it herself? Apparently Sheamathan had to expend a great deal of energy to paralyze or control a human. But the gnomes succumbed if they simply came too close. Rather than share her thoughts, she told him, "At this distance, I don't feel much."

"You're fortunate. I find it hard to think clearly. I'm fighting it, but if I stay here long, I'll be witless and paralyzed."

How much of his weakness was from being near Sheamathan, and how much was from his injuries? She wasn't sure, but the gash on his cheek needed immediate attention.

The stones. They strengthened my knees and healed my bruises. Maybe I can help him.

According to Raenihel, the gnomes had no aptitude for gem powers, so she would have to do this. Unzipping her pouch, she took out her hematite, topaz and sugalite. "Can you reach through the bars so I can look at your injured arm?"

"Are you a doctor?"

"No, but I have Fair Lands gems with healing abilities. I may be able to help you."

The gnome stuck his arm far enough through the bars for her to reach him. She held his arm steady with one hand and applied the stones with the other. The gems grew warm as she held them against his skin, and she knew something was happening when he sucked in his breath.

"Does it hurt? Are you all right?"

"Hurt? No. I feel a tingling heat, and it's growing stronger."

Good. Now if only the guards stayed away until she was finished.

"The cuts are closing," he said in amazement.

"The gash on your face, is anything happening? Can you tell?"

"It's not bleeding now. My face feels warm, though not as warm as my arm."

If only she could put the stones directly on his face. Well, there might be another way. Something just as good. "How's your arm now?"

"Much better. The heat and tingling have stopped."

"There's something I want to try." She put away the stones and reached under her shirt for the Challenger's knife. Why wouldn't it work? The hilt had the same healing stones: hematite, topaz and sugalite. And other helpful stones, too, that would give him strength and courage. She drew the knife from its sheath. Could it be more than just a weapon? Could its abilities depend on the user's needs? She held it up. Right now, she needed it for healing. The blade glowed for a few seconds, and then went dark.

"Come as close as you can. I'm going to hold out a knife. I want you to bring the tip of its blade to your face. Lay it carefully against the wound. Can you do that?"

"Yes."

She held out the knife, her fingers wrapped so tightly around the hilt that the gems pressed into her palm. She closed her eyes to concentrate and felt the blade moving as the gnome drew it toward his face. The gems grew warm, then hot in her palm. *Focus. Focus on the stones' healing powers. Imagine their energy flowing through the blade.*

For a moment she felt dizzy, but the feeling passed, and then energy shot through her. The knife and her hand, they were melding into one, radiating heat and energy!

The gnome cried, "Energy is pouring through every part of my body!"

The heat intensified. She opened her eyes, expecting to find her hand enveloped in flames. But there was no fire. The blade was still dark. Once again the strange knife had surprised her with its unexpected abilities. What else could it do?

Two or three minutes passed, and the whole time it felt like holding a live electrical wire. She wasn't sure she *could* let go. The energy was so intense. Slowly her feeling of being one with the knife faded, the energy flow ebbed, and the gems cooled. When the gnome let go of the blade, she pulled it back through the bars, feeling light-headed. Wow! What an experience. She took a few deep breaths.

"My face is smooth. I feel no trace of the wound," the gnome reported excitedly. "My hand and arm have healed. I don't have any cuts or bruises. How can I thank you? Who *are* you?"

"My name is Lana. What's yours?"

"Theaffar." He cleared his throat and said, "I have a unique problem now. What do I tell the guards when they notice my wounds are gone?"

"Tell them the truth. I healed you with Fair Lands gems." She laughed. "They'll be shocked and amazed. Which is good for my reputation."

Their conversation ended when heavy footsteps approached. One guard carried two metal tankards, two others followed with meal trays, and more tagged behind. Regurgitate moved to the front of the procession and approached her cell.

"Breakfast! How thoughtful, Regurgitate," she said cheerily. She was sure Theaffar would think she was crazy.

Regurgitate grunted and fumbled with the lock while the rest of the breghlin gawked at her.

"Wally made yer breakfast, "Ferdinand announced. "Regurgitate woulda let ya starve."

Wally, holding one of the trays, looked at her sheepishly and then cocked his head at Grace. "Was partly Grace's idea. Brought some for the gnome, too, just this once."

"Prisoners ern't fed much," Grace explained. "Water and stale bread. Once a day."

She bit her lip to keep from laughing. The rapport she had built so far might save her life. In any case, she and the gnome had breakfast.

Wally and Ferdinand carried in her tankard of water and a tray holding a shallow earthenware bowl and a metal spoon. She looked into the bowl. Pieces of stringy, raw meat floated in a pool of blood, along with a mound of blood-spattered, lumpy green porridge. On top of it all sat a pink blob that looked suspiciously like brains. Ugh. The food had an unfamiliar, pungent smell, somewhere between unpleasant and revolting. She wanted to smile politely but her face had frozen. Maybe this was a breghlin delicacy, but she'd rather starve than eat it. Wally and Ferdinand set the tankard and tray on the floor, and then moved to Theaffar's cell.

After a moment Theaffar's door clanged shut. He called, "Thank you from both of us. I think Lana is overwhelmed by your generosity."

The breghlin exchanged puzzled glances. Wally nudged Grace and said, "I think he means she likes what we brought her."

She finally found her tongue. "Umm, yes. I'll eat it later. When I can savor it properly."

"Save it all ya want," Grace said, "but it don't get no better from sittin'."

The group, except for Regurgitate, left the room. Regurgitate stood in front of Theaffar's cell. "Hey gnome, didn't you have a big cut on your face?"

"Yes, I did."

"Don't got one now."

"No. The cuts on my hand and arm are gone, too."

"Lemme see." A pause followed, then, "How'ja do that?"

"I didn't. Lana did."

Regurgitate looked into Lana's cell. She smiled sweetly.

"How?" He glared at her.

"I have powers you wouldn't understand." She held his gaze until he began to shift uncomfortably from one foot to the other. When she turned and walked to her bed, she could feel his eyes on her. Settling on the slab, her back against the wall, she folded her arms and closed her eyes, ignoring him. After a moment she heard him clomping away.

"Well done," Theaffar said. "The guards seem to like you. And fear you. How long have you been here?"

"Only a day. Yesterday I met with Sheamathan. I survived the meeting, but here I am, so I guess that means it didn't go so well. On the bright side, she's not sure what to do about me, and that may be to my advantage."

"She won't send you to the work camps. I'm quite sure of that."

"Work camps. I've heard about them. I wish I could help you escape before they send you there, but I have no idea how to get out of here."

For a while neither spoke, and then she asked, "Are you going to eat your breakfast?"

The gnome gave a derisive snort. "No! Why, do you want it?"

"Want it!" she burst out laughing. "I can't even *look* at mine! Parts of it may still be alive." Before the guards came back she'd dispatch it down the sewer grate, and then eat a piece of dried venison. Raenihel had given her meat, seeds and nuts. It might be dumb to give some away, but how could she eat decent food while Theaffar had nothing but raw meat and green slop?

"I didn't mean to offend you," the gnome said. "I don't know what humans eat."

"The same things you do, like vegetables and meat. But we like our meat *cooked* first." She started giggling. How could he think she wanted a double portion of that hideous stuff? "I have some dried venison. I'll share."

"I couldn't take your food. When it's gone, all you'll have is bread and water."

"Don't worry. I'll be fine. I'll find a way out of here." She retrieved her stash of venison and held a piece through the bars. "Here. Please. I insist."

Theaffar took it and said, "Bless you. You're very generous."

She wolfed down a piece and then dumped her breghlin food down the sewer, leaving a little in the bowl so it looked like she'd been too full to finish it. A moment later she heard the metallic scrape of Theaffar's spoon as he emptied his into the sewer.

"Mercy or kindness from a breghlin is almost unheard of," Theaffar said. "I feel guilty throwing this away."

Breghlin voices drifted down the passageway and she tilted her head to listen. In the distance, cell doors clanged. Maybe prisoners were getting their bread and water rations now. How many gnomes were here? Probably most were in work camps.

About an hour later, Regurgitate walked into the cellblock, swinging his keys. He looked disconcertingly happy. He walked toward her and Theaffar and said with obvious pleasure, "The gnome comes with me. He's well enough to work now."

Her heart sank. *No! Not yet!* This was all her fault. She shouldn't have interfered. If she'd let Theaffar heal at his own pace, in a day or two they might have found a way to escape.

Regurgitate unlocked the cell and said, "Come along, gnome. Least you got a good meal, first." He gave a harsh bark of laughter. Theaffar walked out of the cell and stopped at Lana's door. He didn't look angry. "Good luck, Lana. And thank you."

Still blaming herself, she nodded numbly. Regurgitate grabbed Theaffar's arm and yanked him away.

Chapter 15

When Wally came back for Lana's tray, he glared at her through the bars and ordered gruffly, "Bring yer tray here. Put it by the door. Then stand back."

She gave him a puzzled look but did as he asked.

"Don't need no trouble. Got enough problems," he grumbled. His floppy jowls and quadruple chins jiggled. "Move away from the door, now. And mind ya, no magical stuff."

So that's it! She stepped back. Her reputation was spreading. Wally was afraid of her.

He unlocked her door and with surprising speed scooped up the tray, and then backed out without taking his eyes off her. Slamming the door, he glared through the bars. "Regurgitate won't be back, 'causa you. *She's* sendin' another head guard." He stomped away with the tray.

It wasn't fair to punish him. It was all so annoying. Just when she had managed to develop a decent rapport with all her guards, including Regurgitate, the least friendly of the bunch, Sheamathan was going to replace him, and the rest of the guards were mad at her. Healing Theaffar had set off a chain of events that she hadn't anticipated. She had made a real mess for herself.

She dropped onto her bed and sat chin in hands, staring moodily at her cell doors. She deserved a moment of self-pity, didn't she? After all,

Raenihel was outside the castle, safe, waiting for her to solve the gnomes' problems, while *she* sat in a cell, waiting to be tortured or executed. How would she ever get out of here?

A scrabbling noise jarred her from her gloomy thoughts. She looked up. What could it be? The noise stopped briefly and then started again. She slid off her bed and walked to her cell door, following the sound. It was coming from out here somewhere. Studying the cellblock's dimly lit ceiling, she spotted a two-foot vent hole. The sounds were coming through that vent, so something had to be up there crawling through the airshaft. An animal? A gnome? The scrabbling stopped.

Something dark dropped from the vent hole. She stifled a scream. Some kind of roach or beetle, and it was *huge*. It was hard-shelled with two segments, dark brown, and the size of a small cat. She was too stunned to move. The bug skittered about, its long, barbed feelers probing everywhere, probably looking for food. Its wings lay folded back over its body, but she figured it could probably fly.

Ugh. She hated bugs. This one looked like something from a science fiction movie—one of those B Grade films where radiation turned normal insects into mutant giants. She watched with horrified fascination as it came toward her. "There's no food here. Go away!"

Can beetles hear? She had no idea. The thing stopped, its feelers probing in her direction, and then it launched itself at her cell. She stumbled back in alarm. The bars rattled as the beetle landed and hung on, its body spanning two bars. Its feelers flicked wildly. She felt its compound eyes watching her.

Shivering in revulsion, she kicked the bars, hoping to knock it off, but it clung resolutely and began to crawl higher. Now what? She looked around, grabbed the tankard Wally had left in her cell, and threw water on it. That ought to get rid of it! But no, the bug withstood the deluge and spitefully hung on.

Frightened and angry, she smashed the empty tankard against the bars. The beetle finally dropped off, but not for long. It flew back and reattached itself to the bars. What kind of beetle was this? So aggressive, like an angry wasp. But if it was one of Sheamathan's creations, that might explain it. "Go away! There's no food here," she repeated. With increasing violence, she knocked it off again and again. Each time it returned, slamming into the bars even harder.

By now she was shaking. She should have ignored the beetle. It might have gone away, but now it was enraged. The attack was no longer about food, if it ever had been. Now it was personal. What could she do to get rid of it? When her guards came back, would they kill it? She couldn't count on that. If she acted afraid, they'd leave it to torment her, and that would end her reputation for bravery.

I might get sprayed with a pound of bug guts, but I've got to kill it.

Willing her hands not to shake, she unsheathed the knife and held it up. The blade began to glow. The situation seemed so surreal, like a bad Sci-Fi movie. Her twisted sense of humor overrode her fear. All she could think of, as she moved into stabbing range, was corny lines like, *Prepare to die, mutant! Fry in hell!* The beetle, at waist level, started to crawl upward. Holding her breath, she jammed the blade deep into its body. The incision immediately sizzled and blackened around the knife. The beetle released its grip on the bars as it died. Holding the knife with both hands she lowered the bug to the floor where it continued to sizzle. She watched, fascinated, as its wings dropped off and the carcass turned into a crispy, beetle-shaped cinder.

Shaking with relief, she pulled out the knife and sat back hard on the floor. It was over. Later she might feel proud of herself, but right now she was too numb to feel much of anything.

Approaching footsteps brought her to her feet. She sheathed the knife, hiding it under her shirt. An unfamiliar breghlin, massively built and intimidating, walked into the room, straight to her cell. His block-shaped head with its low brow, flattened nose, and thick protruding lips, sported a number of scars above a scraggly, black beard.

"Yer not very big," he observed in a deep voice. He smiled at her unpleasantly. When she didn't say anything he looked down at the beetle. His initial glance turned into a glowering frown as he crouched down to get a better look and saw that the bug had been fried to cinders. She'd give anything to know what he was thinking. He stared at the blackened bug quite a while before he stood and met her unwavering gaze. Something flickered in his eyes. Wariness?

"I hope that wasn't a family pet," she said with all the nonchalance she could muster. "It was bothering me."

When he touched the carcass with his foot, it crumbled into a heap of ash. His hands twitched nervously and then his fingers curled into fists. "Not a bad trick," he said in a voice that wasn't altogether steady. "They say ya got powers, but that won't help you. I'll shred yer meat from yer bones. Think you can get outta here?" He looked decidedly uncomfortable as he wet his lips. His voice lowered to a threatening growl. "Wouldn't try it,' if I was you. Ya met yer match."

She was amazed to see fear in the breghlin's eyes, but maybe she shouldn't be. He *knew* what Sheamathan could do to him. He *wasn't* sure what Lana could do, and he didn't want to find out. She studied him thoughtfully. Bob? Nate? Bruce? He looked surprised when she said, "My name is Lana. What's *your* name?"

He scowled. "None of yer business, but my name is X."

Chapter 16

Raenihel woke on hard ground, lying on his back. For a moment he didn't know where he was. The early morning sky along the horizon glowed red and orange. He blinked and looked again. It was morning, and he was outside in an unfamiliar place. Sitting up with a groan, he rubbed his eyes. It all came back—Lana and the Challenger's blade and the journey to Shadowglade. Yes, he remembered drifting off to sleep after keeping watch through most of the night. He had slept fitfully, disturbed by troubling dreams.

Cautiously he crawled to the edge of the embankment so he could see the castle and the surrounding land. Lana hadn't returned. Was she still waiting for an audience with Sheamathan? It wasn't likely. He ran a hand through his long, white beard. Something was wrong. He could allow more time, trusting that she was resourceful enough to overcome whatever difficulty had waylaid her, or he could go look for her. He knew what he *should* do. After all, he had brought her here under false pretenses, letting her think they had come to gather gem specimens, while all along he had planned to take her to Shadowglade to confront the woodspirit. He was not proud of that, but two worlds were in danger. He would wait until midday, and if Lana hadn't returned by then, he would do his best to find her.

Even at this distance, he could feel Sheamathan's influence sapping his strength and making his mind sluggish. The closer to the castle he went, the harder it would be to keep a clear head, and that realization brought a new pang of fear. He moved away from the embankment and turned his back on the castle. If only he could turn his back as easily on the problems the castle and its mistress represented.

When a gnome stood in Sheamathan's presence, and she exerted her full influence, she rendered him witless and paralyzed, as she had done that horrible night when he had first met Lana. No, he didn't want to go into Shadowglade, but there was no one he could send in his place.

Sitting with his back to the castle, he thought about what he must do. A small meal of nuts and venison would put him in better spirits, he told himself as he dug through his pack. Midday, he would take a deep draught of fialazza for courage and set out in search of Lana. If anyone saw him before he reached the castle, he would pretend to be completely under Sheamathan's control, on an errand in her service. Scouts had found such a gnome once, far from the castle. The gnome's mind had become so dulled by Sheamathan's control that he had wandered off and gotten lost. The poor fellow had fallen into a pit, and had no idea how long he had been there. It was a wonder one of Sheamathan's pets hadn't eaten him.

Raenihel chewed a piece of venison and stared blankly ahead. He would fix his mind on Lana, her gems, and the Challenger's blade and fill his mind with positive thoughts to help him resist the woodspirit's power. He *must* find Lana. Meeting her had given him hope for the first time in decades, and he couldn't let her journey to Shadowglade end in disaster.

Periodically throughout the morning he scanned the land between himself and the castle, hoping to spot Lana, but not as much as a shadow moved across the dry, cracked land.

When the sun beat down directly overhead, a blazing orb in the cloudless sky, he knew he could wait no longer. He sighed in resignation and looked for somewhere to hide his belongings. It wouldn't do to walk into Shadowglade with a backpack full of supplies. A few hundred feet away he found a crevice large enough to hold both backpacks. He threw Lana's in, and then rummaged through his own and took out anything he couldn't do without: food, fialazza and a knife.

His wineskin felt about half full, so he would need to drink sparingly. Water was too bulky to carry without his backpack, so he must leave it behind. He took several gulps of water, followed by three sips of fialazza, and then slipped the leather cord around his neck and hid the wineskin inside his tunic. The pouch of nuts, a few pieces of venison, and his small knife fit into his pockets. He dropped his backpack into the crevice and kicked red dirt on top.

Taking a deep breath to steady his shaking hands, he headed toward the embankment. How many of Sheamathan's hideous creations roamed between here and the castle? Pythanium were nocturnal creatures, he reminded himself, but there was no telling what else was out there or, for that matter, inside the castle itself. He dreaded going into the castle. Even if he could slip inside unseen, he still had to locate Lana before Sheamathan's pets or the breghlin found him. It seemed like an impossible mission.

He half-walked half-slid down the steep embankment, raising a cloud of dust that stung his eyes. When he reached the bottom, he dusted himself off and cautiously scanned the desolate land. Most of Sheamathan's abominations hated daylight, so they would look for places to hide from the midday sun. He must steer clear of the wider crevices.

Fixing his eyes on the castle, he walked with sluggish, halting steps, as if he were under Sheamathan's control. The deception came easily. Her evil presence made his body feel heavy and unresponsive and his mind cloudy. By the time he neared the castle it would be nearly impossible to keep his mind on his mission. What would become of him if he truly fell into a trance? Shaking away the uncomfortable thought, he concentrated on Lana and the Challenger's blade. He felt certain it was her destiny to help his people and her own. She had gem powers, and now she had the Challenger's knife. The knife was a powerful weapon. He, a lowly gnome, had used it to kill a pythanium. There was no telling what a human with Lana's gem powers could do with it. She would learn its secrets and master its powers.

Squinting his eyes against the sun's glare, he tried to keep a watchful eye out for danger. The midday heat made him increasingly tired and weak, and between the physical exhaustion and Sheamathan's oppressive control, it was all he could do to make his feet carry him forward.

When he finally approached the open drawbridge, he kept his head down and walked with slow, shuffling steps. If anyone stopped him, he would babble incoherently and pretend to be harmless and dim-witted. He paused for a moment, fighting an urge to turn back. No, he must see this through. His heart beat faster as he stepped onto the drawbridge.

With a strange detachment he listened to the hollow thumps of his footsteps on the aged, splintered gray timbers. Sweat trickled down the back of his neck. He was grateful for the knife-edge of fear that twisted in his stomach. It helped clear the fog from his mind. Once he reached the castle and found a way in, he would find a good hiding place and have a calming drink of fialazza.

He reached the end of the drawbridge without seeing any guards. Wetting dry lips he continued along the front of the castle, fighting the impulse to look up. If anyone was watching from the watchtowers he must look as if he belonged here.

The castle's side wall was impenetrable—no doors, no way inside. Somewhere, there must be a servant's entrance, he thought in frustration. If not on the side, then perhaps in the rear.

When he reached the rear wall, he was relieved to see three doors: farthest away, two massive, recessed doors made of rough-hewn timbers, and much closer, a little door, half off its hinges. What a strange little door, he mused. Providence had provided a way inside and he was grateful. Pushing the door open farther, he stooped and went through, leaving the door open for light.

The narrow, stone-block room looked like part of a storage cellar. Its low ceiling provided adequate room for him to stand. Shelves along the walls on both sides held a variety of tools, crocks, red clay pots, and wooden kegs.

He crept forward and came to a small arched opening between two groups of shelves. Probably another storage room lay on the other side. A few feet away, at the end of the room, stood another door. Later, he would see if it was locked, but now he must rest and drink some fialazza. From here, he could see both doors. If anyone came in, he would crawl through the small arched opening and hide.

He pulled out the wineskin and sat in front of the opening. After two sips he felt his muscles relax. Sheamathan's presence didn't seem quite as oppressive. Another sip brought new energy and heightened awareness. And then he sensed someone close by.

A scuffling sound, not far away, made him tense with alarm. A muffled voice said, "Something's here." Raenihel held his breath and strained to hear more. Another muffled voice whispered, "What is it?" Raenihel looked around, frightened and bewildered. Where were the voices coming from? The first voice answered, "Dunno, but something's blocking our door."

Something jabbed Raenihel in the back and with a startled cry he bolted to his feet.

No longer muffled, a high-pitched voice said, "Sorry, but we didn't know somebody was sittin' there!"

Raenihel asked cautiously, "Who's there?"

"Just Greg and me." A pause followed, then, "Who's *there?*"

The voices didn't sound dangerous or threatening. He answered, "Raenihel. Raenihel the gnome." He paused uncertainly. "*What* are you?"

Soft laughter followed and the sound of scampering feet. What emerged from the hole made him step backward.

"What we *were* is human boys, but you didn't ask that. What we *are* is rats, as you can see."

His revulsion gave way to pity. He found himself at a loss for words. The huge rat that had spoken began to laugh. Being turned into a rat was hardly a laughing matter, and he stared sadly at the creatures before him.

The rats were a foot high and a couple feet long, not including their long, hairless tails. The one that had addressed him was brown, and heavier than its gray companion. Both rats looked at him with bright, black eyes, their long whiskers twitching. Raenihel let out a long, expressive breath and, finally finding his tongue said, "I'm very sorry for you."

The gray rat made a movement rather like a shrug and said in a high, squeaky voice, "Hey, it ain't so bad. After a while you get used to being ugly and repulsive. Jordy here was kinda ugly and repulsive to start with, so it wasn't much of a change for him."

Jordy let out an aggravated squeal. "Hey, being a rat suits you to a T. It wasn't much of a change for you, either."

Raenihel fought back a smile. He was interested in their story, but if they bickered the whole way through, he had a feeling it would be a very long tale. "Well, now," he said, trying to steer the subject to the matter at hand, "I wonder if you know anything about a friend of mine. I think she's being held here—a young human woman. She arrived the other day and probably met with Sheamathan."

"Whoa, whoa, whoa," Greg said, sitting back on his haunches. "Slow down. We rats are none too gifted with brains, you know."

"Speak for yourself," Jordy growled. "Me, I got more brains than a rat's likely to need in three lifetimes."

Greg sputtered, but answered Raenihel's question. "Well, if she's here, she's probably in the dungeon. And yeah, somebody came through the other day. We heard a voice. Not sure if it was a woman. Figured someone wanted us to do something, so we hid." He appraised Raenihel with keen, black eyes and said, "You need any help looking for your friend?"

Raenihel considered. "Well, the castle is vast, and it would be helpful to have someone who knew his way around this maze." Immediately he cringed at his choice of words.

"Sure, we rats are good with mazes, so they say," Jordy said, frowning in self-pity.

"Forgive me. I meant no offense."

"Forget it," Greg said. "We make a lot of rat jokes ourselves."

Jordy grunted and switched his hairless tail irritably.

"Are you volunteering to help find Lana?"

"Sure," Greg said. "Sounds like fun. Besides, what's the worst that can happen once you've been turned into a rat? It sorta colors the way you look at life and danger, if you know what I mean."

"And what about you?" Raenihel asked the other rat.

Jordy snorted. "I'm in. Where Greg goes, I go. I'm not sittin' around this, um, rat hole by myself." He showed his teeth in what might pass as a smile.

Oh, dear. This would be a memorable experience.

"So, let's get going," Greg said.

Jordy lifted one of his pink, front feet in protest. "Wait. Gimme a minute to round up a snack."

"He's gotta get some cheese outta his mousetrap," Greg said sarcastically.

Raenihel grimaced as the rats scampered into their hole. Maybe their help wasn't worth the price.

Greg and Jordy claimed to know every corner of the castle and every hiding place. Several months ago they had discovered the airshaft that led to the dungeon. When they were bored, they hid and listened to the guards. Greg said the dungeon had a network of airshafts. Vents opened in the ceiling of each central hold—cellblocks with a row of cells. Some cells had their own vents, he said, and you could look into them.

Raenihel felt like an awkward, oversized worm as he followed the rats. The airshaft was large enough for them, but he had to wriggle on his belly or crawl on all fours, keeping his head down. The rats could move much faster than he could, and it was difficult to keep up. He was much too old for this, he sputtered to himself. He should have found his own way to the dungeon. Once he found Lana, he wasn't sure what he'd do, but he'd figure it out when the time came.

After what seemed forever, the rats stopped above the first cellblock. The airshaft passed over a vent hole a couple feet wide. Jordy, who had taken the lead, crouched beside the hole. Raenihel and Greg waited farther back where they could whisper without being heard.

"I don't imagine he can see much through that hole," Raenihel said.

"First, he'll listen for anyone talking down there. Maybe he'll hear her, or the guards talking about her. We rats have pretty good hearing."

Trying to find Lana by listening at every vent hole didn't sound very efficient, and it could take a long time. Unfortunately, he didn't have a better plan. How many cellblocks were there? He was afraid to ask. His knees hurt and his back ached, but it was best not to think about that. In a couple minutes, Jordy scampered back to report.

"It's quiet down there. I can see part of the hold if I stick my head down the hole, but I can't get a good look without falling."

"What if the gnome was to stuff you through so you could get a better look?" Greg suggested.

"Why not stuff *you* through?" Jordy retorted. His already high, squeaky voice went up an octave. "Maybe you don't mind your whiskers getting whacked off by a sword. I've become a little attached to *mine*."

"Okay, okay, don't get hot around the collar. Oh, right, you don't have one," Greg said, snickering at his own dismal wit. Raenihel groaned inwardly. There was no end to their "we've been turned into rats" jokes.

Jordy continued to sputter, "If I show my face down there, guards will cut me to ribbons."

"If they cut you to ribbons, I'll wear one on my tail in your memory. Anyway, the guards are probably gone. What a coward."

Tempers were rising. Raenihel said, "Maybe there's another way."

"Oh, I'll go, I'll go. Why not? I have nothing to live for," Jordy said dramatically. "Always the hero, that's me." He walked down the airshaft. "Come on. Just be careful not to drop me. One shake of my tail means stop lowering me. Two means haul me up."

Raenihel discovered just how heavy these oversized rats were once he held Jordy by the hindquarters and started to lower him headfirst through the hole. Jordy flicked his tail once, signaling him to stop. Hanging halfway through the opening, the rat should be able to look around the central hold, and with any luck he might see into the cells. Jordy flicked his tail twice and Raenihel pulled him up.

"Well?" Greg asked impatiently.

"Nothin' down there. No guards. No prisoners."

Raenihel said, "On we go, then." He finally brought himself to ask the dreaded question. "How many central holds are there?

"Wouldn't know for sure. Never counted them," Jordy said. "Probably at least forty."

Raenihel's heart sank at the prospect of dropping the rat down dozens of holes. He said gloomily, "If that's the case, we'd better keep moving."

Chapter 17

Lana paced, trying to channel her nervous energy. Things weren't going the way she had planned. Her idea of building a rapport with the guards, and then bribing or tricking them into letting her go, had fallen apart. She needed a new plan.

Breghlin were mean but they weren't very smart, and better yet, her guards were afraid of her—even X—a fact that continued to amaze her. X was bigger and meaner than the rest and, if she was not mistaken, dumber, too. Somehow, there had to be a way to take advantage of that. Being nice hadn't gotten her anywhere. Now, she'd try a different approach—fear. She would exploit the breghlins' fear of gem powers. What had Jules said? *Knowledge and power, bluffs and bargains.* It was time for bluffs. She wasn't sure what the bluff would be, but she would think of something.

About an hour later, X came in with a piece of dry bread wrapped in a dingy cloth. He shoved the bread through her bars and growled, "There's yer rations." She was willing to bet that Wally and the others hadn't mentioned she'd already had breakfast.

"Where's my water?"

He gestured at the tankard on the floor. "Ya already got yer water today."

"It's gone."

He looked at her through narrowed, distrustful eyes, as if her wanting water was some kind of a trick.

She picked up her tankard and carried it to the door. The breghlin took a cautious step back, watching her carefully.

"It's empty." She turned it upside down and added firmly, "And I would like *more*."

X licked his fleshy lips. One eye twitched nervously. "Prisoners get one ration of bread 'n water."

"Today I will have *two*. I spilled my water. This pest was bothering me." She gestured at the pile of ash that had been the giant beetle and gave the breghlin what she hoped was an intimidating smile.

X looked down at the ashes. She could swear he shivered before he looked up and said, "OK. More water. Just this once."

"Good. And clean up that mess."

X stumped away, muttering.

Well, that had gone pretty well. She grinned and walked back to her bed. But what should she do next? X was purposely staying out of reach. He shoved her bread through the bars. He would probably find a way to refill her water without coming into her cell. If he wouldn't come inside, she'd have to stab him through the bars and then take his keys. She sat on her bed and thought. Okay, supposing for the sake of argument she actually managed to stab and kill him, what if she reached through the bars for the keys on his belt and she couldn't reach them? Or what if he fell so she had to roll his corpse over? How could she do that that from inside her cell? She sighed in frustration. "Rats!"

A high-pitched whisper came from overhead, "Yeah, over here. I didn't think you could see me."

Startled, she leapt to her feet and looked around.

"Up here!" the squeaky voice said.

The air vent! She looked up and gasped. A huge brown rat looked down and said, "Yeah, I'm not happy about the way I look, either, but what's a guy to do?"

Lana stood open-mouthed as a giant gray rat joined the brown one. It peered down, wriggled its whiskers and smiled, revealing sharp upper and lower incisors.

A familiar voice drifted through the hole, "Lana, it's me, Raenihel. These are a couple, um, friends." He continued in an apologetic tone, "They're very nice people, ah, er, rats. They've come with me to get you out."

Usually she babbled when she was nervous, but once in a while words completely failed her. This was one of those times. The brown rat blinked at her and said, "What can I say? He ain't too picky about his friends. If it makes you feel any better, we *used to be* people."

Revulsion slowly gave way to a mixture of pity and amusement. At least someone was trying to rescue her and this was no time to be choosey. For all she knew, if she didn't get out of here soon, she might end up like them. She shivered at the thought. "How do you plan to get me out?" she whispered.

"I'm not sure," Raenihel's voice came through the vent. "First we had to find you."

Her thoughts raced. The seeds of a plan formed in her mind but there was no time to work out details. She'd have to ad lib. "The head guard is bringing me water. I think I have a plan. Keep listening by the vent, and when the time comes, you'll know what to do." She thought for a moment and added, "Your cue will be the words, *spirit powers.*"

A moment later, X lumbered into the central hold carrying a metal water jug with a long, thin spout. As he walked toward her cell, she took a calming breath. Years ago, in the sixth grade, she had played the role of the *Spirit of Christmas Past* in the annual Christmas play. She might not have given an Oscar-winning performance, but she had done all right. This time more than her ego was at stake. She walked to her cell door and launched into her hastily devised one-act play. "Since you've done as I asked, I will show you mercy."

X scowled in obvious confusion.

"I'll give you a chance to walk out of here alive. Is that fair?"

He gave her a 'what are you talking about' look, and his scowl shifted to a look of watchful distrust. "Huh?"

Breghlin had limited vocabularies. She needed to keep this simple. "Your world is strange to me. I needed time to rest, but now I have renewed my powers."

X fidgeted nervously, the jug of water in his hand clearly forgotten.

She reached beneath her shirt and came out with the unsheathed knife. X took a step back. His frightened eyes flicked back and forth from the knife to her face. She lifted the knife over her head. How many seconds before it started to glow? "Powers of the Fair Lands, hear me!" She started a mental countdown: *Ten, nine, eight, seven, six.* She needed a magical-sounding word. *Five, four, three, two,* "Jabberwocky!" she cried, giving the knife a theatrical flourish. As if on cue, the blade began to glow.

X took a giant leap back and dropped the water jug. It clattered to the floor, splashing water over his feet. His eyes, the size of golf balls, remained glued to the glowing blade.

Her accomplices had better be listening. In a loud, clear voice she called, "I, Lana of the Fair Lands, summon mighty beings to defend me. Come, O *spirit powers* of the Fair Lands!"

Thank goodness they understood what to do. Eerie, high-pitched shrieks drifted down from the vent. X cowered, covering his ears. How could she explain her plan to X with his hands over his ears? "Listen to me, X!" she commanded.

X uncovered his ears and stood a little taller. Another ghostly wail circled the cell, and then faded away.

"Spirits!" she called. "Confirm my words. If this breghlin helps me, his life will be spared."

A chorus of ethereal voices intoned, "His life will be spared."

Lana fixed X with a piercing gaze. "Will you do as I ask so I can let you live?"

X nodded vigorously, jowls trembling. His former harsh words, and the threat to 'shred yer meat from yer bones,' seemed forgotten, she thought, holding back a grin.

Now what? She needed an escort out of the dungeon. After that, she could probably manage on her own. Hopefully Raenihel and the rats would find her. "Set me free and escort me from the dungeon," she commanded." If anyone questions you, just say you're taking me to Sheamathan. Do you understand?"

X nodded again.

"Good. Now let me out of here."

X sidled up to the door, reaching for a ring on his belt that held several keys. His hands shook so badly it took a minute for him to find the right key and fit it into the lock. "Ya won't kill me now," he said worriedly. Staring at the knife, he opened the door.

"As long as you do what I say, I won't hurt you."

"Come on, then."

Reluctantly, she slid the knife into its sheath. It wouldn't do for a prisoner to hold a guard at knifepoint.

X took her arm lightly and steered her forward. Just beyond the cellblock, in the passageway that led past several central holds, they passed Grace and Ferdinand. Neither breghlin acted like anything was wrong. Why should they question the new head guard, chosen by Sheamathan? X stared straight ahead and kept walking.

Once they were outside the dungeon, he stopped and dropped her arm. "Sheamathan's afraid of ya," he said slowly, as if weighing his words. He gave her a long look and asked cautiously, "Do you plan to take her place?"

The question surprised her. Did he think she was as powerful as that? "No. But I commanded her to stay out of my world, and I asked her to free the gnomes."

X nodded. "Errr, I see."

"Where does she keep the gnomes? Where are the work camps?"

X hesitated. "They work in her mines. Not too far from here—that way." He pointed, and then glanced about anxiously. "Yer should go," he said, turning toward the broad stone stairway that led to the main floor. "Take these stairs."

"Very well. You may leave now."

He made a funny little bow and hurried away. He hadn't wanted to be skewered by the Challenger's blade or attacked by spirit powers from another world, but what would Sheamathan do to him when she discovered he had let Lana go?

It wasn't safe to stay here, but as much as she wanted to slip out of the castle and head to the embankment, she couldn't leave Raenihel behind. Sheamathan's influence would continue to weaken him and cloud his mind. How would she find him? "Rats," she said gloomily for the second time that day.

A breathless voice came from somewhere overhead, "Hang on, we're coming!"

Surprised, she looked up, searching for an air vent. Sure enough, several feet away she saw a hole in the ceiling.

"Had to follow you through the air-vent system. And your gnome buddy ain't so fast."

She walked to the hole and looked up, oddly happy to see a rat.

"There you are," the gray rat said, puffing heavily. "And all in one piece."

"Move aside," Raenihel commanded. The rat moved away and in a moment Raenihel looked down. "I'm glad you're all right." Sweat glistened on his lined brow. "I'd come down, but I can't fit through the hole. Greg says he'll lead me through this airshaft to a safe place. I'll hand Jordy down and he'll guide you there."

"If that's the only way," she said unhappily.

"It's the *safest* way," Raenihel said. "And we should get going." His face disappeared from the hole. A second later a scowling brown rat glared down at her. "I'm Jordy, and if you're going to drop me, we can forget the whole thing."

Lana said firmly, "I won't drop you."

"Ready?" Raenihel called.

"Ready." As she lifted her arms, the rat's hindquarters came into view. She froze. The rat was much bigger than she'd thought! Its long hairless tail flicked nervously and its little pink feet peddled empty air. Grimacing, she stood on her tiptoes and grabbed him around his middle.

"Easy now!" Jordy cried. "I'm delicate!" Someone overhead snorted at that and she grinned in spite of herself.

"Okay, Raenihel. I've got him." Lowering the rat as fast as she could without dropping him, she let go the minute his feet touch the floor.

Jordy looked up at her and said nastily, "There now. That wasn't so bad, was it?"

She took a step back and shook her head. They weren't getting off to a very good start.

Jordy sat back on his haunches, muttering under his breath, and dusted himself off with his forelegs.

"We'll meet you outside," Raenihel called down. She heard movement overhead as he and the other rat started off.

"Stay close," Jordy said. "If you can stomach it."

The irritable brown rat took off, scampering nimbly up the stairs, and she hurried to keep up. At the top of the stairs he paused, looked both ways, and headed down a hallway. Next, they passed through two vacant, unfurnished rooms and into another narrow hallway that looked like a servant's access. By now she was winded. For all she knew the spiteful rodent was taking the long way to wherever they were going. She kept running. From time to time the rat looked back, and if she straggled he showed his teeth and ran all the faster. Where was he taking her? They came to a narrow, back stairway and Jordy started down in nearly total darkness. Maybe he could see well enough, but she couldn't. She slid her hand along the wall as they descended. At the landing they turned and went down another flight, and then Jordy scampered into a basement storage area that was lit by mineral oil lamps in wall brackets.

"Through here," Jordy said, slowing. He paused near a low doorway and went inside. She stooped and followed him into a low, windowless room. Bags of grain lined the walls and grain littered the floor. In the light that shone from the adjoining room, she saw Raenihel and Greg perched on some bulging sacks.

"Lana!" Clearly relieved to see her, Raenihel came over and hugged her briefly. When he stepped back, Jordy looked up at Lana and showed his teeth. "Seein' as I got you here safe, don't *I* get a hug?"

"Umm, sure."

"Aw, Jordy, cut it out," Greg said. "You weren't always so keen on rats, yourself."

Lana stooped and gave Jordy an awkward pat on the head.

"Nice rat, good rat," Jordy mocked. "Pretend I'm a cat if that helps."

Raenihel shot the rat a warning glance, then gestured toward the bags and said, "Lana, please have a seat." He returned to his spot beside Greg. "Tell me what happened. Did you meet with Sheamathan?"

Lana sat. "Yes, and since you found me in the dungeon, you know it didn't go well. But I learned something useful. You're right—Sheamathan can't touch the Challenger's blade." She wished she didn't have to tell him the other news. "And I learned what became of the Challenger."

Raenihel sat forward eagerly. "Yes?"

There was no easy way to break the bad news. "Your Challenger is Sheamathan's wolfhound."

Chapter 18

Raenihel's brow creased in confusion. "What? I don't understand!"

Lana shook her head, and said with a quiet sigh, "I don't, either, but it's true. While my guards were gone, the wolfhound walked in and came to my cell. It spoke in my mind. This time I listened. The wolfhound's name is Jules. He created the knife—the Challenger's Blade. Don't ask me how he got turned into a dog. He mentioned bluffs and bargains, and called the last hundred years a tragic tale of ignorance and greed, or something like that." She gave a helpless shrug. "I guess it's complicated."

"Complicated! It's a disaster!" Raenihel's lips trembled. His eyes filled with tears. Running a hand over his beard, he stared blankly ahead.

"We still have his knife and I'm learning to use it," she said, hoping to console him. "And Jules thinks I can help him. He wants to regain his human form and confront Sheamathan again."

"After what happened last time?" He shook his head and frowned. "Even if he found a way to become human again, and that seems unlikely, how can he defeat her? And how can you help him?"

She shared Raenihel's bewilderment, but they needed to stay hopeful. "I don't know yet. But I *do* know where to learn more about Jules and the knife. When I get home, I'll find answers."

"I've seen Sheamathan's wolfhound, but I've never heard of a Challenger," Greg piped up.

She glanced at him, in no mood to explain. "It's an old legend."

Greg persisted, "You're sayin' the Challenger tried to defeat Sheamathan, but she won?"

She nodded. "Right. Maybe his special knife wasn't powerful enough."

Jordy said, "Sheamathan can't touch the knife? Why not?"

"It's covered with powerful gems from our world. When evil beings touch the gems, it's like touching hot coals."

"So, the knife is still a threat to her. Wow," Jordy said. "Can I see it?"

She hesitated, but really, what harm could it do? "Sure. Why not?" Bringing out the sheathed knife, she drew the blade.

"Woooow! It's beautiful!" Jordy cried.

"Yeah!" Greg agreed enthusiastically.

The blade began to glow.

"Cool! Look at that!"

The glow faded. The knife went dark.

"So, why does it light up like that?" Jordy asked.

She was about to quip that curiosity killed the cat, er, rat, but decided not to add to their fund of corny rat jokes. "If it senses danger or evil it keeps glowing. If not, it goes dark."

"I guess we're not evil. No matter what my mom says," Jordy joked.

Lana sheathed the blade and gave the pudgy rat a sad smile. "Your mom must be worried sick. When did you get here? *How* did you get here?"

"Around a year ago," he said. "You lose track of time here, especially when you're a rat." Staring at the floor, he wriggled his whiskers. "Yeah, I'm pretty sure Mom misses me. Even though I used to make her mad."

"Of course she misses you." Pricked by her conscience, she looked away. She'd been so worried about saving her own skin she'd barely considered that these were two *boys*, boys with friends and families who missed them. In some ways, they were worse off than the captured gnomes were. There was no rescue from being a rat.

The gray rat said, "One night me and Jordy rode our bikes to County Forest Park." He gave Jordy a sidelong look. "So our moms wouldn't catch us drinking."

"Seemed like a great plan," Jordy muttered miserably.

"Other kids do it. Guess they were luckier than we were. After a few beers Jordy didn't feel like riding home."

"Neither did you."

Greg ignored him. "Anyway, we went for a walk and hung out by the creek. After a while we nodded off. When I opened my eyes, I thought I was dreaming. Horrible, ugly monster-guys were all around us. They had weapons. Knives, clubs, and spears. They grabbed us and brought us here."

Jordy said, "It was a nightmare. Only it was real."

Greg nodded. "Yeah, the trees and even the sky looked all weird. We had no idea where we were."

"Or how to get home," Jordy added.

"Both of us started screamin' and we ran. But the monsters—the breghlin—caught us. They clubbed Jordy over the head and knocked him out cold. Even if I could get away, I couldn't leave him."

"Yeah, like you coulda got away," Jordy said sarcastically.

"I'm not sayin' I could. I'm just sayin' I wouldn't leave you," Greg protested, and he looked at Lana and added. "We've been friends since fourth grade."

Lana said to the scowling gray rat, "I'm sure Jordy wouldn't leave you, either."

"Yeah, only a *rat* would do something like that," Jordy agreed unable, even now, to resist a rat joke.

Raenihel finally joined the conversation. "So Sheamathan turned you into rats."

Greg nodded. "Yeah. Anyone who comes here, or causes trouble, gets turned into something."

"Last year rats were in vogue," Jordy said bitterly.

"The breghlin," Raenihel began thoughtfully, "Do you think they captured you, planning to take you to Sheamathan, like a gift?"

"Yeah, something like that," Greg said. "She was happy to see us at first."

Lana gave the rats a confused look. "Happy to see you? Why?"

"She asked us a lot of questions. Mostly about home," Greg said. "And she seemed really interested in everything we told her."

"What did she want to know?" Lana asked, alarmed. She glanced at Raenihel but his blank look said he didn't understand why she was so worried.

"All kinds of stuff," Greg said, wriggling his whiskers thoughtfully. "Things like how many people there are. Do we live in a forest, or a village or a city? Are there walls around the cities? You know, stuff like that."

Jordy said to Lana, "When you were talkin' about gems and the knife, it made me think. Sheamathan asked us a bunch of stuff about gemstones. Like what kind of gems people have, and if they have a lot of them. My mom has diamonds. Sometimes she wears turquoise." When he paused Lana could see Jordy's mental gears spinning." Cocking his head, he looked at her with shrewd black eyes. "I get it now. I couldn't figure out why the woodspirit cared, but now I do."

Greg gave a squeak of excitement. "Right! She showed us a bunch of gems and asked if we had the same ones back home. Then she made us touch the gems and tell her how they felt. That seemed pretty dumb at the time. I told her they felt like stones—cold and hard. Duh. How *else* would they feel?"

Raenihel still didn't understand. "Why would she question the boys? She learned about the Fair Lands from the Challenger long ago."

"Exactly. Long ago," Lana said. "Unlike here, things change quickly in our world. And what makes you think he told her the truth? I sure wouldn't. Anyway, you're missing the point. She had the boys *touch* the gems. Fair Lands gems and Shadow gems can't hurt them. She knows that. So she had another reason. Don't you see? She wanted to know if they had *gem powers*."

"Ah, I see your point. That makes sense," the gnome said thoughtfully. "It was a test."

"And we flunked it," Greg said.

"Yeah, and a failing grade gets you turned into a rat," Jordy added, flicking his tail angrily.

Greg blinked. "Huh?"

"*Lana* didn't get turned into a rat," Jordy explained impatiently. "She can do stuff with gems and we can't. Plus, she has the knife. Sheamathan won't mess with her."

Raenihel said, "We're still learning about the knife. We don't know what it can do. Maybe Sheamathan doesn't, either. So, anyone with gem powers is a threat."

Lana thought back to her encounter in the throne room. "If Sheamathan had been able to touch the knife, I bet she would have taken it from me."

"She can't touch it. Breghlin can't touch it, either," Raenihel said. He frowned as he added, "Of course, there *is* a way. A human or a gnome could take it to her."

This time, Raenihel was a step ahead of her. Lana hadn't stopped to think about that. "I wonder how long it will take Sheamathan to figure that out," Lana said.

"Not long," Jordy muttered under his breath. He sat up on his haunches and rubbed his stomach with one paw. "All this talk has made me hungry. It's nearly dinnertime and I didn't get any lunch."

Raenihel said, "We won't keep you. Thank you for all you've done."

"Yes, thanks, guys," Lana said. The words sounded so inadequate. "We'll find a way to help you. We won't forget about you, I promise." No, she certainly wouldn't. How could anyone forget these sadly comical rat-boys? But her offer to help was mostly wishful thinking. "We plan on rescuing the gnomes in the work camps, too," she added, remembering what X had told her. She said to Raenihel, "Your people are in a mining camp. I know where it is now. X pointed in the general direction and said it's not too far from here. Maybe we can free them."

"Forget it. It's hopeless. We've seen the camp," Jordy said, shaking his head. "The hills above the mining pit are crawling with breghlin. There's more down in the pits, too, where the workers live."

Her heart sank. A girl and an elderly gnome would never be able to free the gnomes from a place like that. It would take gem powers beyond her capabilities, and an army of gnomes. "I think we've done all we can this trip," she said reluctantly. "I should go home, learn more, and come up with a plan."

"I'm afraid you're right," Raenihel agreed, his shoulders sagging. "I'm tired and discouraged. Your revelation about the wolfhound was a terrible blow. I need to go home and discuss this with my clan."

Greg and Jordy jumped down from the grain sacks and walked to the low door. Greg said, "If you come back, look around here and you'll probably find us." Jordy raised a paw in farewell. Then they were gone, leaving Lana and Raenihel to their gloomy thoughts.

Chapter 19

Jordy led Greg into an empty storage room. "We gotta talk," Jordy said breathlessly. His tail was twitching, a telltale sign he was nervous, but he couldn't keep it still. He was pretty sure Greg wasn't going to like his idea.

"Talk? About what?"

Jordy took a deep breath and plunged in. "I got this idea. Listen up. We go to Sheamathan and offer to steal the magic knife. If we're lucky, we shouldn't have to hurt anybody and—"

"Huh?" Greg cut in. "I don't get it."

"I'm talking about stealing the knife with the gems—the Challenger's knife, dimwit."

"Yeah," Greg said with a fierce scowl. "*That* part I *got*. Are you crazy? Why would you help the woodspirit?"

Jordy sat back on his haunches. Just as he'd thought. This was gonna be a tough sell. "Don't look at me like that. *Think*, Greg. We make a bargain with the woodspirit, and the knife can be our ticket home!" He spread his paws in a helpless gesture. "Maybe *you'd* like to spend the rest of your life as a rat. Not *me*. I wanna go home, ride my bike, and play sports." Meeting a stony silence, he tried a new approach. "Don't you want a girlfriend? One who doesn't have fur and a tail?" It was hard to look his friend in the eye and see such disappointment and disgust. "Look, it's easy. Sheamathan turns us back into boys and we steal the knife and take it to her. Lana and the gnome won't even know it was us that did it." He was hoping that last angle would win his friend over.

Greg's answer was frigid. "Maybe not, but *we'll* know. I don't think I could live with that."

"Don't go all soft on me now." Jordy's tail flicked angrily. "When will we get another chance like this?"

"You'd trust Sheamathan? After she turned you into a *rat*?" Greg shook his head. "She'll *never* let us go home, Jordy, no matter *what* we do for her. The minute we give her the knife, she'll turn us back into rats."

Jordy wasn't an idiot. He'd thought about that, but as long as there was a shred of hope, they had to try. "You don't know that for sure. Besides, what do we have to lose? Look, I'm cutting you in on the deal 'cause you're my friend. Stay here and be a rat if you want. I'll go by myself."

"Once you're a boy again, Lana and the gnome won't recognize you. But *I* will," Greg said quietly.

"Um, right. Is that a threat? If you're gonna *rat* on me, my plan isn't going to work." Bad enough Greg didn't want to play along, but to actually turn against him? He'd better be bluffing.

"You've talked me into a lot of stuff I wasn't too happy about, but this is over the top. *Way* over. Sheamathan pretty much destroyed *this* world. *Ours* may be next. How can you help somebody like that?"

"'Cause I don't want to be a rat for the rest of my life," Jordy said irritably. His thoughts snagged on those last words and his stomach did a slow, sickening roll. "Hey, how long do rats live?"

Greg wriggled his whiskers thoughtfully. "Cats and dogs live ten to twenty years. I dunno about rats."

Jordy's trembling voice was no act. "Well, what if rats only live three or four years?" He paused, letting his words sink in. He'd never really thought about that. They were just kids, he and Greg—miserably unhappy turned-into-rats kids, but still. As long as nothing made a meal out of them, they'd be fine. Well, not fine, but *alive,* anyway. Now he wasn't so sure. "Just because *humans* live to be seventy or so doesn't mean *we* will. We're *rats* now. Maybe we only *got* a couple more years."

Greg looked decidedly alarmed. "Gee, I never thought about that."

"If we don't do something soon, it may be too late."

"Maybe you're right."

"Of *course* I'm right." This was the only argument that had fazed Greg so far, and Jordy clung to it. "We're wasting time. Are you in or out?"

"You win," Greg said miserably. "I'm in."

"Lana and the gnome will have to do without the knife. Let's get going. Before you chicken out."

Jordy led the way to Sheamathan's chambers, running as fast as his short legs would go. They had to cut the deal right away before Greg lost his nerve. Lana and the gnome were headed to the portal, so there wasn't much time. He didn't *want* to see Sheamathan. She was *mean.* He and Greg hadn't done anything to deserve being turned into rats. Like, what could a person even do that was bad enough to deserve something like that? They would escape, as soon as they gave her the knife. Before she did anything even *worse* to them. Sheamathan *had* to go for this bargain. She just *had* to. He and Greg knew where to find the knife. They couldn't steal it, though, unless she turned them back into boys.

They'd get the knife away from Lana—somehow. He didn't have a plan, exactly, but he'd make one up on the fly. He bared his teeth in a snarl. The gnome was just a little guy, and pretty old, so he shouldn't be much of a problem. And Lana, well, she was a *girl*. Yeah, she was older than he was, but he could take her, for sure.

The knife with the jewels was a totally awesome weapon. Too bad he couldn't keep it, 'cause it would be *by far* the coolest thing he'd ever stolen. Way cooler than the iPad or the DVDs, and the jeans and sneakers he'd lifted from the department store were too boring to count.

Breathing hard and starting to tire, he ran down the hallway that opened to the throne room. A terrible thought came to him. What if the guards wouldn't let them in?

"Wait up," Greg called, panting heavily a few feet behind Jordy.

Jordy stopped and looked back.

"Let me catch my breath."

Jordy gave his friend the once-over. Greg wasn't just tired. He was scared. Reaching out a paw, he touched Greg's back, and it felt like Dad's recliner on the vibrate setting. "Just think. After this, I won't pick on you anymore for havin' red hair and a big nose. No matter *what*, you'll look better than you do now."

"Gee, thanks."

"Sorry for the way that sounded, but you know what I mean."

He was scared too. Only an idiot *wouldn't* be. His stomach was going around like a sock in the dryer. Holding his head high, he trotted to the throne room's massive, closed doors. Since he couldn't knock, he'd have to shout and hope the guards could hear him. Right now, no one would be able to hear him. Not over the loud voices in there. He sat back on his haunches and motioned for Greg to be quiet and listen.

"She said she had powers." The voice was deep, guttural, definitely a breghlin. "There was voices from nowhere."

He and Greg exchanged wide-eyed glances. The breghlin was talking about *Lana*!

"Enough excuses!" Sheamathan shouted. "You let her go. You *helped* her escape! It was a trick. I can hardly believe you could be fooled so easily."

The breghlin's voice shook with fear. "She had the knife, and it glowed! I was afraid!"

"I will give you something to be afraid of," Sheamathan said, her voice cold and dangerous. Jordy shivered, glad it was the guard facing her and not him. Maybe she'd turn the guard into a rat or a snake or a toad. He cast a quick glance at Greg who sat quaking beside him. "A year or two in a cell will give you time to gather your wits, assuming you *have* any," Sheamathan continued.

Another voice spoke. "My Queen, sssomething mussst be done."

"Done about what, my pet?"

"The woman and the rumorsss ssspreading through the castle. We know that the Challenger wasss defeated. He can no longer vex you. But can another Challenger arise?"

"Unlikely. Gem powers are not common in humans. We must put an end to the rumors. The woman has stirred up more trouble than I anticipated." A pause followed. "X, tell me, do the rumors say that she speaks on *behalf* of the Challenger, or that she *is* the Challenger?"

"I've heard both."

"Sssshe is dangerousss."

"We do not know everything there is to know about the blade. Perhaps neither does she. The knife would be safer in my possession, but that poses a problem. Guards, escort this buffoon to the dungeon. Put him in the woman's cell."

"You are merciful, My Queen," the breghlin groveled.

"I will have your head, fool, when the image of your head on a pike brings me more pleasure than the thought of you rotting behind bars."

Jordy let out a squeal when the doors burst open sweeping Greg and him aside. They rolled and floundered, trying to get to their feet. The guards flanking X frowned down at them with a look of disgust, and then marched X away. The doors began to swing shut.

"Hey, wait!" Jordy shrieked.

The doors stopped as another breghlin looked out. He curled a lip when he saw them. "Off with you!"

"We have something to tell Sheamathan! It's really *important!*"

The breghlin's sneer reminded Jordy of a snobby butler. "Important? Is that so?" he growled.

"Please let us in. It's about the Challenger's knife."

Sheamathan commanded, "Let them in. I will see them."

Shaking with a mixture of fear and relief, Jordy gave Greg a "don't mess this up" look and walked into the throne room. This place had bad, bad memories. He felt like running away, but he couldn't afford to be a wimp. Taking a deep breath he looked across the room at Sheamathan on her throne.

"Come along. Do not keep me waiting."

A pythanium rose up behind her throne, weaving sinuously. Jordy let out a terrified squeak. The serpent's wide, flat head bent protectively over Sheamathan's throne. Shivering with dread, Jordy prodded Greg to move. The pythanium's watchful yellow eyes followed them as they crossed the room. Then, from the shadows, the black wolfhound appeared and sat down at Sheamathan's feet.

Sheamathan looked down at Jordy and Greg in front of her throne and leaned forward, eyes intent. "Now, what is your news about the

Challenger's blade?" she asked, almost kindly. "What do you know of it?"

Jordy tried to keep his whiskers from twitching at the poisonous glint in her black eyes. Those eyes gave him the creeps. He felt like he was staring into a dark well and if he dropped a rock in, it would fall and fall and fall and fall. Long waves of black hair tumbled around her shoulders. Her skin was white and lifeless—like skin under a week-old bandage. Her black dress seemed to absorb the torchlight. Looking at her made him feel weak and numb and it was hard to think. The dog showed its teeth, which didn't help, either. Dogs didn't like rats. And the pythanium was staring at him like hot food on a buffet line. It stunk to be on the bottom of the food chain.

"We have a deal for you!" The rest poured out in a jumble. "We met the woman—Lana—the one with the magic knife. Me and Greg know where she's going. Turn us back into humans and we'll bring you the knife!"

Sheamathan had been watching him with a flat, dead smile. Now, her expression grew interested. "How do I know you can get it away from her? Or that once I change you into boys you will bring me the knife?"

He trembled under the intensity of her gaze. "We wouldn't think of betraying you and sneaking off or anything like that. We want to go home. If you agree to our bargain, you can send us home after you get the knife. That will be our reward."

Sheamathan angled her head and studied them, wetting her lips. The motion, and the coldness in her eyes, looked reptilian. "An interesting proposition. Tell me where to find the girl."

"She's with a gnome. They're headed to the portal. But knowing where she is won't do you any good since, well, since you can't touch the knife. You need us to bring it to you."

"Do not be impertinent; I am quite aware of that." If being blunt offended her, he couldn't help it. She had to realize she *needed* them. Sheamathan's eyes narrowed as she regarded him thoughtfully. He looked back with keen, bright eyes. Trustworthy eyes, he hoped.

The woodspirit swept back her hair, and Jordy saw a gray metal necklace close around her throat and an assortment of longer necklaces with pendants holding gems. The gems glinted in the wavering torchlight in a fascinating display of shapes and colors. She lifted her arms upward, and then moved them slowly outward, her palms facing the rat-boys. The motion made her wide, sheer black sleeves slide back, and his eyes flicked to the gem-studded silvery bands encircling each upper arm and the stacks of gem-encrusted bracelets on her wrists.

A wave of energy washed over him. One moment he was a rat, the next, his old self again. He staggered—his balance on two feet suddenly unreliable, but after a moment he felt steadier. He looked down. He was wearing the clothes he'd worn when he arrived—the same dirty jeans and worn-out sneakers. Running his hands excitedly over his unruly dark hair, he felt for that place where his hair never quite laid down. Still there. So was the big zit on his left cheek. And the dirt under his nails that his mother always nagged him about. He felt like shouting for joy but he just grinned.

Beside him, Greg examined his own transformation with equal excitement, and Jordy had to admit his friend looked darn good despite that awful red hair. Greg never got zits—almost never, anyway. And honestly, his nose didn't look all *that* big. It was amazing what being a rat for a year could do to your point of view.

"There. Just as you were when you arrived," Sheamathan said coldly, "although I see very little improvement in your appearances. Now hurry; bring me the knife. You will become rats by sundown tomorrow unless you return with the knife."

He and Greg raced from the room, nearly knocking over the guards by the door.

"I still don't like this," Greg said as they ran down a flight of stairs.

"Me neither. I happen to like Lana even though I give her a hard time. And I like Raenihel, too. But we *have* to do this, Greg. We just *have* to."

"I know. Just don't expect me to feel good about it."

They headed toward the castle's rear doors.

Chapter 20

"They're gone. I'm not sure whether to be sad or relieved," Lana said. She owed her unusual rescuers a debt of gratitude, but rats, especially giant rats, creeped her out.

Raenihel slid off a pile of grain sacks and dusted himself off. "If it hadn't been for them, I'd probably still be looking for you." His voice was tense. "We should leave. If Sheamathan turned a gem master as powerful as the Challenger into a dog, she's more powerful than I thought. I shouldn't have brought you here."

"Your Challenger is my nightmare beast." She hadn't gotten used to the idea herself. Sheamathan had defeated the gnomes' hero. Worse, turned him into a *dog*. Yes, Raenihel had good reason to be depressed, and afraid. How could they defeat someone with that kind of power? "I know you were afraid to come here, Raenihel. Thank you for not abandoning me." She could picture herself as a giant rat, living here in this basement with Greg and Jordy. The mental image made her shudder.

"It was the right thing to do. Thinking about you and the knife gave me strength and helped me fight her control."

He looked so haggard. This ordeal had taken a lot out of him, and it wasn't over yet. She stood and made sure the Challenger's blade was safely hidden under her shirt. In a tone more cheerful than she felt, she said, "All right, I'm ready to go."

"Just a moment." Raenihel reached for the leather cord around his neck and pulled out his skin of fialazza. "Leaving the castle may be a lot harder than getting in." He took a drink and offered her some.

He was right. A couple gulps to boost her courage couldn't hurt. She drank and handed it back, appreciating the way it settled her nerves. "Security is bound to be tighter once Sheamathan finds out I'm gone. If she raises the drawbridge, we'll be trapped on this side of the moat."

"My thought exactly. We need to get away before she knows you're missing."

They ducked through the low opening, and she followed Raenihel through the basement until they came to the storeroom with the small door. "It's still open," she whispered, taking the lead. This time she didn't crack her head on the ceiling and she didn't need the knife to light the way.

After peeking outside, she turned to Raenihel. "I don't see any guards. Let's go." They slipped through, and walking single-file they proceeded cautiously along the castle wall.

The afternoon sun shone fitfully through drifting bands of clouds. Swirling particles of dirt carried on the wind quickly covered them with a film of grit. Lana swept back wayward strands of hair and kept her head down enough to keep the dirt out of her eyes.

Raenihel's plan to threaten Sheamathan had been hopelessly naïve, she thought once again with a touch of annoyance. How would it have looked if Sheamathan had let Lana deliver the gnomes' ultimatum and then just walk away? Weak, no doubt about it, and Sheamathan would never allow herself to look weak.

Glancing over her shoulder to make sure Raenihel was keeping up, Lana discovered that he was disturbingly far behind. "Hurry up," she mouthed. He nodded. His face looked deceptively calm but she knew he was scared, and he had every right to be. He risked being sent to a work camp.

The next time she looked back he had fallen even further behind and she muttered irritably under her breath, "What is the matter with him? He can walk a lot faster than this. I've *seen* how fast he can walk." In fact, at times she'd had trouble keeping up with him. She motioned impatiently. His lined face looked unusually pale. He leaned forward as if fighting a strong wind and finally closed the distance between them.

"What's wrong?" she demanded. He answered, "I'm all right," but his eyes had a blank, distant look that troubled her and his hands were trembling. No, he was definitely *not* all right.

Every moment they delayed increased their risks. Even if they got safely past the castle walls it was still a long way to the portal. Sheamathan might send breghlin after them—or worse—pythanium. Lana wet suddenly dry lips, wishing she hadn't thought of that. How did you outrun something that could fly? Her hand instinctively moved to the Challenger's knife. Its solid form under her shirt felt comforting. In the dungeon she'd spent hours theorizing about how Fair Lands gems worked in Shadow, and how the Challenger's knife worked. If she and Raenihel made it safely to the portal, they might have her theories to thank for it. She'd explain everything to him later, but she couldn't expect him to know whether or not she was on the right track.

Most Fair Lands gems had multiple abilities. Three, at least, and some as many as six. The way she saw it, without input from the user a gem produced each one equally. But what if a skilled user could direct all the stones' strength into only one or two abilities? That ought to amplify the selected powers. Combining gemstones with similar properties should also have an effect, the way combining drums, a guitar, and a keyboard created similar but more complex music than each alone.

An aspect of her theory, based solely on instinct, was that combining gemstones with different abilities resulted in new powers. Their interaction would alter them, she reasoned, creating a phase transition into something different. The possibilities were mind-boggling. But until she could find and read Elias's writings, all she had were theories.

She drew the knife from its sheath and took Raenihel's arm. The blade glowed briefly and then went dark.

"Now we head straight for the drawbridge," she whispered to Raenihel. "Don't stop unless I tell you to."

The Greeks believed that topaz could make the wearer invisible. Invisibility seemed pretty hard to believe, but what if people looked at you and your presence simply didn't register? Maybe that's what invisibility really was. If not, it would be just as effective. She focused on that concept and held the knife tightly. Raenihel's form wavered and became insubstantial. She could see through him. He looked at her and then down at himself, and let out a cry of distress. She tightened her grip on his arm. "I'm trying to make us invisible. I don't know if it's working properly, but something is happening. Hurry. I don't know how long I can keep this up."

Maybe onlookers couldn't see them at all, and they could only see each other in this ghostlike form because they were aware of the others' presence. She had no idea, and there was no way to test her theory at the moment.

They walked the remaining length of the side wall. When they rounded the corner, she was relieved to see that the drawbridge was still down.

As they neared the drawbridge, Raenihel's steps began to falter and his breathing grew labored as she tugged him along. All at once she understood. The woodspirit's presence, like gravity, was trying to hold him here. Well, it wasn't going to work, she thought angrily. They'd fight it together.

Dragging him along was like towing a concrete pillar. With every step he felt heavier, and the effort of pulling him while trying to maintain invisibility was making her dizzy. This would never do. She had to forget about invisibility for now and focus all her attention on drawing strength and stamina from the knife.

Letting her mind go blank, she drew several deep breaths and then refocused her mind. She pictured energy running from the knife through her whole body, pooling in her hand, and then flowing into the gnome's arm.

Energy streamed through her and she let out a startled gasp. Every nerve in her body was on fire! Raenihel became no heavier than a rag doll. After a few minutes she discovered she didn't need to pull him. He had stopped panting and was walking normally beside her. The burning sensation dampened to a tingle, which was good, because feeling like she was on fire was a bit disturbing.

They crossed the drawbridge and kept walking. "How do you feel now?" she asked.

"Better. Much better."

She believed him. The distant, blank look was gone. He seemed more relaxed. Still, she didn't let go. Holding his arm as they passed through the groves of dead trees, she steered him toward the opening in the castle's outer wall. The fallen bricks from the formerly bricked-up doorway still lay on the ground where they'd dropped. She climbed through the opening with Raenihel right behind her, and they scanned the surrounding land. Nothing moved across the bleak landscape.

"Well, we made it this far. I hope our luck holds," she said.

They set out toward the embankment where Raenihel had camped after she left. The rush of adrenalin had worn off. She felt tired and jittery and was tempted to stop for a while but they really couldn't afford to. Not here in the open. They had to keep moving.

When they reached the base of the embankment she asked, "Can you keep going, or are you too tired?" Raenihel had kept up remarkably well, especially considering his age, but she didn't want to push him too hard.

"Let's keep going. I feel quite well." She studied him quickly. He was breathing hard, but so was she. He could probably make it to the top and then they could rest.

They scrambled up the steep hill and kept walking. "I can make it to our campsite," Raenihel said. It wasn't much farther, but her legs ached from climbing the hill. Still, if he could make it, she could.

When they reached the site, Raenihel coughed several times, clearing his lungs, and gave a shaky laugh. "What a relief to be back. I think we're safe here."

She bent, bracing her hands on her thighs while she caught her breath. It seemed like days ago she had left Raenihel here and set out for the castle alone. When her heart rate slowed, she and Raenihel crouched down to scan the land between themselves and the castle. No sign of anyone following them. Maybe they were safe for the moment.

"We should rest and have something to eat," he said. "And I need some fialazza to settle my nerves."

She brightened. Yes, a meal and a few swigs of fialazza would do both of them worlds of good.

Raenihel led her to the crevice where he had hidden the backpacks. She sank gratefully to the ground while he pulled up the backpacks and took out some dried venison. Plenty left. Good, because suddenly she was starving. After handing her a wrapped portion, he pulled out his wineskin and helped himself to the first drink. No such thing as ladies before gentlemen today, she thought with amusement. Not after what he'd just been through, and she didn't blame him.

After a minute he sat down beside her, slipped the leather cord over his head and handed her the wineskin. She shook it gently to hear the liquid slosh. About a third left. She took two big gulps, enjoying the unique flavor. Amazing stuff. She loved the way it refreshed and calmed her. Paper crinkled as they unwrapped their venison and ate silently, lost in private thoughts.

They still had a long way to go and they couldn't afford to let down their guard. Shadow was a dangerous, inhospitable world. Even if Sheamathan didn't come after them, any number of horrors could waylay them between here and the portal. Lana especially dreaded the weed-covered hills. She could still picture the pythanium rising up behind the boulder.

"I always feel more cheerful after a meal," Raenihel said, interrupting her uncomfortable thoughts. "We'll hike to the portal and wait until nightfall when it's easier to cross."

Reluctantly she stood and put on her backpack. Considering all they'd just been through together, she felt comfortable speaking her mind. "On the way here, I worried about getting separated. If something happened to you, how would I get home?"

"You could find your way back to the portal, especially by daylight. It's not that far away."

"Right, but then what? Without you, how would I get across?"

Raenihel slipped his pack over his shoulders. "Other gnomes would come along. They'd take you home."

She refused to let it drop. "Before or after the mutant bugs attacked me? I'm sorry, but I don't like the idea of depending on you, or anyone else, to get home."

He waved her fears away. "Then you must learn to go through the portal on your own and I will teach you."

"It looked easy enough when we came here. Is it?"

"When the barrier is weak, it is. That's why we cross at night when the portal's energy field is weakest. You simply attune your mind and body to the energy field and step through."

Atune yourself? What kind of mumbo-jumbo was that? "Attune your mind and body and step through," she repeated. Why did she not feel reassured?

Raenihel shrugged. "It becomes second nature after a few tries. Let's go. We should keep moving."

They walked across the dead land, shielding their faces when the wind picked up and pelted them with red dirt. What a miserable place. Long ago, trees and grass had probably covered the ground. It was hard to picture that now.

From time to time she and Raenihel looked back to make sure no one was following. A sense of foreboding that she couldn't shake dogged her steps.

At last they left the barren plain and entered the dreaded "stinking hills." She realized now, after more thought, that the odor came from decaying carcasses, like that horrid skeleton she had tripped over. She shuddered. What better place for a pythanium feeding ground than weed-covered hills scattered with boulders? Fortunately, pythanium hunted at night. But where did they go during the day? Maybe they slept right here in the weeds, behind these boulders. It wasn't a comforting thought.

When they reached the dry streambed and crossed into the flat lowlands, she scanned the terrain ahead and started to relax. Pythanium couldn't hide here. There was nothing for cover except a few thorny bushes.

Raenihel looked over his shoulder. "We have come a long way with no sign of pursuit."

"We had a head start," she reminded him, using her sleeve to wipe sweat from her face. "We shouldn't get over-confident."

"Or let down our guard," he agreed. "We will be much safer in the forest. We can hide there until dark."

She glanced at the darkening sky. The sun was already going down, so they wouldn't have long to wait. The horizon had an orange tint like autumn leaves. As sunset approached, the temperature would drop quickly. Already it was growing colder, but right now she welcomed the cool breeze.

Ahead rose the familiar steep embankment, and at the top stood the forest where they had first arrived. Her heart felt lighter just thinking about the portal. She could hardly wait to get home. She'd gotten away from Sheamathan without being tortured, enslaved, or turned into a giant talking rat. In a couple hours she'd climb into her safe, comfortable bed. At the moment, she couldn't think of anything more appealing. Nothing would keep her away, *nothing*—not even swarms of mutant insects. Tomorrow she'd drink coffee and eat normal food. Best of all, Elias's hidden safe awaited her, and she would find it.

"What's *that*?" Raenihel asked sharply, jerking her back to the present.

In the distance, two forms walked across the lowlands. For now, anyone she and Raenihel met posed a threat. "They look human," she said. "Too tall for breghlin or gnomes."

"Humans near the portal, yes, that's possible," Raenihel conceded, but he looked troubled by the idea.

"How would they get here? Wouldn't someone have to bring them through? Gnomes? Breghlin?"

"Breghlin, no doubt. Gnomes seldom bring a human across. Lately, the breghlin haven't spent much time on your side of the portal, though, so it does seem strange."

"Whoever they are, maybe they've been here a while, hiding in the forest."

The gnome's brow creased. He shook his head. "Not likely. If they escaped the breghlin and tried to live in the forest—well, the insects we saw there are carnivorous scavengers."

"Oh, great," she muttered.

"And then there's the problem of what to eat. Many forest plants are poisonous, and as you can see, there's nothing edible in these lowlands."

"So, whoever these people are, we should be worried."

Raenihel looked increasingly tense. "I'm afraid so. And they're coming our way."

"What should we do?" There was nowhere to hide. The embankment, a few minutes' walk away, would take a while to climb.

"Just keep walking. If they don't seem threatening we'll stop and talk to them, and then decide."

"I'd like to take out my knife, but I don't want them to see it."

"I agree. Keep it hidden unless we have to defend ourselves."

"I have gems. And my bracelet." She touched the malachite. The stone felt unusually warm and her sense of uneasiness grew the longer she touched it. She couldn't hide her troubled expression.

Raenihel asked worriedly, "It warns you of trouble?"

She nodded. "I think so."

The figures continued to walk directly toward them. Definitely human, men or boys. One of them lifted his arm and waved excitedly.

Was it a greeting, or a plea for help? She needed more insights about them, preferably before they came much closer. Taking aquamarines and sapphires from her pouch, she whispered, "Foresight, telepathy, clairvoyance," and held the stones tightly. These were new powers for her, ones she had never tried to use before. Could she do it now, under pressure?

A queasy feeling in the pit of her stomach made her stumble to a halt.

Raenihel grasped her arm. "What is it?"

She held up a warning hand. He nodded and waited silently.

Focus. What did she feel? She took several deep breaths. *Danger.* The impression grew stronger and so did the queasiness. Brief flashes of boys' faces. Harmless looking boys, yet something felt wrong. She couldn't read their thoughts but two impressions came through. *They're hiding something. And they're worried we'll find out.* She and Raenihel needed to get away from these people as soon as possible.

"Whoever they are, they can't be trusted." She put her gemstones away. Her palms were damp. She felt vulnerable, even with the knife. "We need a code word."

He looked confused. "A code word?"

"You know, a signal."

Understanding came into his eyes. "You mean, a way to let each other know something without the strangers catching on."

"Exactly." If either of us thinks we're in danger, we say the word. Then we attack."

"All I have is a small knife." He took off his backpack, rummaged through, and came out with a sheathed knife. "It's small but very sharp." He tucked it into his belt.

"What code word should we use?" she asked as they started walking.

He thought for a moment. "Fialazza. If we think we're in danger, we'll say something about fialazza."

"All right. Good idea." Nervous tension ran through her. She hated uncertainty. Meeting these strangers, not knowing their intentions, was almost as nerve-wracking as facing Sheamathan.

By the time the strangers came close enough to see them well, she and Raenihel had nearly reached the base of the embankment. Both young men waved their arms and ran toward them. Raenihel gave her a sidelong look as the boys stumbled to a halt, panting.

"Hey! Are we ever glad to see *you*!" said the tall, redheaded boy.

The other boy, slightly over-weight, with dark curly hair said, "We haven't seen anyone and we've been wandering for *days*!"

Raenihel shot her a furtive, skeptical glance.

She folded her arms. "How'd you get here? Where'd you come from?"

"From our forest park. A bunch of ugly monsters grabbed us and brought us here," the redhead said. "They looked sort of like *him*." He jerked a thumb at Raenihel, "only way uglier. No offense."

Raenihel cleared his throat but kept silent.

"We fought like maniacs and got away," the other boy said as he dropped to one knee and tied his shoelace.

"Then we hid in the woods. Up there." The redhead pointed to the top of the hill.

Her eyes narrowed. "You've been there ever since?"

The pudgy dark-haired kid stood and dusted off his jeans. "Yeah. What a creepy place."

"Poor things," she said. "What did you find to eat?"

Exchanging a glance, they answered in unison, "Plants!"

"Yes, of course," she said, "which ones?"

The boys shared another quick look. Green ones!" the red-head said." He shifted uncomfortably. "Can you help us get home?"

"Possibly," Raenihel said in a tone that didn't sound very promising. "You haven't been to the castle, or seen the woodspirit?"

"Castle? There's a castle around here?" the dark-haired boy said just as the other boy said, "Woodspirit, what's that?"

Lana raised a brow. She looked at one boy, then the other. They looked decidedly nervous and all of this sounded rehearsed. "By the way, I'm Lana, and this is Raenihel."

"I'm Pete," said the redhead.

"Rob," said the other.

Introductions aside, the conversation stalled. The boys seemed to have run out of things to say. They exchanged sly, meaningful glances and Rob said, "I don't like hanging around here in the open. It's safer in the woods. Let's climb the hill."

"Okay, sure," she said. "You go first. We'll be right behind you."

"Ummm, we're tired and kind of slow. *You* go first," Rob said. Something flickered in his eyes, and then it was gone. He smiled.

Her queasy feeling came back. An image flashed through her mind—the boys springing on them from behind as she and Raenihel climbed the hill. She bit her lip as she looked at Rob, trying to think of an excuse, *any* excuse not to go first. Her mind went blank. "Rats!" she muttered.

Rob paled and Pete's eyes widened in surprise.

And then she knew.

"Raenihel, I need a drink of fialazza."

She kicked "Rob" in the stomach. He doubled over and collapsed, rolling onto his side, howling. She drew her knife. If he as much as *thought* about getting up, she'd skewer him. Behind her she heard the thump of someone hitting the ground, and then shrieks of pain that weren't Raenihel's.

Rob tried to roll over and get up. With a savage grin, she kicked him in the ribs. He collapsed again, moaning. Holding his ribs, he rolled onto his back. She dropped to her knees and brought the knife to his throat. The blade glowed softly. "Are you Jordy or Greg?" she demanded fiercely.

"Jordy!" he gasped. "Please don't kill me!"

"I ought to shred yer meat from yer bones," she said through her teeth. X's threat seemed appropriate, she thought with a grim smile.

"It's hot!" Jordy moaned.

She gave him a puzzled look. "What's hot?"

"The knife!" He tried to move his head to escape the blade, but she kept the knife to his throat. Looking at it in surprise, she repeated, "Hot?"

"Yeah," he gasped raggedly.

"I'll let you up if you promise to march your worthless, rat-tailed butt straight back to Shadowglade. You don't deserve to be taken home." She kept thinking about the knife. Hot? How very odd. It should only be hot when touching evil beings from Shadow.

Getting to her feet, she looked around. Raenihel, still holding his knife and looking angry enough to use it, stood over Greg, his boot planted squarely on the boy's chest.

"I didn't wanna do this," Greg said tearfully. "Jordy said if we didn't steal your knife and give it to Sheamathan we'd die here as rats."

Raenihel's voice shook with anger. "You planned this while we were helping Lana *escape*?"

"No," Greg said, his lower lip trembling. "Jordy thought of it right after we left you."

Jordy looked too bruised and miserable to do much harm. She left him and went to kneel down by Greg. "Tell me," she said, holding the knife to his throat. "Does this feel hot?"

His voice quavered. "Not exactly hot, just warm. Why?"

"Never mind. Just testing a theory." She stood and sheathed the knife.

"What should we do with them?" Raenihel asked angrily. "They betrayed us. Why should I take them through the portal?"

Jordy struggled to his feet, still clutching his ribs, his face white. "We couldn't go home, anyway. The deal was, we bring back the knife or we turn back into rats by sunset tomorrow."

Greg said mournfully, "Only then we'll be dead rats. She'll probably kill us for not coming back with the knife."

Lana said, "I realize that breghlin can't touch the knife, so she couldn't use breghlin to steal it. She needed a gnome or human. But even if you got the knife away from me, I'm surprised she trusted you to bring it back."

Raenihel said with evident alarm, "Who says she trusts them? Look!"

Lana froze as she followed the direction of his gaze. In the distance, row after row of dark forms marched across the lowlands.

"Breghlin!" she gasped.

Chapter 21

Raenihel took his foot off Greg's stomach and said to Lana, "To the portal! Now!"

Greg stumbled to his feet. In a tone a lot like his rat voice he squealed, "You're *leaving* us?"

Lana snapped, "What did you expect?"

"We can't stay and protect you." Raenihel's lined face looked implacable. "We have to save ourselves."

Jordy's eyes brimmed with tears. "That's all *we* were trying to do— *save* ourselves."

"By *attacking* us? And stealing my knife? It's *not* the same!"

Jordy's face crumpled. He let out a sob. "I'm sorry."

"They'll kill us for sure!" Greg's eyes implored her for mercy. "Take us with you. Please!"

"Jordy just said you can't go home," she protested.

"We'll turn into rats tomorrow, but I'd rather be a rat *there* than *here*!"

Jordy's face lit with sudden hope. "Sure! Why didn't I think of that?"

She glanced at Raenihel but she couldn't tell what he was thinking. The boys deserved whatever happened to them. They had planned to attack her, steal the knife, and hand it over to Sheamathan. The very idea made her furious. Let Sheamathan have them, she thought bitterly. She took a deep breath to calm herself and uncurled her fingers, which she had unconsciously clenched into fists.

Across the lowlands the breghlin marched toward them. What *would* become of Greg and Jordy? They had failed to steal the knife. Turning them back into rats might not be punishment enough. Sheamathan might torture or kill them.

Her resolve weakened as she looked at the boys' terrified faces. To be perfectly fair, she told herself reluctantly, they hadn't come to Shadow by choice, as she had. For nearly a year they'd lived in rats' bodies, hiding in the castle, foraging for food, at risk of being eaten by predators. Now, for the first time, they'd found a way to win their freedom so they could be boys again and go home. But they had to hurt—maybe kill someone—and steal a knife for an unthinkably evil being. They might not understand all the consequences, but ignorance wouldn't absolve them of whatever terrible things happened. Lana gave a frustrated sigh. It was easy to say that in their place she wouldn't be tempted, but—

Raenihel interrupted her thoughts. "We don't have time to debate this. The boys are from *your* world, Lana. You decide."

Hands on her hips, she stared at the rat-boys. It was her nature to look for the best in people and give them the benefit of the doubt. She hoped she wouldn't regret her decision. "Go! And if you turn on me again, I'll skewer your hides to the nearest tree."

"Thank you! Thank you!" Jordy shrieked. This time, there was no discussion of who went first. Jordy ran to the embankment and started up on all fours, grunting in pain, muttering curses. Greg followed with Lana and Raenihel close behind.

When she reached the top, she stopped to get her breath. Their pursuers were still a fair distance off, but moving quickly, trying to close the gap. She rubbed her arms, suddenly chilled. Why was she worried? Everything would be fine. Soon it would be dark and Raenihel would attune himself to the portal and lead her and the boys through.

Raenihel motioned for her and the boys to gather round. "I have something to tell you, but we need to keep moving so I'll explain as we walk. Boys, take this path. Lana and I will follow."

The narrow dirt trail led toward the portal. Obediently, Jordy and Greg started walking. "You boys may not have thought of this," Raenihel said from behind them, "but even after you go through the portal you won't be safe. The breghlin will follow us through."

Lana's mouth dropped open in dismay. She hadn't thought of that.

"We'll *never* escape," Jordy moaned. "They're sure to find us and bring us back."

"Not if I take you to the Tree Home," Raenihel said. "Breghlin can't follow us inside."

The Tree Home! Lana's hearted lifted. It would be perfectly safe there and the Tree Home was near the portal so they wouldn't have far to go. "Of course! You'll go back to Shadow before dawn, but so will the breghlin and then the park will be safe until nightfall."

"That's right."

"What's a Tree Home?" Jordy asked.

"You might call it a multi-dimensional refuge inside a tree," Raenihel said.

"Cool!" Jordy breathed.

Lana said, "You didn't like it when Gliaphon brought *me* there. Now you're taking the boys?"

"I see no way around it. The boys need to stay the night. As head of my clan, my decision will be respected, which is not to say there won't be complaints."

"Bringing the boys along was *my* decision. Now I'm making trouble for you."

The gnome said firmly, "You helped my people. Say no more about it."

Without meaning to, she had put Raenihel in an awkward position. Hasty decisions had a way of creating unexpected problems, and she had a feeling this was the first of many. Tomorrow at sundown the boys would turn back into rats. Would Sheamathan send breghlin through the portal to search for them again? Or would she give up, assuming the rats had fled beyond the Amulet? A knot formed in Lana's stomach. Where *would* the rats go? She couldn't take them to their parents. *Here are your kids. I found them in another world. Sorry, but someone turned them into giant, talking rats.* Yeah, that wouldn't go over so well. Could she simply turn them loose outside the park? What did rats eat in the wild? Could they scavenge enough from fields to live? Or eat from village dumpsters? No, the village was out. Populated areas would be too risky. She didn't want Greg and Jordy to end up in a government research lab. *Rats! I shouldn't have agreed to help them!*

Her head snapped up. She hadn't been paying attention. That clicking sound—

Soon, the buzz of wings nearly drowned out the clicking.

"Oh no," Jordy groaned.

Drawing the Challenger's blade, she shouldered her way past the boys, muttering under her breath. She had two delinquent boys to deal with and breghlin in hot pursuit. Compared to that, mutant insects were a mere annoyance. *Carnivorous mutant insects,* she reminded herself. The blade began to glow as the insect army came into view. In their characteristic grotesque manner, they crawled, hopped, and tried to fly. She held up the glowing knife. What exactly did she want it to do? She had no idea. Right now she was so irritated she couldn't think straight. "Out of my way you disgusting bugs!"

An arc of light leapt from the blade, nearly blinding her. She turned her head, squeezing her eyes shut. Even through closed eyelids she could see arcs of light leaping from the blade.

Insects sizzled. The air stank like putrid, burnt meat.

She opened her eyes a few seconds later, reluctant to look. Charred insects littered the trail and hundreds of terrified bugs were fleeing into the underbrush.

She spun to see what had become of Raenihel and the boys. Raenihel uncovered his eyes and gawked at her. The boys clung to each other, their faces frozen in open-mouthed astonishment.

She turned back to the path. "Well. That's something *else* the knife can do," she muttered." Walking again, she kicked aside charred insects. The knife glowed softly. Had the knife acted independently, or had her anger been the catalyst for its reaction? Behind her, the crunch, crunch, crunch of insects told her that Raenihel and the boys were following her.

Fading sunlight gave way to the peculiar silvery haze that characterized Shadow's night sky. The glowing knife did little to light the narrow path. Protruding branches, roots and stones—obstacles everywhere—threatened to trip them and slow them down.

The still night air carried every sound. She turned her head to better hear behind her. The voices were much too close. Guttural breghlin voices were easily distinguishable. They were closing the gap, and they weren't trying to hide the fact. Shouted orders and snapping branches marked their progress.

"They're coming! They're coming!" Greg cried in a terrified whisper, tugging at Raenihel's arm.

Jordy cried, "We gotta get out of here!"

Lana shared their panic. Even with a knife that shot bolts of lightning—and who knew what else it could do—she couldn't take on a regiment of breghlin.

Signal whistles and shouted orders came to her on the wind along with curses and angry threats. They crashed ever closer through the underbrush.

She waved for Raenihel to take the lead and they ran deeper into the forest.

Finally, Raenihel stopped and said between shaky breaths, "The portal is right in front of us. When I'm attuned to the energy field, I'll pull us through, so stand close and join hands."

Sheathing the knife, Lana took Raenihel's hand on one side, Jordy's on the other, and Greg seized Raenihel's other hand. Lana felt Jordy's every movement as he bounced on his toes, shifting from one foot to the other. Taking a steadying breath, she waited. And waited. Why wasn't Raenihel pulling them through? Was there a problem?

Her face and arms tingled from the energy field's vibrations. What would happen if she leaned forward, just a little? She leaned her upper body toward the field and something seemed to repel her, pressing her back. Was this what Raenihel was feeling? Greg mumbled over and over, "Come on, come on, come *on*."

It was dark now, or at least as dark as she'd ever seen it here. "Can you take us through soon?" she asked Raenihel, trying not to sound alarmed. "Isn't the barrier weak enough?"

"To transition between worlds I need to be calm." He glared at the hyperactive boys. "And I am anything but calm at the moment."

The boys stopped fidgeting and fell silent. Seconds felt like minutes. Cold sweat coated Lana's skin as Raenihel stood, eyes closed in solemn concentration. She was sure he could feel her hand shaking. As a last resort, maybe Raenihel could pull them inside a tree on this side of the portal, but she would rather cross and hide in her own world.

"Now would be good!" Greg whispered breathlessly.

Unable to keep quiet any longer Jordy said, "Yeah, like, please beam us up."

Raenihel's voice was tense. "I can't get through yet."

After what felt like minutes, Lana asked thickly, "Still no luck?" Raenihel opened his eyes. His frightened look was answer enough.

The energy field was probably weak enough—he was just too panicky to attune himself to the field. Inspiration struck. "Fialazza!"

The wisdom of her suggestion registered immediately. Raenihel pulled out the wineskin, opened it, drank deeply of the calming fluid, and then let the skin drop under his tunic. After a few seconds he gave her hand a confident squeeze. "Now!"

They stepped forward together. Lana almost laughed for joy as she felt the membrane give way. They stepped though into their familiar forest and Greg and Jordy cheered.

"Now to the Tree Home!" Raenihel called. She and the boys hurried after him. If they hadn't been in such a hurry, she would have stopped and kissed the ground.

Raenihel disappeared inside the Tree Home, perhaps checking to see who was there, and then reached a hand out to pull his guests inside. Lana stepped through last and laughed at the boys' comical expressions. Gawking with open mouths, they craned their necks to take in the Tree Home from top to bottom. Greg pointed at the root tables and chairs sprouting from the floor and whispered something to Jordy.

"Amazing, isn't it?" she said. They flashed her a grin and nodded, then began whispering again as they looked over at the gnomes sitting around the "fire" of glowing stones.

She smiled. They were shocked and amazed, and who could blame them? That's how she'd felt the first time, and she suspected she would always feel that way, no matter how many times she came here.

"Wait here a moment," Raenihel said, excusing himself to speak with his clan.

There weren't many gnomes here yet. That might be a problem, Lana realized. Any that came later might run into the breghlin.

Artham and Terrilem were part of the circle, along with a few males she didn't know. Three females and two young girls sat on tree-root stools, working on hand-sewn garments.

Lana studied the tree for signs of decay. Despite the spreading blight, the Tree Home looked healthy and the air bore a crisp, fresh scent.

"Who would believe you could live inside a tree," Greg said to her quietly as Raenihel spoke with the gnomes.

"It's as strange as Shadow, but in a *good* way," Jordy agreed.

Keeping her voice low she said, "One night I was stranded here in the park. I didn't know it, but a group of breghlin were hunting me. Good thing a gnome found me and brought me here. If he hadn't, I might have ended up like you."

"Yeah, you were lucky," Greg said. "We met a few people that got turned into rats and stuff. Most of them get eaten by pythanium sooner or later."

"Thanks for bringing us back," Jordy said. He stood a little taller and looked her squarely in the eye. "After what we did, most people would have left us there. We'll make it up to you. I promise."

Greg took a shaky breath and stared glumly at the floor. "I'm not looking forward to being a rat again."

"Better a rat than *dead*," Jordy reminded him.

"What a choice, huh?" Greg said bitterly. "Just you wait. Someday, I'll get even with Sheamathan."

"Good luck with that," Jordy said.

Raenihel came back wearing a relieved smile. "Fewer complaints than I thought." He took each boy by the arm. "Come. Have something to eat and drink. Then maybe you'd like to sleep."

Lana followed. "Are more gnomes coming? Will they be safe?"

"Safe from the breghlin?"

"Yes."

"If they *Walk Like the Wind* and stay inside the trees, they'll be fine."

While Raenihel was in a good mood she decided to ask another question. "*Walking Like the Wind*—how do you do that?"

"It takes the same focused, relaxed mind as crossing through the portal, but *Walking Like the Wind* isn't something a human can learn to do. A gnome can take you by the hand and bring you along, but you'll never be able to do it on your own. Nor can the woodspirit. The ability is unique to gnomes." He stopped near the circle of glowing stones. "Join us. I'll bring refreshments once you're situated and I've made introductions."

Lana sat immediately. The boys hesitated, but when Lana motioned for them to sit beside her, they overcame their shyness and sat down cross-legged with the group. Raenihel made introductions, the gnomes murmured polite greetings, and then Raenihel bustled off to get food.

Lana looked around the circle. Most of the gnomes were drinking steaming beverages from earthenware bowls, probably some type of tea or broth. They spoke in quiet voices, engrossed in conversation, either not sure what to say to their guests, or sensing that she and the boys were content just to listen.

She felt herself relax. Being inside the Tree Home was like being inside a cocoon. With her elbows propped on her crossed legs, she leaned toward the glowing stones and closed her eyes, letting the soothing, dry heat bake her face. She almost nodded off in a haze of contented exhaustion, lulled by low voices and laughter, the clink of pottery and the sound of the gnomes sipping their drinks.

Jordy's voice roused her. "This may be our last real meal as humans," he said gloomily. Greg sighed and nodded as Raenihel returned carrying a wooden tray with earthenware serving bowls. The bowls held dried meat, assorted greens, and vegetables. After serving Lana and the boys, Raenihel sat beside them. A female approached and handed them wooden spoons and goblets. When Lana saw the familiar red liquid she smiled.

The boys wasted no time cautiously tasting the food. Grunts of approval followed their first hesitant bites. After that, they shoveled food into their mouths so enthusiastically that she couldn't keep from laughing. The gnomes cast furtive glances at the boys, no doubt amused, but continued their conversations.

Lana ate with greater dignity but just as much enjoyment. What was this meat? Some kind of bird? Squirrel? Whatever it was, it tasted remarkable. Way better than dried venison. Midway through the meal the boys finally remembered their drinks.

"Whoa!" Jordy exclaimed, grinning, after his first sip. "What *is* this stuff?"

Greg sampled his and said with a dopey smile, "Yeah, this is seriously awesome!"

"You're drinking fialazza. A drink prized by the gnomes," Raenihel said.

"No kidding, I can see why!" Jordy took another gulp.

Staring absently into her goblet, Lana thought about the first time she'd tasted fialazza, the unfamiliar but pleasant fruity flavor and the way it calmed her yet sharpened all her senses. She smiled and glanced at the boys. Now that she had grudgingly forgiven them, she actually enjoyed having them here. What good was a novel experience if you couldn't share it with someone and talk about it later?

She watched the boys polish off their dinner and guzzle fialazza. They seemed—much as she hated to admit it—like younger brothers. Annoying younger brothers, but still. As a child, she had wished for a sister or brother closer to her age. Ed and Alex were more like uncles.

More gnomes arrived after dinner. They acknowledged Lana and the boys but made no attempt to start a conversation.

After dinner, Raenihel brought out three bedrolls. She drew Raenihel aside. "Last time I stayed overnight, I woke outside. I don't remember how I got there."

"It's natural to fall into a very deep sleep here." He gestured at the veins of dim light running through the tree walls. "The light has a calming effect, as does the fresh ozone air. You didn't wake when we carried you outside. I don't think you will this time, either."

"The boys and I will still be safe? After you leave?"

"Yes. When you wake, the breghlin will be gone. And I think it's only right that you should keep the Challenger's knife for a while."

She hadn't thought about giving it back. She wanted to study it so she could put it to better use. "Thank you. I'll keep it safe and learn all I can about it." The fact that Raenihel had taken her to Shadow under false pretenses still disturbed her, but the knife *had* protected her, and Raenihel was right—she needed to see the dangers her world faced.

She took Raenihel's arm. "I'm sorry we couldn't rescue Gliaphon and the other gnomes."

"The time will come. Your gem powers are growing stronger."

She hoped he was right. This trip had brought out abilities she didn't know she had. In her world, the knife's powers would be weaker, but even so, she looked forward to seeing what it could do. "There's so much I need to know, and I don't have long. The blight is already destroying the forest."

"I wish I had answers for you."

"The Challenger told me where to learn more about him, and the knife, so that's a start. When I learn anything useful, I promise I'll come back."

"Good. Pursue all knowledge, but pursue it with caution." He gave her a fond smile. "Come now. It's time to sleep."

She lay down. The tree's dim, comforting glow made her sleepy. The woodsy, fresh smell reminded her of the air after a long, soaking rain. It was so soothing, so comfortable here. The floor wasn't hard. The bedroll felt soft against her cheek. She drifted into a deep, peaceful sleep.

* * *

Still curled up in her bedroll, Lana woke and opened her eyes to early morning sunlight. This time she wasn't surprised. Her backpack lay a couple feet away and the boys were fast asleep nearby. She felt for her knife and gem pouch. Both were safe. Good. Sitting up, she yawned, stretched deeply, and looked sadly at the diseased forest. She could picture the way it looked before and it hurt to think that if she couldn't find a way to stop the blight, those days might be gone forever. If the disease continued to spread, acres of valuable farmland would be next. In Shadow, healthy tillable land was rare. The gnomes raised crops where they could, and scavenged for edible wild plants. Would it come to that here? She certainly hoped not. There wasn't enough food now to feed the world's population.

The boys' deep, rhythmic breathing finally claimed her wandering attention. She was tempted to sneak off and leave them without saying goodbye, but there they lay, sleeping so peacefully. No, she just couldn't do it.

She crawled out of her bedroll and sat cross-legged, chin-in-hands, staring at the boys. Speaking of food, what would they eat today? It wouldn't hurt them to go without a couple meals. By sunset, they'd turn back into rats, and rats ate a lot less than teenage boys. Was there such a thing as rat chow? Probably her smart phone was working again, now that she was home. She could run a search for "rat chow."

She reached for her backpack and dragged it over. Her phone was in the bottom along with the dead flashlight. She fished them both out and tried the flashlight. It worked. Odd. The laws of nature obviously worked differently in each world. As soon as she touched the phone's power button, the screen lit.

Rat chow, rat chow, hmmmm. Yep. It exists. Selecting the first link, she scanned the ingredient list: *wheat, corn, alfalfa, peas, beans and oats. This variety encourages a rat's natural foraging behavior. The textures keep continually growing teeth in trim.* She pictured the rats' sharp incisors. *Yuck.* How many ounces of chow per day did a normal-size rat eat? Giant rats like Jordy and Greg might eat *pounds* per day! Well, they had better be good foragers, because she couldn't afford pounds of rat chow. The whole thing gave her a headache. Where would they live? How would she get food to them? It was strange looking at two sleeping teenage boys, planning how much rat chow to buy for them.

Following other links, she found an interesting article about rats verses mice. Mice, it said, were rarely as affectionate as rats. Rats were social animals. You should buy two and house them together. *Already got a pair.* The article recommended fresh fruits and vegetables and a few table scraps to supplement their store-bought seed and grain mixture. Skimming, her eyes fell on a paragraph that read, "A rat will play games with you and chase you from one end of the couch to the other." *Oh, great! Another reason not to take them home!* Which characteristics, human or rat, would be dominant when they changed back? She was afraid to find out. Especially when she read the next part, "Rats love to sit with their human, cuddle, kiss, and nibble whatever you're eating." *Lovely. Count me out!* The urge to sneak off and abandon them was nearly overwhelming. She pictured herself buying a basket, putting the giant rats inside, and leaving them on a random doorstep with a note: *Please take care of my boys. Their names are Greg and Jordy. They like to cuddle, kiss and nibble.*

Her laughter woke the boys. Jordy sat up and rubbed his eyes. Greg rolled onto his stomach and looked up, mumbling sleepily, "What's goin' on? Where am I?"

Smothering more giggles, she stood and grabbed her backpack. "I'm heading out for the day. You'll be okay till tonight, right?"

"Sure," Greg said. "You'll be back before sunset?"

"Yeah. I'm not sure what to do with you, but I'll get you out of here before the park closes."

Jordy looked around and said in a troubled voice, "Hey, what's wrong with the trees?"

Last time the boys were here, the forest had been healthy. The change, even in a few weeks, was alarming. Lana shrugged into her backpack. "Sheamathan came through the portal and did this. She can access more of our world by making it diseased and lifeless like Shadow."

"This is awful. Somebody has to stop her," Jordy said.

"We don't know how yet." An awkward silence fell. "Well, I've got to get going. See you later."

Greg and Jordy looked at her with long faces and she felt guilty leaving them. Maybe she could find them something to eat, first. She usually kept a few beef sticks in her glove compartment. And over by the stump where she'd buried the weird stone, she'd seen a tree loaded with apples. *The stone! I was going to take pictures of it.*

"Come on. Walk me to my car. I usually have some beef sticks in my glove compartment."

Jordy brightened. Greg said, "Thanks. We can see more of the forest on the way. How long has it been like this?"

"Not long. A couple weeks." She looked down. "Bring your bedrolls. Better not leave them here."

Scooping them up, they loped after her. She headed toward Parking Area D, taking the shortest route. Hiking in gloomy silence, they examined the diseased shrubs, trees, and withered brown grass along the way.

Near the parking lot, she pointed to the apple tree. "Grab a few apples. I'm going to dig up a stone I hid. I'm pretty sure it's from Shadow. I've never seen one like it."

"Why'd you hide it?" Jordy asked.

"I couldn't take it home, and I didn't want anyone else to see it." Should she be telling them any of this? What harm could it do? "From what I've seen, you can't take anything from Shadow outside the Amulet. If you do, it disappears when you cross into the Fair Lands."

"Where does it go?" Jordy asked.

She shrugged. "No idea."

"Huh. Weird," Greg said.

"I'm going to take pictures of the stone and do some research at home."

By the time Greg and Jordy had picked a few apples, she'd unearthed the stone. They met her by the tree stump. As she held up her prize specimen, the heat began to drain from her palms.

Greg took one look at the stone. "Hey, that's alamaria!"

She blinked. "You know what it is?"

"Sure."

"You're right—it's from Shadow," Jordy said. "How'd it get *here*?"

She turned the stone over in her hands. Iridescent silver flecks twinkled in its depths. It was so beautiful. Her fascinated smile turned to a look of alarm when Greg said in a troubled voice, "You know the gnome slave camps? Well, this is what they're mining."

Chapter 22

Lana almost dropped the stone. She looked at it with a troubled frown. "Why does Sheamathan want alamaria?"

"Yeah, and why does she need a *lot* of it?" Jordy asked.

"Good point." Lana held the stone out. "Does alamaria come out of the ground just like this? Or is it embedded in rock strata?"

"You mean—do miners chop it out of other rocks?" Greg asked.

"Yes, exactly."

"We've been to the cliffs above the mines. I've seen alamaria on the ground and it looks just like this," Greg said. "The stones get hauled away on a cart. A few always fall off."

"So they're alluvial," she said.

"Huh?"

"Alluvial. You know, worn smooth by rivers and streams and eventually buried in silt." Her hands were becoming numb and cold. "I have to set this down and get some pictures before my hands are completely numb." She set the stone on the ground.

"Numb?" Jordy repeated, looking confused.

She gave him an impatient look. "You've never touched alamaria?"

"Sure, what about it?"

"It makes your hands go numb."

"It does? Felt like a normal rock to me."

"Maybe 'cause we were rats," Greg suggested with a shrug.

She shook her head. "Why would that matter?"

"Duuno, just a thought," Greg said.

"OK if we touch your stone?" Jordy asked.

"Sure. Go ahead."

He and Jordy took turns holding it. Greg said, "You're right. My hands get numb right away."

"But how does it *do* that?" Jordy asked.

Lana frowned. "That's what I hope to find out."

Greg said gloomily, "Well, it didn't feel like this before, so if it feels different to rats we'll know tonight." He put it on the ground.

"Right," Jordy said, folding his arms and giving her a dark look. "You can experiment on us. Rats are good for that."

Oh no! Here come the rat jokes again! "Maybe you won't turn back. Maybe Sheamathan's power can't get to you here."

"Don't get our hopes up," Jordy said. "I bet her spell is like the timer on a bomb. It hits zero and we turn back into rats."

He was probably right. Sheamathan's wolfhound crossed into the Fair Lands and he hadn't escaped the spell.

Crouching over the stone, she used her phone camera to get a couple close-ups. The photos turned out all right but didn't really capture the shimmering iridescent flecks. Well, it was the best she could do.

"Okay, so I'm burying this again, and then I'll see if I have something for you to eat."

The boys were in luck. When she rummaged through her glove compartment, she found a few beef sticks and a handful of hard candies, mostly peppermints. She held them out. "I'm sorry, this is all I have."

"Thanks. After we finish this, we still got apples," Greg said.

She got into her car. "See you later." She couldn't babysit them all day.

As anxious as she was to find the hidden safe, it would have to wait, she told herself as she pulled out of the parking lot. She had a few things to do first. After breakfast she had to start a journal before she forgot important details.

Had both Jules and Elias gone to Shadow? If so, their letters could be full of useful information. She drove out of the park. By the time anyone found her journal, maybe the world would be safe and her journal would have a happy ending.

When Lana got home, she raced up the stairs, and after tossing her backpack in the entry hall, walked around her apartment as if seeing it for the first time. What a fabulous place—screwed-up kitchen, beige walls and all. Trailing her hands lovingly over the worn, non-descript furniture, she kicked off her sneakers and flopped onto the couch.

Last night she'd slept on a stone slab in a dungeon. Who would believe that? She couldn't tell anyone or they'd think she was crazy. But if she kept a journal, she could write whatever she wanted. Putting her thoughts on paper would be therapeutic.

After breakfast, she started writing, and by two o'clock she had written a couple pages under three categories, leaving blank pages for future notes. Section one: a general description of Shadow and the "people" she had met there. Section two: her gemstones, how she had used them, and the results. Section three: the knife and its various reactions—with and without her conscious input. Now she was starting section four—theories and observations about gem powers in Shadow, involving the Challenger's knife and her gemstones. Setting down her pen, she reread the last paragraph:

Jordy said the Challenger's blade felt hot. That concerns me. Fair Lands gems burn evil beings from Shadow. The rat-boys have spent nearly a year in Shadow under the influence of dark powers. Could Fair Lands gems react to them now as if they were natives? If so, Jordy's in trouble. The knife felt hot to him but only warm to Greg, which supports my theory. I don't know everything Jordy's done, but he was willing to attack an old gnome and a woman and give a stolen knife to someone he knows is evil. I'm not judging him. I'm just saying if he's "evil" enough to make the knife feel hot, he may be stuck in the Amulet or Shadow forever. Evil beings from Shadow can't enter the Fair Lands. Maybe he can't, either.

Enough for today. She shut the notebook. Time to do something boring and normal like pick up a few groceries. After that, she'd go to the jewelry store to look for the safe, and the weirdness would start again.

When she pulled up in front of the old, three-story brick store, she felt like a burglar. She scanned the street. This time of day, on a Sunday afternoon, there wasn't much traffic. The surrounding shops on Main Street were closed, so no one would see her go in. Not that it really mattered. She had every right to come here after hours but she still felt uncomfortable about it.

With her empty satchel and toolbox in hand, she nudged the car door shut with her hip and stared up at the store. The old brick building's narrow windows looked innocently back at her as if to say, *No hidden safe here.*

Her heartbeat quickened with anticipation as she unlocked the door and walked in. This wouldn't take long. Half an hour, tops. The office wasn't that large.

She walked through the store to the office in the back, and with trembling hands turned the key in the lock. The familiar smell of old books and lemon furniture polish greeted her. Closing the door behind her, she set down her gear and looked around. *If I were Elias, where would I hide my safe?* Jules had said something about it being behind the paneling.

Moving from one wall to the next, she ran her hands over the wood and examined each rectangular section of walnut paneling. No sign of a removable piece—no mismatched wood or loose moldings. But the safe *had* to be here.

Could the removable panel be under a painting? She checked behind the oil paintings and the oak-framed news article. No luck. The only hiding place left was behind the heavy regulator clock. If the safe wasn't there, she'd run out of places to look.

Getting the clock off the wall to look wouldn't be easy. Someone had screwed it to the wall in addition to hanging it from a heavy nail. She muttered under her breath as she opened the clock case door, screwdriver in hand, and set to work.

Once the screw was out, she faced the task of wrestling the clock off the wall. The darn thing must weigh forty pounds. Good thing she stayed in shape. With a groan, she hoisted it off the supporting nail and then, shaking with exertion, slowly lowered it to the floor. Sliding the clock aside to get it out of the way, she examined the exposed paneling.

A shiver of excitement ran through her.

There! A tiny crack formed an outline around the panel, wider at the bottom so a screwdriver or letter opener could loosen it. This was it. The safe had to be here. How many years had people sat in this office, never suspecting there was a hidden safe?

She slid the screwdriver into the crack, lifted the bottom edge of the panel, and then slid her fingers under and gave a tug. The panel lifted out.

For a moment, she was too excited to do anything but stare.

A black, enameled wall safe, decorated with fancy gilt scrollwork, gleamed in the recess. About a foot-and-a-half square, it had probably held jewelry long ago. She knew the combination by heart: 14-35-72. She rotated the dial. A decisive click of the lock told her she had gotten the combination right.

Please don't be empty!

Holding her breath, she pulled the door open.

Yes! Inside lay two packs of letters tied with ribbons, a hardcover ledger, and a stack of loose papers. Giddy with excitement, she ran to get her satchel.

Her formerly dull life had taken a dramatic turn, she told herself as she packed the satchel. The gnomes needed her help to defeat Sheamathan. She had rescued two enchanted rats who had tried to mug her and steal a legendary knife. Now, a wolfhound, formerly a man, had sent her to find a safe that no one in her family knew about. After she read these papers she would decide if she wanted to help him.

Once everything was packed she shut the safe and spun the dial. Time to tidy the office and lock up. She didn't want Arlene to know she had been here.

At a little after four o'clock she left the store, opened her trunk, and stashed the toolbox and satchel. What secrets did the letters hold? No one in her family knew what had become of great-great grandfather Elias, but she had a feeling she was about to find out.

Glancing at her watch, she sighed in frustration. She was dying to curl up on the couch with her treasures, but she had to meet the boys by dusk. With any luck they would be human, not rats, and she could deliver them to their families.

The sun was setting when she pulled into the parking lot. As she got out of the car her heart sank. *Rats!* Two furry forms raced toward her.

"I told you so," Jordy said, panting. "The timer hit zero. We're rats again."

"Yeah," Greg said dismally. "At least we got to be human for a day."

She couldn't think of anything to say that would make them feel better. "Let's go. The breghlin might be looking for you." She opened the back door. "Hop in." The rats scrambled onto her back seat.

As she pulled out of the lot, she felt thoroughly ashamed of herself. Here she was feeling *inconvenienced*; they were trapped in rat bodies, maybe for the rest of their lives. When she looked in the rearview mirror, she caught a glimpse of them huddled despondently together and it tugged at her heart. She couldn't just dump them in a field. Unfortunately, she'd been too engrossed in her journal to plan what to do if they had turned back into rats. Now she was stuck taking them home.

Driving down the park's main road she remembered that the Challenger's blade had felt hot to Jordy. What if he couldn't enter the Fair Lands? What if he disappeared like the bedroll? Gripping the steering wheel with damp palms, she slowed as they approached the exit.

Jordy let out a yelp.

She tensed. "What's the matter?"

"I just got an electric shock! At least that's what it felt like!"

She glanced worriedly over her shoulder. "Greg? Are you OK?"

He rubbed his paws over his face. "I'm OK, but I felt something, too. Not an electric shock. Just a weird tingle."

Hmmm. She was willing to bet she had just driven through the Amulet into the Fair Lands. Jordy had come through, but he'd been zapped, which was rather troubling.

"So, where you takin' us," he asked.

"I was hoping to take you to your parents. But now that you're rats—" her voice trailed off.

"Yeah, that wouldn't be a good idea," he agreed sadly.

"Looks like I'm taking you home while I find you a place to stay."

"That's real nice of you," Greg said. "Most girls wouldn't take a rat home."

"Not *our* kind, anyway," Jordy said with a squeaky laugh.

"No rat jokes or you won't get your treat," she threatened good-naturedly.

"Treat?" Jordy said.

"As a precaution, I bought you something." She handed back an opened bag of rat chow. "Don't get it all over my seats."

"Gee, thanks!" Greg said, sounding genuinely pleased.

In a moment she heard enthusiastic munching.

No one would believe this, she told herself. Heaven help her if Lillian discovered two giant rats in the apartment.

Lana rolled to a stop in the driveway, and before she let the rats out of the car she gave them a lecture. "I'm letting you stay against my better judgment. Don't make me regret it. You can sleep on my couch. I go to work tomorrow morning at nine-thirty. You can hang out and amuse yourselves, but you'll have to be quiet. And keep your paws off my stuff. Deal?"

"Deal."

"No problem."

"Okay. Let's go before someone sees you."

After she let them into the apartment, she went back for the toolbox and satchel. By the time she returned, Greg and Jordy had settled onto her couch.

"Nice place," Greg said.

"It has that homey, lived-in look," Jordy said.

"No cracks about my housekeeping or out you go."

"It wasn't an insult," Jordy protested. "I like it here. My mom is a neat-freak."

She looked around. "Um, what do you need for, well, bathroom arrangements?"

"A box with some shredded newspapers will do," Greg said. "Actually, we could probably jump up on your toilet."

She pictured herself walking into the bathroom in the middle of the night and finding a giant rat perched on the toilet seat. "I'll make you a litter box," she said hastily.

She came back from the basement with a few old newspapers and a box from her last mail-order shipment, put the box in a corner of the living room, and shredded a couple newspapers into it. "How's that?"

"Great. Thanks," Greg said from the couch. Jordy lay next to him, blinking contentedly.

She got her satchel and stopped by the couch on her way to the bedroom. "Is there anything else you need before you go to sleep?"

"My mom usually kisses me goodnight," Jordy said hopefully.

She grimaced. "Don't press your luck." She went into her bedroom and locked the door behind her.

Chapter 23

L ana promised herself she would only spend a couple hours reading. Tomorrow, she could finish the rest. Of course, after two hours she was too fascinated to stop. By two o'clock she was fading fast and knew she had to sleep. She wouldn't need opalite jasper tonight, she thought with a sleepy smile. She turned off her bedside lamp and fell asleep in seconds.

When the alarm went off at eight-thirty, she rolled over, slapped the snooze, and spent a few groggy minutes mulling over what she had read the night before. It was so safe and uneventful here. No gnomes, breghlin, pythanium or heroes turned into dogs.

She sat bolt upright.

But there *were* talking rats! In her living room. On her couch! She had to get rid of them, but how?

Slipping out of bed she fumbled through her closet, too distracted to care what she wore. Where could she take the rats? A pet store? Tempting, but no. A traveling circus? *Step right up. See the giant, talking rats!* No, but the rat-boys *would* be entertaining. Hopefully, she'd think of something at work.

Settling on black pants and a red, long-sleeved blouse, she lay her clothes on the bed and tiptoed to the bathroom. Yawning, she cranked the shower to full blast and watched the bathroom fill with steam. A scalding hot shower would be a sure-fire way to wake up after reading half the night. She stepped into the shower. Water thundered against the ceramic tiles, but there was nothing she could do about it. She hoped it didn't wake the rats.

Energized, she stepped out of the shower, toweled off and then hesitated before switching on the hair dryer. Oh, well. No time to air-dry today. She pushed the "on" switch and cringed. The dryer sounded like an airplane turbine at liftoff.

Miraculously, the rats slept through everything. She looked at them on her way to the kitchen. Their eyes were closed, and except for the occasional twitch of a leg or their whiskers, they lay motionless.

Lana took a container of yoghurt from the refrigerator and stood at the counter, eating out of the container while her coffee brewed. When the coffee finished, she put the yoghurt away and poured a mugful, and with a big yawn, turned toward the table, and almost fell over two rats.

"Whaaa!" she cried, sloshing hot coffee onto her hand.

"Sorry!" the rats cried in unison.

"We smelled the coffee, and we woke up," Greg said.

Jordy nodded. "Yeah, it was like the old days, being at home."

She looked at them uncertainly. "You don't drink coffee, do you?" Setting the mug on the counter, she ran her scalded hand under cold water.

"Not usually. Especially now," Jordy said.

"Caffeine? With these little bodies? No way, "Greg said. "There's no coffee in Shadow, anyway, so it's a good thing we aren't used to it."

She dried her hands and carried her coffee to the table. The rats followed and jumped onto the chairs across from her. For a moment they all looked at each other awkwardly.

"Um, do you want more rat chow?"

"No thanks," Greg said.

Jordy said, "We just want to hang out with you. If that's all right." He wriggled his whiskers and showed his teeth. Lana nearly spilled her coffee. She would never get used to that smile.

"Sure. No problem. It's kind of nice having company," she said, thinking back to the Tree Home and the three of them having dinner and drinking fialazza with the gnomes. "You'll probably be bored while I'm gone. I can leave the TV on low. Just remember, my landlady lives downstairs and I don't want her to know you're here."

"TV!" Jordy clapped his paws in delight. "That would be great!"

"Don't worry. We're used to just hanging around," Greg said. "Sometimes breghlin made us carry messages. Sometimes they had us spy on other breghlin to see what they were up to. Other than that, we just slept, explored, and tried not to get eaten by anything."

She leaned forward, elbows on the table, and looked at them thoughtfully. "You knew your way around the castle pretty well."

"Yeah," Greg said. "Especially where to find food and hiding places."

"And we kept track of everybody worth keeping track of," Jordy added.

She sipped her coffee, watching the rats over the rim of her mug. If she asked the right questions, Greg and Jordy might know something useful, but she wasn't sure what to ask. If only they could write. Imagine how many journal pages they could fill after living in Shadow so long.

"I'd better get going." She brushed back a wave of hair and carried her mug to the sink. After filling the rats' food and water bowls, she turned on the TV. "See you around six."

As Lana parked her car and walked into the jewelry store, she fought an irrational fear that Arlene would know someone had been in the office. It was silly to worry. Even if Lana had left something out of place, Arlene would probably never notice.

All morning Arlene bustled about in a self-important manner, making sure Lana knew she was keeping an eye on her. Mondays were always slow, so the two of them were the only ones working, and when Arlene disappeared for a two-hour lunch, Lana secretly rejoiced.

The day dragged. The hands on the clock seemed glued in place. By four, Lana had waited on only three customers, but she had rearranged the contents of two showcases, vacuumed, and even cleaned the rest room. She still had an hour to kill.

Trying to come up with more busy-work, she decided to clean her jewelry bench. She sat and put tools away, and then sorted through a stack of sticky-notes. Under an advertising circular she found a handful of lapis lazuli stones she had removed from a damaged bracelet weeks ago. She scooped up the scattered stones and looked at them absently, her mind straying once again to Greg and Jordy. The rat-boys couldn't stay with her indefinitely. Where could she take them? She'd thought about it on and off all day but hadn't come up with a good solution, and she had to tell them *something* tonight.

Partially formed thoughts and impressions tugged at her mind. She felt uneasy about the rats living somewhere else. They should stay. She needed them. Why, she couldn't exactly say.

Looking down at the lapis in her hand, she stiffened. Where had those thoughts come from? She *needed* the rat-boys? They should *stay*? The dark blue stones flecked with gold felt unusually warm. *Lapis Lazuli: strengthens total awareness, creativity, ESP, helps to expand viewpoint.* She hadn't been consciously drawing their power, but she *had* been thinking about the rats. Were these stones impressing on her that she should keep the rats a while longer? That three heads were better than one?

Shortly after five she left the store. Maybe she had lost her mind, but she would keep Greg and Jordy for now. To be perfectly fair, they had already been helpful. They had identified the alamaria stone, and maybe they knew other useful things. She stopped at the grocery store and bought food for the week. Fortunately, Greg and Jordy were happy with rat chow and table scraps.

When she walked into her apartment she found them sprawled on the couch in front of the TV, fast asleep. She turned off the TV and they woke with a start.

"Hey, I was watching that," Greg protested sleepily.

She smiled. Her dad used to say the same thing when she found him "watching TV" asleep in his recliner. She looked around. No messes. Good.

"Did you have a good day? Where do you work?" Greg asked.

"At the family jewelry store," she answered on her way to the kitchen with the groceries, "And yes, I had a good day. Thanks." She put everything away and made a big salad topped with diced chicken. As before, Greg and Jordy joined her at the table.

"After dinner I need to read. I can't have any interruptions, okay?"

"Okay, we understand," Greg said, sounding disappointed.

Compared to Shadowglade there wasn't much for them to do, and her apartment was small, especially after living in a castle. They couldn't explore, forage, and spy. The novelty of living here, even with TV, would wear off soon. They'd need fresh air, exercise, and something to do, but she didn't want to think about that now.

After dinner she turned on the radio, found a channel they liked, and escaped to her bedroom. She could finally relax and take another look at her treasures. Sliding the satchel out from under the bed, she emptied its contents onto the bedspread.

Last night she had skimmed through everything. The hodge-podge of information was confusing, but she was starting to piece together Elias's story and how Jules fit in. She understood why the letters had been separated into two groups. Not only had Elias saved all of Jules's letters, he had made hand-copied duplicates of his own replies. The ledger was also a duplicate, given to Jules for safekeeping, in case anything happened to the original. Apparently Elias shared her obsession for keeping records, she thought with a grin.

She slid onto the bed, got comfortable, and arranged her treasures around her. The ledger smelled musty, so she laid it on the nightstand. It held a wealth of information about gemstones, and she planned to read every word.

Jules's mysterious comment about pitying both men still circled in her head, and she hoped that by the end of the night she'd understand what he meant. Most likely he was trying to say that eventually both men had traveled to Shadow, and they had gotten in over their heads. Shadow held dangers that few people could handle, even with gem powers.

Propped up against her pillows, she thumbed through the loose notes and drawings. Jules had made the drawings, and last night she had found a sketch of the Challenger's blade and a letter about it. She looked for the sketch again, found it and studied it briefly, and then reread the letter.

Elias,

After our last conversation, I have been thinking about making an object that incorporates some of the most powerful gemstones. As a blacksmith, I find myself intrigued by the idea of fashioning a knife. Not only would I set gems into the hilt, I would incorporate them into the blade itself. I plan to grind the gemstones and mix them into the steel. I believe that blending the stones will affect the way they perform, and I am anxious to see what occurs. Placing the blade into a hilt inlaid with gems should amplify the blade's power. It should prove a fascinating experiment. This would surely sound like madness to anyone but you, my dear friend and mentor.

Very Truly Yours,

Jules DeLauretin

This letter explained the cryptic note that Jules had written to Elias—the note with the list of gemstones.

Jules's letters explained a lot of things she had wondered about, like how he had gotten involved with Elias. They had gotten to know each other through their local Odd Fellows Lodge. When Jules learned that Elias was a jeweler, and that they shared an interest in gemstone folklore, they struck up a friendship. Eventually Jules shared his theory that combining stones could change or enhance their powers. Was this a new concept for Elias? Lana wasn't sure, but last night she had seen gemstone groupings in Elias's ledger, so he had probably experimented with gem combinations.

Some gemstones in Elias's ledger were obviously Shadow stones because he used the phrase, *gemstones from the other side.* She began to think in terms of Fair Lands gems and Shadow gems. According to Elias, combining Fair Lands gems and Shadow gemstones sometimes produced unpredictable results. He also noted that the results of his Shadow gemstone experiments differed according to *which side he was on* when he conducted the experiments. That was a fascinating concept.

Unless things had changed between his time and hers, Elias couldn't take specimens outside the Amulet, but as far as she knew, experiments *within* the Amulet would demonstrate what happened *on our side.*

She tilted her head back against the pillows, thinking. Alamaria had felt strange to her and also to Greg and Jordy when they were *boys.* But in their *rat*-forms, in Shadow, alamaria had felt like any other stone. Why? Because they were *rats,* or because they were *on the other side?* Now that Greg and Jordy were rats again, she could take them to the park, dig up the stone, and conduct her own experiment. But that would only answer one question, and a few others came to mind. Was the numb sensation the *only* characteristic that changed between worlds? Could Alamaria have completely different properties here on our side? Who had carried the alamaria into County Forest Park? And why?

She shut her eyes for a moment, feeling a little overwhelmed. If she hoped to make sense of the information, she needed to read systematically. First she would finish her "reread" pile. Then she would read Jules's letters from start to finish, followed by Elias's replies. She sighed. Impatience had always been one of her weaknesses—a weakness she fought, because it often got her into trouble.

Reading Jules's letters in order proved enlightening. His first letters were cheerful and enthusiastic. Like her, Jules had been amazed to learn that Fair Lands gems had far greater powers in Shadow. He told Elias to take the jeweled knife and compare its abilities in both worlds. Both men were stunned by the exponential increase of the knife's powers in Shadow. Jules wanted to know whether mixing ground gems into the steel blade had anything to do with it, or if it was all due to the gems in the hilt. To find out, Elias conducted additional experiments using a group of loose stones. The knife out-performed the stones. Jules wrote:

I am delighted to learn that my knife's unusual abilities are due to its unique construction. I dreamed one night of creating a gem-infused steel blade. When I woke, I gave it some thought and decided to try it. It was a logical next step to set the gem-blade into a gem-hilt.

My father and grandfather were both blacksmiths, so despite it being a dying trade, my father expected me to continue the tradition. If I followed my heart I might be your apprentice. I have always loved gemstones and their folklore. As a boy, tales of medieval knights and ladies and their weaponry, ornaments, and jewelry captivated me.

After a few letters, Jules didn't sound so enthusiastic. Apparently, Elias had written more about the world on the other side and Jules found the description alarming.

I could never sleep a wink in such a place as you describe! Poisonous plants, grotesque malformed insects and flying serpents! Could Hell itself be any more frightful?

Jules seemed even more troubled by his friend's obvious disregard of the danger. Lana could see why. Most people would be uncomfortable in this diseased and dying land, but the destruction, the mutant insects, and the poisonous plants didn't faze Elias. As weeks turned into months, and Elias's letters came less frequently, Jules wrote:

Since I haven't heard from you in quite some time, I stopped at your store the other day, hoping to see you. Your note on the door advised: 'Back on Thursday.' Forgive me for meddling, Elias, but people say your boy spends a great deal of time with relatives and neighbors while you are away, and he has become wild and undisciplined.

Elias was just as wild and undisciplined, she thought irritably, only in a different way. He had set up a "study" inside a cave a few miles from the portal, and she was disturbed to read that he had enlisted gnomes to wait on him and gather specimens for him to study. How did the gnomes benefit from the arrangement? They didn't. Jules wrote with evident sarcasm:

I thought it was your aim to help the inhabitants, but it appears I misunderstood. The small people serve your every need and bring you gem and mineral samples so that you can devote every moment to your ledger. These gentle beings need your help. Will you ever have time for them?

In another letter, it was obvious that Jules was worried about Elias. Elias had stopped experimenting with Fair Lands gems and was studying native stones, many with disturbing powers. Jules understood his friend's quest for knowledge, but was appalled that Elias would keep experimenting with stones that had harmful properties.

It is impossible to know the long-term effects of using gemstones from another world. Even if they were all benign there would be risks, but many are clearly dangerous. You wrote about a mottled red stone that filled you with blind rage and gave you the strength of three men. You told me that another stone made plants shrivel within a radius of several feet. I would avoid stones that bring out adverse emotions or have destructive effects. No good can come of them, and I shudder to think what mayhem combining such dangerous stones might produce.

Jules's warning fell on deaf ears, as she expected it would. In his next response to Elias, Jules reprimanded Elias for using the gnomes as test subjects. Elias had found stones that made him a conduit of negative emotions. Anyone with the misfortune to stand near him suffered from insecurity, jealousy, discouragement, depression, hatred, paranoia, or other such destructive emotions. "The small ones," as Jules and Elias called them, found the tests disturbing and reported feeling ill for days afterward, but Elias insisted that his research was necessary, and threatened to hand them over to Sheamathan if they refused to cooperate. Jules condemned him in no uncertain terms:

No benefits from these stones can ever justify tormenting these poor creatures that have suffered so much already. How are you any better than the woodspirit? Your motives may be better, but you are no less a monster in their eyes.

Lana wasn't sure which disturbed her more, the idea that negative energy stones existed, or that Elias would threaten the gnomes to undergo his experiments. To the best of her knowledge, our world didn't have gems with negative powers. Fair Lands gems relieved stress, promoted emotional balance, and even brought happiness and love. Had the negative energy stones always produced unpleasant characteristics, or had Sheamathan corrupted their previously helpful powers? Either way, she could think of few legitimate uses for such stones. Elias should steer clear of them.

She didn't realize Elias still had Jules's knife until she found a letter asking when Elias planned to return it.

In your last letter you promised to visit me. It has been far too long since we met in person. I hope you are coming soon. Quite frankly, I would like you to return my knife. When I displayed it in my shop it generated several sales. Few things give me as much pleasure as crafting a knife. I make all too many fence gates and such, so I am pleased to receive requests for knives and daggers. I make a few for myself when time permits but it is better to be paid for my efforts.

With each letter their friendship seemed more strained, and she doubted they could reconcile their differences. She found herself siding with Jules, and although it bothered her to turn against her ancestor, she couldn't help herself. She was glad Jules stood by his principles and opposed Elias. If only more people had such courage.

One of Jules's letters openly condemned his friend's single-minded ambition:

You excuse your obsession with power by telling yourself that you will become the most powerful being, and when you are in control you can right all the wrongs. In the meantime you exploit the small ones and do nothing to help them.

No good could come from Elias's obsession with power. She felt certain of it. Jules's final letter not only confirmed her opinion, it gave a clue to Elias's disappearance from the Fair Lands. At the bottom of the second page Jules wrote:

What price are you willing to pay for power? Don't be a fool. You write that gems from our world have become hot to your touch. Surely you know what that means. Before long, you will be trapped on the other side.

Yes, her ancestor was a fool! She felt like throwing the letter across the room. Her theory was right! If you immersed yourself in Shadow gem powers, Fair Lands gems would begin to react as if you were a native. If you were a good person, you had nothing to worry about, but Elias had become corrupt and obsessed with power, hurting others to advance his own goals. In the end, it had separated him from his son. She fumed silently. Jules had thought she'd read this story and feel sorry for Elias? Hardly! She despised Elias, relative or not!

Before she realized what she was doing she had crumpled the letter without reading the last page. Elias would never help the gnomes, she realized, disgusted. No wonder Jules had stepped in. Elias, idiot that he was, had lost the ability to touch Fair Lands gems, which had been his only real advantage over the woodspirit. Limited to Shadow gemstones, he was no match for Sheamathan who had far more knowledge and experience. Taking a deep breath, Lana smoothed the crumpled paper and forced herself to read the last page.

Thanks to you, Sheamathan has followed her breghlin scouts through the portal to spread death and destruction. You foolishly told her that few people in our world command gem powers. Now she believes that humans are weak and easily dominated. It falls to me to help the gnomes and stop Sheamathan. The woodspirit's destructive forest blight serves to expand the Amulet, which gives her greater access to our world. I must act quickly while she knows little about me or my abilities. You have written that even with my blade I am no match for her. No doubt that is true, and while greater powers might be mine if I used gems from the other side, I refuse to do so. Dare I say, if you are any indication, the hazards outweigh the benefits. I shall meet her with only my knife and other Fair Lands gems.

Jules had been willing to fight a nearly impossible battle. Most people would have walked away and told themselves not to get involved. She wished Jules were her ancestor instead of the detestable Elias.

Would she be just as angry when she finished reading Elias's letters? Could he say anything to redeem himself? She read his first letter slowly, trying to keep an open mind. Whatever kind of person he was, at least he was interesting. She read his first letter twice. It told how he had learned that County Forest Park was an unusual place, and how testing Jules's newly completed knife at the park had led to discovering the portal.

The first time he had gone to County Forest Park, he had gone to hike and fish. He took jasper to protect him from snake and spider bites, chrysocolla to give him intuition to know where the fish were biting, and rhodochrosite to improve his eyesight so he could better enjoy the park's beauty.

He walked the trails and discovered, much to his amazement, that for the first time in twenty years he could see quite well without his glasses. He had a wonderful day and caught so many fish he released all but three. Other fishermen were envious of his success. Certainly this was an extraordinary place, he wrote, and he was anxious to return with other gems.

On his second visit, despite a troublesome day at the store, his hematite dispelled all his negative thoughts. The chrysocolla relieved his arthritis, and his sugalite filled him with such an intense feeling of well-being that he caught himself whistling a popular tune—one he didn't even like. He was convinced that the park was a strange, mystical place. Henceforth, he would conduct any important gem tests at the park.

While testing the knife, hoping to learn whether this combination of gems amplified the stones' known properties or created any that were unexpected, he discovered the hideous savage creatures, the small people, and the existence of a portal to another world. Naturally, Elias could only share this bizarre story with one person—Jules.

Elias wrote:

The knife enabled me to discern areas of the forest that produced unexplained anomalies. I felt energy that made my hair stand on end, and occasionally the blade gave off static charges. Then it began to glow. I noticed that the needle in my compass swung wildly. At nightfall, the anomalies grew even more pronounced. Fascinated, I stayed past sundown and the knife's powers became stronger. I was filled with strong emotions, chiefly a keen premonition of danger. Near midnight, the blade glowed brighter than before, and I heard noises in the woods. Through the trees I spied hideous creatures. At first I thought my eyes played tricks on me, but the savage brutes were all too real. I fled before they saw me, vowing I should never again step foot in that accursed place.

Lana laughed, remembering her own experiences—her mixture of curiosity and fear. Of course, like her, Elias's curiosity had overcome his fear. After a couple weeks he decided to go back.

During my second trip, which took place after sunset, I met the gentle small ones. Perhaps the knife's power drew them. I sensed they were not dangerous and that they meant me no harm. They said that the hideous creatures I had seen were evil, but had once been like themselves. My beautiful, unusual knife fascinated the small beings. They claimed that the hilt contained gems they had never seen, and that in their world gemstones had amazing powers. They assumed, after seeing the knife, that I had the ability to use their gems, and that I might become a valuable ally.

The small beings needed help in overcoming a powerful being of a different species, called a woodspirit. She had brought blight upon their land and corrupted many of the inhabitants—who then became the aforementioned evil savages—and she had made herself queen. I confess that I was enthralled by the story, and I agreed to be transported to their world.

The farther she read the more annoyed she became. Elias had never seriously planned to get involved in the gnomes' problems. He didn't care what the woodspirit did to them. By his own admission, after the gnomes took him through the portal, he went his own way and delved into his research. His gemstones were far more powerful in this new world. That, in itself, was a thrilling discovery, but then he located native gems that had astounding abilities. No, the plight of an oppressed people didn't matter to him. He had a world full of fascinating gems to study—gems that would give him godlike powers—and he didn't have time for anything else.

He learned that using gems in this new world produced an unexpected benefit. His body became infused with their powers. Soon, he could perform amazing feats without even touching them, but if he went too long without handling the gems the infused powers faded.

Elias had spent most of his life studying and experimenting, convinced that gems held the arcane properties his books claimed.

Now, he had discovered a world where gems were more powerful than he had ever dreamed. Lana understood how excited he must have felt, but he had taken crazy risks, hurting himself and others in the process, hoping to become invincibly powerful. His smug, over-confident attitude in this passage really irritated her:

I have met the woodspirit being, Sheamathan, many times, and she believes I am a powerful gem master from the Fair Lands. Why must you always worry needlessly? I am not afraid of her. I have an advantage. You see, I am able to use gemstones from our world as well as from hers, whereas she cannot touch ours. She is corrupt, and touching our gems burns her. Equally troublesome to her, I have discovered that gemstones from Shadow often behave in an unpredictable manner if they interact with gems from our world. She would be wise to fear me.

Lana sighed over his lost opportunities. How could he have been so blind? He should have used Fair Lands gems to disrupt Sheamathan's powers before he lost that advantage. If he had caught her off guard, he might have defeated her, but he hadn't even tried. In his final letters, Elias finally seemed to understand what a mess he had made of things, and he decided to hide his ledger and letters in the jewelry store safe.

I had planned to learn all I could and develop my powers, and once I was certain of my abilities I would have dealt with the woodspirit. Time seemed of no importance. But now, suddenly she has ambitions to rule our world, and time is of the essence. She must not be allowed to study our world as I have hers. Her lack of knowledge is our best, and perhaps our only *defense.*

Lana blinked. A sudden chill swept over her. She stared blankly at the letter in her lap, thinking with a sick feeling in the pit of her stomach that the similarities between Elias and the man Raenihel had described were too numerous to be a coincidence. If she was right, though it seemed impossible, Elias was still alive, and in Shadow the gnomes called him Folio. She thought back to Raenihel's words: *"Would you risk becoming like the old fool, Folio? All his studying got him nowhere! A curse upon him! He lives in isolation in Strathweed, compiling folios full of knowledge that might have saved my people from torment and bondage.*"

If Elias *was* alive, it was due to gem powers in Shadow. The temptation to live several more decades, or perhaps even centuries, would probably be hard to resist.

Elias's letters had ended abruptly, and she understood why. Once he had become too corrupt to enter the Fair Lands, he couldn't pass beyond the Amulet, so he had no way to get letters to Jules. Maybe they had spoken in person afterward, though, in Shadow. When Jules realized that Elias couldn't defeat Sheamathan, he had gone to Shadow to challenge Sheamathan himself.

Lana scrubbed her face wearily. The gnomes believed that Jules had driven Sheamathan from the Fair Lands. That didn't make sense. The start of a headache throbbed dully at her temples. The woodspirit had turned him into a dog. So how could he have driven Sheamathan from the Fair Lands? *Something* had happened, though, because the woodspirit had withdrawn for generations. Lana shook her head. How would she learn the whole story? She might have to get answers from Jules. Judging by his letters, he was trustworthy.

Jules planned to pit himself against Sheamathan again, which seemed a doomed mission, but maybe he didn't care if he died fighting the woodspirit. Lana frowned. Even if he broke the enchantment—and that was a big if—he would age normally. Life would be different now. Blacksmithing didn't exist. The world had changed radically. With the exception of Elias, every friend and family member he had ever known was dead. Maybe he felt he had nothing to live for. That thought made her sad. After reading his letters, she felt she knew him.

She laid her head in her hands. Jules was right; she had misjudged him in his wolfhound form, assuming he was evil. He was honest, brave, and compassionate. He stood up for what he believed in, despite great personal loss. She felt shallow and selfish by comparison.

On the next full moon she would go to the park and wait, hoping that the wolfhound she had always feared would come through the portal.

Chapter 24

Lana smiled as she walked into the living room and let Greg and Jordy know she was home. They weren't pets, they were boys, but sometimes it was hard to remember that. While she made dinner they chased each other around the furniture, squeaking playfully. She hoped Lillian couldn't hear anything downstairs.

The rat-boys enjoyed mealtimes with her. It seemed cruel to eat human meals in front of them, but they didn't seem to mind. Sometimes they all sat in the living room and watched TV while they ate, but usually they sat at the kitchen table. She had stacked pillows on the chairs for them.

After bringing her bowl of chili to the table, she poured rat chow into two bowls, added a few greens, and called the rats to the table.

"I have to read after dinner again," she told them as she stirred her chili. She didn't have time to entertain them and she felt guilty.

"Gee, you sure read a lot," Greg said, clearly disappointed.

Jordy stopped munching his rat chow long enough to say, "No problem. We won't bother you," but he looked dejected.

Should she tell them about Elias? What harm could it do? She blew on a spoonful of chili and studied the rats thoughtfully. Of the two, she trusted Jordy least. Aside from trying to attack her and steal the knife, she pegged him as an instigator. The boys' under-age drinking party at the forest had probably been his idea because, quite honestly, he struck her as the type who did what he wanted and worried about the consequences later. That attitude could be trouble, she knew all too well after reading her ancestor's experiences. Would the boys take Elias's tragic story seriously and learn a lesson from it?

"I'll read in the living room. I know you get tired of being alone so much. At least we'll be together."

"Great! If you want, you can read to us," Greg said hopefully.

"It's pretty complicated stuff."

"So why do you want to read it?"

"Because I need to learn things," she said, and then paused. "I may find a way to turn you back into boys."

Jordy coughed a piece of rat chow across the table. "What?"

"Wow! What kinda book are you readin'?" Greg asked excitedly.

"It's not a book." She gestured with her spoon. "I'll tell you what it is, but you need some background first."

They showed their teeth in brief smiles, looking pleased that she'd confide in them, and then began to eat again, crunching noisily.

"When I was in the dungeon, I saw the wolfhound, who used to be the Challenger. He wants me to help him. If he can regain his human form, he plans to challenge Sheamathan again."

"Last time he lost and got turned into a dog. What's he plan to do this time?" Jordy asked.

She frowned. She had asked herself the same question. "I don't know yet."

"Don't interrupt," Greg scolded.

She crumbled crackers into her chili. "He told me a little about himself and the Challenger's Blade. We didn't have much time to talk.

He said there were secret letters that could verify his claims, and he told me where to find them."

"And *that's* what you're reading!" Jordy concluded triumphantly.

She laughed. "Yes, I found the letters. They tell a lot about gem powers. Maybe I can find a way to defeat Sheamathan and break the wolfhound's enchantment." She sipped her water and waited for the rats' reaction.

"Wow," Jordy breathed. He sat back on his haunches, his rat chow forgotten. Greg looked equally intrigued.

"The Challenger's name is Jules," she told them. "He and my great-great-grandfather Elias were friends. Both were into gem lore. When Elias discovered the portal, he took gems to Shadow to see if it affected their powers. It turns out they were *much* more powerful there. Anyway, whenever he came home he and Jules got together, or he sent Jules a letter with the latest news. He expected Jules to be as excited as *he* was."

"But he wasn't," Jordy said when he saw her expression.

She shook her head. "Not after Jules heard about mutant bugs, pythanium, and poisonous plants."

"Shadow was like that way back then?" Jordy asked.

She gave the rats a couple of her crackers and said, "Yes. It was the same as today, but maybe the destruction covers a wider area now."

Greg nibbled a cracker. "Who'd hang out in that creepy place if they didn't have to?"

"Jules felt the same way. The *next* letter he got from Elias was even *more* disturbing."

"What did it say?" Greg demanded eagerly, ignoring his own advice not to interrupt.

"Elias wrote that a lot of Shadow stones had dangerous—harmful—dark powers. But he experimented with them anyway. Worse, sometimes he used the gnomes as guinea pigs."

Ohhh," Greg said. "Maybe he didn't mean to hurt them. At least not at first."

"Yeah," Jordy said, nodding. "He probably figured once he finished his experiments he could make it up to them later."

"Make it up to them? How?" she demanded, disturbed by Jordy's cavalier attitude.

"Dunno," Jordy said, apparently unconcerned, as he nibbled his cracker.

She put down her spoon and leaned forward, staring solemnly at Jordy. "Even if he *could* have made it up to the gnomes, what he did was evil and he harmed *himself*."

Jordy stopped chewing. He cocked his furry brown head and twitched his whiskers. "What do you mean?"

"Once he started doing bad things that hurt others, it changed who he was—in fact, it changed him so much he couldn't enter the Fair Lands anymore. He never saw his son or any of his family and friends again."

"That's awful," Greg said, sounding genuinely disturbed.

"What a lousy end to his adventure," Jordy agreed, avoiding her eyes.

She sat back in her chair and folded her arms. "From what I've read so far, our world—the Fair Lands—is protected by a force field. You know what a force field is, right?"

"Sure," Greg said. "I've watched lots of Star Trek reruns."

"Yeah, me too," Jordy said.

She smiled. "Good. If a person from another world comes through the portal, they enter our protective realm, called the Amulet. If they keep going, they come to the border between the Amulet and the Fair Lands, and then they hit the force field and can't go any farther. They can't get into our world."

The rats exchanged glances. Greg said, "Like how my parents installed an invisible fence for our dog? If it tries to go through, it gets zapped."

She nodded, amused. "Yeah, I guess it's sort of like that. Only it's worse than getting zapped with static electricity. I tried to take something from Shadow into the Fair Lands once and when I left the Amulet it disappeared."

The rats considered this gravely.

"Sheamathan is trying to "trick" this natural defense mechanism," Lana explained. "First, she starts a disease inside the Amulet. Before long the defense mechanism doesn't recognize the corrupted land as part of our world. It stops defending the land, so there's nothing to stop the blight from spreading. As the Amulet gets bigger and bigger, Sheamathan will be able to travel farther into our world."

"Whoa," Greg breathed. "I get how it works."

Jordy flicked his tail nervously. "Once she comes here, she'll destroy everything."

"Yes. And anyone who did things to help her would have a tough time 'making it up to us later.'" She caught Jordy's eye and gave him a meaningful look.

"Okay, I get it," he said grudgingly. "But I didn't know—I didn't think giving Sheamathan your knife was *that* bad."

She said gently, "I don't really know you, Jordy, but I can say with complete certainty that you need to work on who you're becoming. Remember that electric shock you felt when we drove out of the park?"

Jordy nodded silently.

"That was the force field."

His mouth fell open in alarm as he connected the things she'd just said. "You mean it almost didn't let me through?"

"Yes, that's my understanding."

"Wow," Jordy said miserably.

Right and wrong had just become personal, not just a story about somebody else.

"Wow," Greg echoed. The gray rat glanced at Jordy. "I felt a tingle, too. But not as bad as you."

Lana stared into her bowl, idly stirring her chili as she told the rats, "There's a powerful gem master in Shadow called Folio. All the gnomes hate him. Sheamathan tormented and enslaved the gnomes and he didn't try to stop her." She paused, and forced herself to say the rest. "I just found out that Folio is my ancestor Elias."

When she looked up, both rats were staring at her, wide-eyed.

"It's too late for *him* to choose the right path. It's *not* too late for you."

Jordy let out a choked squeak. He ran from the table, jumped onto the couch, and stuck his head under a pillow.

"I guess I'm not very hungry," Greg said. He went and sat beside his friend.

Anything else she had planned to say could wait, she decided. The rats needed time to think, and she didn't feel like talking at the moment. Thinking about Folio left her depressed. She finished her meal without tasting it, loaded the dishwasher, and went to get the ledger. When she came back, the rats were still sitting on the couch, looking glum.

From time to time she stopped reading, looked up, and found them watching her, but they didn't interrupt. After about an hour she found the material about transformation enchantments. She read through the material twice, hoping there was some mistake. This wasn't good. She'd be putting herself in danger if she tried it.

"What?" Greg demanded, breaking the silence. "It's something bad. I can tell."

She looked up, heavy-hearted. "All the transformation enchantments use the bad Shadow stones. The ones with dark powers."

"Ohhhh." Greg's head drooped.

"I wouldn't know where to find the right gemstones," she said, frowning. "I don't even know what they look like. I suppose Raenihel might know." She paused, considering. "If I only hold the bad gemstones a couple times, maybe they won't hurt me."

Jordy let out a squeak and shook his head violently. "Forget it! You're not turnin' out like your ancestor Elias because of me. I feel guilty enough *now*."

She gave him a surprised glance, pleased but sad. "I really wish I could help you."

"I have a feeling that doing a bad thing, even for a good reason, is still bad," Jordy said firmly. "We'll find another way. At least I hope so, or I'll never get to tell people I'm sorry for things I did."

She went over and kissed the top of his head. He looked up, startled. "What's that for?"

"For thinking about who you are and who you're becoming."

He showed his teeth in that strange, disconcerting smile of his and she felt her lips curve in an answering smile. "Get some sleep. We'll get up early and go on a field trip. Would you like that?"

"Yeah, sure!" Greg said. "Where we goin'?"

"Back to County Forest Park to dig up that alamaria. Now that you're rats, I want you to touch it and see how it feels. After that, we'll go to the campfire where I found it and see if anyone's been around."

"Great! Let's do it," Jordy said, and then added warily, "if you're sure I won't get stuck inside the Amulet."

She smiled. "You'll be fine. See you in the morning."

She carried the ledger to her bedroom and set the alarm for five thirty, hoping she could fall asleep right away. She had to be at the store by ten, but that should give them plenty of time.

Chapter 25

Shortly after six, Lana drove out of town with the rat-boys perched on the back seat. They stared out the windows, clearly enjoying their outing.

The sky grew lighter, showing streaks of pinks and orange as they approached County Forest Park. Unfortunately, the rising sun revealed ugliness too, and she felt sickened by the spreading destruction. Looking from one side of the road to the other was a study in contrasts—healthy trees outside the park, diseased inside.

The local paper had run an article about the blight. Experts were baffled, mostly because every kind of tree was affected, not just one kind. And not just trees, either—field grass, shrubs, moss, weeds—all diseased and dying. It didn't make sense so people had all kinds of theories. Like ground water contamination, or buried toxic waste.

"We're here," Lana said, trying to shake off her gloomy thoughts. "We should have the park to ourselves. No one comes this early." *Who'd want to come here, even later in the day? There's no reason to come unless it's to see the destruction.*

She opened the door for the rats. "Meet you at the rotted stump by the trail head." They took off at a run. She followed, taking her time. It was good to see them run and play.

Shuffling through the leaves, she could see brown grass underneath. Brown grass? During a rainy September? Definitely not normal. A cold breeze lifted her hair. She pulled her sweatshirt zipper higher, shivering, and not just from the cold. The park felt tainted with evil. The diseased forest was giving her the creeps. She wrinkled her nose at the sour tang in the air. It smelled like rotting compost.

When she caught up to the rats, they were arguing good-naturedly over who had reached the stump first. She ignored them and started digging.

"Okay. You first, Greg," she called as she set the stone on the ground and brushed dirt from it. "Touch the stone. Tell me what you feel."

He scrambled over and touched it with both paws. After about ten seconds, he said, "It feels weird. My paws are going numb." After another few seconds, "Wow! My paws are so stiff and cold I can hardly move them!"

Jordy circled him impatiently, clearly wanting to try it himself.

"Can I stop now?" Greg asked. "I can't feel anything. My paws are totally numb!"

"Sure. Thanks, Greg."

"My turn!" Jordy sang.

"Okay. Go ahead."

After a moment he cried, "You're right! It didn't feel like *this* before!"

She gave a satisfied smile, but only for a moment. *This is a Shadow stone, the first you've ever seen. Is it a good stone, or a bad one?* Her smile turned to a wary frown. Sheamathan was mining alamaria. Was that reason enough to suspect it held dark powers? The stone was unusual, beautiful, and it either drew energy or interrupted its flow. Handling the stone hadn't produced any harmful side effects so far, but it paid to be cautious.

"You can let go now, Jordy. Our experiment was a success." *And I'm going to bury this weird stone again.*

"We're going somewhere else now?" Jordy asked, chaffing his paws and shivering.

"I'll show you where I found this. First, let me bury it."

The rats' boundless energy made her laugh. As they all walked to the campfire, Greg and Jordy scampered through dead leaves, jumped over fallen branches, climbed onto every stump, and dove squealing and laughing into the leaves. Lana found the destruction too depressing to enjoy the hike. No one, not even the "experts," knew how to stop the blight's progress. How long before it spread beyond the park?

When she found the narrow, unmarked path, she let the rats go first and followed gloomily after them. It was painful to think how much everything had changed. The dense forest had lost its pleasant green canopy. The trees lifted bare branches to the heavens as if in a plea for help.

After ten minutes they came to the clearing where she'd found the remains of the campfire. She stopped short, surveying the scene.

"Someone's been here, all right," Greg said, scooting forward to investigate. A pile of dirt covered in gray ash, and pieces of charred wood sat beside a two-foot-deep hole. Jordy and Greg moved forward and peered into the hole.

"Why would somebody dig a hole here?" Greg asked, glancing back at her.

She shrugged. "I don't know. Maybe whoever buried the alamaria was looking for it."

"I don't get why they buried it," Jordy said.

"Me, either." Were there any clues to suggest who had been here? Anything left behind? She looked around but didn't see anything. "We should start back now." The rats looked disappointed but they didn't ask to stay longer. "We'll do this again," she promised. "Maybe not here, but I'll take you somewhere you can run."

As she drove to the exit, a solemn hush fell over the car. She felt certain Greg and Jordy were thinking about the force field. Slowing to a crawl, she realized she was holding her breath, waiting nervously for Jordy's yelp of pain. They passed the area where he had cried out before and he didn't let out as much as a squeak. How was that possible?

"Ow!" Jordy squealed a moment later, and then he gave a shaky laugh. "Hey, it didn't hurt as bad this time."

"Good," she said in a flat tone. "That's good."

"Then why don't you sound happy?" Jordy asked.

She debated keeping it to herself, and decided against it. "The border of the Amulet has moved," she said in a tight voice. "The Amulet is expanding." Her hands tightened on the steering wheel. More and more land lay unprotected as the blight spread; the Amulet didn't recognize the diseased land as part of its own and had stopped defending it. "Do you understand what this means?" she asked the boys.

"I think so," Greg said slowly.

She looked at the rats in her rearview mirror. Their tails twitched nervously. Turning her attention back to the road she said, "The area of our world that Sheamathan can occupy is *growing*." She felt sick at the thought. Time was running out.

"I don't want her in *any* of our world," Greg said.

"Will she ever—can she get to my parents' house?" Jordy asked in a small voice.

"Yes, if the Amulet keeps expanding."

"Your secret papers, do they mention anything that might help?" Greg asked.

"I wish I could say yes, but I just don't know. I learned it's possible for Fair Lands gems to disrupt some of Sheamathan's gem powers. That might help us. And drawing powers from multiple gems at the same time creates new powers, but I don't know enough about that yet. I learned new ways to use the Challenger's blade." Her voice trailed off. "Bottom line, we don't have much time, and I still don't know how to defeat her."

"So what're we gonna do?" Jordy asked in a panicky voice. "We can't let her come here and take over like she did in Shadow."

Their best hope was the wolfhound, which wasn't very encouraging. "I'm hoping to meet Jules during the next full moon. I think he knows how to break his enchantment, and if I can help him, I will. When he's human again, he'll challenge Sheamathan."

"If he changes back," Greg said, "Will he be more powerful than you?"

She sighed. "I hope so. We'll see."

By the time she took Jordy and Greg home, it was time to go to work. She was in no mood to stand behind a jewelry counter. How would she keep her mind on business?

Driving to the store, Greg's question about Jules circled in her head: "Will he be more powerful than you?" Quite honestly, she didn't know, but she suspected it didn't matter. Neither of them were any match for Sheamathan.

Last time, Jules had faced Sheamathan unprepared. Was it any wonder things had gone wrong? And seriously, was he any more prepared now after spending the last century as a dog? She laughed bitterly. If anyone had ever had a chance of defeating Sheamathan, it had been Elias, back when he could use both Fair Lands and Shadow gems.

She looked down at the speedometer and let off the gas. "Darn that old fool!" she muttered. "If I ever meet Elias, I'm going to tell him *exactly* what I think of him."

Chapter 26

Lana marked off the days on her kitchen calendar with a big, black X. Normally, time flew much too quickly; now, it seemed the full moon would never come. Jules would come through the portal. She felt certain of it. He'd want to talk to her about the hidden papers she had promised to read. This time she would open her mind and listen to him. Together they might be able to break his enchantment. He had better have a plan to stop Sheamathan, she told herself grimly, because the blight was spreading at an alarming rate.

Lately, she'd been sharing parts of the ledger with the rat-boys. They'd become fascinated with gems, and it was nice to have someone to use as a sounding board. She had stopped thinking about finding them another home. They weren't so bad, really, now that she was used to them. They got bored and cranky at times, but thanks to the new pet carriers, she had started taking them to the village park, and that had helped a lot. In the dark, they could pass for dogs.

Emily had called a couple times, wanting to get together. Refusing would have raised questions, so Lana had reluctantly agreed. There was no way she could have company here, of course—not with the rats camped out in her living room, so they had gone out for dinner and then hung out at Emily's.

It was increasingly difficult to keep her mind on business. Between worrying about the rat-boys, County Forest, and Shadow, she was jumpy and irritable, and others were starting to notice. During free moments behind the sales counter, she worked on her gem powers. If Jules needed her, she wanted every possible gem power at her disposal. The only good thing about being distracted all the time was that she hardly noticed Arlene's snide remarks. At the ten-day mark, Lana told Arlene that she was planning to take a few vacation days.

The weekend before the full moon, Lana drove to the forest to speak to the gnomes.

The sun was setting when she arrived at the park, and she hoped the rangers were gone. She didn't want to explain why she was here after hours. As she walked to the Tree Home, she debated with herself. How much should she tell the gnomes? She had promised to share information from the secret papers, but who would have thought she'd learn that Elias was Folio? She didn't want to be deceptive, but she could just imagine Raenihel's reaction if she told him. Still, it seemed the right thing to do.

When she arrived at the Tree Home, Raenihel and other gnomes were outside, examining diseased plants.

Raenihel straightened and held out his hand. "Lana, it is good to see you!"

"I see you're keeping an eye on the blight," she said, clasping the gnome's callused hand. "It's spreading at an alarming rate, isn't it?"

"Yes, it is very troubling. Did you find the secret papers and learn anything useful?" When she nodded he took her arm. "Come. Let's talk inside." He drew her into the Tree Home.

With a growing lump in her throat, she followed him to the circle of glowing stones and sat down with the assembled gnomes. They looked at her expectantly. This wasn't going to be easy.

"I found my ancestor's hidden papers," she said without preamble. The gnomes nodded, clearly up-to-date on her efforts to help them.

They looked at her with hopeful smiles. "The papers described Fair Lands gems and Shadow gemstones, and told about their abilities. I found a sketch of the Challenger's knife, and a letter that explained how it was made, but it didn't say much about what the knife can do." She paused, wishing she could be more encouraging, but there was no point giving them false hope. "I'm sorry, but even after reading everything I still don't know how to defeat Sheamathan."

The gnomes' faces fell. They looked at one another with expressions that said, "*Now what?*" From the beginning they had put too much faith in her and had set themselves up for disappointment. Once she told them about Elias, they would probably hate her, even though she was nothing like Elias. They'd tell themselves that she couldn't be the one who was destined to save them, which is what she had tried to tell them all along. So why did she feel so miserable?

"I learned something that shocked me," she said hesitantly, staring down at her hands. "I'd rather not tell you, but you deserve to know." Hatred for Elias tightened her throat. For a moment, despite her resolve, she wasn't sure she could go on.

Raenihel patted her hand soothingly. "I can see how much it troubles you."

Taking a deep breath, she lifted her head and forced herself to look at the gnomes. "It won't be any easier if I give you all the background, so I'll just say it. Your Challenger Jules, and my great-great-grandfather Elias, were friends. Elias came to Shadow and studied your gems, and he used their powers to extend his life. He's the man you call Folio."

The gnomes' expressions showed a mixture of horror and confusion. She glanced aside at Raenihel who looked troubled, but he kept patting her hand. "No wonder you're upset," he said gently. "The family connection is embarrassing. Don't worry, dear one. You're not to blame for the things he did. And you're nothing like him."

An awkward silence fell but, to her relief, the gnomes didn't look angry with her. A female got up and brought Lana a plate of food and a cup of fialazza, like a mother trying to soothe a child after a bad day at school. If only the matter were as trivial as that. Lana let out a shaky sob and smiled through tears as she took the food and drink.

After a few sips of fialazza that helped settle her nerves, she said to Raenihel, "I know I've asked you this before, but could you tell me about the Challenger's meeting with Sheamathan? Anything you know might be helpful."

The old gnome stroked his beard thoughtfully. "I didn't tell you much because there isn't much to tell, but I'd be happy to recount the tale."

"Thank you, Raenihel." She picked at her food even though she wasn't hungry.

"Here is the tale as my ancestors passed it down," he began. "When we first met the Challenger we didn't trust him. The man we called Folio had misused us, and we had little use for humans. The Challenger seemed very different, however. He knew that Folio had exploited us, and that the woodspirit had tortured and enslaved us. He seemed as concerned about Shadow and our fate as he was about the fate of his own world. My clan held a lengthy council with him, then we took him to some of the other clans, and they told him everything they knew about Sheamathan and her stronghold, Shadowglade. He was disheartened by their reports, but even so he was determined to challenge her."

When Raenihel paused, Lana glanced at the other gnomes. Their expressions suggested that they never got tired of this story.

"The next time my people saw him, a few days later, he was dressed formally in a black frock coat and trousers. His face glowed with a righteous fervor. He wore around his neck and on his arms pieces of jewelry with large gems of various colors, and at his waist he wore the

Challengers blade. Our people were proud that such a good and powerful man would act on our behalf.

"The next day, he came to us again, but he wore no gems. He gave us his jeweled knife and told us to keep it safe—we might need it in the future. We never saw him again." Raenihel sighed. "There ends the tale. There is nothing more I can tell you."

Lana held back a sigh of frustration. The story was interesting, but not very useful. She left County Forest Park feeling discouraged. The original perimeter of the Amulet had failed. The blight now extended beyond the park, which meant the Amulet was expanding and more of the Fair Lands was vulnerable. Before long the Amulet would extend for miles, and Sheamathan would have access to all of that land. The situation looked hopeless, Lana thought bitterly, but she and the gnomes would keep looking for an answer.

The morning of the full moon, Lana got out of bed with a nervous headache, her stomach in knots. She didn't feel like eating, and that wasn't like her.

Why am I up so early? I don't need to leave for hours.

The best therapy for her jittery nerves was activity, she decided. She cleaned the rats' litter box, refilled their food and water, and left an open bag of chow by their bowls. If she didn't come home for a few days, they'd be fine. After that she scrubbed the sink, took out the trash, read all her unopened mail, wrote checks, and then dropped her bills in the mailbox. It was only nine o'clock, and she had run out of things to do.

Collapsing into the chair in the living room, she picked up a romance novel she had started weeks ago. By now she barely remembered the plot. After reading the same paragraphs over and over, she gave up in disgust.

Just then Jordy and Greg finally woke. They jumped off the couch and came over to her chair. She could tell by their quivering bodies and sad eyes that they were wrecks, too.

"I don't want you to go," Greg said, crawling onto the arm of her chair and looking up at her dejectedly. "What if Jules drags you off on some dangerous mission and we never see you again?"

Jordy, near her feet, stared up at her, whiskers twitching. "Now that it's time for you to go, we're scared." He jumped onto the chair's other arm and sat nervously thumping his tail against it.

She smiled at the rodent bookends and patted them affectionately. "Jules might not even show up. I'm pretty sure he will, but who knows?"

"I hope he just wants to tell you stuff," Greg said.

"Well, whatever he wants, I hope I'm ready. I've been working a couple hours a day with the knife and my gemstones."

"You're gonna take the knife with you?" Jordy asked.

"Of course. And I'm taking a pouch with lots of gems."

Greg asked, "Will you be seeing the gnomes in the Tree Home?"

"I hadn't planned to, but if Jules doesn't come, I'll go to the Tree Home and see if there's any important news from Shadow."

After that, the rats watched TV and she watched a couple shows with them just to keep her mind occupied. At one thirty she spent an hour holding gemstones for strength, courage, and foresight. At two thirty she forced herself to eat, and then she filled her canteen, put on her travel pouch, and packed her backpack with things she'd need if this turned into an overnight trip.

Last time she'd seen the wolfhound at about three o'clock. So apparently, unlike the gnomes, he had no problem using the portal in the daytime when the energy field was stronger. If he normally came in the daytime, the gnomes probably never saw him.

After checking her provisions one last time, she walked into the living room. Greg and Jordy sat near the door, looking like two orphans about to lose their only friend. Actually, she thought with a heavy heart, that was painfully close to the truth.

"I'll ask Jules if he knows how to turn you back into boys." It was the only comforting thing she could think to say. The rats nodded.

She put on her brown jacket with the fleece lining. The color blended well with the dead forest, she thought grimly. Her khaki pants and dirty, well-worn sneakers would blend in, too. The essentials she usually carried in her purse were in her backpack. *Stop stalling. Say goodbye.*

All week, while holding her gems, she'd had the same premonition—she'd leave tonight with Jules on a campaign to defeat Sheamathan. Greg and Jordy had sensed something was up, and they had fretted for days. It seemed only fair to be straight with them.

Kneeling, she looked the rats in the eye. "I have a feeling we're saying goodbye for a few days."

They nodded glumly.

"I'll come back as soon as I can, but our world is in danger. I have to help." She held out her hand. Jordy sat back on his haunches and stuck out a paw. She thought she'd feel silly shaking a rat's paw, but she didn't, and then she shook Greg's. "I'm going now before we all start blubbering."

"Goodbye," Lana. "Be careful," Greg said softly.

"We'll miss you, but we'll be okay." Jordy's whiskers twitched with emotion.

She walked out the door, sorry to leave them and yet anxious to go. This was it—no more days to cross off the calendar. She was going to the portal to meet the wolfhound.

* * *

As expected, the park was deserted. She decided to hang out near the Tree Home since it was close to the portal and a logical place to wait. Finding a stump to sit on, she sat and unsheathed the Challenger's knife. She wasn't expecting danger, but it couldn't hurt to check. The blade glowed briefly and then went dark. Good. That meant she was safe. She sheathed the knife, tucked it into her belt, and took out six sapphires and an equal number of lapis. Holding them tightly, she opened her mind and drew the powers she needed—*telepathy, clairvoyance, and heightened awareness.* If Jules was near, he'd find her or she'd find him. She didn't feel anyone's presence, and she got no thoughts or images that didn't feel like her own. He wasn't here yet, she realized, disappointed.

Twenty minutes passed. She had been so certain that he would come the first chance he got. She chewed her lip and stared into the trees. Something could have prevented him. Maybe he couldn't get here.

Finally, she felt a presence.

Branches snapped. Something moved in the underbrush. Her heart leapt and she jumped to her feet, shoving the gems into her pouch. It was probably the wolfhound, but she needed to be careful. She drew the Challenger's knife and the blade began to glow.

Unlike the last time, it *continued* to glow. With growing alarm she stared at the blade and her fingers tightened around the hilt.

Close by, branches snapped and twigs crunched underfoot. She looked around, frantically scanning the woods. Then, a few yards ahead, the wolfhound emerged from the trees.

"It's you," she said, sagging with relief. "Why is my blade still glowing?"

The wolfhound thought into her mind: *Someone is with me. Don't be afraid.*

An old man stepped from the trees. Lana stopped breathing. His mustache and beard didn't completely hide the wart-like bumps on his face. His nose was broad and flat, and his lips were little more than a gash in his face. Thick gray hair reached to his shoulders. He wore a long-sleeved, green robe that fell loosely around him, but the garment hinted at a surprisingly muscular body. His eyes were the color of his robe, and when he looked at Lana, she felt she had been skewered in place. No one needed to tell her—this man was her great-great-grandfather Elias.

She stood a little taller. "Hello Folio," she said icily, purposely using the name the gnomes had given him. She refused to dignify him with the name Elias. Why was he here? Was this some sort of trick?

He and the dog approached and he said, "You don't need to say how much you despise me, Lana. I know everything you think and feel."

"How convenient." Feeling betrayed, she looked down at the dog. "Why did you bring *him?*"

The wolfhound said in her mind, *I'm afraid we need him, in many ways.*

Her eyes narrowed. "Name one."

You and I can communicate, but I can't speak out loud. At times it will be easier for Elias to speak on my behalf. My meaning must not be mistaken.

His reasoning made sense, but Folio's presence was such a shock that all the things she had planned to say, the questions she had planned to ask, fled from her mind. After an awkward silence she said to Jules, "You said you needed my help to protect Shadow and the Fair Lands. Well, I read the letters and the ledger, and I have more questions than answers. I still don't know how you can regain your human form, or how to drive Sheamathan out of our world and make her stay in Shadow."

The wolfhound walked forward and sat down at her feet. His dark eyes looked trustingly into hers. *We must go to Shadow where your powers are strongest. Then, there's something I need you to do."*

"What?"

I must die and you must bring me back to life.

Chapter 27

L ana stood in stunned silence. Her first reaction was that Jules couldn't be serious. Folio's grim expression said otherwise.

"I wish you weren't serious, but you are, aren't you?" A weight had settled around her heart. It was hard to breathe. "I'm still developing my gem powers." She let out a shaky breath. "What makes you think I can do this?"

"You're stronger than you know," Folio said firmly. "And there's no one else capable of doing this."

You'll be successful, and I'll be human again.

She looked down at the wolfhound. "I see what you mean about having no misunderstandings."

With an expression that said she'd rather not speak to him, she asked Folio, "What happened between Jules and Sheamathan? In the woodspirit's dungeon, Jules told me he'd been the Challenger. Considering his present form, that's a disturbing revelation. He said Sheamathan did this to him."

"It's complicated, as you can well imagine," Folio said. "When I had already missed my best chance to defeat Sheamathan, and we were in danger of losing the Fair Lands to her, Jules decided to confront her. Quite frankly, he had no chance of defeating her. His Fair Lands gem powers were still developing, and he had no experience with native gems." Folio stroked his beard. His gaze grew distant. "We considered bluffing Sheamathan, trying to make her think Jules was more powerful than her, but she would soon learn the truth."

Jules continued, *After conferring with the gnomes, Elias and I came up with a plan. I would tell Sheamathan that I might not be able to defeat her, but my Fair Lands gem powers could disrupt hers and make a fool of her. I would be a continual thorn in her side. I proposed a bargain. To rule Shadow undisturbed, she must forever give up the Fair Lands. In exchange, I would allow her to enchant me so I couldn't interfere with her.*

Lana thought back to her visit with Jules in the dungeon and his comment about bluffs and bargains. It was all starting to make sense. "Sheamathan has a history of dealing with threats by turning people into rats, birds, and lizards, so I see where this story is headed. But if being turned into a dog was your side of the bargain, you got a raw deal."

Folio looked at the dog sadly. When his eyes met Lana's again, he looked defensive. "My relationship with Sheamathan at the time might be called an uneasy truce. She tolerated me mostly because I stayed out of her way. Right before Jules met with Sheamathan, I went to her with a warning: A gem master named Jules DeLauretin, my rival from the Fair Lands, was coming to set up permanent residence in Shadow. He intended to stop the blight in both worlds and end her conquest of the Fair Lands. I told her he had made my life miserable for years, and that the *last* thing either of us wanted was Jules DeLauretin living in Shadow."

"Clever," she said with a laugh, forced to admire Folio, at least this once. "And was Sheamathan worried?"

He chuckled. "Yes. During my early days in Shadow, she had seen enough of my Fair Lands powers to know that I was a threat, and that my gem powers could interfere with her own. She realized, after she thought the matter through, that giving up the Fair Lands to rule Shadow undisturbed was a reasonable trade-off." Folio's expression darkened. "Jules came to the woodspirit wearing gems and fine clothing. He carried the knife and demonstrated a few of its powers. At the end of the interview he gave her an ultimatum. She had one day to agree to his bargain."

"There was no other plan? One that didn't result in *this*?" Lana asked coldly, gesturing at Jules. In Folio's place, she would have tried to destroy the woodspirit, even if it cost her own life. How could he stand by and let Sheamathan turn Jules into a dog?

"Any other plan had, at best, a fifty-fifty chance of success," he answered.

"People have gone to war on slimmer odds."

"You don't understand," he said firmly, his eyes holding hers. "This way, we were guaranteed victory. Sheamathan would immediately withdraw from the Fair Lands, which is a critical point. So far, she knew little about Fair Lands gems. She hadn't spent enough time on our side to know that many gemstones from *her* world behave differently in *ours*. We couldn't allow her to discover that."

Lana nodded reluctantly, seeing his point. In his letters he had written: *She must not be allowed to study our world as I have studied hers.* "I'm sorry, go on."

"The next day she accepted the bargain. Jules would sacrifice himself, and she would relinquish the Fair Lands. I helped Jules devise the spell that bound Sheamathan to Shadow, and I helped Sheamathan construct Jules's enchantment."

"*You* created the spells?" she said in surprise.

Folio gave her a sly smile and a wink. "Naturally, since I could function as a disinterested third party."

Once again, she laughed in spite of herself. "Not so disinterested. You lied to her about Jules."

"Yes, but Sheamathan believed I was on her side as we worked out the details of the bargain." He cleared his throat. "But that was not the case. Today, with your help, we will break Jules's enchantment."

"We break it by *killing* him?" she asked, still troubled by the idea.

Folio gestured at the wolfhound with an age-spotted hand. "In order to break the enchantment, the dog must die. I brought a specially made poison, which I will administer. Humans can withstand a larger dose than a dog, and that's the key to my plan." Folio stood taller and took a deep breath. "When the poison takes hold and the dog dies, the transformation will take place. Jules will return to his human form. We will have a small window of time when Jules, the human, is poisoned and barely alive." His eyes held hers. She had the uncomfortable feeling he was probing her, weighing her skills one last time to make sure he could count on her. "You must use the knife and all your skills to heal him. I have the ability to slow the passage of time, so this, and protection while you work, will be my contribution."

And although she doesn't know it, Sheamathan will help us indirectly.

Lana raised a brow. "How is that?"

She built an alamaria stone obelisk near the portal. In Shadow, alamaria amplifies all gem powers, but it has two shortcomings: You need a great deal of it, and its range of influence is limited. Despite those limitations, it's very effective.

"An alamaria obelisk near the portal," she repeated thoughtfully. "Let me guess. That's how Sheamathan managed to get through the portal after all these years."

"Exactly," Folio said. "Word reached me that the woodspirit had discovered a new stone. Naturally, I was curious. What was it? What did it do? When she began mining large quantities, I grew concerned. I secretly went to the mines and found a stone to study. As soon as I discovered its properties, I knew the Fair Lands were in danger again."

"And you decided to get involved this time," she said stiffly.

Folio sighed as he placed a hand on the wolfhound's head. "You'll have your chance to berate me later, and no doubt I deserve it. At the moment, our time would be better spent changing the future than reliving the past."

You'll help me, Lana?

She looked down at the wolfhound and shoved her hands into her jacket pockets so he wouldn't see them shaking. "Yes, of course I'll help."

Folio took her arm. Together, she, Folio and Jules walked to the portal and crossed into Shadow. She immediately recognized the unusual forest with its huge trees and black moss. Instead of taking the narrow path that Raenihel had used, Folio led them through the underbrush in a different direction. Was this a shortcut? Or was he worried that someone might see them? As far as she knew, no one actually lived in this part of the forest.

In a few minutes they came to the broad path that led to the obelisk and it didn't take long to reach it.

The obelisk stood around fifteen feet tall. Large stones formed the base and incrementally smaller stones rose to its peak. She stared in silent awe at the sheer magnificence of so many black, shimmering stones. When she unsheathed the Challenger's blade and held it up, something unusual happened. It began to glow, and then it went dark. And then the blade began to glimmer with the same iridescent silver flecks as the alamaria. Jules's voice in her head pulled her attention from the blade.

Let's begin, before I lose my nerve.

Folio produced a vial from a hidden pocket inside his robe. He poured its contents into the dog's mouth. Lana held her breath as the poison took effect.

He went down. Drool came from his mouth. His whole body twitched in violent spasms. His eyes glazed over and his breathing became labored. It was horrible to watch. She felt a mounting sense of panic. What if something went wrong? What if she couldn't heal him? Perspiration covered her face. Her hands were damp and she couldn't keep them from shaking. Folio interrupted her panicky thoughts, saying calmly but firmly, "The poison is powerful. This won't take long. Be ready."

She couldn't let herself fall apart. She had a job to do and everything depended on her ability to think clearly and use her gem powers. Reaching into her travel pouch, she searched for gems that would help Jules survive the poison. She wanted to use several loose gems in addition to the Challenger's blade. Lore said aquamarine reduced the effects of poison. She'd soon find out, she told herself grimly. She took out aquamarine, hematite, sugalite, topaz and jasper.

The wolfhound stopped thrashing and lay still. An instant later Jules, as he had looked the day he was enchanted, lay on the ground.

"Now!" Folio commanded.

Lana knelt beside Jules, opened his shirt, and placed the aquamarines on his chest. She didn't think he was breathing. His lips were blue. Even with her help, could he overcome the poison? Could she really bring a man, who appeared to be dead, back to life? Arranging the rest of the healing stones on his chest, she watched his face, hoping for some sign of life.

Maybe it was because Elias was slowing time, but nothing seemed to be happening. Seconds felt like minutes. She concentrated on the gems, doing her best to draw and channel their power. This was no time to question her abilities, she told herself sternly. Jules and Elias trusted her and she had to trust herself. She swallowed hard and took a deep breath. Time to use the Challenger's knife along with the loose gems. She lifted one of Jules's lifeless hands and wrapped his fingers around the hilt. His hand was cold, so cold. She placed her warm hands around his, pressing firmly, maintaining his grip on the hilt.

"Good," Folio encouraged. "Picture healing energy flowing from the knife into his hand."

For an instant her mind flashed back to the day she had channeled energy into Theaffar, and she relived that moment. She felt the same burst of energy and the sense of flames enveloping her hand.

Her frantic need to restore Jules became her guide and she began to work without conscious thought. She pictured the poison weakening and dissipating from his body, and then strength and vitality coursing through the knife and flowing into him. She directed healing to heart, kidneys, liver, and other organs affected by the poison, including his brain. At the end, the dog had suffered convulsions. Could that cause problems after the transformation?

"Good!" Folio boomed.

She spared a brief glance at the blade. It continued to shimmer like alamaria. Now what? Now what? She was running out of new ways to focus the blade's power and she wasn't sure what to do. She looked at Jules's pale face and cried in desperation, "Breathe! Open your eyes!"

His eyelids fluttered, and then opened. Blue eyes looked into hers. She gasped. With a strangled sob, she looked at him through a blur of tears, and her tears began to drop onto his face like rain.

"Oh dear," I seldom have *that* effect on women," he said weakly, giving her the ghost of a smile.

"Dear friend, it is good to see you in your real form," Folio said. "Now lie very still, and mind you, no flirting with Lana."

Jules gave a short laugh and then winced with pain. "Laughter may be the best medicine, but it hurts at the moment." He studied Lana's face and gave her a shaky smile that touched her deeply. "I'm in your debt. Thank you."

She wiped away her tears, feeling awkward all of the sudden as she looked into his eyes. She became very aware of her hand holding his on the knife. She let go and stood on shaky legs. He could manage on his own now. After all, it was his knife and he was probably more skilled with it than she was. He maintained his grip on the hilt and seemed to be breathing easier, but now and then he winced. Lana and Folio watched him silently.

"It's wonderful to be myself at last," he said, his voice weak, but steadier now. "I'll never look at a dog the same way again."

Folio smiled. "The rules of your enchantment and the wolfhound form worked very well, I'd say." In answer to Lana's questioning look he explained, "As long as Sheamathan lived, Jules's human mind returned to him during each full moon. This gave him an opportunity to check on her and make sure she hadn't circumvented their bargain. Every month he inspected the Amulet for signs of blight. Usually he continued into the Fair Lands where he could pass as a normal dog."

"Yes," Lana said. "A normal dog that terrified me."

"There now, what are you doing?" Folio scolded when Jules tried to sit up. "I told you to lie still."

Jules gave him an exasperated look. "I feel much better now."

"Better than what?" Lana asked, concerned. "Better than dead? Better than a poisoned dog? Rest for a while."

"I suppose you're right, but I'm impatient." He sat rubbing his forehead, and he still looked pale.

Folio gave Lana a hesitant smile. "When he's rested, I think he'll be able to walk with support. We shouldn't stay here, and he'd be more comfortable in my cave at Strathweed. We've already imposed on you enough for one day," he said, his voice trailing off.

"I'll go with you," she said with mixed emotions. She still didn't like Folio, but she hated him a lot less.

And he probably already knew that.

Chapter 28

After ten or fifteen minutes, Jules insisted he was strong enough to walk. Lana studied him silently, knowing it was pointless to argue. Maybe the aquamarines had helped dispel the effects of the poison because he seemed to be recovering remarkably well. He was still pale, but who wouldn't be after what he'd gone through? The three-mile walk to Strathweed would be difficult, but he should be in a safe place where he could rest and have something to eat, and where else could they take him?

Lana glanced at the sky. It would be dark before long. If Jules was capable of walking, they should get going.

Folio helped Jules up and grasped his left arm to support him. They began to walk.

"Don't fuss over me," Jules protested. "I'm quite steady now."

"You're just too proud to lean on an old man," Folio grumbled. "I intend to fuss over you for a day or two, so you may as well make the best of it."

Lana hid a smile and put on her backpack. She caught up to them and fell into step on Jules's right side, but she didn't offer her arm or try to touch him. Jules was reluctant to lean on Elias. He certainly wouldn't want her help. She noticed he was still holding the knife, which was a smart idea. He could draw strength and healing while they walked.

They covered the first quarter mile at a moderate speed, or as Jules called it, 'the pace of a pokey old woman.' Lana felt certain the knife was helping him. He didn't seem winded or in pain.

The overhanging bows of Shadow's abnormally tall trees formed a canopy over the trail. In the fading daylight, Lana studied Jules discretely. How ironic that her former nightmare beast was a fine looking man. She had never stopped to picture the wolfhound in his human form, and even if she had, she wouldn't have imagined him this way. He was in his late twenties, she judged, and he had blue eyes, full, well-defined lips and a firm, square jaw. The slight bump on the bridge of his nose might have come from a smithing injury. His thick, light brown hair hung down to his collar and looked rather rakish, actually. He wasn't stunningly handsome, she decided, but he had the kind of rugged good looks that grew on you. His face said, *"Trust me,"* and you knew instinctively that you could.

When he turned his head to look at Folio, she tried to calculate his height. He was about three inches taller than she was. Not that it mattered, she told herself, but her heart was beating a little faster and she couldn't help but notice that his black suit couldn't hide his broad shoulders and powerful biceps. He really looked like a blacksmith. He could have stepped out of a historical romance novel, she thought with a faint smile. She reined in her thoughts and tried to concentrate on the men's conversation.

"She has her breghlin, the pythanium, and other monstrous creatures," Jules was saying. "Now she has alamaria. It won't be easy to defeat her."

"Alamaria overcame her restrictive device. Now I suppose she thinks it's her greatest asset and she can use it to conquer the Fair Lands." Folio gave a short, humorless laugh. "One's greatest asset can become one's greatest weakness."

Jules said, "Is that just a profound observation, or are you hinting you have a plan?"

Folio responded dryly, "You know me too well. I have a plan."

Lana glanced past Jules to look at Folio. The old man looked very pleased with himself.

"Out with it!" Jules commanded. "If I die of suspense, Lana will need to bring me back to life again."

She laughed and he looked at her and smiled.

"There will be time to discuss Sheamathan's defeat tomorrow when you're rested," Folio said fondly but firmly, as he would speak to a son. "It's an ambitious plan, but we can make it work."

"All right," Jules said with good-natured resignation. "It might be too much for me to grasp right now anyway."

It was getting dark and they needed to go slower and watch their step. Folio reached inside his robe and produced a large, clear crystalline gemstone. He cradled it in his palm and it began to glow bluish-white, lighting the path several feet ahead. Sheamathan had held a similar stone, Lana remembered—that night in the forest when Lana had first seen her. She was curious about the gem, but Folio had mentioned Sheamathan's restrictive device, and she was far more curious about that.

"You explained Jules's side of the bargain and I think I get the major points." She ticked them off on her fingers. "Incapable of gem powers. Only rational during the full moon. Unable to speak. As long as Sheamathan was alive, he'd be under the enchantment." She paused, "In exchange, Sheamathan agreed to stay out of the Fair Lands. Tell me more about her end of the bargain. You mentioned a restrictive device. What was it?"

"We weren't foolish enough to trust her," Jules said. "She would have double-crossed us."

Folio said with a note of pride, "Her side of the bargain required her to wear a device that would keep her from going through the portal. When she put it on and closed the device, I melded the ends using gem powers so it could never be removed."

Lana thought back to her meeting with Sheamathan. She didn't remember seeing something like that. "Where does she wear it? What does it look like?"

The bluish glow of the crystal illuminated Folio's face. He smiled and gave a little chuckle. "Jules and a gnome metalsmith made a necklace, like a collar. Particles from two Shadow gemstones are embedded in the metal. One makes the metal extremely hard, impervious to any tool. The other emits erratic bursts of energy." He paused. "I created a spell, you see, so the portal would detect and repel anything with that erratic energy signature. Until Sheamathan discovered alamaria, she couldn't overcome that repelling force and go through the portal."

How ironic! Lana burst out laughing. She tried to control herself but it was no use. Jules looked at her with a bemused expression. Folio just stared. When she finally got control of herself, she gasped, "Invisible fence!"

Both men gave her blank looks. Being from the 1800s, they had no idea what that was.

"Jules, you've been a dog too long!" she said, still laughing. "You made the woman a *dog collar!*" The men smiled faintly but still looked lost. "In my world, we have a way to confine pets," she explained. "It's called an invisible fence. You bury a wire underground, and as your pet approaches it, a transmitter sends a warning signal to your pet's collar. If the pet stubbornly keeps going, it gets a static charge that repels it. What you designed sounds a lot like that!"

"You're right, it *is* ironic," Jules said, grinning.

"Did Sheamathan assume she could get the collar off somehow?" Lana asked, smirking at the idea of the all-powerful woodspirit wearing a dog collar.

Folio rubbed his forehead and said with a wry smile, "I suppose so, but the power that seals the necklace is very effective. Even if she could cut through the collar without slitting her throat, the pieces would immediately meld themselves back together." He cleared his throat. "She never asked me to conspire with her, but maybe she thought I wouldn't *really* meld it shut."

Jules said. "If that's what she thought, she must have been very disappointed."

A gust of wind sent dry leaves and twigs tumbling along the path. The temperature was dropping. Lana zipped up her jacket and pulled the hood over her wind-blown hair.

"Our relationship since then has been strained but polite," Folio continued. The crystal's glow illuminated the toad-like texture of his skin. "I maintain the appearance of being her ally. When she summons me, I visit her. I've also gone uninvited so I could check on Jules." He lowered his voice to a conspiratorial tone. "We never discuss anything of importance. The object is to learn more from the other person than you reveal about yourself. She doesn't know the extent of my Shadow gem powers and I plan to keep it that way." He wrapped his arms about himself and drew his green robe tighter, as if gathering all his secrets and holding them close. "Sheamathan fears what she doesn't know, and what she can't control."

"With only a day to think over the bargain, it probably sounded like a great deal," Lana said. "Sheamathan probably assumed she'd eventually get the collar off or at least break through the repelling field."

"Both sides hoped to out-smart the other," Jules said with a rueful grin. "We thought *we* had an ace in the hole."

Lana gave him a puzzled look. "An ace in the hole?"

"An ace called your great-grandfather Henry."

She frowned in confusion. "Huh?"

Jules said, "You read the letters, so you know Elias was trapped in Shadow."

"Yes," she said slowly, wondering where this was headed.

"Elias couldn't go home to his son, but we hoped someday I could bring Henry to him." He paused to let that sink in. She stared blankly, still confused, because it wasn't that simple.

He went on, "Henry was twelve when Elias disappeared, and like his father, he was interested in gems. We expected Henry to develop at least a measure of his father's abilities. With that in mind, when I made my bargain with Sheamathan, I left all my Fair Lands gems, except the knife, with Elias. We were *so sure* Henry would be able to use them someday."

Folio said, "Our plan was that Jules would communicate with Henry, bring him to me, and together we would free Jules from his enchantment. Then the three of us would challenge Sheamathan."

Lana let out a groan, understanding now. She placed a sympathetic hand on Jules's arm. "But he *didn't* develop gem powers, so you couldn't communicate with him."

"Exactly," Jules said with a frustrated sigh. "Generations passed, and I tried to make contact with others, including your father and brothers. They had only a mild interest in gems and no aptitude for gem powers whatsoever." He looked down at her and their eyes met.

"Finally, I came along, and I had the powers you'd been waiting for, but I was afraid of you."

He nodded and looked away.

"I'm sorry," she said softly. "I really am." She squeezed his arm briefly. She had refused to listen to him that day in the forest, and she could still hear his howl of misery. Tears rolled down her face.

"I've done it again," Jules said gently, "I've made you cry."

"I was so afraid of you," she said in an agonized tone. "But I should have given you a chance to explain." He must think she was a blubbering idiot who cried over everything, but she couldn't stop the tears. "All those years you suffered. I could have helped you."

"Maybe this is the way it's supposed to be, the three of us working together."

Maybe so, but she'd feel better if he shouted at her and called her an idiot. She felt like such a coward, and a self-righteous coward at that. She had despised Folio for ignoring the gnomes' sufferings, but to be fair, she hadn't wanted to get involved, either. Hadn't she told herself that the gnomes weren't her problem? They weren't even human. Why should she care what happened to them? Eventually she had offered to help them, but she had wanted to do it on her own terms, and she had resented Raenihel for asking her to confront Sheamathan before she felt ready. Folio had screwed up. He'd been self-centered and manipulative, but over the years he'd had his redeeming moments. He'd even masterminded the bargain between Sheamathan and Jules. Why was she being so hard on him?

Stumbling over a rock, she shook off her uncomfortable thoughts and forced herself to concentrate on the trail. They were starting down a steep hill and the trail was getting narrower. Walking downhill would be easier and a nice change, she thought as she glanced at Jules. He hadn't complained, and he was keeping up all right, but the long hike had to be difficult for him and they still had a couple miles to go.

Folio moved into the lead, holding his crystal. She and Jules followed single-file, walking carefully and watching their footing. The forest felt less oppressive here than near the portal. The sky's silvery shimmer was a reminder that she was in a different land, but this area didn't seem so, well, creepy. If there were any unpleasant insects or animals in this part of the forest, she hadn't seen any. Maybe Folio's gem powers could keep them away. What would his home, Strathweed, be like? The name didn't sound very appealing, and she hoped it wasn't as bleak as the places Raenihel had taken her. She knew from Folio's letters that he lived in a cave. A lot of gnomes lived in caves, according to Raenihel, so caves must be fairly common.

The trail widened again. They walked silently three abreast for another half mile. Then Folio announced cheerfully, "Halfway there!"

By now she was tired and thirsty. "Let's take a break." If they had another mile and a half to go, she needed a drink. Folio and Jules stopped while she took off her backpack. "Is there someplace we can sit for a few minutes?"

"Maybe I can find a fallen log," Folio said, using his gem to illuminate the edge of the woods. "This way." He led them a few yards off the trail to a fallen tree. She sat with a groan. Part of her problem was the backpack. After a while it felt heavy. Rummaging through, she pulled out the canteen, pulled the stopper, and handed the canteen to Jules.

"No, you first," he insisted.

She drank her fill and passed it to Jules. He took a long drink and sighed contently. When it reached Folio, the old man stared at it wistfully and mumbled, "Fair Lands water." Then he closed his eyes and drank.

"Is water very different here?" she asked.

The old man took several more gulps and answered, "More minerals here. Probably healthy. In any case, you get used to it. I brought a flask of water," he said patting what must be the flask beneath his robe, "but yours is more palatable."

"How do you feel now?" she asked Jules.

He gave a careless shrug. "Fine. A little light-headed sometimes, but it passes. I'll be back to my old self after a good night's sleep."

"You're not in pain?"

"No. Right after you brought me back, I was, but I'm all right now."

They rested five or ten minutes and then returned to the trail. This leg of their journey took them across low, rolling hills. The trees were still tall with huge trunks, but Lana noticed several small clearings, and Folio's light revealed green groundcover that looked quite healthy.

When Folio announced, "Almost there!" she could have shouted for joy. It felt like the wee hours of the morning and she was totally drained. The shock of meeting Folio had taken a lot out of her, but that had been nothing compared with watching the wolfhound die and knowing that it was up to her to restore Jules and heal him.

They rounded a bend and Folio stopped. The light from his crystal illuminated another small hill with rocky outcroppings. "My cave is just ahead," he said with a childlike eagerness. "Jules has been here many times, but it will be new to you, Lana. Come along." He started off again. She and Jules hurried to catch up.

The mouth of his cave was about five feet across and four feet high. A grid-work of small branches, bound with leather thongs, served as a removable door. It probably kept out large animals, but not much else. Folio grasped the door and moved it aside. "Please come in."

Jules walked at Lana's side as Folio led them into the cave. Folio's gem sent light bounding around the cave, revealing minerals on its irregular surfaces.

"This network of caves goes a great distance." His voice bounced off the ceiling and echoed from the walls. He motioned for them to follow.

The cave widened and became higher. There was less evidence of water seepage here. A narrow passageway disappeared into the darkness. "That way leads to an underground stream," Folio said. To the right further back, a wide cleft opened into another part of the cave.

Lana had heard about famous caverns in the United States but had never been inside one. What a fascinating place. How strange to think that her ancestor lived in one in another world.

They stepped through the opening in the rear of the cave and Lana found herself in Folio's home. Blinking in surprise, she looked around in wonder. It was brighter here, thanks to Folio's ingenuity. Glowing, bluish-green lumps every few feet lined the perimeter, shedding light into the cave-room. She was too distracted to ask what they were. So many things fought for her attention; it was hard to take it all in.

"Gnome-made furnishings," Folio said, with a sweep of his arm. "Purchased in my early days here. Naturally, the books and such are from home."

The large, irregular cave contained a wealth of animal skin rugs, some scattered on the floor and others piled beside a chair. Freestanding shelves made of a dark wood held a large collection of books and ledgers as well as tools and pottery. A simple desk and chair, where Folio worked most of the time judging by the clutter, stood near the bookshelves. Gems and mineral samples covered two square tables near the desk.

Toward the center of the cave, four oversized wooden chairs sported tapestry pillows in muted shades of red, green and blue. By the wall, she saw a bed frame with a mattress made of ticking. On the right side of the cave was the typical gnome "fire"—stones that glowed but didn't give off smoke, and a few pottery crocks, probably filled with food. The overall vibe was comfortably bohemian.

"Welcome to Strathweed," Folio said with a touch of pride. "It may not be luxurious, but it's homey." His voice didn't echo as much here, probably due to the rugs and furnishings. "I'll bring you a cup of fialazza and something to eat, but after what we've been through, sleep will do us all the most good." He glanced about. "As you can see, I have plenty of animal skin rugs and pillows but only one bed. Normally I would offer my bed to the lady, but if she'll forgive me, Jules, I think you should sleep there tonight."

"I agree," Lana said hastily.

"That's not necessary. I can sleep on an animal skin," Jules protested.

"Don't argue," Lana said firmly as their eyes met. "I won't listen to your protests, and you know just how stubborn I can be."

Jules laughed and shrugged, giving in with good grace. "Yes, indeed I do."

"With that out of the way," Folio said cheerfully, "Grab a rug and we'll sit by the circle of stones."

After taking off her backpack and coat, Lana chose an animal skin with brown and tan zebra-like stripes, took it over to the glowing stones, and set it down by Folio's rug, which had shaggy, reddish-brown fur that reminded her of a mastodon hide. Jules set his knife on Folio's desk, and then sat beside Lana on a gray skin with large black spots.

"I'll be right there," Folio said.

He brought them root vegetables, greens, mushrooms, and pieces of dried meat mixed together in pottery bowls. Next he filled goblets with fialazza and then he sat and said, "Please eat. I hope you enjoy it."

While Lana ate, her eyes strayed to the cave's eerie lights. "What's the weird glowing stuff?" she asked Folio.

"Foxfire. Do you know what that is?"

She shook her head.

"It's also known as fairy fire. Isn't that a delightful name? A species of fungi in decaying wood creates the bioluminescence. The greenish-blue glow is actually an oxidative enzyme reaction."

"Fascinating," she said and meant it. She had always enjoyed science.

"I like the color. I find it soothing," Folio said with a shrug. "As you can see, I'm partial to green." He indicated his robe and smiled.

"So, you've been to Folio's cave quite a few times?" she asked Jules, trying to make conversation.

"Yes, as Elias explained, every full moon I became lucid. When my human mind returned I found myself in a dog's body, and I usually came here first, and then I went through the portal to check on the Amulet. Sometimes I kept going—into the Fair Lands." He paused, and his voice was a little shaky when he continued. "As time went on, I didn't age, but everyone I knew and loved passed away. The world I knew was gone." He smiled sadly and went on in a steadier voice, "Oddly enough, the one thing that never changed was Grayson Jewelers. The store survived the generations with very few changes."

Lana didn't know what to say. In Elias's case, he'd lost family and friends, but he had no one to blame but himself. She hadn't stopped to think about the consequences of Jules's disappearance. His parents must have been heart-broken. Perhaps he'd had brothers and sisters. A wife and children? A lump formed in her throat. "I'm so sorry," she murmured. "I can't imagine what you've been through."

Folio said, "I didn't try to stop Sheamathan in my early days when I might have had a chance. Once Jules was enchanted and our "ace in the hole" didn't work out, I can't tell you how miserable I felt." There was no mistaking the pain in his voice. "First I had lost my son, and then a dear friend, all because of my own poor choices. I became despondent. I didn't care about anyone or anything. I channeled my pain into further dark powers."

The thought of his wasted years was depressing. The harsh things Lana had planned to say to him a few days ago went out of her head. She didn't condone his experimenting on the gnomes or mistreating them, and he was responsible for Jules getting involved in the gnomes' conflict with Sheamathan, but Folio had suffered for what he had done and seemed truly sorry. If Jules could forgive him, who was she to hold a grudge?

She stared into her bowl. "I didn't mean to upset everyone by bringing up a depressing subject."

Folio said firmly, "None of us can hide from sorrow or mistakes."

"My nightmare is over at last, thanks to you, Lana," Jules said softly.

She could feel him looking at her but she kept her head down. After an eternity of tense silence, Folio said with forced cheerfulness, "Well, I'm about to call it a night. Eat up. I'll rinse the dishes. Then Lana and I will fight over the most comfortable animal skin rugs while Jules climbs into my comfortable bed."

As tired as she was, she was sure she'd have no trouble sleeping. She would have to sleep in her shirt and khakis, she realized. Tomorrow she'd definitely need a bath. Maybe she'd bathe in the underground stream.

After piling three animal skins on top of one another, she took a pillow from one of Folio's chairs and lay down. Folio brought her a woven green cloth to use as a top sheet. She took a last look around the cave room and snuggled into the rugs. Until recently, she'd led a pretty boring life, she told herself with a faint smile.

Clearly, those days were over.

Chapter 29

When Lana woke and opened her eyes, it took a moment to recognize her unfamiliar surroundings. *Strathweed. Folio's cave.*

Maybe it was because no outside sounds could penetrate this far, but she had slept soundly, even on the floor. These animal skins were surprisingly comfortable, she thought as she stroked the dense fur. And they smelled faintly of herbs, maybe from Folio's cooking. Rolling onto her back, she listened to see if anyone was awake. Deep, even breathing came from behind her, probably Jules. She didn't hear anyone else, so Folio might be up.

She yawned deeply and stretched, then threw back the green cover and lay staring at the ceiling. Yesterday had been a day to remember. She had met her ancestor Elias, brought a man back from the brink of death, walked three miles through a forest in another world, and had dinner in a cave with an underground river. Yes, it had been a remarkable day. Today would probably be just as remarkable. They needed to find a way to overthrow Sheamathan—a being with gem powers who had destroyed the gnome world and set herself up as queen, and wanted to rule Lana's world now. It all sounded pretty crazy.

Lana glanced toward the cave entrance as Folio entered from the outer cave carrying a plate of food. He must have been cooking outdoors. Whatever he'd made for breakfast, it smelled wonderful and she was really hungry. *Rats! He won't have coffee! I'll have to do without!*

She sat up and looked around. Jules was sleeping soundly on Folio's bed, with a green cloth pulled up to his chin. Sleep would help him recover, so the longer he slept, the better. She studied his face while he slept. It was still hard to believe that this man had been the wolfhound—the nightmare beast that had terrified her. Would she ever get used to the idea? There was nothing terrifying about him now. Whenever he smiled his whole face lit with warmth and good humor. His penetrating blue eyes shifted in an instant from hard and determined to patient and kind. She felt drawn to him, but he probably had that effect on a lot of people.

Getting to her feet, she looked down at her rumpled khaki pants and brown knit shirt. She looked like she'd slept on a cave floor. Oh, wait. She smiled inwardly, plucked bits of fur off her clothes, and dusted herself off. Hopefully she smelled better than she looked. Taking the hairbrush from her backpack, she pulled it through her tangled waves. *I'd give my right arm for a shower right now.* As quietly as possible so she wouldn't wake Jules, she walked to the glowing stones where Folio sat with his back to her, drinking something from a pottery mug.

"I don't suppose that's coffee," she whispered.

He jumped and looked over his shoulder, startled but clearly happy to see her. "I'm sorry, it's not. But it's very good. Would you like some?"

She was about to ask, "What is it?" but did it matter? Right now, any dark, steaming liquid would do as a coffee substitute. "Sure. I'll try some. Thanks." She sat down beside him, sharing his animal skin rug.

A covered cast iron pot sat on the circle of stones. A tray on the stone floor held steel knives and forks, pottery mugs, plates and a pitcher. He poured the steaming liquid with a flourish and handed her the mug. The aroma was promising. She took a sip and smiled. The flavor was bold but not bitter, and the intensity gave her a pleasant jolt. Suddenly her day seemed brighter. She sighed contentedly. "It's good, whatever it is." She let the steam bathe her face.

"I'm glad you like it. It's the closest thing we have to coffee—roasted rakka root. When I make it strong I don't notice the minerals in the water."

"Where I live, people pay for mineral water. This tastes fine."

"I have rakka in the morning," he said, combing his beard with his fingers. "The rest of the day I drink tea made from herbs."

She took another sip. *I wonder how Greg and Jordy are? They always eat breakfast with me. I hope they're all right.* She hadn't thought about them since leaving home. "I need some advice about dark gem powers," she said abruptly.

Folio's hand jerked. Rakka splashed on his robe and he gave a little yelp. She hadn't stopped to think how that request would sound. He looked visibly shaken.

"No!" she exclaimed, waving a hand to erase the false impression. "I don't want to *use* dark powers; I want to *undo* them. For my friends."

His shoulders sagged with relief. "Ah," he said, letting out a long breath, "in that case, perhaps I can help. Tell me the situation."

"It's a long story, but I was rescued from the dungeon by a gnome—with the help of two teenage boys Sheamathan turned into giant talking rats."

Folio grimaced, "Rats have been a favorite at Shadowglade, lately."

Folio didn't need to know they had tried to steal the knife, so she left out that part of the story. "Breghlin were chasing the rat-boys, so Raenihel and I took them through the portal, and now they're living in my apartment."

It took a moment for her words to register. Then Folio threw back his head and laughed. Belatedly, he covered his mouth, glancing toward the bed. After a moment he whispered, "My dear, you're a wonder!" He set down his mug. "Remind me to never drink hot beverages when you're talking to me." Then he turned serious. "I can undo their enchantment if that's what you're asking."

"It's different from what Sheamathan did to Jules?"

"Yes, completely."

"Great! What a relief!" She could hardly wait to give Greg and Jordy the good news. "I know we have more pressing problems right now, but I'm glad to hear you can help!"

"Sheamathan doesn't know this," Folio said in a confidential tone, "but I've helped a few poor souls like those boys."

Lana leaned toward him. "Really?"

He nodded. "Now and then I find an enchanted creature near the portal. They don't know how to get home, but they remember the woods where they came through, so they often return there."

"I'm sure they'd rather go home enchanted than not go home at all," she said, "but it's wonderful that you could restore them to human form."

"Yes. There's no worse fate than having one's mind trapped in an animal's body."

She couldn't argue with that. Was it worse to be like Greg and Jordy who lived their daily lives knowing they were enchanted, or to 'come to' once a month like Jules and discover it over and over? Lana said, "After you helped some of Sheamathan's victims escape, didn't she wonder what became of them?"

"They're worthless, inferior beings, quickly forgotten," Folio said in a tone dripping with sarcasm. "She turns them into whatever amuses her at the moment and they're left to survive however they can. Most get eaten by wild animals."

Lana shivered. Thinking back, Greg and Jordy had said the same thing.

They had been so engrossed in their conversation that Jules's cheerful, "Good morning!" caught them both by surprise.

"Have a seat, dear fellow!" Folio said with his usual gregarious charm. "We waited breakfast for you."

Jules sat down by Folio. Lana tried not to stare. His black trousers and white shirt looked as rumpled as her own clothing, his hair was tousled, and he needed a shave. His blue eyes were clear and bright, though, and his cheeks glowed with healthy color after a good night's sleep.

Folio opened the cast iron pot to let out the steam. As he reached for a plate, he said in an elaborately casual tone, "Lana and I were just discussing the two young men living in her apartment."

Lana stiffened at Folio's choice of words and glanced at Jules. His eyes widened in surprise, and then he quickly looked away. "Is that so," he said awkwardly.

She felt her face flush. "No—um, they're not exactly young men."

Folio calmly filled Jules's plate, handed it to him, and then served Lana. She took her plate, but she barely noticed what was on it.

"True, the young men aren't quite themselves at the moment," Folio agreed vaguely. He left it at that, dished his own breakfast, and then glanced innocently at Lana. "How's your breakfast?"

She looked daggers at him. He gave her the ghost of a smile and she noticed the twinkle in his eye. He'd done this on purpose, she realized. Apparently the old man had a perverse sense of humor. "Orelia eggs are very tasty," he advised meekly with his mouth full.

When she looked down at her plate, giant orangey yolks surrounded by cream-colored egg whites stared back like two accusing eyes.

If I don't say anything, Jules will think what he's thinking now. If I defend myself, he'll know I care what he thinks. "At the moment, they're not young men. They're, um, giant talking rats," she finished. Staring down at her plate, she took a big bite of yolk and chewed savagely.

"Giant rats," he repeated with a trace of amusement. She looked up and met his eyes.

Folio finally intervened. "You see, Lana couldn't turn the rats back into boys, but she *could* rescue them from Shadowglade. She and her gnome friend took them through the portal."

"They couldn't go home as giant rats," she said with a helpless shrug. "I didn't know what else to do with them, so I took them home."

Jules's blue eyes sparkled and it looked like he was trying not to laugh. "I'll bet they make, ah, interesting companions."

"That's for sure!" It was a relief to clear up the misunderstanding. Everything she knew about Jules from reading the letters, well, he was a decent, honest sort of man. Of course she cared what he thought of her. Why make a bad impression? Returning to her rapidly cooling breakfast, she dug into the ostrich-sized eggs. What did an orelia look like? Maybe it was better not to know.

"Lana will bring the rats to the portal and I'll restore them," Folio said. "It's the least I can do, considering they helped her escape from the dungeon." He paused, fork in hand, and turned to her. "By the way, I would like to hear about your thrilling escape."

"I'm sorry I couldn't be any help," Jules said, looking embarrassed.

"Clearly she managed just fine without you," Folio replied with a shrug. "More rakka, Lana dear?"

She held out her cup. This rakka stuff was really good. Almost as good as coffee. After taking another gulp, she launched into her tale. "At first I tried to get on the good side of my guards. It worked, sort of, until they put a wounded gnome in the cell next to mine. He was in a lot of pain, but I managed to heal him." She looked at Jules and added, "I used your knife."

"There you go, Jules," Folio said in a satisfied tone, "a precedent that she could heal you. No sooner was your knife in her hand than she was using its gem powers to heal people. You needn't have worried."

"Who said I was worried?"

Lana hid a smile. "When the guards asked the gnome what happened to the cuts and bruises, he admitted I'd healed him. Sheamathan heard the story and of course she was upset, so she switched head guards. The new guard was afraid of me."

Folio said, "Breghlin are afraid of gem powers."

"Later, a giant beetle dropped through an air vent and attached itself to my bars. I tried to drive it away, but all I did was make it mad. Things went from bad to worse." She shivered at the memory and looked at Jules who seemed fascinated with her story. "Eventually, I fried it with your knife. All that was left was a beetle-shaped cinder."

"Bravo!" Folio said in delight.

Jules broke into a slow grin. "I'm impressed."

"After seeing what I did to the beetle, the new guard was more afraid of me than before. Long story short, right after that, my gnome friend Raenihel showed up with the rat-boys he'd met in the cellar. The three of them crawled through air passageways to find me."

Folio stroked his beard. "Finding you was one thing, but getting you out was quite another, I imagine."

She tucked a lock of wavy hair behind her ear and smiled. "We tricked the guard. Raenihel and the rats who were up in the air vent pretended to be powerful spirits from my world that had come to help me." Jules and Folio exchanged glances, smiling at the ploy. "After that, I told the guard I'd spare his life if he escorted me out of the dungeon."

Folio let out a hoot of laughter. "Spare his life indeed! Utterly amazing!"

Jules laughed and looked at her with frank admiration. "Who besides you would think of such a thing?"

She shrugged, feeling her face flush, and said lightly, "Probably no one. I can't resist a long shot."

"Good," Folio said. He cleared his throat meaningfully. "Then you'll appreciate my plan to overthrow Sheamathan."

She looked into Folio's green eyes and thought rather than said, *You know the saying, a chip off the old block. Well, I'm looking at the block, and I'm pretty sure I'm the chip.*

Folio gave her a sly smile and a wink.

Jules poured himself a mug of rakka and said to Folio, "Speaking of which, I'm rested now. You promised to tell me your plan."

"So I did, so I did," the old man agreed, nodding. He set aside his empty plate and folded his age-spotted hands. "The plan involves alamaria."

"Alamaria," Jules repeated, running a hand over his stubbly chin. "The stone that amplifies Sheamathan's powers."

"It does so on *her* side of the portal," Folio said, smiling enigmatically. "On the Fair Lands side—" He paused. "We'll need to bury a quantity on the Fair Lands side."

Lana's face spread in an appreciative smile. She understood what Folio was trying to do. "On our side, it blocks power. We'll have an advantage."

Folio looked at her in surprise.

"I found the stone you buried."

"So that's where it went," he said, the corners of his eyes crinkling with laughter. "And you've conducted your own experiments."

She nodded, suddenly worried. "It will block *our* powers, too."

Jules listened to the exchange. It didn't take him long to get up to speed. "You're saying that in *our* world, alamaria blocks power. So, if we bury it, Sheamathan will step through the portal, lose her powers, and she won't know why."

"Yes, good points, both of you." Folio sounded pleased. "Lana, you're right. Our powers will be gone, too." He rubbed his hands together. "But we'll plan accordingly." He looked at Jules. "As you have pointed out, Sheamathan will lose her powers but she won't know why. And she won't know *we* have lost *ours*." Folio paused to let the implications sink in. "So, we'll have a befuddled, powerless woodspirit and a short window of opportunity to take advantage of that. We won't need gem powers to subdue her, but we *will* need to neutralize her, because as soon as we go beyond alamaria's influence, all of us will regain our powers."

"Neutralize her? How?" Jules asked.

"I plan to use a powerful sedative made from local plants."

Jules muttered, "If that doesn't work, I'll use my knife, and I won't need its gem powers."

"Eventually she'll wake up. Then what do we do?" Lana asked. "We can't let her go back to Shadow and regain her powers."

"I've been thinking about that, and assuming we're successful, I have something in mind," Folio said. "We shouldn't be over-confident, though. Remember, we won't have powers. She might come through the portal with breghlin. We should have armed gnomes on hand, just in case."

"Wouldn't Sheamathan wonder why we didn't just use our powers against her?" Lana asked.

"Possibly, but I'd rather reveal we're powerless than be killed by breghlin. While she's confused and vulnerable, we'll attack and sedate her."

"It may be over before she knows what's happening," Jules said.

"Where will we get all the alamaria?" Lana asked. "Greg and Jordy told me the mine is heavily guarded and not easily accessible."

"I can get us down to the mine undetected," Folio said, looking pleased with himself. "We'll liberate a few gnomes to carry alamaria to the portal. Later, when this is all over, we'll set the others free."

Lana said, "The gnomes Sheamathan captured from Raenihel's clan could help us. They'd be honored, and I'd like to get them out of there as soon as possible."

"I have no objection if we can find them without too much trouble." Folio stood. "Now, we need to address more mundane matters. Jules, I have shirts and pants that should fit you." He looked down at his robe. "I seldom wear anything but green robes in Strathweed, but I have plenty of sturdy gnome-made garments. Lana, I assume you came with a change of clothing, but you'd probably like some soap and water, maybe a washbasin. I can show you the underground stream. The current isn't swift and the water isn't deep—maybe three feet in the center—but it's very cold. Or, there's a natural spring near my cave, but no doubt that's just as cold."

She stood, grateful for the chance to wash. Her backpack held a change of clothing, soap and shampoo. Any source of water would do. "An underground stream sounds fascinating. I'll give it a try."

"I'll get a towel and washbasin. If the water proves too cold to submerge yourself, you can resort to the basin. I'll walk you down, and then I'll round up clothing for Jules."

He left to gather supplies and she went to get her backpack. A subterranean river, she thought, shaking her head in amazement. And she was going to bathe there.

With his crystalline gem to light the way, Folio led her through the outer cave and into the passageway. "I have a spare lightgem you can use to find your way back." His voice echoed in the smaller space. The passageway sloped downward, but it wasn't steep. "It's not far. You'll hear the water in a minute."

True to his word, as soon as they rounded a bend she heard the distinct sound of splashing water. Only a little farther, and Folio stopped. As he held up his lightgem and moved his arm in a wide arc, Lana stared in wonder at the eerily beautiful, primitive scene. A river flowed through a low-ceilinged cave. It emerged from utter darkness on her left, apparently coming from around a bend, and on her right it disappeared between two boulders and an overhanging ledge. Chunks of rock had broken free from the ceiling and fallen into the streambed, and the river splashed unperturbed around them. Mineral deposits, here as elsewhere, coated the walls. The water looked perfectly clear, and the stream's relentless journey through the dimly lit cave was almost enough to hypnotize her.

Folio broke in on her thoughts, speaking over the sound of flowing water. "I bathe here daily, so I'm impervious to the cold. I suppose you'll find it shocking."

She enjoyed a challenge. The underground river called to her. She would conquer it. "At home they have something called the Polar Bear

Plunge," she told him. "In the winter, a bunch of crazy people in swimsuits run down the beach and plunge into the ocean. It's usually done as a fundraiser for charity."

"Extraordinary," Folio said. "Have you tried it?"

"Once. That was enough!"

He smiled. "Don your polar bear fur and try my river." He set the supplies on the cave floor and took a lightgem from his pocket. Once it began to glow, he set it on her towel. "Good luck."

She stared at the river for a few minutes after he was gone, working up her courage. A hot shower was more her speed, but this could be fun. She peeled off her clothing down to her underwear, and then walked to the edge of the river and stuck her toes in.

Yep, cold. Very cold. But not as cold as Polar Bear Plunge. I can do this.

With a shout like a battle cry, she dashed into the stream and dropped to her knees, letting the water flow over her. Cold! Yes, breathtakingly cold but exhilarating! A little exhilaration went a long way, though. In a couple minutes she'd had enough, and waded out to get shampoo and soap. Brief intervals, in and out, would be the way to survive this, she decided. First her hair, then her body. Wash, retreat. Rinse, retreat.

When she stepped out of the water for the last time and toweled herself dry, every cell of her body tingled. She had never felt so alive. The air felt chilly enough to be grateful for dry clothing, though, so she dressed hurriedly and brushed her hair.

I'll leave the unused basin for our rugged blacksmith. A devious grin spread across her face. *Will he be tough enough for Polar Bear Plunge?*

When she reached the inner cave, Folio and Jules stood talking. A towel and a pile of clothes sat on a nearby chair. Folio looked up with a twinkle in his eye and said, "Did your polar bear fur keep you warm enough?"

She set down the backpack and replied nonchalantly, "Yes. After you're in for a while and get used to it, the water feels cool and refreshing. I really enjoyed it."

Jules's expression said he didn't get the polar bear joke, but he understood she had bathed in the river.

"Oh," she said, glancing at Jules with a faint smile. "I left the wash basin there." Her smile widened. "In case the river is too cold for you."

Jules drew himself up to his full height and said, "A refreshing dip in the river sounds wonderful." He picked up his clothing and towel and started toward the outer cave. Folio, clearly holding back laughter, gave Lana a knowing smile as he turned to follow Jules. She was sure her answering smile looked a lot like Jordy's disturbing rat grin.

When Jules returned, Lana and Folio broke off their conversation. Folio took one look at Jules, winked at Lana, and asked in an innocent tone, "How was the water, Jules?"

Shivering visibly, Jules strode across the cave. He wore Folio's tan trousers and a rust colored shirt. The pants were a bit short and a couple inches too big at the waist, but the shirt fit fine.

"I won't lie to you. It was cold," he said. "Bitterly cold!" His teeth chattered as he dumped everything on the chair. He rubbed his hands briskly and gave Lana an odd look. "Are you an amphibian?"

She laughed. How refreshing! He had admitted defeat and acknowledged her superiority. Most men wouldn't. He could have forced a smile and pretended the water was fine.

"It's the Grayson family genes," Folio said, chuckling. "We're a hearty clan."

"Apparently so," Jules muttered.

She had only survived the freezing water by wading in and out and wrapping herself in the towel between plunges. But she couldn't bring herself to admit that.

"I'm going out to pick some fresh greens. After lunch, we'll decide if we're rested enough to walk to the mines." Folio bustled off, leaving her and Jules to stare at each other in awkward silence.

Why did Jules make her feel shy and awkward? She hoped it didn't show.

"You should probably hold healing gems or your knife for a while," she said. "It's not every day a man comes back from the brink of death." If she wasn't mistaken, she wasn't the only one who felt shy. Hitching up his too-large pants, he glanced at her and then ran a hand through his damp hair. "Yes, good idea." He smoothed his shirt and tucked it in better, as if concerned how he looked in Elias's hand-me-downs.

"I'm going to use gems for strength and courage," she said as she walked away to get her gem pouch. He must find it strange to be a man again, and now, here he was, hanging out with the woman who had always been afraid of him.

She sat down in one of Folio's comfortable chairs. Jules got his knife and took the chair next to her. Wrapping his fingers around the hilt, he leaned his head back and closed his eyes.

It was hard to concentrate on gems. She stole a few glances at him, reminding herself that here sat the legendary Challenger. Things might not have worked out the way he and Folio had wanted, but the bargain he'd made with Sheamathan had confined her to Shadow for generations. That made him a hero in Lana's eyes. After a few minutes she asked, "How could you speak in my head when you were a dog? You weren't holding any gems."

He opened his eyes and looked over at her. "In Shadow, when you hold gems, your body becomes infused with their powers. Since Elias knew I would need to communicate, he transferred infused telepathic powers to me before I turned into the wolfhound."

"I thought infused powers wear off."

"They do. Folio had to renew the infusion, and quite honestly, it never came easily to me—speaking telepathically."

She had always tried to block his thoughts. "Can you still do it? Now that you're human?"

"I suppose so."

"Try."

He held her eyes, a faint smile on his face. *Lana is an amphibian.*

She burst out laughing.

"Folio routinely reads our thoughts. I've gotten used to it," he said with a shrug. "My private thoughts aren't very interesting, so I really don't care, but I consider it an intrusion."

"Yes, it's creepy. A few of my thoughts about him he probably wishes he'd never heard."

"If so he has only himself to blame. I'd only use telepathy with permission, or in an emergency."

"You have my permission. What am I thinking?" She stared into his eyes and concentrated.

Jules let out a bark of laughter and exclaimed reproachfully, "You devil!"

"What was I thinking?"

"The river was freezing!"

They both laughed. "You don't know how much better I feel hearing that," he confessed, grinning.

"I don't know what got into me. It was a mean trick, but I couldn't resist."

"I've recovered from worse wounds than wounded pride," he said good-naturedly.

"You certainly have."

He switched the knife to his other hand and fell silent, and she went back to using her gems, but now and then she felt him looking at her.

Folio returned with a basket of greens and smiled broadly when he saw Lana and Jules sitting together.

"We're infusing gem powers," Jules announced, as if he needed to explain.

"Good idea. You both need to regain your strength."

Jules sat forward in his chair. "I feel much better after a good night's sleep and that bracing plunge in the river. I believe I'm ready to travel today." He looked at Lana. "It's time someone besides Lana had an adventure with my knife."

Chapter 30

Folio knelt on the cave floor and tied a rope around a roll of burlap bags. "These bags are ideal for carrying supplies," he said. "Fortunately, I seldom throw anything away. The moment I do, I find a use for it." He attached additional ropes so someone could wear it as a backpack.

Lana studied Folio while he worked. He looked quite different today, dressed in a gray, long-sleeved shirt and pants instead of his green robe—less powerful and mysterious, she thought. He wore moccasin type shoes and a black leather pouch on a sturdy woven cord around his waist.

"I refilled your canteen." Folio handed Lana the canteen and something wrapped in brown paper. "Dried meat," he said in answer to her questioning look. "Do you have room in your backpack?"

"Sure, plenty of room." She packed the food and slipped the backpack over her shoulders.

"I believe we're ready," Folio said. "We'll hike at a slow, comfortable pace. I don't want either of you worn out before we're there."

The men took the lead. Jules wore the Challenger's blade tucked into his belt and the roll of burlap bags on his back. Lana was content to follow a few paces behind and she studied her surroundings as they walked.

Strathweed looked different by daylight, almost cheerful. This must be one of the areas that had escaped the worst of the blight, or else Folio had used gem powers to heal the land around his home. The low, rolling hills with their rocky outcroppings didn't look forbidding under a blue, sunny sky. The air held none of the stench of decay she had noticed elsewhere. She could almost forget that Sheamathan had turned most of Shadow into a grim, depressing land full of diseased plants and mutant animals.

Field grasses grew in the rocky soil. One particularly kind dominated the terrain. It stood over two feet high. Sprays of tiny greenish-yellow flowers drooped languidly from its tips. It was quite pretty, she thought with a smile. "Folio, what's this?"

He looked over his shoulder and she pointed.

"It's a weed," he answered, "and very common around here as you can see."

"Does it have a name?"

"Yes, Strath. Strath Weed."

She laughed. So that explained it. He lived in a place named after a flowering weed. Maybe he had a softer side after all.

Rocky ground soon gave way to low, rolling hills. The land still looked reasonably healthy here. Widely spaced trees let in enough sunlight for low, dense plants to grow among the trees.

Farther on they walked through small clearings. The groundcover, which resembled ivy, reminded her of home, and there were lots of shrubs with dark red berries, but the berries might be poisonous, so she resisted the impulse to eat any.

After about a mile, tall, thin saplings rose up amid the gnarled, old trees and prickly undergrowth encroached onto the trail.

At last they came to the long, steep hill she remembered from last night. Today, they'd be walking up it. She wiped beads of perspiration from her forehead and assessed the steep incline with a mental groan. The air had grown uncomfortably hot and humid, but at least there was a breeze.

So far, conversation had been at a minimum, so when Folio spoke in his deep, commanding voice, Lana looked up with a start.

"At the top of the hill we'll veer off the trail and make a beeline for the alamaria mine which lies behind Shadowglade. The direct route, although more difficult, will save us at least two miles."

"Sounds like a good trade-off," Lana said, brushing strands of wind-blown hair from her face as she hurried to catch up with the men.

Jules said, "I used to come to Strathweed by a similar route."

Folio reached out and drew Jules to a halt. "At the top of the hill we'll rest and drink some water. Are you all right? How are you feeling?"

"Fine. I think I'm back to normal."

"I wonder if Sheamathan knows you're gone yet," Lana said, hitching up her backpack.

Jules turned to Lana. "If not, she will soon. At the end of the full moon, I always return to her throne room and sit at her feet, looking up at her mocking face, and then mercifully, my canine mind takes over."

Lana shuddered. "Thank goodness that's over now. You're free of her." How had he kept his sanity through that endless cycle of torment? Few people would subject themselves to that, even to save their world.

As they started up the hill, Jules dropped back to walk with her. "Sheamathan won't expect me to break the enchantment. When I don't come back, she'll probably think I'm lost or injured. It may be a long time before she figures out what really happened."

"I disagree," Folio said over his shoulder. "I think she'll figure it out sometime tomorrow."

"Tomorrow! Why tomorrow?" Lana asked, completely baffled.

Folio answered her question with a question. "When a dozen gnomes disappear from the mines tonight, who do you suppose she'll blame?"

"Incompetent guards?" Lana suggested weakly.

"Gnomes have never escaped before, although they have tried, on their own and with help. Anyone who can whisk away a dozen gnomes without alerting the guards must have extraordinary gem powers— powers most would call magic. Certainly that narrows the field of rescuers."

Yes, that made sense. According to Raenihel, his clansmen had tried unsuccessfully to rescue gnomes from the mining camps. If a dozen gnomes disappeared one night, Sheamathan would assume that gem powers were involved. "Won't she think *you* did it?" she asked Folio.

"I've never intervened before," he called back. "That, and the fact that her wolfhound is suddenly missing may be enough to indict Jules."

Jules said, "Lana has powers. What about her?"

Lana considered briefly. "I don't think I'd be her first guess. I met with her on the gnomes' behalf, delivered their message and went home. She knows that. Her breghlin followed me to the portal looking for your knife. That was a month ago."

Jules shrugged. "Well, if I were her, I wouldn't rule you out, but Elias may be right that I'm the prime suspect. Sheamathan knows I routinely check your side of the portal. I've seen the blight, so I know she's outwitted her restrictive device." He kicked a stone from the trail and frowned thoughtfully.

Folio said, "There's no reason to keep your part of the bargain now that she's broken hers. Naturally, you'd try to break your enchantment."

Lana nodded. "You disappear, and a dozen gnomes escape. It could be a coincidence, but not likely." They walked in silence and then something occurred to her. "Considering the camp is full of gnomes, why would someone only rescue twelve of them? Won't Sheamathan think that's odd?"

"Probably. And she hates mysteries," Jules said with a wry smile. "I almost feel sorry for her. She's on a losing streak. She lost you before she learned anything useful about you. She lost the Challenger's blade, which she wanted so no one could use it against her. She lost me, and now she's about to lose a dozen gnomes."

Lana laughed. "You forgot another loss—Folio. He's helping us, so she's lost him, too."

"True," Folio said. He slowed and turned to them. "I'm her only listening ear, so losing me will be a devastating loss, I assure you. Whenever I visit, she spends the first hour recounting every idiotic thing the breghlin have done since my last visit." He put on a long-suffering expression and smoothed his gray beard. "I make sympathetic comments at regular intervals, so she thinks I'm still listening. The breghlins' lack of ingenuity and witless blunders drive her mad, but she's stuck with them. A more intelligent race would question her orders and rebel against her cruelty, and she's well aware of that."

The group continued up the hill. The mention of breghlin made Lana think about the dungeon. The breghlin were lawless savages, but Grace, Ferdinand, Wally and the gang weren't as vicious as some of the others. Maybe there was hope for them.

Her legs had begun to ache from the steep incline, and it was still a long way to the mine. She stopped to massage her calves. Jules waited for her. "Do you hike much at home?" he asked. "You don't even look tired."

She straightened and started to walk again, more pleased than she cared to admit that he showed an interest in her. "Yes, I like to hike. It's relaxing and gives me time to think." She gave him a sidelong glance. "On the other hand, maybe I should find a safer hobby. Hiking through County Forest Park got me *here*."

"One way or another, you were destined to come here."

"Destiny," she said with a sniff. "I've never believed in it."

"I believe events happen to us when we are uniquely qualified to fulfil a purpose. Call it what you will."

She gave him a long look. She had never thought of it that way.

"You were uniquely qualified to break my enchantment. I needed your help, and I couldn't afford to give up, even though my attempts to speak to you as a wolfhound upset you."

"You're nothing if not persistent," she agreed, giving him a slight grin to soften her words.

A hint of amusement crossed his face. "I can be just as stubborn as you, when I need to be."

When they reached the top of the hill, they found a spot to sit that was free of stones and weeds with thorns.

"Our hike will be more difficult once we leave the trail," Folio said brushing dust off his sleeves and pant legs, "but our object is to reach the mines before dark and assess the situation."

Lana opened her canteen and took a drink, glad she wasn't responsible for their plan. They needed to spirit away a dozen gnomes as well as sacks full of alamaria without alerting the guards. Not an easy task, but Folio seemed to think they could pull it off. She ran a hand over her forehead, wiping away a film of sweat. She had hoped to include Gliaphon in this mission but she realized the more she thought about it that it would be too risky to search for him. They needed to get in and out as quickly as possible.

"Do you think there will be a lot of guards?" Jules asked Folio.

"Actually, no," he said, and Lana looked at him in surprise. "Particularly not on the cliff," he added. "Mining operations stop before sundown. Most guards go home, especially the ones on the cliff. That's why I went in the evening to spy on the mine and collect alamaria samples."

"Why are there fewer guards in the evening?" she asked. "Wouldn't it be easier for gnomes to escape at night?"

"When you see the mine, you'll understand. The gnomes never leave the open pit where they mine the stone. Breghlin haul up the alamaria in a large bag-like carrier made of woven rope. At the end of the day, they haul up the carrier for the last time and it stays on top of the cliff." He spread his hands. "So how can the gnomes escape? They can't scale the cliff, so there's no need for a lot of guards. One or two are stationed on the cliff by the equipment, and a few in the mining camp below."

"So it should be fairly easy to rescue the gnomes," she said. "That sounds too good to be true."

Folio waved a hand, "I wouldn't call it easy, but it's better than attempting the plan during mining hours."

"So, how do we get down to the mine?"

"We'll use the winch and carrier to get down to the camp, and then we'll find our dozen gnomes and bring them up, three or four at a time. This procedure is not without its challenges. Chains and pulleys make a lot of noise." He stood and put out a hand to help her up, as if not wanting to dwell on the dangers and anxious to be off.

"So, the guards will hear us," she said as she stood. "How can we keep our rescue mission a secret?" She put on her backpack and looked at him expectantly.

"With Fair Lands powers on your end and Shadow powers on mine," he said, and she wondered if he was really as confident as he sounded.

Jules, who had listened silently until now said, "Someone will have to stay on the cliff and operate the winch."

Folio didn't answer. He took out his pocket watch and checked it, and then he started walking. "Yes, it will take two people to pull up our cargo," he said as he crossed the trail and started into the woods. "You and I will remain on the cliff."

Jules charged after Folio. "Send Lana down to the mine *alone?*"

She was surprised, too, but it made sense. It didn't take physical strength to find the gnomes, but it did to haul them up. She plowed through the underbrush, trying to keep up.

"We will be watching from above," Folio said firmly. "And as we know, Lana is very resourceful."

"Yes, she is," Jules sputtered, "but gathering alamaria and a dozen gnomes while avoiding capture seems like a lot to ask."

With a strange sense of detachment, she listened to their debate. Imagine, giving *her* the hardest part of the mission. Folio must have a lot of confidence in her abilities, which was nice, but a little unsettling. She would do whatever he asked. Sure, she was afraid. Who wouldn't be? Going down there alone with no backup if something went wrong *was* pretty risky. They'd be watching from the cliff but unless Folio's gem powers worked from a distance he couldn't protect her.

"She may only need to collect the gnomes," Folio said. "The alamaria may be waiting on the cliff."

"Twelve bags worth?" Jules protested in a tone that said Folio was either wildly optimistic or delusional. "A few rocks may fall off a cart, but we need a lot more than that."

Lana ducked under a low-hanging branch and skirted a bush covered with thorns. Jules crashed through thistly shrubs and underbrush, without even trying to sweep them aside.

"I've studied their operation," Folio explained patiently, walking slower so Jules could catch up. "Usually, they leave the last load of the day on the ground, and the cart hauls it away in the morning."

She supposed her job would be easier if she only had to worry about gnomes.

"All right. So, maybe she won't need to bring up alamaria, just gnomes," Jules said irritably. "It's still dangerous. Especially alone."

"I don't deny that, nevertheless, it's the only way."

It felt odd to be the topic of debate. Folio had already made up his mind and it was obvious that he wouldn't back down. Why argue?

Jules made an exasperated noise and muttered something under his breath that she couldn't make out. He slowed his pace enough for her to catch up and she walked alongside him.

"Will you lend me your knife when I go?" she asked, hoping he wouldn't be angry.

He gave her a fierce glance. "Yes, of course. But I'd rather go, myself." He swept an intruding branch aside with more violence than necessary. It broke with a sharp snap.

She understood his annoyance. She was about to play the starring role in yet another adventure with his knife. But she didn't think his protests were all about male pride. The concern in his voice suggested he felt protective of her. She felt unaccountably pleased at that thought.

They walked at least five miles through the pathless wilderness. With every mile the blight grew more severe. The forest was mostly standing dead wood, and the trees, shrubs and groundcover that was still alive looked unhealthy. It was depressing. At least Folio's shortcut avoided the dangerous regions she had traveled with Raenihel—like the pythanium feeding ground.

She knew they were nearing Shadowglade when there were no more trees, and miles of dry, cracked land stretched out ahead. The familiar reddish soil soon covered her already-dirty sneakers and filled every crease in her khakis. Red dirt invaded her nose, ears, and mouth, and filled every exposed pore. It felt disgusting, but on the bright side, she supposed red dirt was the perfect natural camouflage.

They turned their backs to the wind and stopped a moment to rest. "We'll be there before dark," Folio advised. "There's a grove of dead trees near the cliff. We can hide there and observe the operation without being seen."

Lana shook her canteen. How much water was left? Maybe a third. It would never last until they got back to the portal. With any luck she could refill it in the mining camp. If not, they would have to resort to Folio's skill at getting liquid out of plants, which would be time-consuming. She took a few sips and handed it to Jules, but he must have noticed how empty it felt because he hesitated, looking reluctant to drink.

"There will be water at the mining camp," she said. "Workers have to drink. Go ahead. I'll get more."

He didn't look happy about it but he took a few gulps. "Now you're on water detail. In addition to everything else." He shook his head, looking frustrated, and handed Folio the canteen.

Folio took a few sips and after resting a few more minutes started walking again. Lana followed, increasingly nervous, but determined not to show it. She went over the plan in her head. First, they had to get rid of the breghlin guarding the equipment on the cliff. Then, Jules and Folio would put her into some kind of a carrier made of ropes and lower her to the mines, probably several stories down. *That* would be fun, she thought with a grimace. She wasn't afraid of heights, but being stuffed into a rope bag and dropped off a cliff wasn't her idea of a good time. Assuming she reached the bottom in one piece, she must find a dozen gnomes and send them up in the carrier, a few at a time, without being caught.

The sun was going down when they neared the mine. They found the grove of dead trees Folio had mentioned and hid there. Two hundred feet from their position stood the winch apparatus made of giant logs, with a ramshackle building that must be the guard shack beside it. Near the winch lay a pile of alamaria. Lana's heart lifted at the sight of it. Folio had been right, and this would make their mission much easier.

"What did I tell you, Jules," Folio whispered excitedly. "There's your alamaria—more than twelve bags full."

"I don't mind being wrong when being wrong is to my advantage."

"Now what?" Lana asked. Her hands had gone clammy.

"Now I make a discrete visit to that guard shack." Folio chuckled. "I hope the guards are sleepy. They're about to enjoy a very long nap." He stepped from behind the tree and his form wavered, becoming increasingly transparent. The darkening sky and the ground showed plainly through the outline of his body. After a moment, all she could see was a shimmer in the air, which drifted toward the guard shack and then disappeared inside.

"Impressive," she whispered to Jules.

Jules looked equally spellbound.

"Have you ever see him do that?" she asked.

"No. He's full of surprises." He looked her in the eye. "You know, you have the potential to be as great as he is."

"Not if it means using dark powers. I won't go there."

"I'm glad to hear that, but avoiding dark powers doesn't necessarily limit you. Most anything *worth* doing can be done with other gems." He took off his sheathed blade and handed it to her. Her heart beat faster at the intensity of his gaze. "I know you'll put this to good use. Please be careful."

"I will. And thanks." For a moment she thought he was going to say something else, and then he looked away. They sat in tense silence for several minutes.

She didn't see Folio return, but she heard a low voice say, "It's done," and a patch of shimmering air took on a human outline that became transparent, then translucent, and then opaque. "Those guards won't be troubling us," Folio said, sounding rather proud of himself.

Wonderful. Folio had neutralized the guards. The rest was up to her. She studied the winch with growing apprehension. Perspiration beaded on her forehead. She felt light-headed. Taking a deep breath, she unsheathed the knife, desperate to draw confidence and optimism from it. She had a job to do and Folio was counting on her.

"Steady," Folio said gently.

There were times, like now, when she didn't want him reading her thoughts. She grabbed the canteen and stood. "I'm all right. Let's go," she said with more confidence than she felt.

By now the sky was as dark as it ever got here in Shadow. The characteristic silver shimmer provided enough ambient light to see where they were going. They walked toward the winch apparatus, which looked disturbingly like a giant Lincoln Log creation. Jules carried the sacks. While he and Folio waited for her to send up a bagful of gnomes, they could bag some alamaria. She smiled in spite of herself. Humor was good. For a moment her hands shook a little less.

Tilting back her head, she looked up at the winch. Was she crazy? She was about to entrust her life to this contraption. She pressed a hand to her chest but it didn't keep her heart from pounding. Two gigantic thirty-foot logs formed an A-shaped support structure, braced by a one-hundred-foot perpendicular log stretching out behind the A. The other log arm would swing her out over the cliff. She studied the pulley system warily. Chains controlled an iron hook that held the woven rope carrier. She looked over the cliff and instantly regretted it. The ground was sixty or seventy feet down. She wasn't sure she could do this.

Folio didn't give her time to talk herself out of it. He took her arm. "Now listen carefully. Breghlin are a predictable lot. Dinner was two hours ago and that's when they started drinking. By now they're playing cards or dice and they're too drunk to pay much attention to the gnomes. One or two guards will stay sober enough to make rounds and check the shacks every couple of hours."

She nodded and took a shaky breath. Folio's assessment sounded encouraging. Maybe this wouldn't be as bad as she thought.

"Have you ever used Jules's knife to create invisibility?"

"Yes, but the way I do it is different than yours. If someone looks at me, my presence doesn't register."

"Show me."

It was hard to perform on demand, especially when she was nervous, but she had managed it while escaping from Shadowglade, and she had been just as scared then. Gripping the knife firmly, she closed her eyes to concentrate and channeled its power. Energy hummed through her and she was pretty sure something was happening.

Jules drew in a sharp breath and Folio said, "Yes! Good!"

As soon as she stopped concentrating she felt the energy ebb. She opened her eyes and looked at Folio and Jules.

"Put the knife away until you get to the bottom," Folio advised, "and then I want you to use the invisibility, just as you did now, and head straight to the mining shacks."

Once again she looked over the cliff. She could make out ten squat, wooden mining shacks that looked big enough to bunk six or eight gnomes. A few hundred yards to their left stood a larger building that might be guards' quarters. A structure with a steeply pitched metal roof stood off to the right, away from everything else. The front two-thirds didn't have walls, just support beams, and it reminded her of a picnic pavilion. The shapes beneath the roof looked like tables, so it was probably a communal dining area, with a kitchen in the rear. A covered well stood next to the pavilion.

"Bring four gnomes at a time, surrounding them in your aura of invisibility. Once they're safely in the carrier, Jules and I will haul them up."

"What about noise?" she asked, remembering his comment about chains and pulleys.

"I've given the matter a great deal of thought. I will confine the equipment's sound waves within an energy field. No one outside the boundary will hear a thing."

She raised a brow. Folio was full of surprises. If no one could hear the winch, that left only the risk of someone seeing the moving carrier. But in the dark, it wasn't likely that anyone would notice it. It was time to go, before she lost her nerve. "I can think of a hundred "what ifs," but I should get going."

Folio spread his arms as he surveyed the boom and winch, and the air began to vibrate with energy. The hair on Lana's arms stood up.

After a moment Folio lowered his arms and said to Jules, "It should be safe to bring down the carrier."

Lana tried not to fidget as Folio and Jules worked the chains. The boom passed horizontally over their heads, and then the rope basket began to descend, stopping a few inches off the ground.

Folio and Jules held the carrier to steady it. Lana swallowed hard and climbed in. Her weight made the baglike structure close in around her. It was like crawling into a hammock that perversely tried to trap you inside.

No turning back now.

She signaled she was ready, and watched with nervous fascination as Folio and Jules manipulated the arm that held her carrier. As the carrier began to swing out over the cliff, she looked up at the hook, hoping the carrier was secure. Fine time to worry about that now, she thought grimly. In any case, staring at the hook was better than looking down.

The carrier's ropes creaked ominously, and when her hammock prison began to swing in the empty air, she shifted her position ever so slowly and wound her fingers through the ropes in a death grip. *Don't panic. You're fine.* She took several deep breaths and looked back at the cliff as the carrier began its descent. Jules stepped forward, watching her with a look of despair. She tried to smile reassuringly but it felt like grimace. Chains clanked and the pulley squealed. Hopefully, no one outside the boundary Folio had created could hear all this noise.

After an eternity of dangling in the air, she reached the bottom. It was a struggle to climb out of the rope bag, but she finally freed herself and sighed with relief at the feel of solid ground under her feet. She drew the knife and clasped the hilt firmly, concentrating on the invisibility effect as she scanned the camp.

There was no sign of movement. She walked to the closest shack and hesitated when she reached the door. Should she knock or just walk in? She hadn't even planned what to say. Opening the door slowly, still invisible, she slipped inside and left the door ajar.

"The door just opened! Who's there?" a gnome called.

"I don't see anyone."

"Quiet," Lana said softly. She should have rehearsed a speech. "I've come to rescue you, but I can only take a few of you right now." She paused, realizing what she needed to say. "The Challenger is waiting at the top of the cliff."

In typical gnome fashion, they all began to talk at once, but they had the good sense to keep their voices down. "The Challenger!" one whispered excitedly. "Has he returned?"

"Begging your pardon," another said timidly, "but who are you? And *where* are you?"

She dropped the invisibility field. "I'm Lana, the Challenger's ally." Eight gnomes looked at her in shocked amazement. "And this is the Challenger's Blade." Holding it up was like flashing an ID badge, she thought as she watched the gnomes' expressions. They'd obviously heard of it. *Great! Instant credibility! As long as I don't mention Folio.*

"The Challenger needs twelve of you for a special mission. Can one of you get four more to go with me? Just bring them. Don't explain why."

A black-haired gnome with a long, tangled beard said, "I'll go."

"Remember, only four."

"Yes." He slipped silently from the shack.

She told the remaining gnomes, "The Challenger and his companion will pull you up with the winch and carrier. You'll go up in groups of four." *They're going to see Folio when they reach the top. Even if they don't know who he is his lumpy skin and odd features will remind them of a breghlin. I'll let Jules and Folio talk their way around that.*

"You mentioned a special mission," one of the gnomes said. "Can you tell us more?

"We need you to carry sacks of alamaria. The Challenger will explain why."

The gnomes fell silent. They waited patiently for the others to arrive. In a few minutes the door opened and more gnomes crowded inside. She repeated her message for the benefit of the newcomers.

"I'll take the first four now. I'm going to make us invisible. To do that, we have to stay close together."

The gnomes glanced at one another and then the closest four stepped forward. She clasped the knife tightly, closed her eyes and concentrated on invisibility, and when she heard a confirming gasp from the gnomes, she pictured the field expanding until it included the four gnomes going with her.

They left the shack, and she was relieved to see that they matched her pace, forming a tight knot around her. She headed directly toward the winch.

Folio and Jules stood near the edge of the cliff, ready for her cargo.

The gnomes wasted no time scrambling into the carrier. With or without a special mission led by the Challenger, they'd be happy to leave this place. Once they had settled into the carrier, she dropped the invisibility field and signaled for Jules and Folio to raise the carrier.

It was too soon to pronounce the mission a success, she told herself, feeling relieved as she watched them ascend, but at least one load was on the way up to safety. She started back for the next group and realized when she was halfway to the shacks that she didn't hear chains and pulleys. Folio's sound boundary worked. A grin broke over her face.

By the time she came back with the second group, the carrier was waiting a few inches off the ground. Even though she and the gnomes were wasting no time, this process felt nerve-rackingly slow. Guards might start making their rounds at any moment. "Hurry up, climb in!" she whispered, grasping the carrier to steady it. When they were all inside, she dropped the invisibility field, waved her arm, and the carrier began to rise.

One more group.

Even then, she wouldn't be finished, she reminded herself. She would have one more duty to perform: water detail, as Jules called it. Folio could extract water from plants, but why not take some while she was here?

As she walked toward the shack, she scanned the camp. Everything had gone remarkably well so far. Maybe that was why she felt edgy. It seemed too simple. That was silly, of course. They deserved to pull this off without a hitch.

For some reason, it seemed farther to the shacks this time. What was the matter with her? Her legs felt increasingly heavy, and try as she might, she couldn't make her feet move any faster. Panting with exertion, she finally reached the shack and stepped through the door. Maintaining invisibility wasn't easy. How would she ever walk to the portal once this was over? *You have to keep going. Don't think about that.*

It was all she could do to keep her voice from shaking with exhaustion. "Everyone is safe at the top," she said to the last group. "You're next." She wanted desperately to sit for a moment and catch her breath, but there wasn't time. She had to get the last four gnomes up the cliff. Delays could put the mission at risk. "Remember," she told them, "stay close."

She simply couldn't walk fast, but she tried not to worry about that. Speed wasn't as important as invisibility. Part way there, she thought about stopping to rest, but she didn't want to alarm the gnomes. Breathing heavily, she pressed onward. She gripped the knife hilt so hard it hurt, trying to draw strength while keeping the invisibility field intact. The effort made her dizzy, and after a moment she gave up.

Her vision had grown annoyingly blurry. She blinked a couple times. *Almost there. Just a little farther. You can do it.* Just ahead, the carrier hung waiting. She glanced up, making sure Jules and Folio were ready. A few gnomes stood at the edge of the cliff with them. Hopefully the alamaria was bagged and ready to go. As soon as she came back with water, everyone could leave.

Once again she gave the signal. Chains rattled as the pulley took up slack. The carrier lurched off the ground. With weary satisfaction she watched the gnomes rise. Funny, she didn't remember the gnomes getting into the carrier. Oh well, they were on their way. Now what was she supposed to do? Oh, yes. Water.

She turned toward the building that looked like a dining pavilion, remembering that the covered well sat beside it. *Cold water.* Until now, she hadn't realized how thirsty she was. Taking several deep breaths, she aimed herself toward the well. Her legs felt weak and uncooperative but she forced herself to walk. The well was further away than the mining shacks. Maybe she should forget the idea of refilling the canteen. No, she thought with a frown. The next source of water might be miles away, and until they got there they could rely on the canteen.

When she finally reached the well, she found the empty bucket sitting on the rim. She eyed the dining pavilion cautiously, but as Folio had said, dinner had been hours ago and everyone was gone. Satisfied, she tucked the knife into the sheath on her belt. It wouldn't do to drop the knife into the well.

Grabbing the rope with one hand, she slid the bucket into the well and was relieved to hear a reassuring splash. The pulley squeaked and squealed as she hauled up the bucket with both hands, the rope biting into her palms. She had forgotten how heavy water could be.

When the bucket reached the top, she set it on the stone rim, plunged her hands into the water, splashed some on her face, and then drank a handful. It tasted like minerals, but it was icy cold. After filling the canteen, she decided to drink a few more handfuls from the bucket.

She bent over the bucket and something sharp jabbed her in the back. A guttural breghlin voice demanded, "Who have we here?"

She froze as a long, thin blade appeared near her face. A second voice growled, "Answer the question."

Chapter 31

Lana's heart raced. If she reached for her knife the breghlin would slit her throat. She couldn't run, bent over a bucket with a knife in her back. And she couldn't call for help. Who would hear? Folio might be watching from the cliff—or not. He was busy with twelve gnomes and a pile of alamaria. And for all she knew, there was nothing he could do to help from that distance.

The knife in her back jabbed more insistently. The air reeked of alcohol and breghlin filth. She gasped out, "My name is Lana!"

Instantly the knife at her face and the blade in her back retreated.

"Grace! It's Lana!" said the guttural voice in amazement.

"Lana? Here?" the other said. "Don't hurt us! Didn't know it was you!"

Lana straightened and turned to face the breghlin.

Grace and Ferdinand stared at her blearily. Grace sniffed, and then wiped his crooked, pocked nose with his sleeve. "Sheamathan sent us here," he said in answer to her stupefied look.

"After *you* got outta the dungeon," Ferdinand added meaningfully. "Larry, Danny, and all of us is here." His fleshy, protruding lips trembled.

"Yeah, all us *oafs*. *She* called me a *useless* oaf," Grace said, slurring his words, "So that must be the worst kind." Grace looked a little unsteady on his feet. Lana studied him, thinking furiously. Maybe she could walk away. He might not stop her. An hour from now, he might not even remember seeing her. "Did you just come from this building?" she asked, pointing toward the dining hall.

Grace nodded.

"Is anyone else there?"

Grace shook his head. "The others be at the barracks."

She took a deep breath and let it out slowly. It wasn't safe to stand here. Someone might see them. "Let's go inside," she suggested.

Grace said, "Sure, c'mon. Have a drink. We got plenty of beer."

Lana took a quick glance around. They led her through the pavilion and into the enclosed part in the back. As she suspected, the back room was a kitchen. A huge, rectangular wooden worktable with massive legs stood in front of a grimy, cast iron cook stove. A stack of pots and pans sat on one end of the table, and metal tankards littered the rest of its marred surface. Cabinets without doors hung on one wall. A disorganized array of supplies lined the sagging shelves. The walls looked greasy. Clearly, cleanliness was not a priority here. Her feet stuck to the creaking floorboards as she walked to the table and sat down. Grace and Ferdinand plopped down across from her and each picked up a tankard. Globs of grease, bits of meat, and other unidentifiable bits of food clung to their black beards. She tried not to look.

Grace drank deeply, smacked his lips, and then grabbed a tankard from further down the table and shoved it toward Lana. "Have some!" It skidded to a stop in front of her. She looked down. Several inches of someone's unfinished beer sloshed inside. Hiding her disgust, she looked at her companions. "Thanks." She leaned forward, elbows on the table. "I'm glad you're still together, but I suppose you'd rather be working at the castle."

Grace shook his head. "Nah. It's better here. Night duty's easy." He took another gulp of beer as if to prove his point.

"So your punishment isn't so bad," she said.

Staring at her rather glassy-eyed, both nodded. Ferdinand slurped his beer and then set down the tankard and stared into it moodily. "*She* is afraid of you," he announced. "You have the Challenger's knife. You have powers." He looked up and his lips twitched nervously. "Beings with powers always hurt others. But *you* didn't hurt us. You was *nice* to us."

"That's right," Grace said, nodding vehemently. "You was nice."

"*She's* never nice," Ferdinand grumbled. He took another drink of beer and then slammed down the tankard. Lana jumped. His protruding lips parted, showing yellowed stumps of broken teeth. His black eyes flashed. "You gived us *names!*" He began smashing the tankard with each word for emphasis. "You! Gived! Us! Names!"

"That's more than *She* ever done," Grace agreed mournfully. He took a gulp of beer and frowned into the tankard, as if in its depths he could see images of his thankless, dismal existence.

Neither of them seemed to notice that she wasn't drinking.

Ferdinand's shoulders sagged. He let out a long, shuddering breath. After a moment he sighed heavily and chugged his beer. Resignation seemed to have replaced anger. Tankard in hand, he looked at Lana and asked, "Whatcha' doin' here?"

She had expected this question long before now. "Checking things," she answered vaguely.

Grace belched loudly. "What kinda things?"

She cast about for a reply. "Um, gnome working conditions. Got a call from OSHA. You have violations here."

The breghlin exchanged blank looks. Ferdinand swayed slightly. His head dipped once. He caught himself and sat a little straighter, but clearly he was having trouble staying awake. *In a few minutes he'll be snoring on the table.*

This would be a good time to slip out. She was certain they wouldn't stop her. "It's nice to see you again, but I really should be going." She reached across the table and gave Ferdinand's arm an affectionate pat. "Thanks for the beer. Don't get up. I can see myself out."

Maybe Folio could wipe this meeting from the breghlins' memories. She had a feeling it wouldn't be necessary. Sliding off the bench, she cautiously headed for the door. Neither breghlin said a word.

She couldn't resist looking back. Ferdinand sat slumped over the table with his mouth open. Grace swayed slightly, his head nodding sleepily, still clutching the tankard with both hands. *Pleasant dreams, guys.*

She pulled out the Challenger's Blade. She was exhausted, but the adrenalin rush of being captured had cleared her head. Concentrating on invisibility, she stepped through the door and shivered as the cold canteen touched her side. Everyone had better enjoy this water. It had nearly gotten her killed.

Halfway to the winch, her legs started feeling rubbery again. Staring straight ahead, she willed herself to keep going. When this was over, when she was safely on the cliff, she could use her gems and the knife to get her strength back. Hopefully it wouldn't take long. It wasn't safe to hang around here, but she couldn't walk far in this condition.

As she approached the cliff, she looked up. The gnomes had clustered around Jules and Folio and were staring out over the mining camp, probably wondering where she was. The carrier, fifty feet away from her, waited near the ground. She pushed herself forward and dropped the invisibility field, and then climbed awkwardly into the carrier and collapsed. This time she didn't mind being entrapped in the hammock-bag. Its clinging embrace felt reassuring. With trembling hands, she slid the knife into its sheath.

The carrier jerked once and started its ascent. The pulley squealed and the chains rattled violently, but she was too exhausted to worry about plunging to her death. The carrier swung slightly each time the men pulled on the chains, and she felt like a fish inside a net being hauled into a fisherman's boat.

When the carrier reached the top, the log boom began to swing inward, so they could bring her over the ground. A moment later she looked down and saw Folio, Jules and the gnomes. Wrapping her arms around the canteen, she waited for the carrier to stop. Where would she find the energy to climb out?

The gnomes crowded around, all of them talking at once. Behind them, Folio barked, "Move away! Let her get out."

"Let me through," Jules commanded brusquely. The gnomes parted and he strode toward her. His expression was unreadable. He might be angry, annoyed, or relieved; she wasn't sure. Struggling to sit, she held out the canteen and said weakly, "I got us water."

Jules made a sound—something between a moan and a sob. He reached into the carrier and lifted her out as if she were no heavier than a sack of alamaria.

"We need to move. Now," Folio said in a low voice as he picked up Lana's backpack. "Let's go back to the grove of dead trees." The gnomes grabbed the sacks of alamaria and hoisted them over their shoulders. Folio led the way. Lana expected Jules to set her down and help her walk, but he hurried after Folio and the gnomes, cradling her to his chest.

"I can walk," she protested, embarrassed.

"And you will, later, after you rest." His tone clearly said 'don't argue with me,' but she found herself arguing, anyway.

"We may not have time to rest."

He dropped his voice so only she could hear. "Good, then I'll carry you."

She looked up into his face. A merry twinkle danced in his blue eyes.

"Invisibility is draining," she said, abandoning any idea of protest. "After the third trip, I was a wreck. Walking to the well was one trip too many, but at least we have water now."

"I don't think I can drink it."

"Why?"

"It almost cost your life. I saw what happened."

"But I escaped."

For a moment he was silent, and then he let out a frustrated sigh and shook his head. "You're either the luckiest or the most resourceful person I know."

She laughed. Tension drained from her body.

He laughed too and said in a lighter tone, "Later, when you're rested, you can tell us about it."

They had reached the grove of dead trees. Jules carried her to the tree where Folio stood and set her gently on the ground. She felt a bit unsteady on her feet after her ordeal, but she supposed there could be another reason for feeling weak kneed. She could feel Jules's eyes on her.

"I'm glad I didn't bring a thirteenth sack," Folio said, giving her a sly wink. "I expect you're a more pleasant burden than a sack of alamaria."

She felt herself blush. Folio loved to tease her. "I can walk. I'll be fine. I just need to get my strength back. Let me use my gems or the knife for a few minutes." She sat on the ground, pulled the knife from its sheath, and wrapped her fingers around the hilt.

"We can't stay long," Folio said, "but we'll take frequent breaks. The gnomes are each carrying heavy loads, so they'll need to rest, too."

She closed her eyes. For the next fifteen minutes she would concentrate on strength and healing, and maybe she'd recover enough that she wouldn't be a burden to the group.

The time went too quickly. Before long, Folio's voice broke her focus. "We should go," he said gently.

Jules held out his hand and helped her up. "Now that I don't have the burlap bags, I can wear your backpack."

"All right."

"How do you feel?" He studied her face, looking concerned.

"Better."

"Well enough to walk?"

She nodded, feeling herself blush. "Yes."

"You're very sure?" he said, with a playful look in his eyes.

She couldn't mistake his meaning. She looked away, hoping she didn't start stuttering and said, "As long as we take frequent breaks, I'll be fine."

He gave a wistful sigh. "If you change your mind—"

The group set out with Folio in the lead. Jules walked beside her at the end of the procession. She wasn't always shy around men, so it must be the whole wolfhound thing. As a dog, he'd been terrifying. But as a man, he was surprisingly hot.

She drew strength from the knife as she walked. The night air had cooled. There was no hint of a breeze now. The cooler temperature made their hike easier and she was glad the wind had died down. They'd be crossing the plains of red dirt again, and she had eaten way too much dirt the first time.

"If you're up to it, I'm ready for your story now," Jules said.

"Was Folio worried about me?" she asked before she launched into the tale.

"Yes, of course."

"Did he know what was happening? Could he read my mind?"

Jules shook his head. "No. From that distance, he couldn't read your thoughts, just your emotions, which he said ranged from terrified to elated." He paused and gave her an appraising look. "So what happened? We saw you at the well. Two breghlin came out of the building, and it looked like they marched you away at knifepoint. How did you get away?"

"They didn't march me away exactly. They asked me in for a beer."

"What?"

She glanced at his astonished face and tried not to laugh. "I knew them. They were my guards in the dungeon. Remember I told you I tried to get on my guards' good side?"

He nodded, "Yes, I remember but—"

"When they saw it was me, they dropped their weapons and asked me not to hurt them. They have a healthy fear of my gem powers, and your knife." She paused, reflecting on the encounter. "But it wasn't just that they're afraid of me. Being nice to them made a greater impact than I realized." She would never forget Ferdinand's pain-filled outburst as he smashed his tankard on the table: *You! Gived! Us! Names!* "No one has ever been nice to them," she said sadly. "They're just tools. Sheamathan uses and discards them. They've lived their whole lives without a kind word."

"But they're just witless savages," Jules said, clearly perplexed by her passion.

"What do you expect, with the way they've been treated?" she asked indignantly. "Sheamathan encourages their savagery. She thrives on evil and destruction." She gave a frustrated sigh and added, "Don't forget, long ago the breghlin were gnomes."

Jules didn't answer. He looked at her thoughtfully and rubbed his chin. "I see your point, but I question their ability to change. Or their desire to."

"Maybe they like being savages. Most of them probably do. But from what I've seen, some of them show promise."

"If we're lucky enough to defeat Sheamathan, they'll lose more than a leader. They'll lose their purpose in life. They may be worse off than now."

She shook her head. "I don't think so. There's no reason they can't grow crops, develop skills, and become self-sustaining. We'll see."

"I admire your optimism." He gave a short laugh. "I just realized. You never explained. How *did* you get away from them?"

"They got so drunk I just said goodbye and walked away. I doubt they'll remember any of this tomorrow."

"Lucky or resourceful," Jules said, looking at her intently as if trying to decide. "Both, I think." He shook his head. "In any case, I've never met anyone like you."

Chapter 32

As they walked to the portal, Folio told the gnomes more about his past. Lana noticed he didn't gloss over his shortcomings. With that out of the way, and seeing that the gnomes still supported him, he launched into a discussion about their mission. Naturally, he couldn't disclose the details, but he made it clear that he, Jules, and Lana hoped to overthrow the woodspirit and strip her of her powers.

After that Jules told the gnomes about his bargain with Sheamathan. He admitted he'd been the wolfhound. As expected, that was a disturbing revelation. The legendary Challenger had never been as all-powerful as the gnomes had thought. Worse, Jules's ally was the now-repentant but much-despised Folio. The gnomes bore up under these disturbing revelations remarkably well and only asked a few questions. For the most part, they kept their thoughts to themselves.

The gnomes had stories to share, too, and Lana was happy to learn that one of the gnomes she'd rescued today was from Raenihel's clan. Dardeneth, a middle-aged gnome, had spent more than two years in the mining camp, and he'd had his share of run-ins with the guards. When Lana asked him about Gliaphon, Dardeneth said he was there, unharmed but miserable and depressed.

To her surprise, Gliaphon had told the miners about her. He said a woman named Lana with gem powers had gotten involved with his clan.

When Theaffar arrived in camp, claiming a woman named Lana had healed him in the dungeon, the miners assumed it was the same Lana. But if Lana had gem powers, why was she in the dungeon? Couldn't she save herself? And if she couldn't, how could she help them? Today, when Lana arrived, claiming to be the Challenger's ally, they thought the Challenger had freed her. Jules set them straight.

The group arrived at the Shadow side of the portal at about four in the morning. The gnomes dropped their heavy sacks on the ground and gathered around Folio.

"I know you'd like to rest, but you only have a little further to go," Folio told them. "Carry your sacks through the portal, leave them on the ground, and then you're free to go. When you get home, tell everyone the Challenger rescued you."

"And you'll free the others, like you promised?" one of the gnomes asked.

Folio met their eyes unflinchingly. "You have my word. We will rescue the other miners soon. I must caution you—not a word to anyone about bringing alamaria here."

The miners looked at one another and nodded.

"It was an honor to help you," one of the gnomes said, standing a little taller.

Folio gestured toward the portal. "Shall we go through now?" He took Lana's hand and they stepped through the portal. Jules and the gnomes followed. The gnomes set their sacks on the ground, and after a few parting words they retreated through the portal.

Folio looked at the sacks full of alamaria and gave a weary sigh. "This is a great accomplishment, but it's just the beginning."

"Unless you're planning to conjure up shovels, I need to go home and raid my landlady's garden shed," Lana said.

"Actually, that would be a great help. Get some sleep first. I'll place a ward around the alamaria until you come back."

"I hate to leave you here. I'm sorry I can't take you home where it's more comfortable."

"I can't leave the Amulet," he said, "but I'll sleep well enough here. Perhaps you can take Jules with you. I'm sure he'd like to meet your, er, roommates," he added with a chuckle.

She hadn't thought about Greg and Jordy for hours. Her heart leapt at the thought of telling them that Folio could break their enchantment. "If I bring Greg and Jordy back with me, will you turn them back into boys?"

"Certainly," Folio said. His face brightened. "Then we'll have two more workers to bury alamaria!"

She laughed. The boys would be more than happy to help.

"You can sleep on my couch," she said to Jules. "Greg and Jordy are probably sleeping there now, but the minute I walk in they'll be wide awake and talking their whiskers off."

Jules smiled. "If it's no trouble, I'd be happy to go."

"When you come back," Folio said to Lana with a beseeching look, "bring me a cup of coffee."

* * *

Greg and Jordy must have heard footsteps. They were waiting eagerly by the door. "Lana!" They cried in unison. Both showed their teeth in happy rat smiles, and then looked warily at Jules.

"Guys, this is Jules, the Challenger. Jules, the gray fellow is Greg, and the brown one is Jordy."

"Nice to meetcha," Jordy said.

"Yeah. Lana read us a couple of your letters," Greg said.

"I've heard quite a bit about you," Jules told them with a grin. "And I'm happy to meet you."

"Won't you come in," Jordy said with an expansive wave of his paw, as if he owned the place. "It shouldn't stink much," he added. He looked at Lana. "I mean, you weren't here to change the litter, so sometimes we used your toilet."

"Thanks for the warning," she said. "By the way, I won't be buying you any more rat chow."

"Why not?" Greg asked.

"You're going to be eating burgers and pizza!"

Their eyes widened. "We're gonna be boys again!" Jordy cried ecstatically.

"Yes!" Lana said, laughing. Their joy surged through her heart. They would be normal teenage boys again. She had no idea how they would explain their absence to their parents, but it didn't matter. They would be home at last, and she was sure it would be an emotional reunion.

"*You're* gonna change us back?" Greg asked Jules. Jules shook his head.

"Jules can't do it, but Folio can. He helped me break Jules's enchantment. He's done a lot of good things lately. He's waiting for us at the park."

Jordy said, "I'm glad to hear he's a better person than you thought."

"Me too. Now, if you'll excuse us, we need to get a few hours' sleep. Then we'll go to the park."

"Lana promised me your couch," Jules said to the rats. "I hope you'll forgive me."

"No problem," Jordy said, giving Jules his disturbing rat grin. "We never peed on the cushions or anything, so you don't need to worry about that."

"Ah, um, good," Jules stammered.

"I'll bring you some bedding," Lana said, trying to keep a straight face. When she returned, the rats were on the overstuffed armchair, watching Jules. Could Jules sleep with giant rats staring at him? "I can lend you opalite jasper to help you sleep," she offered.

"Thanks, but I doubt I'll need it."

Probably not. He had to be exhausted. In addition to wearing her backpack, he'd carried alamaria for a while when one of the gnomes needed a break. "I'll wake you in a few hours," she told him.

By the time she crawled into bed it was five forty-five. She set the alarm for eleven so they could get back to the park by noon. Reaching into the nightstand drawer, she took out her opalite jasper. Good thing Jules hadn't wanted it. She slipped it under her pillow. The wolfhound was here, sleeping on her couch. That was enough to keep her awake.

* * *

When the alarm went off at eleven, Lana woke feeling headachy. Late morning sun shone through her windows. She turned off the alarm and reached under her pillow for the opalite jasper. "Good job," she said. "I was out the minute my head touched the pillow."

Shower. Clothes. Coffee.

The steaming shower got rid of her headache, and she stepped out feeling refreshed and energized. After hurriedly brushing her hair, she put on clean jeans and a royal blue, V-neck sweater and headed for the kitchen. Jules was still fast asleep on the couch. The rats were watching a Tom and Jerry cartoon with the sound off. They looked up at her and showed their teeth, clearly pleased with themselves for watching TV without making noise.

Jules looked so peaceful she hated to wake him. For a moment she stood staring. Maybe he sensed someone looking at him because he stirred, opened his eyes a sliver, and then wider when he saw her. "How long have you been standing there?" he asked sleepily. "I hope I wasn't snoring or drooling on myself."

She laughed and shook her head. "Only a few seconds. I hated to wake you." She glanced at the rats. "It's OK to turn up the sound now."

When the sound came on, Jules sat up, looking amazed as Tom and Jerry cavorted across the screen.

"A lot of things will be new to you," she said, realizing he had never watched TV. Until last night, he hadn't ridden in a car. So many things would be new to him. No doubt the modern world would seem like a wonderful but frightening place.

While he showered she made scrambled eggs, toast, and a full pot of coffee. She hadn't forgotten Folio. He wanted some, too. Jules came into the kitchen, clean-shaven, with damp, towel-dried hair. He looked disturbingly handsome despite wearing yesterday's clothes.

"The boys always eat with me," she told him, making no apologies as she poured two bowls of rat chow. "Chows on!" Greg and Jordy scampered to the table and hopped into their usual chairs. She carried plates of eggs and toast to the table and Jules followed with coffee.

"I'll drive you home to your parents after Folio changes you back," she told the boys while they ate. "What will you tell them? How will you explain where you've been all this time?"

Greg thought a moment. "I guess we'll say we ran away from home."

"Yeah. We took a bus to a big city," Jordy agreed.

"Maybe New York," Greg suggested.

Jordy said, "Right! New York would be good. You can hide in a big city. Nobody finds you there."

"And we ate out of dumpsters and lived in a big, abandoned building," Greg went on, warming to the tale.

Jordy laughed. "Yeah, a building with *big rats*."

"You have to admit, there's a kernel of truth to the story," Jules said.

Lana smiled. True. The boys *had* made their home in a big building far from home and had eaten leftover scraps of food. And there *had* been rats. *Big ones* indeed.

* * *

When Lana was ready to leave, the rats climbed into their pet carriers. It was time for the rats to become boys. Lillian wasn't around, so Lana borrowed the shovels and left a note on the garden shed door.

When they reached the park a little after noon it was deserted. With a travel mug of coffee for Folio in one hand, and the carrier with Greg in the other, Lana started walking. Greg weighed a ton. Jules carried Jordy since Jordy was even heavier. She wished she could open the carriers and let the rats run, but she didn't dare.

"Man, you've been eating too much chow," she grumbled, struggling uphill with Greg.

"Just wait till I'm full of burgers and fries," he retorted.

"I won't be carrying you, then. When Folio turns you back into boys, you can get the carriers and shovels from the trunk. I'm already tired."

They found Folio sitting, arms crossed, with his back against a tree, resting comfortably.

"Hi! I have coffee!" Lana called.

His eyes snapped open. He looked up with an eager smile. "Bless you for remembering!"

They set down the carriers and she handed Folio his coffee. "Sorry. I had no idea how you like your coffee, so I left it black."

"I'm not particular. Thank you." He sipped the coffee, looking contented. "It's been a very long time," he said with a sigh.

Lana was surprised that the rats didn't say a word. She tended to be grumpy until she'd had her morning coffee, so maybe they figured they'd better be still until Folio drank his. After a moment Folio said, "Now then, let's take care of your friends."

Lana unfastened the carrier doors and Greg and Jordy scrambled out, trembling with nervous anticipation. Jordy said in a small voice, "We're very grateful for your help, Mr. Folio."

Folio wore the gray shirt and pants he'd worn since they'd left Strathweed. His gray hair hung to his shoulders, and his long, gray beard covered most of his toad-like skin. When he drew himself to his full height and looked down at the rats, he looked like a towering gray thundercloud. "We need to move away from the alamaria."

He walked a distance through the woods and the rats followed. Lana and Jules trooped behind. "Far enough. This should do," Folio said. He stretched his arms upward, then slowly outward, palms toward the rats. Lana felt the air vibrate. One moment Greg and Jordy were rats, the next they were human. The boys fell into each other's arms, sobbing.

This was the second time she'd seen Greg and Jordy as boys. She smiled through her tears at the redheaded Greg with his prominent nose and the stocky, brown-haired Jordy. Their nightmare was over. They could go home.

Lana felt an arm slip around her shoulders. Surprised, she looked up at Jules. "I'm always crying about something, aren't I?"

He brushed a tear from his own eyes and said softly, "That's one of the things I like about you." She gave him a skeptical look, but he squeezed her shoulders reassuringly and said, "You feel things deeply. You think that's a weakness, but it's not—quite the opposite. Your depth of emotion makes your gem powers stronger."

She looked down, too overcome to speak. Was he serious? She cried whether happy or sad. Her friends said she was a good listener because she was so empathetic, and maybe they had a point, but sometimes it was embarrassing. Now he was suggesting that her "weakness" made her powerful. That was hard to believe.

The boys finally stepped away from each other and Greg sniffed and said, "We'll get the shovels now."

Lana handed her keys to Greg. "Take the pet carriers with you. You won't be needing them anymore."

Chapter 33

Lana, Jules, and the boys buried the alamaria in a wide, shallow hole just outside the portal, and then carefully replaced the sod so the ground looked undisturbed. Standing back, arms crossed, Lana inspected the ground and smiled with satisfaction. "Good work, guys."

Digging had left her tired and sore. Any other time she'd use a few of her gemstones to ease the pain and give her energy, but if this alamaria worked the way it should, her gems would be useless. Time for a test, she told herself, reaching into her gem pouch. She found a fire agate that normally gave her energy and stamina and closed her fingers around it, trying to draw its power. The stone felt cold and lifeless in her hand.

"It works," she announced triumphantly.

"What works?" Jules asked.

"The alamaria. It's blocking the power from my fire agate."

"That was smart—testing it," Jules said, leaning on his shovel. "If the alamaria doesn't work, it's better to know it now."

"I was sure it would, but I still had to check," she said, putting the fire agate away. "When you get this many stones together, they're really powerful."

"Like Sheamathan's obelisk." Jules put down his shovel and walked over to her. "What about infused powers? Are we sure it will block them, too?"

Folio, who was busy tamping down two pieces of sod that refused to lie perfectly flat, looked up and said, "Yes. I ran a test of my own." He gave the offending sod one more determined stomp and continued, "I restored the boys outside the range of the alamaria and left my gems there. Normally, I could read your thoughts without my gems, but now I can't."

"So your infused powers are gone. Good to know," Lana said with a grin. "Now you can't hear what we're thinking about you."

He gave her a sly look. "Enjoy it while you can, my dear."

Jordy piped up, "I'd love to see Sheamathan's face when she finds out her powers don't work."

Greg grumbled, "Me too, and we have to miss it."

"We don't know when she'll show up," Lana said, "so you can't hang around and wait. You need to get home."

"I know," Jordy said with a sigh, "but you guys are gonna kick her butt, and I'd give anything to see it. Promise to tell us every juicy detail." His smile reminded Lana a lot of his rat grin.

"I promise," she said, wishing she were as confident of their success.

"I've been thinkin'," Greg said. "Could you take us to the bus station—instead of home? I need to come up with a story about living in the city and all that, and I'm not sure how you'd fit in."

"Yeah, sure. Good thinking." She reached into her jeans pocket and pulled out a five, a few ones, and some coins. "Here. You'll need money for a phone call, and besides, you can't go home penniless. After you paid your bus fare, this is what you had left." She gave Greg a conspiratorial wink.

Greg hesitated.

"Take it," she insisted.

He took the money and stuffed it into a pocket in his tattered jeans. "Thanks. I'll pay you back."

Jordy grinned. "And we owe you for a bag of rat chow."

She shrugged. "No problem. Someday you can take me out for pizza."

"Deal," Greg said.

"So, now what?" she asked Folio who was listening with an amused smile.

Why don't you and Jules take the boys to the bus station. I'll head back to Strathweed, and you can come when you're ready. We'll discuss how to lure Sheamathan through the portal. I have a few ideas.

"All right with me," Lana said. She had two more vacation days, followed by the weekend, and Mom and Dad weren't expecting her to do chores. She said to Jules, "If you'd rather head back with Folio, I don't mind."

"Elias is used to traveling in Shadow and knows the dangers. I don't mean to offend you, but you really should have an escort." He paused and gave her a sidelong look. "Have you ever gone through the portal by yourself?"

Her face fell. "No, that's a good point. I've always crossed with Raenihel or Folio. I guess I need you." Besides, he had the knife now, and all she had was a bag of gems. It would be better to stay together. She turned to Folio. "After we take the boys to the bus station, there's something I need to get from home before I come to Strathweed. It's critical."

He looked concerned. "What?"

"A bag of coffee."

"Ah!" His face lit. You'd think she'd volunteered to bring a sack of rubies. "Do hurry back," he said and walked through the portal.

* * *

Elias walked the last stretch of the trail feeling unusually cheerful. The prospect of guests lifted his spirits. A hermit's life could be tedious. The thrill of examining new gems and unlocking their secrets had kept him busy for decades. But even in the early days he had sometimes felt lonely and despondent. His isolation had grown harder to bear the longer he was trapped here. He had lost his home, his family, and his friend Jules. How could he have been such a fool? He heaved a sigh. If he dwelled on his mistakes, he would go mad.

Despite his relationship with the woodspirit and his reputation for dark gem powers, a few gnomes came from time to time, looking for a lucky talisman, an aid to fertility, healing for an injury, or a cure for insomnia. In exchange, they made him clothing and brought him food. Their visits were more business than social; nevertheless, he enjoyed the brief respite from his loneliness.

He rounded the bend, smiling as his cave came into view. This was the start of a new era, and he hoped it heralded the end of Sheamathan's reign. Jules was himself again. Lana was aware of her gem powers and had come to Shadow. Elias had never met anyone like her. Her eyes burned with the fire of a thousand lightgems. When she looked at him, he saw his own selfishness and shortcomings and every dark shadow that lurked in his heart. She had only been here a few days, and she was already infusing Fair Lands gem powers. In time, he could teach her many things about Fair Lands gems and Shadow gemstones as well—if she would let him.

She had despised him at first. Her hatred had been palpable. It had been painful to feel the depth of her disgust and contempt. But her contempt had given way to wariness and distrust, then to grudging acceptance, and now, he thought with a smile, to more promising emotions. She still called him Folio, but someday, he fervently hoped, she would call him Elias.

He approached his woven-branch front door and was about to pull it aside, when something swift and dark overhead made him stop and look up.

"Franklin!" he cried in surprise, recognizing the giant, black bird. How odd. Franklin hadn't signaled that he was coming. The bird circled, wings outstretched, and made a gliding descent to the ground. Franklin resembled a black bird known as a skreet, but he was several times larger. His abnormal size was a hallmark of Sheamathan's enchantments.

"Let's go inside, Franklin." Elias wrenched the door aside. No one must see his feathered messenger. "I'll get you something to eat while you tell me why you're here." The bird followed obediently and they entered the inner cave. Elias poured a handful of seeds into a wooden bowl and filled a goblet of fialazza for himself, hoping it would steady his nerves. He settled into a chair and set Franklin's bowl on the floor nearby.

Hidden among his feathers, Franklin wore a rare purple gemstone on a leather cord around his neck. Elias wore a matching gemstone on a necklace. The gem allowed Elias to open a two-way link. If Elias or Franklin summoned each other, the purple gems grew hot and transmitted each other's locations through visions.

After a moment, Franklin looked up from the bowl of seeds, blinking intelligent black eyes. In a high, musical voice he said, "Sheamathan is sending a cart to bring you to Shadowglade. She wants to speak to you."

Elias leaned forward. "When?"

"Soon. When I left, the breghlin driver was hitching a maraku to the cart."

"I see," Elias said, running his fingers through his beard thoughtfully. "The invitation is timely. I need to speak with her. Unfortunately, two human friends are on their way here, and I don't want the driver to see them."

Franklin rustled his feathers. "Do you want me to warn them?"

"Would you?" he asked, brightening.

The bird bobbed his head. "Certainly."

While Franklin pecked at the seeds, Elias sipped his fialazza, turning the goblet absently in his fingers. "I suppose Sheamathan wants to discuss the missing miners."

"I heard her mention them," Franklin said, sounding apprehensive.

Elias nodded. Being a bird had advantages. Franklin could perch overhead and spy on Sheamathan. "What else did you hear?" Elias asked, frowning.

"The wolfhound is gone. It didn't return after the full moon."

Elias sipped his fialazza. "What does Sheamathan think about that?"

The bird screeched—a sound like laughter. "She says gem powers are at work. She thinks the wolfhound outwitted his enchantment."

Elias smiled faintly. "She's right, he did." His smile faded. "Does she think I had a hand in it?"

Franklin cocked his head. "I don't believe so. She suspects a human woman."

"You've been a great help to me, Franklin. I wish I could repay you. The human woman, and the wolfhound who is now a man, are the ones I'm expecting."

"I'll tell them to hide if they hear the cart."

"Bless you, my dear friend." Their relationship spanned fifteen years. Sheamathan's enchanted victims lived long lives if they managed to avoid predators. Franklin's plight still made Elias furious. Over the years, Elias had restored a few enchanted beings, but Franklin had refused his help. It was beyond Elias's abilities to heal him, and Franklin would rather be a skreet than go home a crippled man. Franklin had spent months in the dungeon, starved and beaten for refusing to give detailed information about his home and family, and the beatings had left him crippled. When Sheamathan had finally seen she couldn't break him, she had turned him into a giant skreet.

Elias said, "You should go. Before the breghlin comes."

"I'll find your friends."

He walked Franklin to the entryway. The bird bobbed his head in farewell, and with a heavy heart, Elias watched him take to the air with rapid beats of his powerful wings. Elias stared after him and then shook himself from his gloomy thoughts to concentrate on the matter at hand. Sheamathan was like an impatient child, he told himself with a sigh. She would expect him to come immediately. If he wasn't home, the driver would wait, but Sheamathan would grow more irritated with each passing hour.

Hurrying to the inner cave to change his clothes, he put on a green robe and a pair of leather sandals, and then brushed his hair and beard. Inside a box beside his bed he kept several ornate gold bracelets set with powerful gems, and a number of heavy gold chains that held pendants with gems. He emptied the box onto his bed. He would wear the entire assortment.

His body had long since become infused with gem powers, but if he went a few weeks without touching the gemstones, his powers began to weaken. Touching the gems boosted his infused powers. With some gems the difference was barely discernible, but with others it was like a jolt of power. Whenever he met with Sheamathan he wore all his gems.

She would be similarly gem-laden; in fact, her array of gems would eclipse his. He smiled bitterly. It was her way of reminding him that she ruled Shadow, and that she was a more powerful gem master. Today, as always, he would avoid looking at her gray metal collar. It galled her to wear the restrictive device and they never spoke of it.

He slipped seven necklaces with pendants over his head and let them lay in plain view on his robe. Four of the gems held dark powers. He never used dark powers these days, and he hoped he wouldn't have to today. He placed four cuff bracelets on his right arm, and three on his left. Even in the dimly lit cave, light flashed from the faceted gems and shimmered across the domed surface of the cabochons. He drew power and let out a long, shuddering breath as strength and vitality surged through him. Tilting his head back, he closed his eyes, drawing intuition, foresight, and confidence.

These meetings were always unnerving. He must measure his words carefully and guard his thoughts. With practice, he had learned to hide his true feelings and shield his mind. Nevertheless, she would try to read his thoughts. He stroked his beard thoughtfully. She would probe, hoping to catch him in an unguarded moment, and he would do the same to her. All the while they would smile and drink tea or rakka, and eat fruit that had survived Shadow's blight. An onlooker would think they were the best of friends. He scowled. Hopefully, this charade would be over soon. Sheamathan was a detestable creature. In his darkest moments, he had been a saint compared to her. With help from Lana and Jules, he would end her reign of terror.

The shrill, high-pitched blast from an animal horn echoed through the cave. The driver was here. Smoothing his expression, he walked to the front door, looked through the woven branches, and said curtly to the breghlin standing there, "Good day. What can I do for you?"

"The woodspirit sent me to get you."

"I see. Give me a moment to refresh myself and I will accompany you."

The breghlin's lumpy, malformed features and dull eyes registered no emotion. Jerking a thumb at the cart, the driver said, "I will wait." The cart was drawn by a maraku—the same kind of animal that Sheamathan used to haul alamaria. The beast reminded Elias of an ox, but it was smaller and less powerfully built. Its thick, curly reddish-brown coat made a fine rug once the animal was too old to work.

Elias hurried to the inner cave and finished getting ready. After taking another drink of fialazza, he slipped a small knife and a few loose gems into his inner pockets and then looked around. What was he forgetting?

Ah, yes. The sedative. I don't know when I'll need it, so I should have it with me.

His pulse raced at the thought of Sheamathan stepping through the portal and finding herself defenseless. With Lana and Jules's help, he would drug her, and then he would ensure she was defenseless—permanently. He retrieved a vial from a high shelf and examined the murky red liquid. The idea of drugging the woodspirit both excited and terrified him. He was nearly certain this potion wouldn't kill her, but it should incapacitate her for two or three hours. He slipped the vial into his inner pocket, and wiped his clammy palms on his robe. Now it was time to go. This visit was essential to their plans, but there were so many things that could go wrong, and the prospect of failure made him numb.

He secured the door to his cave, walked to the cart, climbed in, and sat on the padded bench behind the driver's box. "Go ahead, driver," he called. The breghlin cracked the beast on the rump with a stick and the cart lurched into motion. Elias grabbed the side of the cart to steady himself.

Deep in thought, he stared unseeing at the passing scenery. Sheamathan believed that Jules had broken the wolfhound enchantment and that Lana was involved. That should make the woodspirit feel vulnerable, and he could use that to his advantage. He would convince her that her campaign to win the Fair Lands was in jeopardy now that Jules was human again, and she should check the Amulet to see if he had interfered with the blight. Elias frowned, considering. If Sheamathan was worried enough, she might want to go tonight. Would she ask him to go with her? He took a deep breath and let it out slowly. He had planned to wait for her in the Amulet with Jules and Lana. He had never considered walking through the portal *with* her. It might make little difference, he supposed, as long as Lana and Jules were expecting it.

His hand moved instinctively to the purple gem beneath his robe. If they got the chance to overthrow Sheamathan tonight, he must send word to Lana and Jules, but it wouldn't be easy to get away from the woodspirit long enough to summon Franklin and entrust him with a message. Elias sighed. Lana had a reputation for being lucky and resourceful. "Please let that be something we have in common," he muttered under his breath.

* * *

Lana and the boys spent a moment in tearful goodbyes at the bus station. The boys took her phone number and promised to call. Ironically, a few weeks ago, she had been desperate to get rid of them, and now she was sorry to see them go. She had become surprisingly fond of them, she realized, as she watched them walk into the bus station. How had they won her over? No one had ever been dependent on her, much less looked up to her. Was that the secret? It was nice feeling like an older sister. Sure, she had missed her privacy, but now the prospect of watching TV by herself and eating alone left her feeling empty inside.

Jules laid a comforting hand on her arm. "I'm sure you'll see them again."

She nodded and put on a brave face. "I guess we should get going."

After stopping at her apartment to get Folio's coffee, they headed for the park, and she drove the entire way in pensive silence, feeling tense and jittery for no reason that she could explain. She debated saying something to Jules but she didn't want to alarm him. After all, she had nothing to go on—no dreams, visions, or telepathic messages—just a sense of uneasiness.

When they reached the park and she was about to get out of the car, Jules caught her arm. She turned to look at him and saw the worried look in his eyes. "You've been unusually quiet," he said. She could hear the suspicion in his tone. "You feel it too, don't you?"

She tried to hide her surprise. "Feel what?"

He gave her a look that said she knew very well what he meant.

"Okay, you're right," she said reluctantly. "I feel uneasy. Is that what you mean?"

He nodded.

She looked out the windshield and said quietly, "At first I thought it was something to do with Greg or Jordy, but now I don't think so."

"It could have to do with our trip to Shadow," he said slowly. "It might be a warning." He paused. "Or maybe it's about Elias. Maybe he's in danger."

"See, that's just why I didn't say anything to you." She looked at him and shrugged. "It feels like a warning, but a warning about *what?* Without having some idea, it won't do us much good."

"At least it will make us more cautious," he said as he got out of the car.

They walked to the portal without seeing anyone. Thanks to their gem powers, it wouldn't be difficult to use the portal during the daytime—or so Jules said. She wanted to cross now while nocturnal predators were sleeping. As they approached, she could feel the energy field's vibrations. How strong would the repelling force be? Jules drew his knife and then held out his other hand. She slipped her hand into his and after a brief pause he led her through.

The forest on the other side was quiet, almost serene this time of day. The sky was a pale blue, nearly white, with high wisps of clouds. She stood very still, listening for movement in the trees and underbrush. Jules continued to hold the knife. And her hand. His fingers tightened protectively around hers, warm, strong, and reassuring.

After a moment they looked at each other, a wordless communication passing between them. It wasn't quite mind reading, she thought, and yet they knew what the other was thinking. *It seems safe enough at the moment, but keep a sharp eye out.*

They set out for Strathweed. She still felt edgy. How could she relax when she sensed danger but didn't know what it was?

The air was completely still, without a hint of breeze. As she walked the winding, tree-shaded trail with Jules, the only insects she saw were normal-size. Even so, her eyes flicked nervously over the woods on either side of the trail, and she was especially wary of gullies and thick patches of brush where something might hide.

After a mile or so she felt more at ease. It was almost like hiking at County Forest Park, except the trees were so otherworldly. Just as she was about to comment on how peaceful it was, Jules pulled her to an abrupt halt, his hand tightening around hers. He looked up and scanned the sky, his expression unreadable.

What had he seen? She was about to ask when something dark passed overhead. She tensed, searching the sky for another glimpse of it, but the thick canopy of leaves obstructed her view. Whatever it was, it was far larger than most birds, but too small for a pythanium.

Jules's pulled her into the trees.

There it was again—a black bird, as big as a turkey, circling slowly.

When Jules's hand relaxed, she stopped watching the sky long enough to glance at him. His expression was more curious than afraid, and she found that reassuring. Together they watched the sky for the bird's next appearance.

Wings flapped loudly, and then the huge bird appeared, descending rapidly with a shrill screech. Lana let out a startled cry. The bird flew over the trail, its wingspan nearly as wide as the trail itself.

"Don't be afraid," Jules said. "I know this bird. It's Elias's messenger."

Lana's mouth fell open. Elias had a messenger? If so, the bird must be enchanted. She tried to relax, but it was hard not to feel apprehensive when it landed a short distance up the trail and started walking toward them, its head bobbing in bird-like fashion.

"Hello, Franklin!" Jules called. "Did Elias send you?" Pulling Lana with him, Jules started toward the bird.

"Yes," the bird said in a high, clear voice. "Elias told me to find the human woman, and the man who used to be the wolfhound would be with her."

Lana blinked in surprise at the mention of the wolfhound. Folio must really trust this bird to give out *that* kind of information.

"Is something wrong?" Jules asked.

Franklin bobbed his head. "Sheamathan sent a cart to bring Elias to Shadowglade." He paused, as if to let them digest the information. "He's worried that the driver will see you, so hide if you hear the breghlin's cart."

"We'll stay off the main trail," Jules said.

Lana tightened her grip on Jules's hand. "Sheamathan sent for him? I don't like the sound of that. Should we be worried?"

He shook his head. "I don't think so. Elias planned to meet with her—just not this soon. She's probably worried because I didn't come back. By now she's heard that twelve miners are gone. Strange things are happening, and Elias is the only one who can advise her."

Franklin angled his head and said, "When you did not return on time, the woodspirit retreated to her private chambers to seek knowledge from her gemstones. She believes your enchantment has been broken." The bird's gaze shifted to Lana. "She suspects this woman was involved."

Jules absorbed this information with a worried frown. "Things are escalating quickly," he said to Lana. "Sheamathan thinks I'm human again, and who besides you could break my enchantment? It took Fair Lands powers." He paused. "I didn't think she'd suspect the truth so soon."

Lana twisted a strand of hair nervously. "Folio was right. He said she'd suspect what had happened right away, and I never stopped to think about it, but of course she'd use her gems to figure out what had happened."

The bird screeched—a sound like harsh laughter. "The woodspirit is frightened. She's afraid of people she can't control!"

Jules looked away and folded his arms. After a moment he said, "Elias will meet with Sheamathan in an hour or two, and he'll set our plan into motion."

Did he welcome that or find it disturbing? The thought of confronting the woodspirit so soon made Lana feel numb. "I want to go through with our plan," she said slowly, "but I don't feel ready." Jules looked at her with no trace of fear and she wished she could feel as calm. "We only have one shot at this," she reminded him. "We can't afford a mistake."

He downplayed her concern. "You're viewing this from our perspective—now look at it from hers. After nearly a century, Sheamathan overcame her restrictive collar and started to feel invincible. Then you arrive with Fair Lands gems and the Challenger's blade, and I break my enchantment. How do you think she feels now?"

"Vulnerable."

"Exactly, and Elias will prey on her insecurities."

His optimism was encouraging. "I hope so. We need to keep her off balance."

"She's never known the extent of my abilities. Wouldn't that bother you if you were her?"

Lana nodded. "And over the years, you might have discovered things about *her*—maybe some of her weaknesses."

His expression grew thoughtful. "I wonder if she ever considered that during my lucid periods I might have been studying Shadow gems and plotting against her. Fair Lands gems are a threat, too. That's why she's afraid of you."

Lana laughed. How could the woodspirit be afraid of a twenty-two-year-old gemologist with an old Toyota and a dumpy apartment? It seemed ridiculous.

"Don't laugh. I'm serious," he protested. "Sheamathan doesn't know much about you, but you were able to use the Challenger's blade, so she knows you have gem powers. The idea of us working together, looking for ways to disrupt her powers, has to be unsettling."

"I hope so."

"Elias is sly. When he's through with her, she'll be a nervous wreck."

To Folio's credit, he had already pulled off some pretty good stunts, like the wolfhound enchantment and the restraining collar. Sheamathan had taken his bait and played right into his hands. Now he had to do it again.

"Elias knows Sheamathan's weaknesses," Franklin agreed. "He'll choose his words carefully."

"If it were me," Jules said, "I'd make her question whether the blight is still spreading. We could have reversed it by now. We want her to go there and check."

Lana wet dry lips. The thought of Folio trying to out-maneuver Sheamathan made her stomach churn. He had to shield his thoughts while playing the role of a supportive, sympathetic friend—a deadly game. If Sheamathan glimpsed his true feelings and discovered he was plotting against her, she'd strike him with every dark power at her disposal.

She said grimly, "When Folio needs us, we'd better be ready."

"If I can watch without being seen, I'll spy on the meeting," Franklin promised.

"We can't thank you enough," Lana told him.

"We'll stay at Strathweed until Elias comes home or you bring us a message. I'll leave the door open."

"The woodspirit often serves him tea on the terrace. If she does that today, it will be easy to spy on them. Wish me luck." Franklin bobbed his head and flew away.

"And so we wait," Lana said heavily, watching him disappear above the treetops. "I hate suspense."

Jules took her arm and they cut through the woods, avoiding the trail that led to Strathweed. Her mind kept wandering to Folio. He had amazing powers but the woodspirit was an ancient being, as infused with evil as with gem powers. Folio was about to face that black-hearted abomination. Lana felt a sudden sadness that surprised her. For the first time she saw Folio as a vulnerable old man—a vulnerable old man that she cared about.

Chapter 34

The cart rattled down a narrow path and then circled behind the castle. Elias took a deep breath, willing his pulse to slow. He placed a hand over his stack of bracelets, drawing peace of mind, courage and optimism. Today, of all days, he must appear calm and relaxed.

In a moment the driver would pull up by one of the rear entrances and guards would take him to Sheamathan. Typically, she served him tea on the terrace. A vine-covered arbor shaded the terrace, which sounded quite delightful, but the vines were poisonous like the woodspirit herself. He frowned. Fortunately, his gems would warn him if she served him anything laced with drugs or poison.

As the cart rolled to a stop, he cast a furtive glance at the sky. Twice, he had seen Franklin following at a distance. That meant his faithful ally had already delivered the message to Lana and Jules and now he was here to spy on the meeting.

The cart beast stamped its feet impatiently and let out a bellow. The breghlin jumped off the driver's seat and came back to assist Elias. Elias took his hand, climbed out of the cart, and followed him to the rear entryway. The door opened immediately. Two breghlin with sheathed knifes on their belts stood waiting.

"*She* awaits you," one said in a gravelly voice. Neither breghlin looked Elias in the eye. They were afraid of his powers, assuming that if they offended him, he would punish them, just as Sheamathan did.

"Very good. Shall we go?" Elias followed them into the castle.

When Sheamathan wasn't in her throne room, she was usually lounging on the terrace. It extended from the second floor, supported by stone columns, and overlooked an ornamental garden of poisonous and carnivorous plants. Sheamathan delighted in that garden and often made sketches of it, showing Elias her handiwork with the praise-seeking enthusiasm of a five-year-old child.

Today, four guards stood just outside the terrace doorway. Elias walked past them and paused for his escort to announce his arrival.

"The gem master of Strathweed!"

Sheamathan was sitting on a wrought iron bench with her back to him. The infuriating woman continued to stare at her garden and made no effort to move or reply.

"It's a fine, gloomy day," Elias ventured. The woodspirit hated sunny days nearly as much as cheerfulness.

She finally stood, set something on the bench, and faced him. "Yes, gray skies are soothing," she agreed, and then she looked past him and snarled at the guards, "Stop staring. Call for tea and fruit!"

Elias turned to look at them. "Yes, My Lady," the stouter of the two said, bowing repeatedly. Trembling, they backed through the door, probably afraid to turn their backs on her.

"The dolts seldom remember my habits or anticipate my needs," Sheamathan grumbled.

Here we go again with the list of breghlin offenses.

Unlike the breghlin, he knew her habits and made a point of remembering what pleased her. He walked to the round, wrought iron table and sat down, idly studying the tabletop while he waited for her to join him. Spiders, beetles, and pythanium had been worked into the table's intricate design. As always, a pot of various carnivorous plants— pale green, variegated yellow, and blood red—sat in the center of the table. Sheamathan enjoyed the insects' hopeless struggle to escape before the plants digested them.

She walked toward him, barefoot as always. Wild, untamed waves of jet-black hair hung to her waist. She wore a full-length black dress. Sheer, three-quarter length sleeves covered, but did not hide, the gem-studded silver bands encircling each upper arm. On her wrists, and up her arms nearly to her elbows, she wore gold and silver bracelets encrusted with every color gem. Gold rings with gems adorned three fingers and both thumbs. She wore fewer necklaces than he did. Four large pendants with gems hung from intricate silver chains. The grayish metal collar, her restrictive device, lay smooth and flat against her collarbone, her only jewelry without gems.

Sheamathan chose her usual chair facing the garden. From this vantage point she could study his face while enjoying the scenery behind him. Her black eyes flicked over his face. Below the surface of his mind flowed an undercurrent of thoughts that he hoped she couldn't penetrate. He allowed a few unimportant thoughts to float along the surface, like breadcrumbs on a pond.

"If I imprisoned every incompetent breghlin, I would have no one left to serve me," she said irritably.

"They're afraid to act without orders," he said with a shrug.

Sheamathan waved a dismissive hand. "I don't mean the fools who just left. They're the least of my problems. I had a security breach at my work camp."

She never called it a mining camp, even though they both knew it was, Elias thought with a touch of amusement. And they never discussed alamaria. No doubt she hoped to keep him in the dark about its powers. "Security breech?" he repeated blankly.

Her index finger absently traced the outline of one of the wrought iron beetles in the tabletop. "Twelve gnomes disappeared the other night. The guards didn't see or hear anything." She looked up and her eyes glittered angrily.

Elias asked placidly, "How is that possible?"

"Gem powers," she snapped. One hand strayed to the stack of bracelets on her arm, and her fingers played nervously over them. "How else could twelve gnomes escape from a pit, especially without making a sound?"

He stroked his beard, making sure he looked very concerned. "Who could free them? And who would want to?"

She leaned forward and her probing black eyes met his. She was trying to read him. A prickle of fear ran up his spine. Her eyes held his for an uncomfortably long time but he remained calm and didn't look away. She sat back in her chair, apparently satisfied and said, "I have another piece of news that may answer your question."

Trying to look only mildly interested, he waited patiently.

"The full moon is past and my wolfhound did not return." She frowned and added, "You, of all people, should know what that means."

It was time to feed her fears. He gave her a worried look. "That is troubling on many accounts. I assume you're implying that he's human again. You think *he* freed the gnomes?"

"Yes. Exactly." Perspiration glistened on her brow. She stared moodily at the carnivorous plants on the table, perhaps hoping he'd tell her that she must be mistaken.

He cleared his throat. "Well, that's certainly a disturbing theory."

She raised her cold, black eyes to his and he fiddled with his pendants, purposely looking nervous. "If you're right, the missing gnomes are just the beginning. Gem Master Jules will cause you no end of trouble." He spread his hands in a helpless gesture and asked bleakly, "But how could this happen? How could he break the enchantment after all these years? It hardly seems possible."

Sheamathan's eyes narrowed. "The woman I told you about is mixed up in this. I am sure of it. There is no other explanation." The woodspirit's lips curled in a snarl. "She has the jeweled knife. How did she get it? Where has it been all these years?" Sweeping back a wave that clung to her perspiring face, she leaned forward again, her eyes filled with hatred. "I should have been more concerned when she showed up with the knife, claiming to be the gnomes' messenger. She told me—" She stopped short, her attention drawn to the doorway as two female breghlin walked in. One carried a tray with ceramic cups, silverware and a silver teapot. The other carried a tray with bowls of mushy-looking fruit.

"Hurry up," Sheamathan snapped. "The dead move faster than you."

The breghlin servers wore gray pants and tunics with their name— HB and TA—stitched on the tunics, if you could call their letter designations names. A leather cord held back their dark brown hair. Their malformed, repugnant features contrasted sharply with Sheamathan's sterile beauty. Elias knew how much that delighted her. The servers shuffled to the table with their burdens, avoiding their queen's eyes, and with trembling hands, unloaded the contents of their trays.

"Where is *Elias's* fruit? You *know* he dislikes rotting fruit!" She grabbed HB's arm, her nails digging in savagely. The pitiful creature gave a strangled sob and said, "I's sorry. I'll bring more right away."

Sheamathan released the server's arm and slapped the breghlin's face. "In the meantime, he'll have nothing to eat with his tea."

Elias stared down at the table. He knew from previous attempts that it was pointless to intervene. Nothing made Sheamathan angrier, and it did more harm than good. The best he could do was say calmly, "I don't mind the occasional piece of, ah, overripe fruit." He tried not to look at the contents of the bowls. Patches of furry mold covered most of their wrinkled skins and they had oozing, discolored spots. Insects crawled on the fruit and buzzed around the bowls.

"Fresh fruit! Now!" Sheamathan ordered. Wrinkling her nose she added, "Bring the disgustingly *sweet* fruits, if we have any." She glanced at Elias and shook her head, as always mystified at his preference for sweet over sour.

TA, who was about to serve their tea, shook so badly that Elias wondered whether any tea would land in the cup. Breathing with shaky gasps, she tilted the teapot with exaggerated care and managed to fill two blue ceramic cups without spilling any. She set the cups gently in front of Elias and Sheamathan, placed the teapot on the table, and stepped back.

Sheamathan took one sip and exploded. "This isn't hot enough! Is it so difficult to boil water?" Grabbing TA's upper arm, her fingers tightened like a vise until the poor creature wailed in pain. Tomorrow the breghlin would have bruises shaped like Sheamathan's fingers. He looked away and sipped his tea, which was just short of scalding. Clearly, the woodspirit's mood was darker than usual and no one could satisfy her.

"Should I brings more water?" the server asked, snuffling as she stared at the floor.

"No. Once the dolt returns with Elias's fruit, I don't want any more interruptions."

He looked at Sheamathan's fruit, wishing the breeze would carry the odor away. How could she eat something that smelled like dirty socks?

"Yes, Mistress." The servant grabbed the empty tray and fled from the room.

"Now, then, where were we?" she asked irritably.

"We were discussing your dog—former dog," he corrected himself, "and the woman with his knife."

"Oh, yes." Her face darkened. "I believe Gem Master Jules found a way to break his bargain once he learned I had broken mine."

"And you think the woman had a hand in it. That concerns me all the more." He shook his head. "I don't like the sound of this. Not at all."

Again Sheamathan's eyes met his in a cold, probing stare. *Had he heard anything about this? Was he really as disturbed as he seemed?* He let a few troubled thoughts float on the surface of his mind.

Sheamathan looked away, sipped her tea, and then took a mushy, plum-sized fruit from one of the bowls. The fruit had rotted and burst open. Tiny insects feasted on the juices that oozed out. Elias watched transfixed as she popped the fruit into her mouth and swallowed it whole. "*You* may have reason to worry," she said as she reached for another fruit, "but he won't trouble *me*. Lately, I have become much more powerful."

And I know why. "Be that as it may," he said, trying not to watch her eat, "Fair Lands gems can disrupt Shadow gem powers. The fact that you're more powerful won't change that."

Her face fell. Perhaps she had forgotten that.

"Jules won't bargain with you again," he advised. "He'll try to disrupt your powers and make you look foolish." He looked her in the eye. "If you're right—if Jules really set the gnomes free—that was his opening shot in the war."

She said in a dangerous tone, "He won't trouble me. I won't give him the chance." She smashed her fist on the table, making the teacups jump, and her eyes took on a wild, unreasoning look that made Elias shrink back in his chair. "This time I'll crush him! He's no match for me!"

Elias grabbed his cup to steady it, and quickly mastered himself, resuming his plan of attack. "Don't underestimate him. When he regained his wits during the full moons, he may have learned new gem powers to use against you. He's dangerous, especially if he has the knife."

"The knife," she repeated, her frenzied hatred visibly leeching away. "A marvelous weapon that should be mine." Her expression took on a brooding sort of gloominess, and he fought back a smile.

"Sadly, neither of us can touch it," he said calmly.

She sighed. "We would be wise to destroy it. If we could."

Yes, she would be safer if the knife were destroyed and safer still if no one could use *any* Fair Lands gems. He had been a threat to her upon his arrival in Shadow, and he would have remained so if he hadn't become corrupt like her. She had rejoiced when she saw his toad-like skin developing and his facial features began to change. She knew what it signified. Once he lost his ability to use Fair Lands gems she became complacent, knowing no one could challenge her power. But those days were over he mused, carefully shielding his thoughts. Jules was human again, and Jules and Lana posed a threat.

He resumed his attack. "The woman carries the Challenger's Blade, you say. How powerful is she?"

"I am not sure. I read her mind easily. On the whole, I found her frightened, timid and uncertain. And she did not know much about the knife. I was amazed it responded to her at all, considering her ineptitude." She shrugged. "Either she is not as ignorant as she seemed, or her command of the knife improved quickly. She caused no end of trouble in the dungeon, as I told you during our last visit." Scowling with disgust she added, "I cannot believe my dimwit guard set her free."

"Has it occurred to you that her ignorance was a carefully contrived act? And her claim to be the gnomes' messenger was a clever deception?"

Sheamathan gave him a dark look, and he thought she was about to reply when the serving female returned with his fresh fruit. The breghlin set the plate in front of him and waited anxiously for his approval. He selected a firm, purple fruit and nodded contentedly as he ate.

"Go now," the woodspirit snapped. HB bowed and scurried away as fast as she could without running.

"The human is no match for me," Sheamathan said, picking up the thread of conversation, "even if she *is* more powerful than she lets on."

He made a split-second probe of the woodspirit's mind and came away with no specific thoughts, just a general sense of uneasiness. "My main concern is that the two are working together."

Feigning unconcern, Sheamathan ignored him. Her eyes roved to the pot of carnivorous flowers. She plucked a large, half-digested, hard-shelled beetle from the mouth of a pitcher plant and, holding it inches from her face, studied it. Elias lifted a brow. What could be so fascinating about a half-digested bug? Then her long, sandpapery tongue shot out, snatching it from her fingers. Munching contentedly, she sighed in satisfaction.

"What if they find a way to reverse the blight?" Elias continued, trying to keep the conversation on track despite his revulsion. "That would ruin your plans. When was the last time you checked the Amulet?"

She looked at him. Concern flickered in her eyes. "A week ago. The blight was still spreading."

He drummed his fingers on the table. "That was before Jules reversed his enchantment."

"Yes," she conceded unhappily. She swept back her hair. The gray metal collar gleamed around her throat and he dropped his eyes before she caught him looking at it. The collar reminded him—he had overlooked a question she would find disconcerting. "What if they tamper with the portal, and strengthen its ability to repel you?"

Her head snapped up. For an instant, fear flashed across her face, and then she hastily looked away. "Is that possible?" Her hand strayed to her chest, her fingers closing around a dark green pendant whose stone he recognized due to its distinctive shade. It gave the user foresight. After a moment she let out a shuddering breath and released the pendant. "They can't stop me from crossing the portal. I'm much stronger now." Clasping her teacup with both hands, she drained it and stared into the empty cup. Her hands were trembling noticeably. *Good. Very good.* His worries were beginning to infect her, and apparently the insights she had received from the green gem had been less than reassuring.

He let two thoughts drift to the surface of his mind. *Check on the blight to make sure it's spreading. See if you can still pass through the portal.*

She looked up and her eyes locked onto his. He knew she had read him. Wariness flickered in her eyes. *Relax,* he cautioned himself. She must only read the thoughts he wanted her to read. *Try to breathe normally.* She was still probing his mind and he must pretend he wasn't aware of it. He concentrated on shielding his private thoughts while allowing random thoughts of friendly concern to float on the surface. Finally, she looked away. It was all he could do not to sag in relief. A sick feeling churned in the pit of his stomach. What would happen if she discovered he was baiting her?

"I suppose it pays to be cautious," she said after a moment. "I have no idea where the wretched troublemakers are or what they plan to do."

"There's no mystery about Jules's intentions. He will try to keep you out of his world."

She absently touched the metal collar, then snatched her hand away and poured more tea. "I have not checked the Amulet since the wolfhound disappeared. No doubt everything is fine, but I should take a look, just to reassure myself."

Good. Yes. She was playing into his hands.

"I will go tonight," she said with a careless shrug. My driver can take us."

"Us?" he asked.

"Yes. Us. You should see for yourself that everything is fine."

"Begging your pardon, but in the unlikely event that something *is* wrong, what then?"

"Then you will help me!" she snapped.

"Certainly, certainly," he agreed meekly. "Jules and the woman are working together. Why shouldn't we join forces?"

"An alliance—a *brief* alliance," she amended pointedly, "would benefit both of us."

"No doubt. And I would be happy to accompany you tonight." He was sure she would wait until dark when no one was likely to see them. Eventually, she would show herself openly, but not yet. He poured another cup of tea to have something to do with his hands. He needed to get a message to Franklin, saying Lana and Jules should go through the portal well before dark and wait on the other side. He looked up, scanning the tangle of vines covering the arbor. Was Franklin overhead somewhere, listening? Even if he were, this wasn't a safe place to converse, and slipping away unattended to speak elsewhere was out of the question.

Sheamathan rose. "Have all the fruit you want. The sweet fruit always goes to waste." She smoothed her dress, smiling slyly. "I have a new morgul stone I would like you to see."

"A morgul!" he said appreciatively. "Quite a find."

"Twelve carats and flawless, and the deep blue color is exceptional, especially for a stone so large."

"Amazing. A breghlin found it for you?"

"Yes. Occasionally they do something right."

"I don't believe I've ever seen a morgul larger than five carats."

She walked away, a self-satisfied smirk on her face, and he smiled too as he watched her go. Their rivalry over gems had started decades ago. She owned the largest, finest gems, and the rarest gems, which had amazing powers. How she loved to torment him with each new treasure. Undoubtedly, the morgul was locked in her private chambers. She would have to get it herself and that would take a few minutes.

He stood and paced the terrace. He was finally alone, but not for long. He could summon Franklin, but whispering was risky since breghlin guards had distressingly good hearing. He could read the bird's mind, but Franklin couldn't read his, despite the purple gem that linked them, so telepathy wouldn't work.

Lucky and resourceful. Lucky and resourceful.

He headed toward the edge of the terrace. Maybe inspiration would strike while he gazed at the gardens.

Something dark moved above him in the vines. He looked up and glimpsed black feathers. Franklin! If Franklin had been listening, there was no need to warn him that Sheamathan would be back soon. Elias continued across the terrace.

Lucky and resourceful.

When he reached the bench where Sheamathan had been sitting, he glanced down and saw a sheaf of papers and a drawing pencil. She had been drawing again, but not the garden this time, and her sketch was disturbing. It looked like a city block in the Fair Lands, but the buildings were very tall and some appeared to be made almost entirely of glass. Strange conveyances lined both sides of the street—sleek, squat forms with small wheels. He drew a deep breath and let it out slowly, shivering with dread. She had gotten these images from someone's mind, and clearly not his.

Never mind the drawing, however disturbing it may be. Here is your luck, Elias. Take it! He snatched up a blank piece of paper, folded it to a more manageable size, and with her pencil wrote in large, block letters:

LANA AND JULES, GO TO THE PORTAL. CROSS AND WAIT. I'M COMING WITH SHEAMATHAN TONIGHT.

He looked up. Franklin was directly overhead, watching through the vines. After a moment Franklin nodded that he understood. Elias probed the bird's mind briefly: Lana and Jules were waiting at Strathweed. Franklin would take the message there.

The bird flew away. Elias walked to the edge of the terrace, tore the message into confetti, and watched the wind carry it away. Feeling as if a burden had lifted from his chest, he walked back to the table and sat down to wait for Sheamathan to return with her morgul.

Chapter 35

Sheamathan walked to her private chambers, fuming silently.

That devious old fool is up to something. His mind was swept so clean there was nothing to find but dust in the corners. When has he ever gone to such great lengths to shield his thoughts? It can only mean one thing. He is hiding something. She let out her breath in an angry hiss and whispered, "What is he hiding?" The stone passageway echoed her whisper, mocking her.

Her eyes narrowed. One hand strayed to her chest. She curled her fingers around the dark green gem, feeling more and more alarmed. *We had been discussing Gem Master Jules and the woman Lana when the gem showed me I was in danger.* She wet her lips nervously and released the stone, afraid to receive further troubling premonitions. She was being challenged on all sides. What had Elias said? Jules would try to disrupt her power and thwart her ambitions. The old fool did not need to tell her that. Of course Jules would try to break her grasp on the Fair Lands. Otherwise, a hundred years of his life had been spent in vain. And then there was the woman. The wretched gnome-lover. Sheamathan ground her teeth in frustration. *She demanded I liberate the gnomes and treat them kindly! What a ridiculous notion! The gnomes are weak, useless fools—worse than breghlin.* Sheamathan's eyes narrowed. How she despised weakness! Her hand moved to the gray metal collar and she cursed under her breath. The loathsome thing would not come off, and it was a symbol of weakness, but at last she had overcome it. Under no circumstances would she ever submit to such humiliation again.

She walked faster, hardly noticing the cold stone on her bare feet. A soft breeze from the open terrace blew through the passageway, faintly stirring cobwebs on the ceiling. Soot had darkened the upper walls. A few torches flickered. Murky light played over the stone blocks.

Elias was the only one who accepted her for who she was, she thought grimly, and now he was behaving suspiciously. *Why is he so worried about the blight's progress? Nothing can stop its destruction.* Satisfying images flashed through her mind: dead grass, rotting fungi, mottled diseased leaves, and trees with bare, lifeless limbs. Soon all the forest's plants and trees would be dead. The disease would march onward like an advancing army, destroying everything. Before long starvation, poverty, and chaos would allow her to conquer and pillage the humans' world. Humans were almost as weak as gnomes, she thought with disgust. It was hard to say which would be more satisfying—using her powers to paralyze them, or turning them into creatures that amused her.

A scornful laugh escaped her lips as she thought of her first interview with the human boys. *They thought they were being clever. They knew they should not tell me about their world, but their minds were full of useful images.* How unfortunate that the woman Lana had escaped. She might have provided fresh information.

Sheamathan frowned. If only she could get mental images from the wolfhound, but his dog mind was useless, and during his lucid periods he managed to keep his mind nearly blank. It would have been easier to make her conquest of the Fair Lands long ago when their world had been more primitive—more like Shadow. Now, judging by what she had seen in the boys' minds, the human world had many advanced countries. She would face weapons and technologies that had not existed in Jules's day, but it did not matter, she told herself. Modern weapons were merely an inconvenience. If necessary, she could reshape their atoms into something harmless. More likely, she would simply subvert high-ranking officers and take command of the humans' weapons. In every world there were those who would remain "gnomes" and those who would become "breghlin." Her brief study of humans suggested that she would find no shortage of "breghlin" to serve her.

Stopping at her chamber door, she gave a mental command to the lock. In response, the tumblers clicked and she opened the door, revealing the comforting darkness of her private sitting room. Urns with wilted flowers and stalks of dead weeds stood along one wall. In the center of the room stood a low couch of brown leather stretched over a frame of animal bones. Two matching chairs faced the couch. Books, maps, and stacks of sketches filled several freestanding bookcases. A few of her favorite sketches hung on the stone walls. She frequently sketched images she had seen in humans' minds: houses and tenement buildings, stores and factories. Many human cities had regions that were delightfully squalid. She would need to destroy the human transport devices, which allowed them too much freedom of movement. People could travel well enough on foot, or they could use animal-drawn carts, as they did here.

The sleeping room, beyond her sitting room, held a writing desk and her vault. A soft, fabric webbing, that encompassed her like a cocoon, hung from the ceiling. Neither room had windows. She preferred semi-darkness. Oil or candles shed enough light to enjoy her sketches and gems.

As she went to get the morgul from her vault, Elias came to mind again. *When I lay claim to his world, he will not care. After all these years, the Fair Lands are just a distant memory.*

It had been easy to corrupt him and trap him here. With little effort she had goaded him into using dark powers. Cut off from the Fair

Lands and unable to use its gems, he was less of a threat. Even still, she kept an eye on him. *He comes when I call, just like the breghlin.*

An uncomfortable thought occurred to her. As the blight progressed she would be able to travel further into the Fair Lands, but so would he. An icy hand squeezed her heart. *He wants to rule! That is what he is hiding!* She should have suspected it sooner. *He will help me fight Jules and the woman, and when they are gone, he will demand a share of my kingdom. He grows bored, and wants power.* She raked her fingers angrily through her long black hair. Elias had lost his ability to use Fair Lands gems, but he had accumulated powerful native gems, and surely he knew how to use them. Her upper lip rose in a snarl. "I will share nothing with him!"

She commanded the vault to open and reached inside for the deep blue morgul stone. *I do not need his help. I am more powerful than ever. I will crush Jules and the woman Lana, and then I will eliminate Elias as well.*

* * *

Lana sat with Jules, leaning against the wall near Elias's front door. They had arrived at Strathweed over three hours ago, and she hadn't stopped worrying since. Had Franklin been able to spy on Elias and Sheamathan? If so, would the bird return with a message? She had held her gemstones briefly several times, but all she had gotten were vague, disturbing impressions.

The unmistakable sound of Franklin's powerful wings pulled her from her thoughts and she jumped to her feet. She ran to the door, calling breathlessly when she saw the bird, "How is he? Is Elias safe?" Her own words caught her up short. She had always called him Folio. Jules motioned for the bird to come in.

"I spied on their meeting," Franklin said. "Sheamathan believes you and Jules are working together. She asked Elias to form a temporary alliance with her, to defeat you."

Jules asked, "Is Elias coming back soon? Did he send instructions?"

Franklin bobbed his head. "Yes. Sheamathan will come through the portal tonight, and Elias is coming with her. You need to get there first and wait for them."

Lana and Jules exchanged worried glances. Jules said, "That's a change of plans. Elias is supposed to be with us when she comes through."

Franklin regarded them with intelligent black eyes. "Elias told Sheamathan she should check the Amulet, and she insisted that he come with her."

"Why?" Lana asked.

"She wants Elias to see for himself that you and Jules haven't interfered with the blight."

Jules gave a sarcastic laugh. "I see. *She's* not worried, but she's checking the blight just to humor him."

"Elias gave her something else to worry about. He says you'll find a new way to keep her from using the portal. She looked alarmed about that."

Lana rubbed her forehead and frowned. "It sounds like the meeting went well, but when I used my gemstones, I got the impression that Elias is in danger."

"What? Why didn't you say something?" Jules demanded.

She gave a helpless shrug. "What could we do about it from here?"

"I hope you're wrong!" Franklin said and let out a mournful screech. "Everything seemed fine between them."

"I want to be wrong, believe me," she said, shaking her head. "He might not be in immediate danger, but I can't dismiss what I felt. I won't relax until Sheamathan loses her powers."

Franklin asked, "How can she lose her powers?"

Lana was reluctant to explain in detail, even though she trusted the bird. "It's complicated," she said, pausing to find the right words. "We learned how to strip Sheamathan of her powers, but when we do it we'll lose our powers, too."

Jules added hastily, "It's not a permanent condition. Once she's defenseless we'll need to *neutralize* her, as Elias would say."

Lana stared at the cave floor. "I have a feeling something will go wrong. I only wish I knew what."

Franklin flapped his wings in agitation. "Tell me how I can help."

Jules said, "Elias suggested that we have armed gnomes on hand in case Sheamathan brings breghlin along. Can you ask some of Raenihel's clan to come?"

"Yes. I'd be happy to do that. I know Raenihel quite well."

"Make sure they don't run into Sheamathan and Elias on the way," Jules cautioned. "Once they come through the portal, they'll need to hide and watch from a distance."

"I'll deliver your instructions."

"I can't thank you enough," Jules said. We'll gather up our gear and head to the portal."

* * *

"You should have told me about your impressions," Jules scolded her as they walked.

"It seemed pointless. What could we do? And I'm not even sure anything is wrong, so why should I worry you?"

"Because we're working together, and you don't need to shelter me," he said, sounding a bit irritated. "You did the same thing this morning. You weren't going to tell me that something was bothering you, but you're too transparent to hide it."

"Transparent as glass, that's me," she said with a half-hearted grin.

In a gentler tone he said, "No more secrets, all right?"

She nodded. "No more secrets."

Half way to the portal, she said, "Let's stop at the obelisk. I don't want to go back to the Amulet yet. I know Elias wants us there ahead of time, but Sheamathan won't go through the portal before dark. We should have plenty of time."

Jules ran a hand through his wind-blown hair and gave her a puzzled look. "I don't mind the side trip, but why don't you want to go back?"

She said quietly, "Think about it. As soon as we go through the portal, we'll lose our powers. We'll be defenseless. We won't even get premonitions of danger."

He nodded. "I should have thought of that. You're right. My knife will be nothing more than a sharp blade in a jeweled hilt. I'm so anxious to get this over with, I'm not thinking straight."

"Wouldn't it make sense to use our gems for a while before we cross? The obelisk amplifies their powers, so that seems like the best place to do it. Maybe we'll foresee something about Elias—something that explains my uneasiness."

"I'm willing to give it a try."

For a while they walked in silence. Was her growing affection for Elias the reason she was worried about him? Was she imagining danger where there wasn't any?

The forest looked deserted as they approached the obelisk, but they scanned the woods for any sign of movement before they left the protection of the trees. She followed Jules into the clearing and looked up, taking in the full height of the shimmering black obelisk. "It's really impressive!"

"It is," he agreed as they stared at it.

"Can you feel it—the energy vibrations?"

"Yes. That's how Elias discovered the obelisk."

"He felt the energy?"

"From a long way off."

As they walked closer, Jules drew his knife. She had used the knife so many times it felt like hers, and seeing him hold it gave her a twinge of envy. The inlaid gems in the hilt and the gem-infused blade were more effective than her handful of gemstones.

"Let's hope this works," she said as she sat on the ground and took aquamarines and sapphires from her gem pouch. Jules sat down a few feet away. She clasped the stones tightly and closed her eyes. *Telepathy, clairvoyance, foresight.*

For a moment nothing happened. Then a cold shiver ran through her. An image flashed in her mind: Sheamathan and Elias at a table, somewhere with vines overhead. Everything seemed fine. Neither one looked angry or upset. Lana deepened her concentration. She didn't get any disturbing impressions, but even so, she felt edgy.

Next, she saw Sheamathan walking down a dark passageway, scowling. Something was definitely wrong. Lana tensed as emotions slammed into her—anger, bitterness, and distrust. She frantically searched for a reason to explain this sudden change. Could there be a connection between the two visions? Elias had been sitting with Sheamathan and everything seemed fine until Sheamathan was alone. Now the woodspirit was angry—furious! But why?

Lana pushed herself deeper, reaching out with her mind, hoping to make sense of it. Maybe that wasn't wise. Violent emotions surged through her, more intense with every passing moment. She started to shake, but even so, she held tightly to the stones.

Cold, unreasoning hatred exploded in her mind. Hatred so intense it took her breath away—a vicious malevolence, incapable of guilt or remorse—malice so deep, nothing but death would satisfy it.

Lana realized dimly that she had to break the mental connection and sever herself from these emotions. She wanted to let go of the stones but her hand had gone numb and her fingers wouldn't open.

An evil presence, dark and depraved, enveloped her. She couldn't relate to the entity's depraved feelings, but she understood its emotions. It couldn't comprehend love. Noble sentiments were repulsive. It hated cheerfulness and laughter.

She felt herself sinking further into that terrible, festering blackness and tried to scream, but there wasn't enough air in her lungs. Once more, gasping for air, she tried to let go of the gemstones.

When she opened her eyes she was sitting on the ground, dizzy and nauseous. Jules sat beside her, propping her up with a steadying arm around her shoulders. She managed to say weakly, "What happened?"

He let go and shifted position to face her. Tension showed around his eyes and mouth. He looked nearly as pale as she felt. "You cried out and started shaking all over. I came over, but I didn't know what to do. Maybe you didn't want me to interrupt you. I had no idea what you were seeing and feeling. Your lips were moving, but I couldn't hear anything. Then you started gasping for air and you dropped the gems and fainted." His eyes searched her face. "I'm really sorry. I should have broken in, shook you—stopped it somehow. Are you all right?"

She took several deep breaths. "Yes, I think so. And it's okay. I'm glad you didn't stop me." He looked relieved that she wasn't upset with him. She managed a faint smile. In his place, she wouldn't have known what to do, either. The obelisk had amplified her gem powers, all right—maybe a little *too* much. In a minute or two, when her head stopped spinning, she'd try to remember what she'd seen.

Before he could question her about what she'd seen, she asked, "How about you? What happened? Did you get any impressions from the knife?"

"Yes—what you sensed earlier—that Elias is in danger. I got one particularly strong impression, but it didn't make sense."

"What was it?"

"Jealousy." He gave her a look that suggested *she* might be able to make sense of it.

"Jealousy," she repeated. "Why would Sheamathan be jealous of Elias?"

He shrugged and shook his head. After a moment he said, "Maybe the word I'm looking for isn't jealousy. Maybe it's rivalry."

She nodded thoughtfully. "You mean, he's not her equal, but she sees him as a rival, anyway."

"Yes. Thinking back to my own case, she knew she was more powerful than me, but she didn't want any competition, and I was a potential rival."

"Right. She had to be pretty worried—or insecure. She agreed to wear a *dog collar*."

He smiled at that, and then grew serious again. "One thing still doesn't make sense. She asked Elias to form an alliance with her. Why would she do that if she sees him as a rival?"

"Well, it sort of makes sense. He's the only one who can help her." She tried to put herself in Sheamathan's place. "It must be unsettling to think she *needs* an alliance. It's like admitting she's vulnerable. But Elias has gem powers, and she needs him right now."

"So, anyone powerful enough to *help* her is powerful enough—"

"To be a rival," Lana finished for him.

"Okay. That makes sense. You know, I think you understand what goes on in Sheamathan's mind better than she does."

Those words touched a nerve. *Yes, I understand her. I was inside her mind. Now* she remembered. She had glimpsed the utter blackness of Sheamathan's soul and felt the smothering weight of pure evil. No one could understand who hadn't felt it. Cold sweat beaded on her face and arms, and she started to shake again.

Jules reached out to steady her. "Lana, what's wrong?"

It was hard to get her breath. "I remember now," she said in a tight voice. "What I saw. What I felt. Mostly it was emotions—*her* emotions."

Jules said gently, "Tell me."

"Anger. Distrust. Then vicious, unreasoning hatred." She felt dizzy as she relived those emotions. "Evil. A smothering, hungry darkness that feeds on pain and despair." She looked at Jules and swallowed hard, afraid to tell him what she had learned at the end, as she passed out. But she knew she had to. No secrets, she had promised.

"She wants to kill us, Jules. Not just you and me—Elias, too."

Chapter 36

Lana and Jules hid in the woods near the portal, waiting for Elias and Sheamathan. Raenihel's clan had arrived just after dusk, armed with knives, swords, clubs, pikes, and crossbows. After speaking briefly with Lana and Jules, the gnomes had fanned out into the woods to watch the portal from a distance, and Franklin was with them.

Lana hadn't been sure the gnomes would come. If something went wrong with the plan, and Sheamathan didn't lose her powers, the woodspirit could paralyze them. For that matter, how did they know this wasn't a trap? The gnomes had newfound respect for Elias after the mining camp rescue operation, but Lana wasn't naïve enough to think he had completely won them over—not after decades of mistrust. Until recently, Elias and Sheamathan had appeared to be on friendly terms, and it might be hard for the gnomes to believe that Elias had always hated her.

Lana chewed her lip. They should be here soon. The tension of waiting was almost unbearable. Her heart raced every time she heard a noise. She couldn't stop worrying about Elias. Sheamathan wanted to kill her and Jules. That was no surprise, but why had she turned against Elias? What had happened between them, and more importantly, did Elias *know* something was wrong? That last question chilled her to the bone. If he *didn't* know, he was far more vulnerable. After touching

Sheamathan's mind, and feeling the depth of her hatred, Lana was even more afraid of her than before. The only comforting thought was that Sheamathan needed Elias, at least for now, so he might be safe for the moment.

Jules hadn't said a word in the last half hour. Lana glanced at him. She didn't need to read his mind to know he was as nervous as she was. He and Elias had been friends for a very long time, and few friendships had survived so many hardships.

She glanced at her watch. Another fifteen minutes passed. What if Sheamathan didn't come? No, she told herself sternly, Franklin was sure they were coming tonight. Whatever had happened between Elias and Sheamathan, Lana could only hope it hadn't jeopardized the plan. She shivered, frustrated and miserable. There was nothing worse than waiting. Jules wrapped an arm around her shoulders in a futile attempt to warm her. "It's getting colder," he said quietly. "You're shivering."

"It's mostly from nerves."

"I thought they'd be here by now." He looked as tense as a bowstring ready to fly. He'd burst into motion the moment he saw Sheamathan.

"I'd feel better if I knew what to expect," she whispered. "You and Elias were supposed to overpower Sheamathan together and pin her down, hold her at knifepoint, knock her out if you had to, and then sedate her. Now Elias is coming through the portal *with* Sheamathan. That bothers me. We don't know what he'll do. Will he pretend to be examining the Amulet so we have time to move in? Or will he attack her right away by himself?"

"I don't know. I've thought about that, too. All I know is, we'll have to act fast or we'll lose the element of surprise."

And then it happened.

Elias stepped through the portal with Sheamathan right behind him.

Jules shot to his feet. Lana got up, but her muscles were sore and cramped, and she felt like she was moving in slow motion.

Sheamathan held up a lightgem and looked around, apparently assessing the progress of the blight. Elias spun to face her and punched her in the stomach with more force than Lana thought possible for an old man.

Sheamathan screamed and doubled over, dropping the lightgem as she stumbled backward, clutching her stomach. Elias leapt forward and swung again, but she recovered enough to straighten and block the blow, and then she hastily backed away, her face contorted with rage. "What treachery is this?" she screamed. "I knew I should not trust you!" Lifting her arms, palms forward toward Elias, she appeared to be calling up her dark powers, or maybe creating a ward to protect herself, but nothing happened.

Jules raced forward. Lana ran after him, trying to keep up.

Sheamathan let out a furious shriek when she saw them coming. It was obvious now that Elias had joined forces with the wolfhound and the woman who had escaped from the dungeon, and this deception made her even angrier.

Sheamathan faced them, and it brought to mind the day in the throne room when she had swept her arm in an arc, and a wall of energy had slammed into Lana, lifting her off her feet and hurling her backward. Now Sheamathan made that same motion, but nothing happened, and Sheamathan's howl of rage echoed through the forest. Lana was close enough to see that the woodspirit was not just angry— she was frightened. By now it was apparent to everyone, including Sheamathan, that she had no powers. No wonder she looked so frantic.

The fallen lightgem's bluish light cast an eerie glow over the scene.

Lana heard pounding feet behind her and looked back. Fifty grim-faced gnomes raced toward Sheamathan. What were they doing? They were supposed to be *hiding* unless breghlin came through the portal. Their jubilant cries nearly drowned out Sheamathan's furious screams. Elias had told the gnomes he would strip Sheamathan of her powers, and it was obvious now that his plan had worked. Lana supposed the gnomes couldn't resist this chance to attack their life-long foe.

Rage, confusion, and panic warred across the woodspirit's face. She had suspected Elias of subterfuge, but clearly nothing like this. Even the gnomes were involved, and they had always hated Elias—nearly as much as they had hated her. Sheamathan launched herself at Elias and Lana saw something gleam in his hand. A knife! He hadn't come unarmed.

Sheamathan raked her nails savagely across Elias's face but that didn't stop his own attack. He ducked under her outstretched arm and slashed his knife across her ribs. The woodspirit shrieked and grasped her side. "Fool! I am not made of flesh," she snarled. "I do not bleed."

Maybe she didn't bleed, but she certainly felt pain or she wouldn't have cried out when he cut her, Lana told herself.

Elias slashed again, aiming for the woodspirit's face, and his knife opened a gash along her jawline. Something sprayed out, a colorless fluid that wasn't blood. Lana couldn't believe her eyes. Of course Sheamathan wasn't human, but just what *was* she? If her woodspirit body wasn't flesh like a human or gnome, was she more like a plant or a tree?

Sheamathan sprang forward, grabbed Elias's knife hand, and managed to wrestle the knife away from him.

Lana's heart hammered in her chest. *No! You should've run! You're an old man!* She and Jules were only a few yards away, but it might as well be miles because they weren't going to get to him in time. Sheamathan had grabbed a fistful of Elias's robe and yanked him forward, bringing the knife to his throat.

Lana's eyes widened and her mouth opened in a silent scream. Sheamathan would slit Elias's throat with no regrets and laugh as his blood poured out.

"How?" the woodspirit screeched. "Why?" She slipped behind Elias with the knife still under his chin and spun him around to face her attackers. "Stop or I will kill him right now!"

Lana and Jules were so close that Lana was tempted to throw herself at Sheamathan and go for the knife. Shaking with emotion, she stopped, and Jules stopped, too. But would the *gnomes* stop? They had always despised Elias. They might be tempted to stand by and let Sheamathan kill him. Afterward, they could overcome Sheamathan and kill her.

As if reading her mind, Raenihel shouted, "Stand down!"

A hush fell over the forest. Holding the knife firmly to Elias's throat, Sheamathan said, "*None* of us have powers. Tell me *why*."

In a defiant voice Elias said, "Gem powers don't work here anymore. We have negated every gem power in the Fair Lands, so you'll have to be content with ruling Shadow."

Lana's mouth fell open. What? Where had he come up with that? *Knowledge and power, bluffs and bargains.* If Lana weren't so worried about Elias, she would have laughed out loud at his gambit, and at Sheamathan's confused expression.

"That is not possible," Sheamathan protested.

"Obviously, it is. We have no powers—you just said so yourself," Elias replied reasonably, as if speaking to a small child.

For a moment the woodspirit stood speechless. Then she asked in a venomous tone, "Negated all gem powers? How have you done this?"

"With help from my old friend Jules, and my great-great granddaughter Lana. I hear you've met her. You're outnumbered, Sheamathan—outnumbered and powerless. Give up with good grace."

Sheamathan's face contorted with hatred. Surely the woodspirit would kill Elias now. The look on his face said he expected her to and he didn't care.

Sheamathan edged closer to the portal, dragging Elias with her, and Lana stiffened with dread, not only fearing for Elias's safety, but terrified that Sheamathan would retreat through the portal and escape. Elias had said that Sheamathan's powers wouldn't work here, but that she could still rule in Shadow. He shouldn't have said that, shouldn't have planted that thought in her mind. If she went back through the portal now they would lose this opportunity. They couldn't afford to let her get away.

Lana debated trying to pull the woodspirit away from the portal, but if she did that, Sheamathan might slit Elias's throat. But if she did nothing, and Sheamathan escaped, her reign of terror would continue. Lana stood in an agony of indecision.

A thunderous beating of wings drew her eyes to the night sky, and a piercing screech split the air. Franklin flew directly toward Elias and Sheamathan with rapid strokes of his powerful wings. The woodspirit gaped at the feathered missile and her knife hand slipped from Elias's throat. Elias twisted out of her grasp and darted aside seconds before Franklin crashed into Sheamathan, knocking her legs out from under her. She went down in a flailing black heap.

Even before Sheamathan could roll over and grab the knife, Jules was on top of her, pinning her to the ground. Sheamathan cursed and snarled, but she couldn't move with Jules's knee on her chest and his powerful hands pinning her wrists to the ground. Through clenched teeth Jules said, "It's over, you despicable creature."

Lana dropped to one knee beside the woodspirit and slapped Sheamathan's face so hard her hand stung. "That's for all the gnomes you've tortured, and for the way you've treated the breghlin."

Sheamathan struggled futilely to retaliate. Lana stared unafraid into the woodspirit's hate-filled eyes. "Go ahead. Do your worst."

Jules said to Lana, "Remind me never to make you angry." She looked at him and found him smiling with amusement.

Elias approached, holding the glass vial, with Franklin close behind. Crouching beside the woodspirit, Elias said cheerfully, "You mustn't upset yourself so. Fortunately, I brought something to settle your nerves." He shook the murky red fluid near the woodspirit's face and laughed.

How would Elias ever get the sedative down Sheamathan's throat? She'd bite him or spit it out. And what if the potion didn't work on a woodspirit? This was pure guesswork. He couldn't possibly know what to expect.

"If her body isn't like ours, how do you know this stuff will work?" Lana asked.

"Her flesh is fibrous, rather like a plant, and her circulatory system pumps a fluid more similar to sap than blood, but she is generally humanoid," Elias said. "This sedative would put a human in a coma." He smiled down at Sheamathan. "And it's a very effective weed killer."

Sheamathan's face twisted in fury, but she didn't say a word. Her eyes darted about, looking for a means of escape.

"She should take her medicine," said a familiar voice. Lana looked over her shoulder and saw Raenihel—along with several gnomes including Artham, Terrilem, and Dardeneth. "Can we help?" Raenihel asked.

"Can you hold her mouth open?" Elias asked.

"With pleasure," Dardeneth growled. The gnomes gathered by Sheamathan's head. Dardeneth picked up a small stick and smiled grimly. Sheamathan struggled, but Jules only tightened his grip on her wrists and bore down harder with his knee. If it hadn't been such a tense moment, Lana would have laughed as Terrilem yanked Sheamathan's head back and Artham forced her mouth open. Dardeneth used his stick to hold down her tongue, and Elias poured the potion down her throat.

"There now, that wasn't so bad," Elias said with his best bedside-manner. "You'll be feeling better in no time at all."

As if on cue, Sheamathan convulsed and went limp. Lana shot Elias a questioning look and he said, "Yes, apparently it works that fast."

"I don't trust her. What can we use to tie her up?" Jules asked. "Even if she isn't faking, she might recover faster than we think."

"Give me your knife," Lana said.

"Take it; I don't dare let go of her. What do you plan to do?"

Pulling the knife from its sheath she made an incision near the hem of Sheamathan's gown, and with a yank, tore off a long strip. "Roll her over. We'll tie her hands behind her back."

"You seem quite experienced at this." Jules observed. "It's rather disturbing." His lips twitched with amusement.

"I watch a lot of TV."

Jules rolled the woodspirit over and wrenched her hands behind her back. "Am I doing this right?"

"You're a natural." She wrapped the fabric around the woodspirit's wrists and secured it with a couple knots.

Elias said, "Now, to carry out the rest of my plan, we must carry her beyond the range of our alamaria."

"May *we* carry her?" one the gnomes asked.

"Yes," Elias said. "But make sure you don't drop her—very hard."

The gnomes laughed nervously, and eight of them gathered around their helpless foe and bore her away. The rest followed, smiling and laughing. Jules, holding his knife, walked beside Lana, bringing up the rear. Lana was tempted to break into a chorus of "Ding, dong, the witch is dead!"

"As soon as we're out of range, my knife will glow," Jules said. He glanced at her. "What do you think Elias is planning to do?"

"No idea. But he doesn't plan to kill her, or he would have done it already."

"It might be safer for both worlds if he did, but I suppose she might prove useful later."

"Useful for what?"

"She might have done something with dark powers that Elias can't reverse without her, or she might have important information that no one else knows."

"Even so, keeping her alive is a risk, and I hope we won't be sorry."

"I haven't seen this side of you before," Jules said with a playful smile.

"I left my kind, benevolent side in Shadow." She felt a bit offended, even though she knew he was just teasing her. "You said I feel deeply, and you're right. Today I'm feeling deeply about justice. Sheamathan can't begin to pay for all the terrible things she's done."

"No, but she'll be gone and the gnomes will have a better life now."

"And so will the breghlin."

Jules's knife began to glow. He called to Elias, "We're clear of the alamaria!"

The party walked a little further and then the gnomes laid Sheamathan on the ground and everyone gathered around. Lana looked down at Sheamathan's white, bloodless face. It was like being at a funeral, only there wouldn't be a eulogy. No one had anything good to say about Sheamathan.

Elias said, "This is a momentous day and I'm grateful to all of you." He paused and looked around the group, his expression serious. "As you know, I've turned away from dark powers, but today I will make an exception."

A startled murmur ran through the crowd, and Jules shot Lana a questioning glance, but she had no more idea than he did what Elias was planning.

"I will give the woodspirit an enchanted form—one as repulsive as *she* is," Elias continued. "She will retain her mental faculties and her ability to speak."

Someone gasped and everyone took several steps backward, as if the spell might affect anyone who stood too close.

Elias moved his arms over the woodspirit. The air shimmered. Sheamathan the woodspirit vanished and in her place appeared a giant beetle, complete with a restraining collar that fit her new form. All her gem-filled jewelry lay on the ground.

The stunned gnomes stared at the being who had terrorized them all their lives as Elias gathered up the woodspirit's jewelry and placed it in his pockets.

Lana shivered with revulsion. The repulsive beetle lay motionless on her back, her six legs, covered with thick spikes of hair, sticking up in the air.

Jules stepped forward and he and Elias rolled Sheamathan over. Lana had to appreciate Elias's handiwork. The beetle's hard-shelled body had a front segment that consisted of a broad flat head with compound eyes and two long, barbed feelers. Her wings folded back over the rear segment, and she had to weigh six or seven pounds.

Jules walked back to Lana and said quietly, "I think she's paying for her crimes now, don't you?"

That shattered Lana's horrified stupor. "Boy! Is she going to be mad when she wakes up!"

Everyone laughed, breaking the tension.

"Excuse me a minute," she said to Jules. "I want to talk to Elias."

Elias looked pleased as she approached. "Things were rather shaky for a moment, but everything worked out all right," he said with a twinkle in his eye.

"Very shaky. She almost killed you. Thank goodness for Franklin." Lana took a deep breath and said, "Jules and I stopped at the obelisk today, and I had an idea as we were leaving. I know you've always wanted to heal Franklin, but you said you couldn't fix his crippled body. What if you used your healing gems near the obelisk?"

Elias looked at her with serious green eyes and pursed his lips thoughtfully. "We know the obelisk amplifies all gem powers. It might not amplify them enough, but it's a good idea."

Lana looked around for Franklin and found him still studying the beetle who in woodspirit form had turned him into a bird. Lana called him and motioned for him to come over.

"I have a theory that using healing gems near Sheamathan's obelisk might boost their power to heal you. Would you let Elias try?"

"I suppose. If it doesn't work and I'm still a crippled man, he can turn me back into a bird."

"Good. We'll stop at the obelisk on our way to Strathweed," Elias said." I don't think our beetle friend will mind the delay."

Lana said, "I still have pet carriers in my trunk. We can use one for Sheamathan."

"Good idea." Elias handed her a lightgem to light her way to the car. "Our friend should sleep for two or three hours. You don't need to hurry."

Jules went with her to get the carrier, and when they got back, Raenihel and Artham were talking with Elias and Franklin. The rest of the gnomes had gone.

"My people went back to the Tree Home to celebrate," Raenihel said to Lana. "You're welcome to join us—tonight or any other night."

Artham cleared his throat. "I owe you an apology, Lana. I was wrong about you. You're a true friend to the gnomes. We'd be honored to have you celebrate with us." He held out his hand in friendship.

"Thank you," Lana said, shaking his hand. "I certainly feel like celebrating, but I'll have to come some other time. I'm going to the obelisk with Elias and Franklin."

Elias looked at her in surprise. He'd never heard her say his real name. His eyes took on the telltale sheen of unshed tears.

She looked away, embarrassed by his unexpected reaction, and knelt to unfasten the pet carrier's door. "I'm not touching her. Someone else will have to put her in here."

Jules carried the beetle over and shut her inside. "Ready when you are," he said as he lifted the carrier.

Raenihel said, "I hope to see you soon." His glance included Elias and Jules as well as Lana. He and Artham left for the Tree Home.

"Sheamathan's driver will be waiting on the other side," Elias said as they walked to the portal. "I had forgotten about him." He gave a little chuckle. "I imagine he'll be shocked to see Sheamathan in her new form."

"Will he believe it's her?" Jules asked.

"There are no beetles like this in Shadow. I think he'll believe us."

"You're going to keep her at Strathweed?" Lana asked.

Elias laughed. "Heavens, no! Tomorrow I'll take her to Shadowglade. I need to shut down the mining camp, release the gnomes and free the prisoners in the dungeon. What good timing," he said, "Sheamathan will have her choice of cells."

They crossed through the portal and found the driver in his cart, as expected. Jules took out the lightgem as they approached the driver.

Elias said in an authoritative voice, "Go back to Shadowglade. Your queen doesn't need a ride back, and she won't be giving you any more orders. We've turned her into a beetle."

Jules held up the pet carrier. The breghlin looked inside. His eyes widened in stunned disbelief.

Elias said, "Go now and spread the word. I'll bring her to the dungeon tomorrow."

The driver hesitated, his eyes still locked on the motionless beetle. Jules handed Lana the lightgem and drew his knife, which began to glow. That jolted the breghlin from his stupor. He gave the cart beast a jab with a stick and the cart lurched into motion.

"Onward!" Elias said cheerily.

Lana carried the lightgem and Jules lugged the pet carrier, grumbling good-naturedly all the way to the obelisk.

When they arrived, Franklin said, "I'm almost afraid to try. It seems hopeless."

"Listen to me," Elias said firmly. "I've given the matter more thought. Lana got the idea to heal you after using her gems here, and I don't think her inspiration was a coincidence. The obelisk amplifies all gem powers, including foresight."

A shiver of excitement ran through her. Foresight? It made sense, but it hadn't occurred to her that the idea hadn't been her own.

Elias said, "I'll turn you back into a man, and then I'll leave you in the capable hands of Lana and Jules."

Lana shot Elias a worried glance. He wanted her and Jules to heal Franklin?

"Your Fair Lands healing gems are more powerful than my healing gems from Shadow," he told her matter-of-factly. "I suspect that's because sickness is common in the Fair Lands and rare here. Lana, you healed Jules. Together, you and Jules can heal Franklin."

She glanced at Jules who gave her a determined look. Together they would make this work, she promised herself, because Franklin deserved it. She set the lightgem on the ground and took the healing stones from her pouch. Jules held his knife.

Elias said, "Enough of Franklin the bird. Let's see Franklin the *man*." An instant later, a thin crippled man with graying hair lay on the ground. His legs were twisted, particularly his left leg, which was rotated, making his foot point sideways. His paralyzed and atrophied left arm was half the size of his right arm, and the fingers on that hand curled like claws.

Jules immediately went to work, following the example Lana had set when she healed him. He wrapped Franklin's good hand around the knife hilt, and clasped his hands around Franklin's to maintain a tight grip. Lana felt overwhelmed when she looked at Franklin. The damage was too great. For a moment all she could do was stare.

Jules said in a hoarse voice, "Lana, help me."

She knelt and laid an assortment of healing gems on Franklin's paralyzed arm and on his misshapen, twisted legs. How had she ever thought they could heal this poor, broken man? And yet, hadn't she brought Jules back from the dead? Jules with his jeweled knife was adding his strength to hers. Maybe that would be enough.

Turning her attention to Franklin's arm, she pressed down on the gems and pictured healing power flowing into his arm and fingers. The stones grew warm and then hot. His stiff, clawed hand began to straighten, then his fingers moved slightly and his arm twitched. It was working! She left those gems where they were and moved down to his legs.

Jules's efforts with the knife had already brought results. Franklin's legs had straightened some, but his left leg—the most damaged and twisted—still looked pretty bad. Lana pressed the healing gemstones against Franklin's leg and concentrated, picturing the bones shifting into proper alignment. The gems vibrated under her palm and grew so hot she could hardly touch them.

She willed the gem's energy to radiate through damaged nerves, bones, tendons, and ligaments, and she watched Franklin nervously. Was that movement? Had she seen Franklin's hip move? If she wasn't mistaken, his leg had rotated somewhat in the hip socket, but it still wasn't right. She glanced at Jules. He looked worried, probably thinking, as she was, that maybe this was the best they could do. No, she refused to give up until Franklin could stand and walk. Franklin hadn't said a word. Maybe he was afraid to disturb their concentration.

On an impulse, Lana let go of Franklin's leg and knelt beside Jules. She looked into his eyes, saw a stubborn determination as great as her own, and wrapped both of her hands around his. Together they held Franklin's hand on the knife hilt.

Energy like a lightning bolt slammed through her! They gasped in unison. Healing power seemed to flow from every part of her body, coursing through her hands. Their gem powers were combining into a single, powerful force, she realized in amazement. She glanced down at

Franklin's legs, feeling giddy and light-headed, as his bones shifted and straightened. In a moment his legs looked perfectly normal and his formerly clawed hand lay flat.

Through her tears she saw Jules shaking his head in amazement.

Elias came over and said in a trembling voice, "Franklin, you look like a new man."

Lana got to her feet, brushed tears from her face, and smiled. Jules stood and sheathed the knife.

"Do you think I'll be able to walk now?" Franklin asked in a tremulous voice.

"There's only one way to find out," Elias said. He bent and held out his hand.

Gripping Elias's hand with both of his, Franklin struggled to his feet. He paused to find his balance, and then with Elias supporting him, took a few tentative steps.

"I can walk! I can walk!" he cried, looking stunned. "How can I ever thank you all? I never expected to walk again!"

Elias said, "After you rest a bit, do you think you can walk to Strathweed? I hate to ask, but it isn't safe to stay here. I'll help you, and I'm sure Jules will, too."

Franklin's face glowed with excitement. "I'll slow you down, but yes, I think I can manage it."

Jules said, "I only need one hand for the carrier. I can help you."

"So it's settled," Elias said. And what about you, Lana? Will you be going home now?"

"Not a chance," she said. "I want to see you free the gnomes and throw Sheamathan Beetle in the dungeon. I have the weekend off and I can't think of a better way to spend it."

"I would be delighted to have you," Elias said. "You can make coffee in the morning," he added with a grin.

"Coffee," Franklin said wistfully.

"May I have a word with you?" Jules asked Lana. He took her arm and steered her away. "After this weekend, I hope you'll be a regular visitor at Strathweed. I know Elias's past upsets you, but he's changed. Give him a chance to prove it."

"Yes, he's different than I expected, and I'm really starting to like him, even though I *hated* him before. I—" She stopped. She could say almost the same thing about Jules. As the wolfhound, he'd frightened her out of her wits and she'd hated him, but not anymore.

His eyes were dark with emotion. "Have you had a similar change of heart for me?"

She gave him a shy smile and said, "Read my thoughts."

As his eyes met hers, a slow smile spread across his face. He hesitated a moment, then pulled her toward him and kissed her, first tenderly, and then with a hunger and passion that took her breath away. When he let her go, he said, "Lana, you've had a special place in my heart for years, even though you were afraid of me."

"I'm not afraid of you now."

He took her hand and pressed it affectionately. "I'll be staying with Elias for a while, and we'd both enjoy your company, so I hope you'll come often."

"I'd like to get to know *both* of you better," she said.

They rejoined Elias and Franklin.

"Shall we go?" Elias asked. "Franklin says he's ready, and I'd like to get Sheamathan back to Strathweed before she wakes. I'll put her carrier in the cave with the underground river. I don't think we'll hear her screams of rage from there."

Lana laughed. "Jules, you and Elias can help Franklin, and I'll carry our new pet."

"If you want her, she's all yours," Jules said. "We'll take turns when you get tired."

The group had nearly reached Strathweed when a high-pitched voice shrieked, "This is *not* amusing!"

Lana set the carrier on the ground and they bent to look inside.

Elias shone his lightgem on the furious beetle. "Actually, it's *quite* amusing!" he said. "Lana, what shall we name our new pet?"

Lana stared at Sheamathan, trying to think of a good nickname. For a moment, nothing suitable came to mind, and then Ferdinand's haunting cry rang in her ears. "*You! Gived! Us! Names!*" Lana frowned at Sheamathan. The heartless wretch didn't deserve a name.

"From now on we'll just call her "S.""

Join us online to find out about the exciting sequel to *Beyond the Forest*!

Shadowglade

by Kay L. Ling

Visit us at

http://www.kaylling.com/newsletter.html

for more about gemstones and a sneak peek at Lana's upcoming adventures.

Lana will return in **Shadowglade** *in Spring, 2017.*

Chapter 1

Waking to discover you're a giant beetle could ruin anyone's day.

The imprisoned beetle, Sheamathan, circled her cage, feelers flicking with impotent fury. Lana watched with a satisfied smile. The cage was an artistic masterpiece, but the former Queen of Shadow didn't seem to care. Gems of various colors twinkled from within the iron scrollwork, and the iron itself, infused with minutely-ground Fair Lands gems, sparkled with subtly shifting colors. The cage, four feet high by four feet wide, was a generous size, but too small for the despicable beetle to retreat from curious eyes.

When Sheamathan stopped circling the cage and turned toward her, Lana fought an irrational impulse to back away. Sure, the beetle couldn't hurt her, but Lana had never liked bugs, and this one was the size of a small cat. It might be Lana's imagination, but hatred seemed to gleam from Sheamathan's compound eyes. Two long, curving, barbed feelers extended from the beetle's broad, flat head. Her wings folded back over an elongated rear segment and spiky hairs covered all six legs. Lana grimaced. A hideous being deserved a hideous body.

In the dimly lit library, the cage seemed to sprout from the table since both were black. The table's ebony-like wood had been carved around the perimeter with a vine and leaf design, and the table legs were shaped like gnarled roots.

Lana had suggested keeping the cage in the library. Sheamathan's fortress-like castle had no cheerful rooms or pleasant alcoves, but the library was tolerable. Granted, the furniture was creepy—leather stretched over frames made of animal bones. Seriously, who but Sheamathan would find that attractive? But the rest of the room wasn't bad. Not that anyone cared about the beetle's comfort, but others had to look after her, and they deserved pleasant surroundings.

Floor-to-ceiling bookcases held several hundred leather-bound books, piles of scrolls and sketches, assorted curios, and small showcases filled with gems. Maps and tapestries hung on one wall. Everything looked ancient, and probably was.

Lana stepped closer to the cage. "Your library has a lot of reading material. I'd bring you a pair of reading glasses, but they don't make them for compound eyes."

The beetle made a strangled noise. "Laugh now while you can. You will be sorry you did this to me."

Not likely. The beetle deserved worse. The thought of killing her had been tempting, but actually, this was a more fitting punishment. "You turned Greg and Jordy into giant rats and Franklin into a bird. Now you know how it feels. I don't know how many years you'll live in your new body, but I hope it's a very long time."

"Change me back. Your misguided ambitions will destroy you."

"We'll take our chances."

The beetle waved her feelers angrily. "The breghlin will avenge me."

"You're kidding, right? They're glad to be rid of you!" Actually, that wasn't entirely true. Despite Sheamathan's cruelty, some breghlin were still loyal to her, and Elias and Jules worried about an uprising.

"Liar!" Sheamathan rustled her wings irritably. "The breghlin fear and revere me."

Lana gave a derisive snort. "You got the *first* half right—they feared you."

The beetle moved to the opposite side of the cage as if trying to escape the unpleasant truth of her reign. "If the gnomes are foolish enough to come out of hiding, the breghlin will kill them. Gnomes are weak, defenseless creatures. Your revolution will end in bloodshed and the gnomes will never be free."

"We'll see." It wouldn't be easy to create a functional gnome society. Lana was well aware of that. The gnomes had spent generations enslaved or in hiding, but they were capable of ruling themselves, and properly armed, they should be able to hold their own against the breghlin.

Footsteps echoed down the passageway and a familiar masculine voice called, "Lana, are you here?"

"In the library," she called back, running a hand over her chestnut waves and hoping she looked presentable in faded jeans. She'd purposely worn a green sweater to compliment her eyes.

Jules strode through the door. What had he been doing? Cobwebs clung to his tousled, light brown hair, and he had dirt smudges on his face. His tan shirt and brown pants were positively grimy.

Great-great grandfather Elias came in behind him, wearing his usual green robe, but it was filthy along the hem. Cobwebs clung to his untidy, shoulder-length gray hair. Under the best of conditions Elias wasn't much to look at. After all, he was 170 years old, with warty, toad-like skin, a nearly lipless mouth, and a broad, flat nose. The gem master's best feature was his intensely green eyes, like Lana's. It wasn't nice to say, but with a face like that, dirt and cobwebs were the least of his worries.

"Looks like you've been cleaning the dungeon," Lana said, laughing.

"Good guess," Jules said, dusting off his clothes. "We just came from there, but we weren't cleaning."

"No, we were dealing with prisoners," Elias said. "The most troublesome breghlin are behind bars now." He looked pleased with himself. "So far, we have thirty, and I hope there won't be more."

"Where did the rest go?" she asked.

"Back to their clans, I suppose."

"They have clans around here?"

"Yes—within a day's walk."

"They won't make trouble? The ones who left?" she asked.

"Impossible to say," Elias replied with a shrug. "They're still in shock, trying to grasp the fact that we defeated their queen and turned her into a beetle."

"It seems to have taken the fight out most of them," Jules said.

"Even so, we're taking every precaution," Elias assured her. "Armed gnomes are stationed throughout the castle, particularly in the dungeon."

"I can't get over it—gnomes guarding breghlin," Lana said, shaking her head. "That's certainly a role reversal."

Casting a meaningful glance at the cage, Elias said, "Perhaps we should speak elsewhere."

"Good idea," Lana said. Although Sheamathan—now known simply as S—was harmless in beetle form, the less she overheard the better, if for no other reason than it infuriated her not to know what was going on. With one last glance at the cage, Lana followed Jules and Elias out of the library.

Torches in brackets cast flickering shadows on the stone passageway's soot-stained walls, and cobwebs hung from the ceiling in eerie festoons. The stagnant air smelled like smoke and mildew.

When out of earshot of the library, Jules said to Lana, "We freed more gnomes this week."

"From mining camps?"

He nodded. "Yes, and some from the dungeon."

"The dungeon? Didn't you release them all last week?"

"We couldn't. Some needed medical care and the infirmary was full."

"Sounds like you had a busy week. I wish I could help more, but I've already taken off too many days from work."

"When are you taking over the store?" Jules asked.

"Not for a few months, but I'm spending more time there lately, getting ready for the transition."

"That's understandable. Don't worry. Just come when you can," Jules said. "How did you get here tonight? Did Raenihel bring you?"

"Raenihel brought me through the portal and Artham was waiting with a cart. I couldn't believe it—he had a breghlin driver! A female, but still!"

"We kept a few breghlin staff. The gnomes aren't happy about it, but they don't complain much in front of us. We'll fill you in later."

"S says the gnomes are weak and can't stand up to the breghlin. I hope she's wrong." Lana said. "Gnomes have the upper hand now, and they'd better act like it."

"How do you like S's cage?" Jules asked.

"It turned out great. When did you finish it?"

"Yesterday. S spent the night in the dungeon, and we moved her upstairs today."

"A simple iron cage would have held her," Elias said, "but infusing the iron with Fair Lands gems adds another layer of protection. Jules made a wooden floor insert, which is the only area she can safely touch. If she or the breghlin touch the cage, the gems in the metal will burn them."

Distant voices echoed down the passageway. Lana tilted her head, listening. Probably guards making their rounds. It hadn't been easy to talk gnomes into working here. Sheamathan had enslaved generations of gnomes, and Shadowglade represented everything they feared and hated. But jobs like guard duty couldn't be assigned to breghlin.

"Even if this regime change proves relatively non-violent, we'll still have some serious challenges," Lana said. "The blight in my world has been stopped, but it will be years before the forest fully recovers, and the damage here is a thousand times worse."

"Reversing generations of destruction will take a long time," Jules agreed. "Maybe gem powers can speed the healing, but we don't know what gems we'd need or how to go about it."

"Right now, I have other priorities," Elias said. "Rats, birds, and lizards have been coming to my cave, hoping I can change them back into gnomes."

"I'm glad you can help them," Lana said. Elias had restored some of the pitiful creatures to their rightful forms, but Sheamathan's pets had eaten the majority and the thought made Lana sick.

"I'll need to divide my time between here and Strathweed," Elias said as they entered a connecting passageway. "The gnomes aren't capable of running things on their own yet, and I expect it will be a while before they are."

"When things settle down, we want to explore the castle," Jules said. We're sure S has resources we can use, but it may not be easy to find them."

"Resources?" Lana repeated. "Like what?"

"Weapons," Jules said, "and caches of common but useful gems. S wouldn't leave valuables lying about, but they're here somewhere."

Lana said, "The first place I'd check is S's private chambers? Have you been there yet?"

Elias gave a grunt of annoyance. "Yes and the door is locked but there's no keyhole, so I suspect she used a mirkstone lock."

This world had hundreds of unique gems and minerals, and Lana couldn't keep their names straight, much less their powers. For the most part, her gem studies had been limited to Fair Lands gems. "Mirkstone?" she asked. "What's that?"

"It's also known as "memory stone." The gem retains verbal or mental commands," Elias explained. "Without the correct command, the gem won't release the lock."

Lana smiled appreciatively. "A password gem. Fascinating!"

Jules said, "If Elias can't guess the password, we may have to break down the door."

"So where are we headed now?" she asked. It felt strange to walk unchallenged through the castle. She kept having flashbacks of her stay in the dungeon.

"The throne room," Elias said. "Frankly, we haven't been anxious to go there."

Lana shivered. She felt the same way, and it was easy to understand Jules's reluctance. He'd spent nearly a hundred years by the woodspirit's side as an enchanted wolfhound.

They reached the throne room and stepped cautiously inside. Torches in iron brackets flickered from all four walls, and curling streams of smoke rose in the stagnant air.

"I had breghlin light the torches," Elias said, "but no amount of light can chase away the gloom."

Lana agreed. She felt small and insignificant as she looked up at the huge stone columns that supported the wooden ceiling beams. Their scrolled capitols, shaped like coiled serpents, looked disturbingly realistic. The ancient walls, made of massive stone blocks, had darkened from soot and grime.

Across the huge hall stood the familiar dais that held the woodspirit's throne. Even though the throne was empty now, Lana's mouth went dry.

For a moment no one moved and she fought an impulse to turn back. A brooding malevolence hung over the throne room, as if centuries of malice had seeped into the walls and could never be eradicated.

Elias murmured, "Let's have a look around, shall we?" He started across the room and Lana followed reluctantly. She glanced at Jules. His expression was apprehensive.

As they approached the massive throne, her eyes passed over the hideous carvings that covered every inch of its surface: winged serpents, giant insects, and malformed birds and animals. The carvings represented living abominations created by S during her reign. Lana took a steadying breath. Jewels imbedded in the creatures' eye sockets flickered in the torchlight, and she felt certain they were jewels with malevolent powers.

From behind the dais, stone gargoyles leered down at them. The group stopped at the dais steps, and Lana tried to dismiss her sense of foreboding.

"I'd like to take an axe to this thing," Jules said, frowning at the grotesque throne.

Even Elias looked disturbed, as if the lingering taint of evil had infected him as well. He straightened his shoulders and mounted the dais.

"You're not going to sit on that thing, are you?" Jules said in a tight voice.

"Certainly not," Elias answered hastily. He looked up at the gargoyles. Their eyes, though sightless, seemed to be watching him. Quickly, he looked away. Rubbing his arms through the sleeves of his green robe as if suddenly chilled, he proceeded to inspect the throne. When he reached the back, he called out, "Here! What is this?" His tone was more curious than afraid.

Jules shot Lana a nervous glance and together they climbed the steps and joined Elias.

Behind the throne stood a broad column about three feet high made of translucent, black alamaria stones. On top rested a large, black book with gemstones set into its ornately-tooled leather cover.

Lana wiped damp palms on her jeans. "Is this what I think it is?"

"It must be S's spell book," Jules said.

"With centuries of gem knowledge inside," Elias said in a tone of awe. He reached toward it.

Lana stiffened. "Is that a good idea?"

"What harm could it do?" Elias asked, but his voice held a note of doubt. His fingers traced the design worked into the leather, and then he slowly lifted the cover.

The first two pages showed grotesque creatures—like the ones carved on the throne. The next two pages were blank—at first.

And then words began to form.

Ommort Mirkstone

Elias stepped back, his face suddenly pale.

"We know what a mirkstone is," Jules said. "But what does ommort mean?"

In a tone barely above a whisper Elias said, "Ommort is a rare variety of mirkstone." He wet his lips. "I call it 'deadman's switch.' Specific actions within a warded area trigger commands stored in the gem. In this case, opening the book was the trigger."

Lana froze as the pages began to turn, faster and faster. The motion finally stopped, and the book lay open at the last two pages which showed ornate weapons and jewelry set with gems. Were these treasures hidden somewhere within the castle?

In a low, menacing tone the book said, "You are not Sheamathan. Ommort Mirkstone *activated*."

Acknowledgements

My sister, Marie Clapsaddle, my biggest fan, provided invaluable feedback and spent more hours reading and editing this book than either of us can count. Thanks!

Lowell Ling, my wonderful husband, provided daily motivation by asking, "Do you have another chapter yet?"

Dennis Morris, owner of Geyser Gem and Jewelry, in Victor, N.Y. answered many questions about gems and inspired in me a deeper love for colored gemstones.

I'd like to acknowledge the "noblebright" trend, which is the opposite of "grimdark." Reading tastes differ, and one style of book isn't inherently better than the other, but for those of you who enjoy main characters who have heroic hearts, this book is for you.

A Note from the Author

Thank you so much for reading *Beyond the Forest*! If you enjoyed it, I hope you will spread the word by posting an honest review on Amazon or Goodreads. You don't need to write anything lengthy or profound. Even a simple statement like, "I enjoyed this book and I think you will too," will encourage readers to pick up *Beyond the Forest*. Lana, Jules, and Elias thank you in advance, and the gnomes and breghlin do, too!

About the Author

Kay L. Ling began writing fiction at an early age. In grade school, her stories evidenced a sense of wonder and love of adventure. In one, mythical creatures lived and traveled inside a rainbow, and in another, a bored sixth-grader turned her teacher into a maroon sofa and then teleported herself to London. As she grew up, Kay never lost her ability to imagine strange and wondrous peoples and places, and now she would like to share her unique fantasy adventures with others.

Visit Kay online:

- Website – http://www.kaylling.com
- Facebook – http://www.facebook.com/KayLLing.author
- Twitter – http://www.twitter.com/polly_metallic

CPSIA information can be obtained
at www.ICGtesting.com
Printed in the USA
LVOW11s1625200317
527826LV00004B/969/P

9 781539 729235